"In The Root of A[...] [for]ces ranged against Da[vid as never] before. Explosive [...] [fo]r the future.

An engrossing, su[spenseful...] [the]mes are noticeably more prominent than in a regular thriller. Very enjoyable, as usual."
Alastair Mabbott, book reviewer for *The Herald*

"Think clerical sleuths and you think of Father Brown, or perhaps James Runcie's Grantchester series. Intuitive and driven by justice, but genteel. Les Cowan's David Hidalgo, an Edinburgh pastor, takes us into Rankin and MacBride territory when crime is hard-boiled, and fair play won by a whisker...

Compelling characters ensure a plot moving on skates through plausible twists and tangles. Crime-solver, yes, but Hidalgo has insight and compassion, too, helping him face up to chaos and evil by understanding its causes and consequences. No glib pieties here spoil the pace but subtly ask readers to look again at the strength that faith might have to offer."
Stuart Hannabuss, writer and reviewer

"Les Cowan throws his man of faith back into a dark world where he needs to question, "Why me?" This latest David Hidalgo adventure takes the unassuming pastor and his wife into a world of crooked politicians and elderly churchgoers with surprising secrets and crooked cops. Could they have been chosen for such a time as this, and what does that mean for their future?

Another amazing, page-turning adventure, with a slice of wry humour running through its very core."
Rob Allwright, blogger and presenter of the *One Man in the Middle* radio show

Praise for the David Hidalgo series:

"In David Hidalgo, Les Cowan has a unique take on the crime busting religious protagonist... he has crafted a clever, twisted game of cat and mouse where you're never quite sure who is the cat and who is the mouse."
Gordon Brown, author of *Darkest Thoughts*

"Exciting and thoughtful... and also gentle probing of how faith and conscience work in the face of obsession."
***Press and Journal* Saturday magazine**

"Another cracker from Cowan... pacey and relentless... The author has found a rich seam of crime fiction."
Scots Magazine* review of *Sins of the Fathers

"Les Cowan is daring in engaging with controversial and complex themes that are patiently rooted in the familiar and recognisable. This means the story is not just exciting but credible and engaging."
GJ Martin, author of the Orcadian Trilogy

"Truly a breath of fresh air from the hard-man-style detective novels, yet the undercurrents it creates are just as threatening. Masterful."
***Living Orkney* magazine**

"A unique combination of spiritual journey and fast-paced crime. Very mature writing: an outstanding achievement."
Ron Ferguson, author and columnist

> To Kathleen!
> Happy Christmas 2022
> with love, Will & Pat xx

The Root of all Evil

Les Cowan

Les Cowan

A David Hidalgo Novel

R

The David Hidalgo series:

Book 1: *Benefit of the Doubt*
Book 2: *All that Glitters*
Book 3: *Sins of the Fathers*
Book 4: *Blood Brothers*
Book 5: *The Root of All Evil*

Short stories:

"David Hidalgo and the Badvent Calendar"
"David Hidalgo and a Case of Forgetfulness"

Non-fiction titles:

Loose Talk Collected
Orkney by Bike

Text copyright © 2022 Les Cowan
This edition copyright © 2022 Rammigeo Books

The right of Les Cowan to be identified as the author of this work has been asserted by him in accordance with the Copyright, Designs and Patents Act 1988.

All rights reserved. No part of this publication may be reproduced or transmitted in any form or by any means, electronic or mechanical, including photocopy, recording, or any information storage and retrieval system, without permission in writing from the publisher.

All the characters in this book are fictitious and any resemblance to actual persons, living or dead, is purely coincidental.

Published by
Rammigeo Books
3 Hill of Heddle, Finstown,
Orkney, KW17 2LH, Scotland

ISBN 978 1 73913 670 3
e-ISBN 978 1 73913 671 0

First edition 2022

Acknowledgements

The Authorized (King James) Version of the Bible ('the KJV'), the rights in which are vested in the Crown in the United Kingdom, is reproduced here by permission of the Crown's patentee, Cambridge University Press. The Cambridge KJV text including paragraphing, is reproduced here by permission of Cambridge University Press.

A catalogue record for this book is available from the British Library

Printed and bound in the UK, October 2022

But they that will be rich fall into temptation and a snare, and into many foolish and hurtful lusts, which drown men in destruction and perdition. For the love of money is the root of all evil: which while some coveted after, they have erred from the faith, and pierced themselves through with many sorrows.

**First letter of the Apostle Paul to Timothy,
Chapter 6 verses 9-10 (KJV)**

For the English chatters of Madrid and Ribadeo

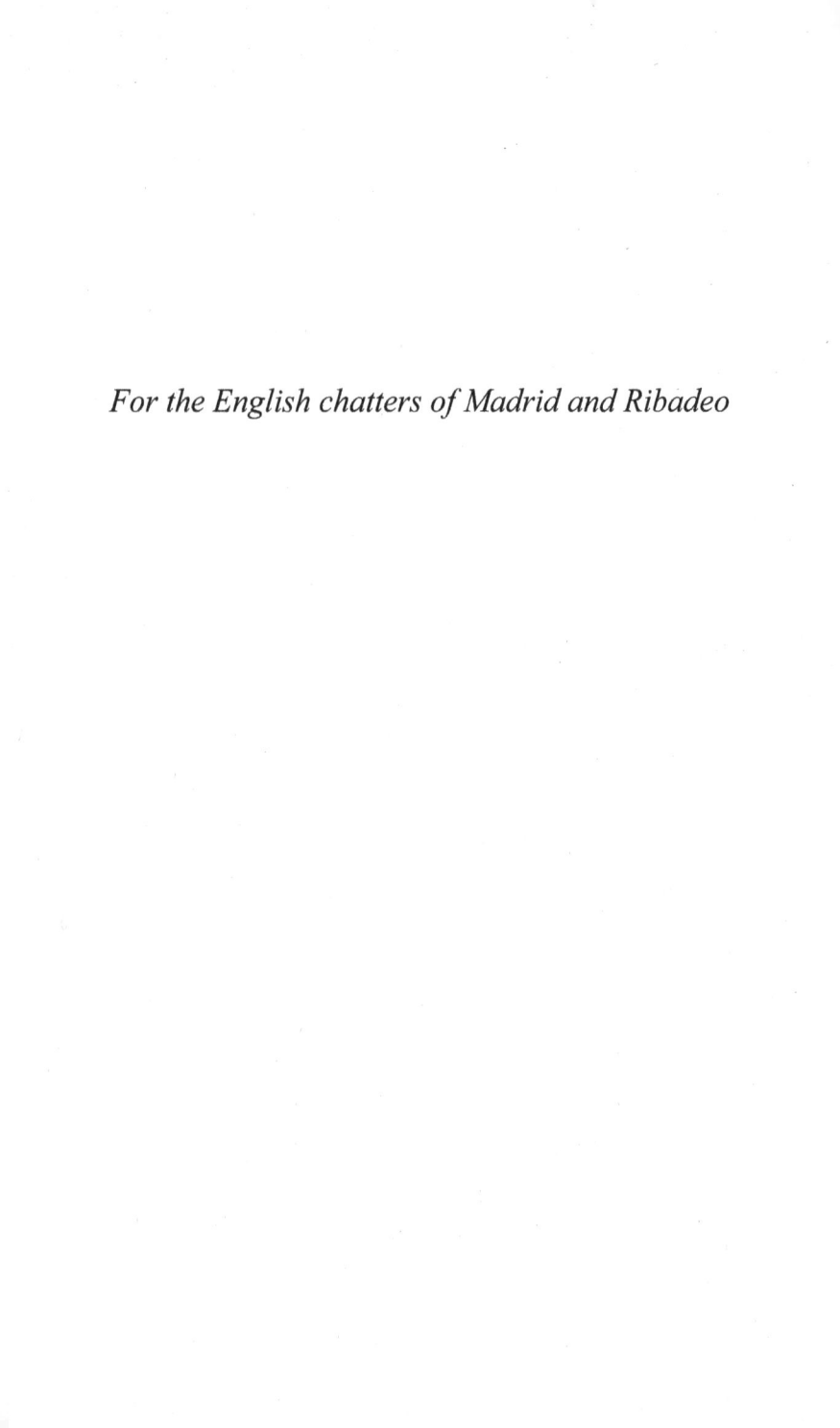

Acknowledgements

Grateful thanks once again to those who have helped in one way or another in the evolution of David Hidalgo, even just by reading a book and posting a review.

Specifically, I am grateful to those who took the time to read and comment on early drafts, in particular Fiona Cowan, Angus Mackay and Mija Regoord.

Also Jessica Gladwell, Joy Tibbs, Mike Belcher, Fiona Veitch Smith and Julie Frederick for supporting the Hidalgo series. I would like to express particular appreciation to Phoebe Swinburn from Midas PR for the amazing feat of obtaining reviews and exposure where I thought none was possible. Also thanks to Ron Ferguson for continued encouragement and reassurance that David Hidalgo had indeed something worthwhile to say.

Finally, thanks to many wonderful friends in Madrid, Galicia, and all over Spain for their kindness and generosity in sharing their culture with me, which has enabled David to go where he goes and do what he does.

Prologue

Casino de Madrid

The surroundings of the *Conde de Malladas* library in the Casino de Madrid were nothing if not appropriate to such an occasion. The lunch upstairs had been sumptuous. This wasn't *Casa Pepe* or even the Jockey Club. Apart from the official royal residences, there probably wasn't a more prestigious location in all Madrid. And why shouldn't he be here? This was the culmination of a long career of public service. The man in the dark blue suit was known among his peers and his juniors as 'The Great Survivor'. His political opponents and rivals within the Party called him 'Teflon Man' because nothing seemed to stick. His closest friends and political allies knew him as almost miraculously sure-footed. For throughout his time in politics, since shortly after the death of Franco and the re-establishment of a constitutional monarchy, he had consistently demonstrated an uncanny sixth sense for minor niggles that might become major headaches, and had moved carefully, but also ruthlessly, when required to make sure they never did. The commentators of *El Mundo* and *El Pais* sometimes wondered aloud why he had never been up for the top job, but this too was part of his instinct for self-preservation. Why expose yourself to all the mud-slinging and responsibility for others' incompetence when you can enjoy all the trappings of power from the much safer bunker of the *Palacio de la Marquesa* and live to tell the tale? This was the crowning moment of all these years of slippery guile.

"Well, this should certainly be enough to guarantee a long and happy retirement," the man opposite remarked, passing a dark leather attaché case from the side of his armchair to that of his guest. "And thoroughly deserved, might I say."

"You don't want me to sign for it, do you?"

The Party treasurer laughed, only slightly self-consciously. "Very funny," he smiled. "I think not. So, what now?"

"Oh, some dotting of i's and crossing of t's. Nothing more. A few courtesy meetings. It's nice to leave things tidy."

"And then?"

"A long holiday, I shouldn't wonder. The *Señora* thinks I've been working too hard for the last ten years and has been plotting some escape for months now. I've just been hanging on since the election to make sure things are tidy for my successor. I thought Monte Carlo, but she seems to favour California. I just hope we don't have to put up with a queue of ghastly celebrities!"

"There'll be those who want to meet the former Minister for Justice and Vice President of Spain in the hope of a word or two in the right quarter, no doubt."

"Oh, I'm past dishing out favours. It's so tiring keeping track of who you owe and who owes you. I'm really looking forward to private life. Honestly."

"Nothing you're going to miss?"

"Not a thing. With the very generous provision the Party has seen fit to direct my way in here…" he reached down and patted the case, "… I'm expecting plain sailing and time to smell the flowers."

"Well, on behalf of the entire Party, we certainly wish you all the best. You have defended our interests and values with great distinction. Take it easy and enjoy it."

They were both old players of the game and understood each other well. Sometimes it might be called 'Let's Get Rich', other times 'Let's Change the Nation', but whatever it was, the bottom line was always the eleventh commandment: 'Thou Shalt Not Get Caught'. What they were doing inevitably carried a degree of risk – and the consequences of anything unfortunate would be ghastly – but on the other hand they were adept enough at covering tracks.

Hence the need for the transaction to be in cash rather than traceable bonds or identifiable securities, and the need for a person-to-person hand over.

However, the *Casino de Madrid* was a perfect venue. Hidden in plain sight, as they say. Both men were well known in its hushed bars and corridors, so a meeting like today's would attract absolutely no attention. As regards age, perfectly tailored dark suits, greying hair and a few kilos more than their doctors wanted, they fitted in perfectly. One slightly taller, one with slightly less hair, but that was of no consequence. What they shared greatly outweighed their minor differences. And principally what they shared wasn't anything as crass as merely money. It was what that money, power and privilege brought them: the right to rule.

The two men stood and shook hands with a degree of formality, but also some personal warmth, then strolled down the grand double staircase, through the foyer and out into the Madrid sunshine. The black case was dropped casually into the back of a chauffeur-driven car. Perhaps the minister would have handled it more carefully had he known its future trajectory.

Chapter 1

Borders

David Hidalgo crammed one last box into the very limited space left in the boot, added a crushable raincoat into the cranny beside it and stood back to examine his work.

"That has to be it," he announced with a shade of satisfaction. "I defy you to get another salt-and-pepper set in there."

Dr Gillian Lockhart surveyed the jam-packed storage space of her silver MX5 with a grave expression.

"I suppose we'll be leaving this behind, then?" she remarked, nonchalantly holding up a bottle of chilled cava in a cooler. "I was planning it for the picnic on the way."

David groaned. "You know my weak spot," he muttered and pulled out the coat. "Whether or not it's wet outside, we need something nice for wetting the inside," he said. "Anyway, maybe it won't rain."

"Look, stick it in here," Gillian replied briskly, pulling open the passenger door of the two-seater and shoving the coat down behind the seat. "Voila!"

"The thought of a picnic is the only thing that's keeping me going," David commented gloomily, climbing in after the coat.

Gillian closed the boot, walked around the long, low bonnet, and slid into the driver's seat. She started the engine and pulled smoothly away from the residents-only parking on Marchmont Road, up the hill onto Grange Road, then left towards Dalkeith Road – the A7 – heading south. David slid a Stan Getz CD into the slot and tried to relax.

"I really don't know why you get so worked up about it," Gillian remarked, smoothly overtaking a dithering bloke in a flat cap driving a Morris Minor. "It's just a visit to see your mum and dad at their holiday cottage. What's not to like? They'll be gracious hosts and we'll be grateful guests. We'll visit some stuff, go for walks, eat your mum's best home cooking, listen to your dad's journalistic war stories – *again* – then go to bed and sleep late. We'll stay for a few companionable days, then come home. Job done, everybody's happy."

"*Ojalá*," David remarked drily. "If only."

"And why not?" Gillian pressed him. "We just need to be nice to one another for a week, then it's over for another year. Bear in mind that your dad may not have too many of these left. We have to enjoy it while it's still possible, then we'll have some happy memories. I always get on very well with him, and of course your mum's a delight."

"Well, he loves you," David conceded.

"And he doesn't love you?"

"Love wasn't a word that cropped up very much in the Hidalgo household."

Gillian pursed her lips as David took another deep breath and tried again to relax. Stan Getz was easing through "The Girl from Ipanema", which did help, then Gillian started humming along softly. She remembered the writer of the book of Proverbs had pointed out that there is a time to speak and a time to be silent. She slammed on the brakes, pulled over, jumped out and had the top down before David quite knew what was happening. Then back in, power on and away again, this time with the sun on their faces and the wind in their hair. The day had a few clouds but wasn't cold, as summer coughed and tried to summon a last burst of energy before the leaves started turning and an icy blast came in over the Forth, freezing the regular Edinburgh shoppers and the returning students.

David drummed his fingers along to the salsa beat and gnawed again at the bone of what made him so uncomfortable in his own father's company. Here he was, not far from sixty, previously successful and well thought of in his chosen field within the evangelical community in Spain. Then, suddenly knocked for six by a personal tragedy there was no way he could have either anticipated or stopped, he'd had to run for his life – almost literally – back to his childhood home in Edinburgh to hide. *Huir* was the Spanish verb. In English, 'flee' sounded like something from a fairy story or a melodrama, but in David's life it had turned into an all-too-cold, contemporary reality. After running from one unexpected reality, he had found himself suddenly thrust into another he had likewise not chosen and could not have anticipated. But this time it had been life-giving. Dr Gillian Lockhart had appeared like a beneficent spirit in the middle of Spanish verbs and pronoun practice at his extramural Spanish conversation evening class. It had started with conversation right enough and ended... well, it hadn't ended yet.

Their life together seemed to insist on producing more drama than you could shake a Holmesian deerstalker at. A missing girl had started it all. Then a fake church and forced prostitution; a paedophile priest bent on revenge; and, most recently, two young Muslim men tricked into a terror plot they had no real interest in or understanding of. But somehow things kept on working out. Surely it would all slow down eventually. He certainly felt he was slowing down these days, though Gillian – more than ten years his junior – showed no signs of it yet, and kept winkling him out of his curmudgeonly comfort zone into frightening things like sailing, bridge, alternative poetry readings and art-house movies. He glanced across as she swung round roundabouts and bends a good bit faster than strictly required, took a second to hook a stand of dark hair behind one ear, adjusted the silk scarf at her neck and put her foot down on the straights. 'Lucky', 'fortunate', 'blessed'... there wasn't a word he could think of that really summed it up, but 'happy' was somewhere in the mix.

With so much going his way, why couldn't he just turn up like a dutiful son, say and do the right things, hug his mum – no difficulty there – and shake his father warmly by the hand? Why not? Among the 'bare essentials' crammed into the boot was a very expensive wooden box of imported Havana cigars, a fine bottle of single malt and a rare, early Lope de Vega edition. He knew very well that this was all bribery to help ease the tension, but justified it as the easiest option. Gillian often told him to let it roll over him – "Water off a duck's back," she would whisper in his ear as soon as they were alone – but there was just so much baggage, so much history, so much family angst… and it felt like his dad kept jabbing at his internal alarm button just to see what would happen. When Gillian had first cottoned on to this state of guerrilla warfare, she had innocently asked what was going on.

"Well," David had replied wearily, "it's a long story…"

More than fifty years earlier, Ricardo Hidalgo Espina had studied journalism in Madrid, then worked first with a provincial daily mainly focused on farming and football before he eventually – what he'd really wanted – got a staff desk on a national. As the new boy, he'd ended up with the society gossip and official occasions. With Franco still at the height of his powers, there had been no shortage of military anniversaries, parades and ceremonies, with all the trappings of a stable and successful dictatorship. However, surprisingly, he had begun to find this rather fascinating instead of a waste of time. The more time he spent in Franco's company – albeit at a distance – the more intrigued he had become. Asking probing questions was neither the done thing nor even remotely safe, so when he'd produced his first story there had been a moment of shocked silence. However, he had argued the case and protested that they had a journalistic duty to at least try to probe the regime's defences every now and again. So, they had published a highly edited piece, simply reporting the facts about troops, trials and allegations of torture, and let readers make up their own minds. Franco was no fool, however, and the owner had been warned, the editor fined and the new reporter sacked.

Ricardo had decided that he was never really meant for a quiet life and had turned to freelancing, and in the evenings he had hung about the bars frequented by the regime. Slowly but surely, connections had started to be made. A bodyguard with the build of a boxer had told him about trips across the city at three o'clock in the morning to drag suspects out of bed and take them for trips they would never forget but would never be able to tell anyone about because they never came back. "We sort them all out," the bodyguard had boasted, "poofs, poets, politicians and protestants," laughing as if the phrase were common stock.

Ricardo's first substantial article had appeared in *Newsweek* and it caused a sensation. America was used to the brutal repression of Khrushchev's Soviet state, but jeez, honey, this was Europe; its ally against communism.

However, international attention cut no ice in Spain, so the writing appeared on the wall and Ricardo had realised he couldn't stay. One drunken night at an international conference on human rights in Edinburgh, he'd had an argument with a lamppost and needed treatment at the Royal Infirmary. A very pretty student doctor with an absolutely charming accent had stitched him up remarkably well, and even more remarkably agreed to check on the stitches at the Deacon Brodie pub on the Royal Mile the following evening.

Several months later, when Ricardo had been forced to run for his life, she was still stitching, swabbing, cleaning and curing, and they had taken up where they left off. Fourteen months later they had married. Less than a year after that, baby David had been born and then, two-and-a-half years later, Roberto.

Eventually it had become possible to travel in Spain again. The kids were fully bilingual, largely bicultural, and loved Spain and the Spanish. Maybe too much. When Roberto, at age fifteen, got a neighbour's daughter (aged sixteen-and-one-week) pregnant, Helen was horrified, but Ricardo hadn't made too big a deal of it. Roberto had taken this as a green light, and further trouble followed.

David, on the other hand, had always toed the line, which seemed rather boring to his father, who had also been a rebel. His older son was studious, cautious, reserved, measured, shy with girls, and seemed to prefer teenage attempts at philosophy and jazz to rock 'n' roll and rebellion. He had made it to Edinburgh University, and Hidalgo senior hadn't been surprised when young David opted to go back to Spain to seek his fortune. However, trouble was on the way. Some family drama or other – Ricardo hadn't really troubled himself about what it was – led David's first wife Rocío to try to end it all early in their married life – unsuccessfully, as it happened. Then, presumably on the rebound from the distress, she had found solace in religion. That wasn't in itself a good thing, as far as Ricardo was concerned, but it had become a positively bad thing when David, raised in the good European liberal tradition of religious scepticism, had decided to join her.

Meanwhile, Roberto had continued to be the bad boy, but in his case, crime seemed to pay very nicely. To add to the pleasure he had undoubtedly enjoyed with young Antonia among the hay bales, he had found his true love – cash. He had lied about his age, falsified documents and got a trading account with a firm of stockbrokers in Charlotte Square. He had read the *Financial Times* instead of *Smash Hits* and watched *Panorama*, not *Top of the Pops*. By the time they caught him, he had a bank account under an assumed name with £18,000 and some small change in it. Ricardo had tried to be stern but was secretly tickled. Mum had read the riot act while Dad had winked in the background. Roberto had been expelled from school, received a suspended sentence and, at age seventeen, joined his older brother in Spain using cash from another account the authorities hadn't found. Ricardo couldn't keep from laughing at the audaciousness of it all. Once Franco was dead and, democracy in the ascendant, there were opportunities to take and money to be made. Ricardo had wished his younger son the very best and taken great delight in his early successes.

David's pedestrian trajectory importing jam and shortbread had seen Ricardo rolling his eyes and yawning. And a few years later, when David jacked in his job to become a pastor, Ricardo had thrown up his hands in horror. What David had come to call 'the cold war' started then, and it hadn't stopped yet. Roberto and David could have supported each other in crazy, hedonistic Spain during the 1980s, but they didn't. To David's recollection, they met precisely three times before Roberto's disappearing act. About eighteen months into his time in Spain, he had simply vanished. Letters weren't answered, he had no employer to give an address, and the room he'd been renting was given up but none of the official bodies were notified of a change. David had pleaded utter ignorance – truthfully enough – but somehow Ricardo had held him responsible all the same.

Then a simple signed card had turned up that Christmas without any address or greeting – just a name – and had continued to appear every year since. It appeared that Roberto wasn't dead but had just decided to be 'disappeared' and stay that way. Ricardo wondered if this was to make Roberto's nefarious money-making easier and more secure, and to avoid the need to even appear to stay on the right side of the law, but that was speculation.

David turned all these things over in his mind for the umpteenth time as he and Gillian left the middle-class, south Edinburgh suburbs behind, passed through the industrial small towns that had grown on mining and textiles south of Edinburgh, and continued into the rolling grasslands of the Southern Uplands towards the Borders. Gillian suggested they divert into Melrose for the picnic she'd made up and David absent-mindedly agreed.

They found a sunny spot with benches and a table, then pulled out avocados and prawns in Marie Rose sauce, honey ham, crisp lettuce, crunchy celery, tiny plum tomatoes, parsnip crisps, crusty bread with Lurpak and black cherry yoghurts, all helped on its way with a half bottle of cava that still held some of its chill. Gillian took the merest sip, then moved on to Tesco's best sparkling elderflower, while David attended to the remainder of the bottle.

The sun grew warmer. Flies buzzed. Magpies started an argument in the tree above their heads. The breeze died, and life seemed not so bad after all.

Gillian twisted round and put her head on his lap, drawing her knees up to fit her feet onto the end of the bench. "Let's try to keep the peace this time," she murmured.

Normally, David would have protested and insisted that it takes two to tango, but the well-planned picnic had done its job and he just let out a dreamy "mmm" sound and said, "I'll do my best."

"That's all I'm asking," she added. "I know it's not easy. Just do your best. I'll try to divert things if they get too difficult. I've been in touch with your mum and she understands. We'll all have a nice time and mend some bridges."

"Anything you say," he responded, as if she had asked his opinion on jeans or a skirt – something he didn't tend to have strong opinions on, believing she looked a total knock-out in either.

They sat and lay silent for some minutes. Gillian found herself almost dozing off. David meditatively stroked her hair and acknowledged that sometimes life really did deserve the benefit of the doubt. Love had come his way not once but twice, and that was something to marvel at and give thanks for. He felt like the subject of the Old Testament writer who said, "You have put eternity in the heart of man," as if this moment of harmony with nature, God and true love might indeed last forever.

Then his mobile rang.

"David! Where the hell are you? Your mother's been preparing all morning. You were supposed to be here at two!"

The peace was shattered. David made excuses and apologised. He woke Gillian, feeling like a balloon with the air let out, and they got back in the car. As they say, the impossible we can manage; miracles take longer.

Chapter 2

Salamanca

Oscarito Fernandez de la Roda knew very well the common expression that 'money makes the world go round', but disagreed with it. Not that he thought it totally misguided – just incomplete. Some people said it was love that kept us all spinning, but, by the age of thirty-four, Oscarito had still to experience that overwhelming dreamy feeling the rest of the world seemed to obsess about, so he had to be sceptical on that one. Truth, faith, beauty, art and patriotism were other options he had rejected as insufficiently universal and pervasive. Money remained the primary candidate, but it, too, ultimately failed the test. That's to say, money was *included* in the answer but wasn't itself the heart of the matter. In short, it wasn't the limited specific of money that made the world go round, but the more global, universal and harmonious concept of *numbers*. It was certainly numbers that made Oscarito's world go round, and, he reasoned, everyone else's too, even if they didn't see it quite as clearly as he did. Money was, in fact, an interesting subset, but numbers in general were so much more universal. They included cash, dates, times, durations, quantities, volumes, capacities, numerical aims and objectives, budgets, targets, percentages, projections, rankings and ratings, and if the definition was slightly extended to include Boolean numbers, then also true and false, and hence the whole wonderful world of logic and proofs.

Oscarito concluded that there was nothing that numbers couldn't be applied to and illuminate. He'd even heard that guys rated girls from one to ten, so sexual attraction turned out to be numerical, too.

Scientists claimed that the fundamental language of the universe itself was mathematical, but Oscar was enough of a realist to accept that the world of 'really hard sums' was beyond him, so he had accepted that he needed to set his sights lower, at more terrestrial numbers, and had chosen to study accounts and public administration. His father told him the family was on cloud nine, so it turned out that numbers even measured and defined human happiness.

Oscar senior was a street sweeper but did not consider this a menial job, since technically he was a *funcionario* or civil servant, employed by the local authority, which meant he had a guaranteed job for life. He and Carmen had a comfortable *piso* suitable to their needs. They did not live beyond their means, and he was inordinately proud of both his boys. Sweeping leaves, rubbish, and even used and discarded condoms, and cleaning up after the giant rubbish containers had been emptied by a fleet of garbage lorries, left him plenty of time for thinking and philosophising. One of his key philosophies was the 'round peg, round hole' view of life. He had readily accepted that he was of a certain shape that fitted fairly well into the slot marked 'street sweeping'. Carmen was of a shape that fitted perfectly into cleaning the offices of the giant wedding cake Telefonica building on Gran Vía in the centre of Madrid. And she was of a shape that also perfectly fitted his shape when they snuggled up in bed together after another hard day of sweeping and dusting. Andres, the older boy, had kept a low profile through school, enjoyed making little knick-knacks for his *mamá* in handicraft classes and had eventually got a steady job with Nacho the carpenter round the corner. Round peg in a round hole. Andres appeared to be perfectly normal in every way, and soon joined his father in philosophising at the *Rincon de Rafa* bar once he had completed his quota of windows and doors.

Oscarito, on the other hand, had always been a bit of a mystery to his parents, neighbours and friends. He had shown not a shred of interest in girls, football or beer; the great triumvirate of Spanish obsessions. No Real Madrid posters on the wall, no girly magazines in the cupboard and no *botellón* in the park – literally 'the big bottle', slang referring to kids who were out to get smashed at the weekend in a secluded corner of a public place – a normal rite of passage for Spanish youth. True, he had shown a brief flicker of interest in the Christmas lottery – another Spanish obsession – but by age fourteen he had explained to his parents that he statistically had less chance of winning than of finding a single designated grain of sand on the beach at Portonovo in the Ria de Pontevedra, where they went on holiday every year. He never took part again, despite Oscar senior's attempt to explain that it had nothing to do with statistics – it was luck. If you were lucky, you won… whatever the statistics.

However, when it came to numbers that could be made to behave in a more co-operative fashion, little Oscar – Oscarito, as he was universally known – was a whizz. Adding up enormous lists in his head, multiplying three-digit numbers and announcing the percentage of the route to Portonovo they had completed at intervals of three kilometres until everyone wanted to kill him, these were the games Oscarito loved. Oscar senior simply shrugged his shoulders, had another beer and gave thanks to San Antonio (patron saint of lost causes) that his younger son was another round peg who seemed to have found his round hole.

Oscarito had sailed through university, unencumbered by matters of the heart, matters of illegal chemistry or the tedious business of going to parties where you were expected to drink, dance and devise some means of getting a member of the opposite sex into the sack. He had stayed home and worked on the odds of the various football teams in La Liga ending up in a particular order. Not that he was interested in football, but the trick was to find bookmakers somewhere in the world who offered significantly different odds from what he had worked out, then bet on being just a little bit closer to the final result than they were. He put every cent he could save into a once-a-year bet, which inevitably came up. This meant he didn't have to scrimp and save quite so much the following year. Oscar senior couldn't believe that his son had repeatedly been so lucky.

After university he had got a job as a junior accounting clerk at a small bookkeeping firm and continued his otherwise untroubled life. Carmen made him a *bocadillo de jamón*, tortilla or Manchego cheese every morning, wrapped it carefully in tin foil and left it out for him, along with some fruit and a carton of chocolate milk – his favourite since childhood, and one of his few self-indulgences. Oscarito took it to work, arriving precisely ten minutes before starting time, then opened whichever Excel spreadsheet was needed that day and spent an entirely satisfying four hours making the numbers line up and behave before eating lunch at his desk. He eschewed the traditional long lunch break with colleagues (plus possible siesta), choosing to complete the remaining four hours as quickly as possible before returning home. Some days he hardly exchanged a single word other than *hola* or *buenos días* with colleagues, which was exactly how he liked it and what they had come to accept. Isabel, the single, middle-aged receptionist, had shown some interest. However, her flirty chat was so thoroughly lost on Oscarito that she had given up in frustration and instead had to revert to trying her blandishments on sixty-four-year-old Alberto the caretaker, who was happily more receptive. Oscarito was not invited to the wedding, which was perfect as he would have had to make up an excuse not to go.

Finally, after four years in the same office doing more or less the same thing every day, but with steadily increasing competence and confidence, Oscar senior came to the conclusion that his son was expanding his skills and was ready for a bigger hole to fill. One night he came back from the monthly Party meeting with a flyer in his hand, which he showed first to Carmen and, a short, whispered conversation later, to Oscarito.

"Look at this, *hijo*," he said. "They're looking for a senior accountant at Party headquarters. You've passed all your exams. You're ready for something new. I think you should apply."

Oscarito glanced briefly at the paper, noting the relevant numbers in the terms and conditions, and, without even consciously thinking, did a quick mental calculation. It was 56.4 per cent more than his current salary, with 25 per cent more holidays. There was access to a pension fund at 12.5 per cent of his monthly salary, which would eventually lead to a pension of 65 per cent of his closing income in thirty-one years.

"OK," he said. "How do I apply?"

"I was chatting with Miguel, the district secretary, this evening," his father replied. "He knows your work at the office. He says you just need to go along to Party headquarters in Salamanca and take all your papers. They'll deal with everything. He'll have a word and let me know when would suit."

The following evening the secretary had a further word with Oscar, who then had a word with Oscarito, who asked for the afternoon off, went to the very posh two-story premises in its own grounds in one of the beautiful leafy suburbs of north central Madrid, and laid his papers out on the table with a slightly shaky hand. Party headquarters. In Salamanca. Perhaps the leader of the Party – the Prime Minister himself – might drop by. His father had been a loyal supporter since the Party was founded after Franco's demise, and even he'd never got this far.

Señor Ibañez, the office manager, glanced over Oscarito's papers in a cursory way, asked him a few questions about his current job and out-of-work interests, then left the room. He caught up with Señor Gonzaléz, Party treasurer, on the first landing up the stairs.

"I've got the new accountant in," he said. "I think he'll be perfect. It's just like Miguel said; he's a robot. He'll just add up whatever you put in front of him without the slightest interest in what it means or where it comes from."

"Capital," the treasurer agreed. "To be honest, the numbers are all growing bigger and it's getting a bit beyond me. A calculating machine that doesn't ask questions is exactly what I need."

"I think we've found him," Ibañez replied, smiling.

"OK. On you go, then."

"Do you want to come in and meet him?"

"Do I need to? Well, I suppose I'd better. If he's going to save my bacon and everyone else's."

So Señor Gonzaléz popped his nose round the door of the interview room, beamed at Oscarito, shook his hand warmly and welcomed him aboard – to the latter's evident bewilderment. Was that the interview over? Had he passed?

Although the Party had just won the election, Gonzaléz explained, it had cost a fortune and there would need to be a major recruitment drive to rebuild their financial base. This would be crucial to their chances in the next election, and hence crucial to the future well-being of Spain. That task successfully completed, the Party would be in a position to show its gratitude and advance careers. He hoped Oscarito could be part of the winning team. Oscarito smiled dutifully through his confusion and stuttered that he would do his very best. Señor Gonzaléz pressed the flesh one more time, beamed again and left the office with his colleague.

"Not so much a robot as a zombie," he muttered once out of earshot. "However, so much the better, I suppose. I guess we won't find him trying to get his own snout in the trough or having it off with the secretaries in a cupboard. Do the necessary and let's get him in as soon as we can. I've a shopping bag full of papers that need sorting and a suitcase full of notes that needs an identity."

So, Oscarito handed in his notice at the bookkeepers – his former colleagues hardly noticed the difference – caught the metro for Salamanca, changing at Chamartin, and started working his way through the backlog, only pausing briefly each day for the *bocadillo de jamón* and his chocolate milk.

It was a mess. They didn't even have an up-to-date version of Excel and there was no office networking. The secretaries were still on XP, and a couple of old CP/M consoles, which probably used to run VisiCalc, sat in the corner. As for the actual accounts, Oscarito had seen more order in his family's recycling bins. However, on the plus side, his new salary was a huge step up and Ibañez, who was his day-to-day boss, never said no when asked for new software, hardware, network cabling or a higher-speed internet connection.

The only early surprise came when Ibañez produced a confidentiality agreement that he insisted all new staff had to sign. Oscarito asked to take it home overnight so he could read it, but Ibañez suddenly got very shirty and more or less insisted he sign there and then if he wanted to continue working. Oscarito was nonplussed. Why should he not be permitted to read a legal document he was being asked to sign? In the end he was allowed to cast an eye over it, gravely informed that it was strictly forbidden to make a copy and told to be ready to sign in ten minutes. By the time Ibañez got back, pen in hand, Oscarito had only got as far as the frankly dire list of penalties that would kick in should the signatory be found to be in breach of any of his obligations. Alicia, the blonde secretary and Rosa the brunette secretary looked up warily from their typing while Oscarito duly signed; still unhappy, but at a loss as to how to handle it. Ibañez folded the document, put it into his briefcase and resumed his former benign, avuncular persona. Oscarito went home that night pondering the day's events, without the slightest idea what to make of it.

Days at Party headquarters quickly became weeks, then months, until his first half-yearly evaluation was due. Ibañez invited Oscarito into his office, made him a coffee, offered a chocolate biscuit and asked him to give his own evaluation of what he thought he had accomplished since he began.

"Well, Señor Ibañez," Oscarito began hesitantly, "I think I've made quite good progress."

Ibañez nodded encouragingly, so he continued.

"All of our software is up to date now, and I think the secretaries were happy with the training I gave them. We have a much better filing system for word-processed and spreadsheet documents, with sensible naming conventions. I've caught up with all the accounts, which should be ready for scrutiny by the external auditors next month. I can do reports on cash flow, debtors and creditors, accounts outstanding, expenses and allowances – in fact, almost anything you want to ask. If we don't already have a report for it, I can write one quite easily. I don't know what else I can say. I think it's all going quite well."

"Excellent, Oscarito," Ibañez beamed. "All you say is quite true. 'I'm more than happy with your progress and what you've achieved. However," he added somewhat more gravely, "that you and I are happy is not the final aim. The goal we both share is that the Party should be happy, and that means the Party treasurer."

Oscarito felt sweat forming on his brow and ran a hand around the back of his collar, wondering what was coming next. He needn't have.

"But I can tell you," Ibañez continued brightly, "that Don Gonzaléz is in fact more than happy. He is delighted, and only told me this morning that the accounts have never been in better shape. You should be very pleased and proud of what you have achieved."

Oscarito was relieved. "I... I am," he stuttered. He had expected things to be generally OK, but hadn't expected such a level of appreciation. He knew his father would be pleased, too. He felt he could begin to relax.

However, Ibañez wasn't finished. "Now, Oscarito," he pressed on. "In my conversation with the treasurer this morning, he told me that because you have more than rewarded our trust in you, he thought the time was right to entrust you with a crucially important matter."

"Certainly, Señor Ibañez," Oscarito said, feeling more confident, while wondering what might be coming next.

"Let me explain," the office manager began, taking a sip of his coffee and settling back into his sumptuous black leather executive chair. "Well-ordered accounts are of course important, and of course we need to keep a tight grip on expenditure, expenses and so on, and pay our bills on time. But there is something much more important. Indeed, it is our life blood. Do you know what that is?"

Oscarito shook his head. As far as he was concerned, every single entry in an accounting system was just as important as any other.

Being even one cent out was unacceptable – like going to work with only one sock on, which had happened once or twice.

"I've no idea, Señor Ibañez," he confessed.

"Well, let me tell you," Ibañez lowered his voice, adding further gravitas. "In a word: donors."

"Donors?" Oscarito repeated blankly.

"Yes, Oscarito. Donors. And I'm not talking about kebabs." Ibañez permitted himself a smile at his witticism. "Nor," he continued, "little old ladies who leave us €5 in their wills. Substantial donors are our lifeblood. By them we stand and fall, live and die, breathe and move. No donors and the Party dies. It makes no difference how many Spaniards consider themselves our natural supporters or how good our policies may seem. Without donors we have no Party machine, no canvassers, no publicity, no advertising, no publications, no telephone lines, no computers – in fact, no hope... and even no you and me. Who do you think pays your wages, Oscarito?" He lit a long, thin cigar.

"I've never really thought about it," the accountant replied. "I suppose it just comes from Party funds."

"And where do Party funds come from?" Ibañez pressed him, breathing out a long cloud of aromatic smoke.

"Erm, donors?" Oscarito ventured.

"Exactly, my boy. Exactly. You are undoubtedly a quick learner. Donors. Our system in Spain is one of mixed funding, in that the State does fund political parties according to their representation in parliament; however, individual membership donations are also permitted. We cannot increase our funding from the State, so what can we do if we have higher costs or want to mount more extensive campaigns?"

"Increase the number of donors?"

"Exactly – and increase the average level of donation. That's why we place considerable emphasis on donors and their place in the Party machinery. So let me ask you another question, Oscarito. Who are the donors and what do they want?'

"I suppose they're people who support our policies," Oscarito ventured. "And who are interested in the welfare of the country."

Ibañez smiled indulgently. "Partly. Yes, they do want specific policies and the welfare of the country in general terms. As they say, 'A rising tide lifts all boats.' However, there are other things they want, too. They want influence. They want the Party's ear – up to and including the Prime Minister's ear. And of course, that means they want things to go their way, to benefit their industry or business, to move Spain in a direction that accords with their interests. But donors are a very mixed bunch. Some want one thing, some another. It's practically impossible to satisfy all needs and desires. In fact, it's a constant struggle to keep them all on board and assure them that what each of them wants will be given the Party's – meaning, of course, *the government's* – closest attention. But in the end that's a matter for the Party hierarchy and the politicians. And you and I are not politicians, are we?"

By this time, Oscarito felt as if he were being admitted to matters of higher policy and the inner workings of power. It was exhilarating but also terrifying. He could only nod, then shake his head vigorously, hoping that one or other would be the right response.

"Exactly," Ibañez continued, apparently unconcerned by the level of confusion facing him from across his desk. "We are not. We are merely humble servants of our political masters. Our job is to help them do their job, knowing that we are taking care of the nuts and bolts behind the scenes. Correct?"

Oscarito didn't dare risk a wrong response and remained rigidly upright and immobile. Again, Ibañez didn't seem to notice.

"So, I come back to my point, Oscarito. Donors largely want different things, some of which may be mutually exclusive, but that is not our problem. However, what is most definitely our problem is the crucial thing that almost all donors want. Can you think what that might be?"

Oscarito dumbly shook his head.

"Anonymity," Ibañez intoned gravely. "Anonymity, confidentiality, security – call it what you will. They give money to the Party to achieve certain goals, and in all but a few cases they do not want the outside world to know what they have given: when, where, how much or how often. There are a small number of highly visible public figures who want the whole world to know about their generosity, but even then they want to do it on their own terms. To declare what they want to, when they want to and not to have it published in a list in *El País*. Do you follow me?"

This time Oscarito thought a quick nod was required and offered it.

"Now that presents us – that's to say you and I – with a certain problem, Oscarito," Ibañez continued. He took another draw of his cigar, laid it in the ashtray, lowered his voice still further and leaned forward, hands clasped on the mahogany desktop before him. "The public code for political parties requires us to place severe – indeed unreasonable – limits on the donations and membership fees we can accept. And we have to make all donations public over a certain figure, which in reality means all the donations that really matter. But donors want anonymity. So, what are we to do? The law requires us to disclose; the donors require us not to. Any ideas, Oscarito?"

Now the accountant was actually being asked for some substantive response he paused, licked his lips and thought. "We could simply not declare the higher donations," he started, "but that would be against the law, wouldn't it?"

"Indeed it would," Ibañez confirmed, watching him closely.

"Or we could split up higher donations into smaller sums and spread them over a longer period so they no longer qualified as over the threshold."

"Good," Ibañez smiled. "Keep going."

"Or, I suppose we could assign a smaller amount to the main donor and perhaps have the bulk assigned to a series of proxy donors known to the main donor, keeping all amounts below the threshold."

"Very good indeed." Ibañez smiled broadly this time and sat back in his chair.

"I knew you were good, Oscarito, but I wasn't sure how good. Excellent. In fact, we do both of the latter. We do not break the law, but we work around the law; like any legal team, any tax management firm, any large corporation and indeed like most of the citizens of Spain. The treasurer has been very impressed with your work and has asked me to give you responsibility for those we refer to as our 'gold star donors'; those who give sums that would nominally take them over the threshold but who wish to keep their anonymity. Naturally, that means keeping records, as we would for any financial matter. However, in this case the Party takes very seriously the wishes of our donors, and these days, sadly, we also have to take into account threats from hackers and hostile bodies, either in this country or abroad. Just think about leaked political emails as an example of what can happen. So, for that reason we do not put any of this on the computer at all."

"At all?" Oscarito asked, incredulous in spite of himself.

"At all," Ibañez confirmed. "Everything is manually recorded." At that, he unlocked and opened a desk drawer, pulled out a large, old-fashioned folio ledger book with dark leather covers and a single gold star on the front and laid it on the desk.

"These are the records," he said, pushing the book across the desk. "And they are now part of your job. As I hope I've made clear, these are the lifeblood, continued existence and hopes of success of the Party. They are only to be attended to outside of normal office hours. This book, and subsequent volumes, must never leave the office. When not in use it remains in my safe. You will no doubt remember that your confidentiality agreement covers the need to maintain privacy and security in matters of the Party as you are directed, Oscarito. With respect to these accounts, you are now so directed. We have confidence in you, but you must understand that the Party cannot tolerate breaches of security in matters as important as this. The consequence would be very serious, I have to inform you. For you, for your future career, for anyone you might divulge the information to and indeed for those around you, whom I'm sure you would not want to see becoming embroiled." Ibañez paused and drew from his cigar again. He was no longer smiling. He had picked up a brass letter opener and was holding it in his right hand and tapping it against the palm of his left. He held Oscarito in an unflinching gaze. "Do I make myself clear?" he asked quietly, pointing the opener directly at Oscarito.

The accountant was struck dumb, glued to his chair. This sort of thing had never been mentioned in *Principles of Ethical Accounting 101*.

"I... I, erm... Yes, sir," he finally replied.

Ibañez pushed the accounts book further across the desk. Oscarito feared it might be electrified, as if touching it would send 10,000 volts up his arm. But Ibañez was waiting, still silently staring at him.

Oscarito had not had a classical education but knew enough to be reminded of Caesar and the Rubicon. Picking up that book would commit him. He could hardly come back to his boss and say he'd changed his mind. Now was the moment to stand up and say:

"I'm sorry, Señor Ibañez. I don't think this is what the Cortes intended when it enacted these laws to protect our democracy from being bought by unscrupulous partisan interests. As a law-abiding citizen, I'm afraid I can take no part in this. Now, if you'll excuse me, I'll clear out my desk. A letter of resignation will be in the post tomorrow morning."

Instead, he leaned forward with moist palms and picked up the book. "I'll do my very best, sir," he said hoarsely. Then he stood up on shaky legs and made for the door.

Ibañez stopped him. "In the safe," he said sternly.

Oscarito bent down, placed the book in the open safe in the corner and closed its reinforced steel door.

If he'd felt nervous signing the confidentiality document, that had been a walk in the park compared with this. Oscarito understood little of office power and politics, but one thing even he grasped. The Party was no longer simply his employer; it now owned him. In taking the book he had taken the thirty pieces of silver, and the safe in the corner now held his future and what was left of his conscience.

"If you don't mind, sir, I think I need some fresh air," he said, leaving the office.

"Are you all right, dear?" Rosa, one of the secretaries, asked as he brushed past her desk. "You look like you've seen a ghost."

Oscarito shook his head. "I need to get out of here," he said, heading for the main door.

Back in his office, Ibañez smiled slowly and picked up the phone. "All done," he said quietly. "I've frightened the living daylights out of him. I think I can safely vouch for his level of terror, if not his actual loyalty. And if he doesn't behave, I'll string him up myself."

Chapter 3

Country Cottage

The property David's parents had rented for a few weeks to escape the summer heat and crowds in their year-round flat in Malaga was perfect. It had private parking at the rear, a small, secluded garden, barbecue space and comfortable garden furniture. The building was of a long, low cottage style with dormer windows – allowing a couple of small upstairs bedrooms – and was constructed from warm, rose-red sandstone with an old-fashioned wooden porch painted moss green.

Gillian crunched to a halt on the gravel driveway and they both climbed out. David's parents were sitting at a garden table and his mum jumped up immediately to welcome them.

"Wonderful to see you both. Gillian, you look younger every year, not older. What's the secret?"

David's dad struggled out of his low deck chair and shuffled over, peering at his watch. "Better late than never," he conceded grudgingly. "*Hola guapa*," he said to Gillian and gave her the customary Spanish *dos besos* – two kisses – then shook David by the hand. "What'll it be, then?" he asked. "G and T, *vino*, or Helen's made a jug of Pimm's."

"The Pimm's cocktail sounds great," Gillian replied. "I've been working on the new term's lectures all week. I'm just ready to unwind."

"Great."

Ricardo disappeared inside and David was about to go and help when his mum stopped him.

"Just let him," she whispered. "It's occupational therapy. You know what he's like. Pottering around calms him down."

David nodded and all three sat down at the garden table.

"How are you, Mum?" David asked. "Was the flight OK?"

They spent the next few minutes catching up. Helen spoke about one or two aches and pains, but a really nice new doctor who'd arrived in their *pueblo* was taking a proactive approach to the problems of ageing and seemed to be sorting things out. Gillian updated her on university politics and her latest research, and David mentioned the chance of a six-week study trip to Mexico that had come up and he was thinking about. In the meantime, Southside Fellowship, the small, unexciting but entirely suitable church David pastored, was plodding along. Numbers were slowly rising and there was a very nice mix of ages and social backgrounds.

"So, the Kingdom of God's still alive and prospering?" Ricardo asked coming out with a tray. "I thought God had deserted us years ago."

"Well, reports of his death may have been greatly exaggerated," David replied genially, keeping his cool and handing over the miscellaneous gifts.

Ricardo grunted again, the words "thank" and "you" apparently not in his vocabulary.

"You know, I completely fail to understand it," he continued, unwrapping the cigars. "With all the evidence we have from science, how people insist on maintaining a bunch of superstitions that would have embarrassed Galileo. And you say you have more young people than ever? What's the attraction? I suppose it can't be the charismatic preaching, can it?"

David grimaced but tried to take the question at face value. "You're right," he said, taking a sip of the Pimm's and a nibble of home-made cookie. "I think things are changing in a way nobody would have predicted. My theory is generational. At least in the UK, previous generations – like your grandparents, Mum – previous generations kind of took it all for granted without thinking too much about it. Then the rise of modernism – you know, Freud, Darwin and Marx – that generation thought anything you couldn't see and measure didn't exist. So, faith was meaningless and outdated."

"Quite right," Ricardo grunted.

David ignored him. "Then the postmodern generation – that's today's eighteen to thirty-five-year-olds – they've grown up without any of the trappings of religion at all. Which means that on the one hand they are incredibly ignorant, but at the same time they're open-minded. They have neither the prejudices of their parents nor the nominalism of their grandparents. They are dissatisfied with materialism, disgusted with corruption and anxious about climate change – all products of modernism, I think."

His dad grunted again. "I think they're just getting hoodwinked all over again. Science may have caused some of our problems, but the way out isn't religion – it's better science. And corruption isn't a new phenomenon. At least in Spain, kings and courtiers have been on the make since forever. Democracy hasn't done much to change that, and there are as many tele-preachers on the make as deputies in the *Cortes*, I can guarantee you."

David opened his mouth to respond, but both women got in first.

"Another cookie, anyone?" Helen asked, holding up the plate.

"How are things in Spain, Ricardo?" Gillian interjected. "More revelations?"

The women shared a second of eye contact and a flash of eyebrows, as if to say, *Well done. You thought of it, too.*

Ricardo grunted yet again, which seemed to be his general-purpose response to anything that didn't come out of a bottle of single malt.

"Horrible," he said. "At least Franco didn't pretend. Now everybody's got their nose in the bucket while maintaining their innocence. Local mayors are being investigated for awarding contracts in exchange for 'donations' and the main parties are accused of having slush funds to reward the faithful. There's even a suggestion from some that there might be organised crime connections. That strikes me as a bridge too far, even for the present bunch – but you never know. They're all feathering their own nests, that's for sure."

"That must be so disappointing," Gillian put in, "especially when you were trying to get rid of Franco and bring in the new constitution with the idea that everything would be different."

Ricardo shrugged. "Well, like I say, it's been part of Spanish society for so long. I'd love to be back in the game, though. Ferreting about. There must be so much to find out if you could just look in the right places and ask the right questions of the right people. There are always some who want to talk. Who can't bottle it up any longer. Who have a story to tell. If I was thirty-five now, not in my eighties, I'd be pestering them till they thought I was their best friend. We make friends with the little fish to catch the big fish." He stared up at the ceiling, as if remembering his history and relishing the idea. Then his head sank and he let out a long breath. "There was a day, but I'm too old and broken now. Younger guys have to take it on. If there are any... That would be a better contribution to society – not more religion."

David finished the cookie he had in his hand and gazed up over the little pine wood behind the cottage. *He doesn't miss a chance*, he thought. *Not one. It's as if he has a personal beef and needs to get a good kick in whenever the opportunity presents itself. If it were anyone else I'd be patient and talk it through, but this is impossible.* He sighed and said nothing.

That thought continued as they unpacked upstairs after another twenty minutes of idle chit-chat.

"Well done, honey," Gillian said, hanging up a beautiful, floaty, printed dress she'd got at the Cancer Research shop on South Clerk Street the week before. A wash and iron, and it would have done for a premier.

David came round behind her and put his arms around her waist. "You are my anchor," he said. "I'd have been off on another pointless quest to make him see sense if you hadn't come in. Honestly, you're the best there is."

She finished tucking the hem of the dress into the wardrobe, which wasn't quite deep enough. "It's just family," she said. "Love them or loathe them, you can't ignore them. And your mum's a delight."

"True, all true. But when I didn't have you, I was adrift. About to go under. You worked the miracle."

"With some divine help, I believe," she corrected him.

"That's right," he replied. "You know, I spent an hour in prayer every morning for a gorgeous girl who wanted to learn Spanish, cook paella and move in with me. Then, bingo! I got the jackpot!"

"Huh. That's gilding the lily somewhat, *Señor*. I did move in, but only once we'd done it right. Happy with the result?"

He reached round and gave her a peck on the nose. "Most days I suppose it's generally bearable," he said with a straight face.

She made a mock lion growl towards his face. "Watch yourself, mister," she said. "Remember you're in my power!"

* * *

They went out for dinner that night and mostly behaved themselves. Ricardo kissed Gillian's hand at the start of the meal and paid the bill at the end, managing to hide his customary reluctance to get his wallet out. In between, he was the genial host and told jokes about now-famous Spanish politicians he had known either when they were students or struggling to find a constituency. The Rioja flowed freely at triple the price of a restaurant in Spain. However, that was to be expected, and besides one more grunt when Ricardo saw the bill, they managed to eat a nice dinner without open warfare breaking out.

Back at the cottage – a taxi ride later – Ricardo excused himself and painfully climbed the stairs. Gillian sat down in the lounge and keyed in the cottage Wi-Fi code to catch up on emails, leaving David and his mum unoccupied.

"Fancy a walk, Davie?" she asked.

"Sure. I'll get a jacket."

The stars were out, along with a new moon, as they wandered along the gravel path at the back of the row of cottages, then through a gate and onto a bridle path leading along a stream.

"How are you really, Mum?" David asked. "And how is he? He sounds like he's in pain."

"Oh, I'm fine. Aches and pains, as you'd expect. I'd like a couple of new hips and knees. And eyes and ears. But I get on with things. I'm not so bad."

"And Dad?"

Helen pursed her lips and took David's arm. "Well, your guess is as good as mine," she said. "Grumpy, of course, but I'm used to that. In fact, I knew that before I married him. But there's something else wrong and I don't know what it is. He won't talk to me, and as far as I know he won't see a doctor. There's something eating him. Something physical, I think, but also something emotional. You know your dad always considered emotions a waste of energy, but there's definitely something. You and Gillian seem to be doing incredibly well, so he's not worried about you. In fact – though he'd never admit it – he reads the Edinburgh papers online. Your crime-fighting exploits have even reached the *pueblos* of Malaga. He's proud of you. He just can't say it."

"I always thought that was just a Scottish problem," David remarked. "Not being able to say how you feel."

"Believe me, it's international," Helen laughed, echoing the gurgling water of the burn. "It's a man thing. Not that we're sexist about it, of course!"

David smiled.

"Yes," he said. "I've heard there are some differences in the electrics, not just the plumbing."

They walked on in companionable silence, arm in arm, absorbed in the symphonies of the night – nocturnal birds, the water in the burn, leaves and twigs under their feet.

"Is it Roberto?" David asked suddenly, then caught himself. "I'm sorry. If you'd rather not talk about it…"

She gripped his arm more tightly. "No, it's all right," she said softly. "Not talking about it doesn't make it go away. The cards come every Christmas, but nothing more. Your dad hired a private investigator a few years ago, you know. It cost €20,000 but found nothing. And it's so long ago nobody would even know what he looks like now – assuming he's alive, of course."

"But the cards?"

"Could be a lawyer. It would be easy enough to prepare them – one for every year until we weren't likely to be alive any more, and the lawyer simply sends them on the due date, paid upfront. And Roberto does whatever he does and goes wherever he does. I don't suppose money would be a problem. Though he may have finally tangled with the law in a way he couldn't get out of and be in a Spanish jail. Who knows?" She gave a heavy sigh. "Your father doesn't talk about it, but I know it plays on his mind. You mustn't judge him too harshly."

"I try not to," David replied, "though it's not easy sometimes. It's very clear that he doesn't rate what I do at all. A son likes to hear that his father's proud of him."

"Oh, he is, Davie. He is. I know he can't say it, but he is. He just doesn't hold with religion. You know that."

"Yes, I'd noticed."

"But all the stuff that's happened since you went back to Edinburgh. The missing girl, the chain of brothels. You know, he used to take the Edinburgh papers to his club in Malaga and translate them for all his friends. 'Crime-fighting curate', they called you, or something like that."

"I think it was 'saintly sleuth'," David remarked dryly. "Anything for an alliteration. Should we head back now? I think I was just dive-bombed by a bat."

They made their way back to the cottage and Helen heated enough milk for three hot chocolates, Ricardo having retired some time before. Then they kissed goodnight, and David and Gillian took theirs upstairs.

"Well, a good heart-to-heart?" Gillian asked, undressing.

"Mum's a gem," David replied, sitting on the bed and pulling his shoes off. "I'd call her a saint if I believed in them."

Moments later they were tucked up, each with a Kindle in front of them.

"I don't think I can be bothered with the history of the crusades tonight," Gillian remarked after a few seconds. "What are you reading?"

"Ted Gioia's *The History of Jazz*. For the third time. There's so much in it, it takes a reread to piece it all together. But it's not exactly riveting by this time, I'll admit. Any better ideas?"

"Maybe I could think of something."

"Mmmm, temptress. Can I finish my hot chocolate first? It's an aphrodisiac, you know."

"Are you suggesting you need one?"

"No, I mean you can paint it all over."

"Yuough! Sticky! If your congregation were to find out what goes through your head!"

He grinned and tipped up the mug. "Lights out," he said. "Let's see what develops!"

* * *

The next few days unfolded in a consistent manner. Ricardo seemed to grow more easily irritated and irascible day by day, while David found himself rising all too quickly to the bait, despite his determination not to. The women tried to keep the peace by changing the subject, proposing outings, making light of things, and keeping the food and drink flowing. They visited the local sights and did country walks and town shopping.

Melrose Abbey, according to Ricardo, was not a beautiful remnant of an age of harmonious classical style built by master craftsmen who had learned their art at Chartes or York Minster, but a hideous skeleton of the corpse of European religious superstition. Local museums weren't fascinating insights into a simpler time of country skills and interrelationships, but monuments to the oppression of the rural working class. Local independent clothiers weren't selling good-quality items at a bit of a markup to ensure their survival through the leaner times until next year's tourists arrived, they were ripping visitors off for goods probably made in the sweatshops of Bangladesh. And no subject of his ire failed to have some religious aspect that he could latch on to in order to criticise in a way that was clearly directed at David.

Gillian had begun the week knowing it would be a challenge, but had been bright and optimistic, thinking to herself, *This might be awkward, but it's not impossible. We can do this.*

After three days she was beginning to see things more from David's point of view. Every day she tried to propose something that seemed so totally neutral it should have been interesting and fun all round, only to find it twisted by Ricardo's habitual grunt, followed by some sour comment. Once again, she realised the truth of David's assertions that his mum was truly a saint in the flesh. He had called her an oak tree in the wind, and the analogy seemed apt.

Every evening, when forbearance had yet again worn paper-thin, Gillian would whisper in David's ear, "Just four more days" or "Just three more days".

By Wednesday night, David went to bed fuming. "This really is above and beyond the limits of filial duty," he muttered, sitting on the edge of the bed and shaking his head. "One more comment like today when he said being a pastor was more or less the same as being a public professional liar and I'm really going to let rip."

"Which you'll regret."

"I'm sure I will, but I'll enjoy it at the time. They say smiling uses fewer muscles than frowning, but sometimes it's worth the extra effort."

"Just two more days, honey," she said. "Tomorrow's Thursday. Then Friday. Then we go home Saturday morning."

He let out a muted "Grrr!" that made them both laugh.

"I'm proud of you," Gillian said. "You're doing well against overwhelming odds. Don't let it be the basis for a bad memory."

He sighed again. "I'll try. But for you – not for him."

They got ready for bed. David climbed in, set his pillows up against the headboard and opened the clamshell of his laptop to try to divert his mind before sleeping. He checked through the BBC News, looking for more ridiculous political nonsense, then popped his email open. Fantastic-value wine offers – only a few bottles left. Dinner for two at an award-winning French restaurant overlooking the Royal Mile – last few days. Then, remarkably, one message from a name he recognised. It was from Mariano, who had taken over leadership of Warehouse 66, the church David had helped found just outside Madrid more than twenty-five years ago. He clicked it open and read.

"Ha! Look at this, Gillian. Well I never. The end is in sight."

"What?"

"It's from Mariano. Seems the Spanish Minister for Justice, who has religious entities in his brief, wants a farewell meeting of all the religious leaders, including evangelicals, before he retires. Mariano's invited but wants me to come too, for the sake of the origins of the church. He's doing all the legwork. Flights for two from Edinburgh on Saturday morning if we agree. Back Monday night. We just need to say yes and he'll arrange it all and pay for it. What do you say? It feels like a godsend, I must say."

Gillian was seated at the dressing table, combing her hair. She stopped mid-brush.

"Hmm. Well, it sounds great. A way out with honour. It's really short notice, though. I'm feeling like I can't lose many more days of prep for the new term."

"Well, according to this you'd only lose Monday. We'd go back up to town on Friday for an early flight on Saturday. That means one day less. Hallelujah! Then church on Sunday, the meeting on Monday morning and home early on Tuesday. You'd only lose one day – or even none if you can work while I'm at the meeting."

"Seems a long way to go for a two-hour meeting."

"I suppose it is, but it's all paid for. Whip over to Madrid. Wined and dined at government expense. Meet some friends. Church at Warehouse 66, meeting Monday morning, then home asap afterwards, loaded up with good *jamón* and a couple of bottles. I'm not preaching on Sunday and we meet our friends. It's a gift. What could go wrong?"

David broke the news at breakfast the next morning with an appropriate expression of regret. "It's probably going to be two hours of sheer tedium," he explained, "but when the minister calls... It might be the last opportunity to put a word in for more religious equality."

Ricardo gave him a very sharp look but restricted comment to his customary grunt at the mention of religion. Helen's face fell and Gillian felt sorry for her, then very guilty. Helen had probably been counting on them to make the rest of the week tolerable. Gillian couldn't imagine what it must be like to live with this the whole time – though maybe having David around made it worse. She reached out to take Helen's hand but missed as David's mum abruptly got up and headed outside. Gillian followed her, leaving David and his father alone.

"Very ingenious," Ricardo commented dryly. "I don't blame you." He got up painfully. "Give me a hand with the breakfast dishes. I think your mother needs some time off."

* * *

The rest of the day went better than any so far. Ricardo seemed to have been silenced at last. Gillian had her arm through David's on one side and Helen took his other arm as they had a lovely riverside walk and a picnic, then went shopping in Hawick. The afternoon was warm and drowsy, and everyone ended up napping when they got home.

David had found a nice-looking restaurant within walking distance that they had noticed driving past but not tried yet. He got the last table for eight thirty and everyone dressed up. Ricardo complemented

Gillian as they headed out and even seemed to treat David with a modicum of respect. They dined well. The conversation was gentle and restrained, and before long everyone seemed to relax. Ricardo insisted on paying again and they walked home in what felt like some semblance of a truce.

As Helen was making the hot chocolate, Ricardo came over to where David was standing. "Come outside with me," he said without any preamble. "We need to talk."

David's stomach turned to something hard and heavy. *Here we go*, he thought. *I'm not getting off as lightly as that.* "Sure," he said.

Helen looked round as the door opened but didn't say anything. David caught Gillian's eye and gave her a hopeless glance. She tried to look encouraging but didn't entirely manage it.

Ricardo led the way and they sat on the garden bench. The air was warm and scented. Ricardo pulled one of the cigars David had brought him out of his pocket and lit up. They remained silent for some moments.

Ricardo broke the silence. "I suppose you think I'm a bitter, bad-tempered old man."

David paused for a second. "Something like that had crossed my mind," he said.

Ricardo puffed on the cigar and blew out a cloud of aromatic smoke.

"I have my reasons," he said at length.

"Really?" David replied, then decided to press on, throwing caution to the wind. "Did you know that your consistent bad temper has ruined this week for everyone? Gillian and Mum as well, but I suppose most of it's aimed at me. I was hoping we might have a peaceful father and son holiday week, but I can see now that the idea was unrealistic. You may not agree with some of the choices I've made but they're my choices, and you should at least have the decency to respect them." He stopped, red in the face, wondering if he'd gone too far.

"Fair comment," Ricardo replied quietly. All the fight seemed to have gone out of him. "But like I say, I have my reasons. Or at least I have my excuses."

"Interesting," David countered. "And what might those be?"

"I'm dying."

Ricardo's words dropped like a bomb.

David opened his mouth but nothing came. Ricardo blew out another cloud of smoke.

"Well, that's a conversation stopper," David finally managed. "What is it? How long have you known? Does Mum know?"

"No, she doesn't. She knows I'm in pain, which I try to hide, but she's a medic, of course, so can't be fooled. In any case, she knows me better than I know myself after fifty-odd years. I guessed about a year ago, but it was just confirmed last month. She wants me to go to a doctor but I've refused. I went for some tests privately without letting on. They confirmed it."

"So, what is it?"

"Cancer, of course. That's what everyone gets, isn't it? Turns out I've got the full monty – lungs, liver, bowel. Brain and balls seem to be the only things that are still intact, though what good they'll do me I've no idea." He took another long puff. "So, if you think I'm even more miserable than usual, that's why. I may be eighty-three, but I'm not ready to go yet. There are things I still want to do. Things I want to find out. Your mother thinks I should apologise to you."

"And is this it?"

Ricardo grunted again. "Closest you'll get," he muttered. "Anyway 'men must endure their going hence', as I believe the Bard once said. But I didn't ask you out here for sympathy. There's something I want you do for me. I've been reading your press cuttings and you seem to have a talent for it."

"What?" David asked, curious in spite of himself. "And why should I help you?"

"Because it affects you, too. I want you to find Roberto. I think he's alive. Probably filthy rich somewhere or else in jail. Or both.

He's your brother and my son. I want to see him again before I die. Make my peace. I've never told you this, but we had a blazing row the last time he came back from Spain. Harsh things were said. He was only interested in money, and I told him that was what had ruined Spain in the past. Rebuilding the country meant engaging with the common interests of everyone, not just the rich and powerful. He said making money means jobs and livelihoods. The poor aren't capable of raising themselves; they need entrepreneurs and investors to put them to work. I told him that was pure exploitation, as bad as the slave owners, then we started shouting at each other. I've regretted it every day since."

David said nothing for a moment. An owl hooted, perhaps having just ended a mouse's midnight jaunt.

"And what hope do you think there is? I expect you've already involved the police."

"Police and private investigators. Every contact in the press I still have. Even the Salvation Army, pity help me. Nothing. But you're different. You'll do it because he's your brother and it's your job. And like I said, it seems you have some talent for that. According to the Scottish papers, anyway."

David remained silent again.

"You must be mad," he finally said. "Mad to think that I could do it and mad to think that I would even try. I lost my bother because you couldn't control yourself and keep your mouth shut. *You* did the damage. *You* sort it out. I'll see you in the morning."

David went to bed fuming, telling himself every word was entirely justified, while knowing perfectly well it wasn't. He tried to put it out of his mind and sleep. The crazy ravings of a disappointed old man.

Chapter 4

Warehouse 66

Oscarito's acquaintance with the work of Austrian paediatrician Hans Asperger (1906–1980) came as the happiest accident he could remember, and he couldn't imagine how there could have been a happier one. Up until that point he had tended to accept his father's broad-brush 'pegs and holes' philosophy. He was simply a funny-shaped peg that just didn't fit in with most of the world around about him – girls, friends, girlfriends – the social life of bars and restaurants, football, handball, any kind of ball, dress sense and what went with what – in fact, any kind of thing that normal people did and talked about. However, he finally seemed to have found a suitably funny-shaped hole in accountancy, and that was that. As regards relationships with the opposite sex – or even his own sex, and indeed often himself and his own feelings and reactions – that would simply have to remain stuck to the wall as a mystery. No harm in that. Religion was full of them.

Likewise, when a work colleague was aiming for an amusing overstatement like, "I have more work waiting at home than the combined labours of Hercules", he would have to look up what the labours of Hercules had actually been, then try to relate a pile of washing and ironing to the task of cleaning out the Augean stables. *Ah*, he'd finally conclude – *it just means lots of work*. He had come to accept the fact that most humour involving anything other than the crudest slapstick or most childish wordplay seemed to be beyond him.

The same applied to the more subtle and generally considered more important codes of liking and disliking in general, and expressing sexual interest in particular. Oscarito was 34, still lived with his mum, was physically slight to the point of being frankly skinny, already receding at the temples, wore terrible suits and mismatched socks, and had less conversation than an adding machine, but unaccountably, from time to time, someone decided he might make a steady date and possibly even a reasonably reliable domestic provider. Laura from Basic Business Practice had made efforts to sit next to him in lectures, to utterly no avail. He had paid less attention to her than to beggars in the metro. Olivia from his final-year business placement had tried to share her Swiss dark chocolate surprises, but found them insufficiently surprising to catch his attention. Even Sasha, who had the world's largest collection of Bee Gee's silk scarves, had been unable to raise any interest in Oscarito with the suggestion they try a night out at a very interesting disco he frequented in the gay district of Chueca. Oscarito didn't get the nuance and Sasha didn't get a date. Oscarito didn't spend his days and nights yearning for something that never happened; he simply didn't notice it passing any more than you might a high-flying jet heading for New York in the middle of a foggy night, obscured by heavy cloud during a Real–Athletico derby, while dealing with burglars and suffering a head cold. It just wasn't, as they say, on the radar.

However, on the wet and windy Saturday afternoon immediately after Señor Ibañez's revelation about the Gold Star Donors book – while keeping boredom and depression at bay by rhythmically hitting the 'Random Article' button on Wikipedia with just enough frequency to skip past Bulgarian Castles and Alien Races encountered in *Star Trek* – Oscarito landed on an article describing Asperger's syndrome and paused long enough for it to pique his interest. He read on through the overview, characteristics, treatment, classifications and terminology, including how it was now considered part of broader autism spectrum disorders. Then he noted the features of social interaction, the often restricted and repetitive interests (he stopped mechanically tapping his right foot at this point and glanced nervously at his wall chart of the Fibonacci sequence), speech and language issues, motor and sensory perception, and finally causes (which seemed a bit speculative) and history (remarkably recent) and sat back, stunned.

It's me, he thought. *Me. It's exactly me. I'm not just weird, it's a syndrome. And there are others like me, too. Thousands, maybe millions. In Europe, in Spain, maybe even here in Madrid. In Carabanchel. Wow!*

It took some time to absorb. It was the key to the treasure, the Holy Grail, the *Art of War*, the *Desiderata*, the four Gospels and the Academy Awards all in one. It was a passport to understanding and a moment of epiphany. He opened another carton of chocolate milk and let the revelation settle, like leaves softly landing on the forest floor. After everything he'd been through at school, at university and in his working life, it turned out he was, after all, a member of the human race. But with something extra. A syndrome.

He immediately jumped to Google and typed in "Famous people with Asperger's syndrome" and the results almost blew his odd socks off. James Taylor, the songwriter, was claimed for the clan; Dan Aykroyd, the actor; Susan Boyle, the Scottish singer; Bill Gates, one of the richest men alive; Einstein (Oscarito's hero); even Marilyn Monroe, apparently. The list went on and on. Successful people. Famous people. Important people. Brilliant people. And they all had Asperger's. They were like him and he was like them. Maybe it was unlikely that he would become an iconic scientist or groundbreaking entrepreneur any day soon, but still, he might do something worthwhile, not just beaver away at trivial numbers all his life – fascinating as they were.

Double wow.

Oscarito took his new self-knowledge into work at Party headquarters the following Monday. He attempted a smile at the secretaries instead of ignoring them. He whistled as he opened his desk drawers and turned on the computer. Excel had never seemed so perfectly harmonious and alive with possibilities. What would he do today? Cure cancer using numerical analysis or merely predict the winner of all future lotteries? How to choose? And what would he do about the Gold Star book?

He beamed at Señor Ibañez when he came in, fifteen minutes late as usual, to the latter's bemusement, and drank two chocolate milks before coffee time. *Hurray!* At last, against all odds, the world made sense. And he knew his place in it. His place, it turned out, was not to be blindly and uncomprehendingly complicit in money laundering, which he had concluded was certainly what was going on here, but to do something – right now he still wasn't sure what – to stand up for the constitution, Spanish democracy and the values his grandfather had died for while fighting Franco. Oscarito was suddenly no longer a bean counter but a warrior. Fate had somehow placed him at the heart of darkness, and it was his job to bring light and expose the slithery swamp life he was surrounded by.

It all seemed so simple until Señor Ibañez, somewhat alarmed by Oscarito's new-found gaiety, summoned him into his office and gave him a half-hour lecture on the importance of taking his responsibilities seriously. A copy of the signed confidentiality agreement was waved under Oscarito's nose and he was reminded of its direst contents. Back at his desk, Oscarito cursed the fates that had revealed his true nature to him the weekend *after* rather than *before* the Gold Star Donors book had landed on his plate from above. However, on the other hand, he now knew what he knew, which Señor Ibañez did not yet know, which gave him a strategic advantage (he had actually read *The Art of War* and Machiavelli's *The Prince*). And for the first time in his life, while continuing to input numbers and formulae, he began to investigate. And to plot.

After everyone else had left the office, Oscarito made himself a coffee and started work on the Gold Star Donors book Señor Ibañez had handed him. He opened the cover somewhat reverently; not because he believed the contents to be sacred, but simply because he had never before come across what he assumed to be utter lies masquerading as truth. Especially in the hallowed surroundings of the Party, which his father had favoured all his life and regularly contributed to, sometimes, in Oscarito's childhood, even up to a deficit in *garbanzos* and *carne*. He had actually gone hungry to feed the Party. Now the lifeblood of the Party was laid out before him in a book. What would he do with it? His own career now seemed of little importance. Oscarito was not used to naked numbers – only those decently dressed up in an Excel spreadsheet cell. So, despite what Señor Ibañez had told him under pain of death, that's where he put them. Then, with the help of the Microsoft Corporation, he read and reread, typed, entered formulae, drew charts and then, finally, tentatively, began to draw conclusions.

As fate or random happenstance or the gods or even perhaps God himself might have planned it, Oscarito's luck continued and his second miracle happened on the Tuesday evening. There was a quiet knock at the door. It opened, and a pretty face, bordered by hair that was blonde up to about an inch from the roots, looked around it.

"*Perdoname, Señor,*" a high-pitched, girlish voice with the accent of a non-native speaker said. "I am Marta. I am the new cleaner. I come in to clean. Yes?"

Oscarito glanced up, utterly uninterested until he saw who was speaking to him. Even with his limited experience and general rule of thumb to avoid all interaction with most humans, he realised someone utterly lovely had walked into his world.

"*Si...* Yes, of c-course," he stammered. "I'm just working a bit late. Please."

Marta smiled gratefully, pushed the door wider open and brought her bucket and mop, furniture spray, dusters and black rubbish bag in with her. She smiled, and Oscarito tried to do what he thought was expected and smiled back. She nodded and Oscarito lost interest in Excel spreadsheets. She bumped the door getting everything past the self-closing mechanism and he jumped up to help her. She started emptying wastepaper baskets into her bag and he waited earnestly for her to empty his. She sprayed and wiped desks, and he cleared away all extraneous material to make her job easier when she arrived in his corner of the room. *All glory be to Señor Asperger*, he thought. *Thank you. Thank you so much.*

She chatted as she worked, asking him things, making comments, telling him about her son, remarking that she hoped one day to win the lottery and not to have to clean offices any more. This was something he had never experienced before. His father's friends mostly ignored him on the rare occasions he was dragged out for a drink and couldn't get out of it. But here was a member of the opposite sex showing an interest in him and sharing details of her life. He had no idea how to react. He tried to err on the side of caution by keeping a smile on his face, nodding and commenting on the extreme unlikelihood of winning the lottery. Marta, however, didn't seen at all fazed by these responses and cheerfully informed him that she had been here all of three years now. Her son was four and had just started *guardaría*, meaning she could now look for work and, "*gracias a Dios*", had been able to get this job in the evenings while a neighbour looked after him to supplement her daytime income from cooking at a restaurant. As regards her job in Romania, she had a master's in statistical probability and had taught mathematics at the university. Of course, she'd understood that she would have to start on a lower rung here, but she still hoped eventually to use her skills in a more appropriate way.

Oscarito couldn't believe it. She loved numbers just as he did. He was undoubtedly on a roll. He felt like asking her what the chances of arriving at his moment of crucial self-knowledge and meeting his soulmate in the same week were but managed to restrain himself. Perhaps she might not see it as clearly as he did. However, he did refill the coffee machine and make her a cup as she worked, and after he had put the odious Gold Star book back into Ibañez's safe and spun the dial – he had already dropped the 'Señor' in his mind – they took a break together. Then he went home, walking on air, with thoughts of seeing her again tomorrow night. And the forbidden job of putting the figures onto the computer was already well underway.

The next night, Marta tentatively asked about him. She was tentative because she had found that office workers often didn't care much for chatting with lowly immigrant labourers, but she needn't have worried. Oscarito had spent the entire day waiting for this moment and had made her another coffee, having already emptied his own bin and wiped his own desk. He told her everything she asked and more, and she in turn bubbled over with information about little Marco, how she missed her family and about the evangelical church she had found, which met in an old NATO warehouse out in Torrejón. Imperceptibly, they bonded over quadratic equations, probability theory, the mystery of Fermat's last theorem and Bonka Spanish coffee.

On the third night he clumsily took her hand, wondering if that were the appropriate thing to do. On the fourth he was beginning to stress over the idea that kissing might come into it somehow, but it turned out he needn't have worried. By the time he realised what was happening it already had happened, initiated entirely by Marta. And it hadn't been nearly as uncomfortable as he had expected – almost pleasant, in fact.

By the end of the week she had invited him to church. They were to have a special speaker – David Hidalgo, founder of the church, visiting Spain from his current home in Edinburgh, Scotland – for a series of special meetings.

"Pastor Mariano," Marta said that Sunday as they were all milling around the foyer, Mariano having just arrived with Maria and another couple. "Can I introduce my boyfriend, Oscarito?"

"Congratulations, Marta." Mariano smiled, gave her two kisses and reached out to shake the hand of the slim man standing slightly behind her. "And welcome, Oscarito." Then he turned and presented David Hidalgo, whom Marta had heard about but never met.

She was slightly shy and nervous, but they exchanged *dos besos* all round, including with the woman she assumed was David's wife. Oscarito stayed in the background, glancing at the chart of the fundraising appeal for a new drug rehab house. Then they heard the band strike up inside.

It wasn't like anything Oscarito had ever experienced before, but then times had moved on, and to be fair he hadn't even been inside a Catholic church for twenty years. Maybe they were all like rock concerts now. On the other hand, he'd never been to a rock concert either, so who was he to tell? Nevertheless, given that his world had been turned entirely upside down in the last week and so far he hadn't fallen off, he didn't complain. He even tried to sing along a bit to what felt like religious karaoke. Marta took his hand on one side and little Marco took the other. Like so many things in recent weeks, this was an entirely new sensation. He stifled his discomfort, tried not to shudder or pull away, and counted prime numbers to help himself stay calm.

Eventually, the singing, the announcements and the whip-round (that bit he understood perfectly) were over, and Mariano bounded up onto the platform and introduced the couple who'd been with him as they came in: David Hidalgo and his wife, Dr Gillian Lockhart. Mariano invited *un aplauso* and the congregation complied enthusiastically. Then Mariano launched into a brief bio for those not in the know. Apparently, the congregation had gone through another fit of growth recently and new folk like Marta might not know the full history. Then, in a sort of onstage chat show, he asked some leading questions about how things were in *Edimburgo*, where it seemed the visiting couple now lived and worked. Finally, curiosity assuaged, David and Gillian were permitted back into the congregation while the kids went out to Sunday school and Mariano continued reading from the Bible and talking about what he called "the stewardship of money". Oscarito paid close attention. The coincidence to his present circumstances was all too relevant. Marta glanced at him out of the corner of her eye, but he was engrossed.

Then there was a bit more karaoke and it was all over. They went back to Marta's *piso*, where a leg of lamb was in the oven, cooking slowly with white wine, traditional herbs and thick slices of Romanian *lardo* from the corner shop that stocked Eastern European foodstuffs. The rest of the white wine went the way all white wine should, Marco was sent off to play, and Oscarito and Marta sat together on the sofa in the quietness, letting the delicious food digest. Finally, after a bit of kissing and fooling about – all entirely new to Oscar, and blissfully sweet and nostalgic of her teens for Marta – Oscarito took a deep breath.

"There's something I need to tell you, Marta, before we go any further," he announced gravely.

"You're married already?" she asked playfully.

"No chance of that – so far," he muttered.

"You're a serial killer?"

"Not that, either."

"Well, you're an international money embezzler, then?"

Now he wasn't smiling. "Maybe," he said. "Something very strange has happened to me recently. I... I'm not sure how to explain."

Marta waited patiently, but Oscarito seemed to have hit a roadblock. He avoided her gaze, then opened and closed his mouth a few times, like a goldfish, but no words would come.

Finally, she realised she would have to help. "Is it something in the office?"

Oscarito nodded.

"Something you've been asked to do?"

Another nod.

"What sort of thing?"

But here the roadblock kicked in again.

Marta took his hand. "OK," she said. Let's imagine this isn't you. Whatever's happened has happened to someone else. Tell me what happened to them."

Oscarito took a deep breath. This suggestion seemed to help. "OK," he began. "An accountant at Party headquarters has been told to work on some highly confidential accounts. Then one day he notices a name he recognises in the income column. A regular donation, €500 every month. It's from the mother of a neighbour he hasn't seen for a while. This seems incredibly generous for an old lady who must be in residential care or something and probably doesn't have much in the way of income. On the other hand, she probably doesn't have much in the way of expenditure either if the family is taking care of the fees. So, he thinks it would be a nice gesture to express the Party's appreciation, and the next time he meets that neighbour in the lift he says what a generous woman her mother must be. The neighbour gives him a very funny look, but he's so stupid he just keeps on going. 'Very generous,' he says, 'to give €500 every month to Party funds when she probably doesn't have much. It's been making a great contribution,' this idiot accountant then says, despite the fact the neighbour is now looking upset and angry. Finally, he realises his words of thanks aren't having the desired effect.

"'What are you talking about?' the neighbour asks in a less-than-friendly way. 'My mother's been dead for more than six years.'

"Now this neighbour isn't so friendly any more, and it's the accountant's turn to be confused. He goes back to his office and starts following up the other names, cross-referencing them with the voting rolls and Party records. It turns out there are hundreds of Party 'donors' who don't exist at all. Or at least maybe in purgatory, but not still operating bank accounts. It's not too hard to see the pattern. Then he starts looking into the laws that govern funding of political parties and finds that it hasn't been legal to accept substantial private donations since 2008. Membership levies are allowed, but nothing more. Parties are funded by the state based on how many seats they have in parliament. But if a party borrows money for the election, hoping to win more seats but not getting them, they finish off worse than they began. Up to their ears in debt. So they have to get money from somewhere. There are donors who want to contribute to get their voices heard, but they don't want anyone to know. So, the dead are enlisted in the service of the living. And any entity bidding for a government contract is strictly forbidden from contributing to Party funds in any way whatsoever – but many do."

"I didn't know that," Marta said quietly.

"Nor did I," Oscarito admitted. "But I'll tell you one thing. The Party treasurer knows exactly what the law is. He just doesn't pay any attention to it."

From there, he told her everything he had so far been able to glean in the short time since he'd had responsibility for the Gold Star book.

Once he had finished, about an hour later, Marta sat back, holding his hand in hers, and considered what he had told her, staring out of the window at the high-rise blocks across the road. When she suggested telling someone, he reacted strongly, gripping her hand until she winced.

"Are you joking?" he asked. "The Prime Minister is leader of the Party and the Minister for Justice is vice-chair. I can't imagine an accountant in Party headquarters would get far with reporting the matter to the local police."

"Well, I'm sure there must be someone else who knows about this who could do something," she finally concluded after Oscarito had vetoed every suggestion. "I'll be praying about it for you. Is telling God OK?"

He finally managed a smile. "I guess so," he replied. "If you think it'll do any good. And so long as he doesn't tell anyone else."

Chapter 5

Palacio de la Marquesa de la Sonora

Gillian Lockhart reached up and straightened her husband's tie. "Got to look the part," she said.

David Hidalgo groaned and looked at his watch. "Forty minutes to go. Mariano, where are you?" he asked no one in particular.

The flight from Edinburgh to Madrid had been totally straightforward. They had paid for coffees – nothing free on budget airlines – and settled back.

"Do you not think it's a bit weird snuggling up to the Minister for Justice when there's so much scandal about political corruption in Spain these days?' Gillian had asked as the plane climbed over the Firth of Forth. "It seems to be in the news every other week,"

"Without a doubt," David agreed. "Jobs for the boys, cross my palm with silver, and plain brown envelopes have probably always been around in one form or another in Spain. But yes, you're right. It does seem to be particularly bad right now."

"What's the latest, then? Is the guy you're going to meet up to his neck in it as well, as far as we know?"

"As far as we know he's not, but there's far more that we don't know than we do, I'm sure. There are some very high-profile, ongoing trials, but the big fish mainly seem to have kept themselves out of it. So it's more like regional mayors, officials responsible for handing out government contracts, branch secretaries; that kind of level. The actual ministers and treasurers seem to have managed to keep their hands clean – at least in public and as far as the judicial process is concerned, anyway. Of course, there are always rumours and innuendos. Some of the papers have printed allegations and been sued, so people are being careful. The other big problem is that it can take years for cases to come to court in Spain, and that means the truth takes a lot longer to come out, which delays incriminating other people higher up the tree."

"Justice delayed is justice denied, then."

"Absolutely. And there's even been a backlash against investigating prosecutors who are tempted to push their methods a bit too far. One of them, a guy called Balthazar Garzón, has now been banned from the bench for something like fifteen years for bugging a lawyer's consultations with the bad guys and trying to prosecute crimes committed in the Franco era."

Gillian gave a theatrical gulp. "I thought that was all supposed to be off-limits to try to heal the past."

"It is. But Garzón took the view that international human rights took precedence over the laws of Spain. Remember, he's the guy who went after Pinochet under international law, although his crimes had been committed in Chile, not Spain. So he's made a lot of powerful enemies. Then when the wiretapping thing came to light they just threw the book at him."

"But he's not in jail?"

"No, though the consequences were probably just as bad from his point of view. Reputation shot to blazes and unable to practise. I think he's lead counsel for some international criminal now."

"He must live an interesting life!"

After that the topic seemed too depressing, so they dropped it and let the engine hum woo them to sleep, despite the constant chatter about special offers, cut-price gifts and supporting this year's nominated charity.

Mariano, David's successor as lead pastor at Warehouse 66, met them at the airport and, since he and Maria had in-laws staying, drove them to a church *piso* they kept for visitors and occasional emergencies. It was a small but comfortable flat a few streets back from Avenido de Constitución in Torrejón de Ardoz, which, while nominally a separate municipality, was in reality part of the growing Madrid conurbation.

"Sorry this isn't the *Palacio* Hotel," Mariano apologised. "It was just what we could get for the money. We have some older church members who've lived in these blocks since the Civil War, you know. If only bricks could talk!"

They went out together to a very traditional Andalucian restaurant for lunch, then Mariano delivered them back. By unspoken agreement, the couple had a nap in the afternoon to recover from their early start, took a *paseo* – the traditional Spanish late afternoon stroll – in the evening warmth, then retired early.

Sunday was Warehouse 66 and the usual warm welcome for David – and now Gillian, too. David had pleaded for nothing more than a brief mention in the welcome; however, Mariano insisted on a platform introduction and a few questions. It was soon over, to David's great relief, then it was the obligatory rock-band worship, which Gillian seemed to be enjoying but David was increasingly finding far too loud for his tastes and far too individualistic for his theology. Then Mariano preached on life journeys and how to bring key decisions under the values of the Bible and the guidance of the Holy Spirit – particularly in relation to money.

Once the service was over it was like a queue for lottery tickets with the number of people who wanted to speak to David, either to renew or to make their acquaintance. Many had become close friends over the years, while some had to remind him and others he'd definitely never met before. The latter often seemed the keenest to make contact, so he tried to be patient. David and Gillian had been introduced to a new couple he didn't know – Marta and Oscarito – before the service and ended up talking to them a bit more afterwards. Marta explained how she had come to Spain and Oscarito talked about where he worked.

"Party headquarters?" David repeated with half a smile. "That must be interesting."

"It is," Oscarito replied with a very serious look. "More than you could guess."

"Well, I won't pound you for inside information."

David had been aiming for a joke, but Oscarito just looked glum and said nothing.

Marco was, by this time, almost pulling Marta's arm off, so David let them go and moved on to the next in line. Nevertheless, the thought of what information might cross the Party accountant's desk didn't quite drop out of his mind, but merely settled and was absorbed, like snowflakes on a lake.

***

Mariano had offered to pick David up an hour before the meeting the following morning to allow plenty of time for travel and parking. However, he was more than twenty minutes overdue. Turning up late for a meeting with the minister – even an outgoing minister with a relatively informal agenda – was not the done thing, even in Spain. David was getting very jumpy, so Gillian tried to distract him. She looked down at the invitation on the table.

"*Palacio de la Marquesa de la Sonora,* Calle de San Bernardo 45, Barrio Justicia. Very posh. Isn't that near Chueca?"

"Yes, but I doubt the minister spends a lot of time there. Far too bohemian. Or maybe he does... Who am I to know?"

"Well, you should just relax and enjoy the experience, even if nothing worthwhile comes of it. Nice lunch on the house, pleasant surroundings and some interesting people. Who else is on the list?"

David reached down, lifted the invitation and read some handwritten notes on the back. "Chief rabbi, the imam from the Central Mosque, some Buddhist guru or other, Cardinal Monserrat, and one or two lesser players."

"We aren't lesser players any more?"

"Ah, well, slip of the tongue. I'm sure we still are. But the minister seems to want to emphasise the law of religious equality just before he goes. So we'll be sitting in a circle, regardless."

Gillian glanced up at the clock, made a quick calculation and put some coffee on just in case. "But times have changed," she said. You've got to admit it."

"Absolutely. This could never have happened in Franco's time. There's no doubt the evangelical voice is being heard more loudly. Mariano's always talking about 'normalising' relationships. Making it so natural for us to be included in things that nobody bats an eyelid."

"Well, he's the one in the driving seat now, so he should know."

"I guess so."

Gillian poured the coffee while David drummed his fingers on the table, then they sat in silence for some moments.

Gillian glanced out of the window. "OK," she said abruptly, "time to go. Mariano's just pulling up." She leaned over and kissed him on the cheek. "Enjoy yourself. Here's your case."

"OK. I'll try to pop a set of Ministry for Justice coasters inside it if you like."

"You'd better not!"

Mariano was full of apologies; not because he was particularly worried about being late, but because he knew David was. However, the ride to the ministry was problem-free, to David's great relief – no traffic jams for a change and the car had air con, which the *piso* lacked.

Pulling into the private car park with a flash of the invitation, it was impossible not to be impressed by the ministry building. The eighteenth-century facade of the *Palacio de la Marquesa de la Sonora* was huge and imposing. The tasteful balance of red brick and white stone, with restrained and harmonious decoration, did exactly what it was supposed to do. It reinforced the power and importance of those who did business there in comparison with the supplicants who came to plead their cases.

No, we're here by right, David had to remind himself as security ushered them into the building. *We're here because the evangelical community is growing in Spain.* After years of no meaningful choice – National Catholicism or nothing – there was a blossoming of diversity in the faith discourse and individual church attendances were often numbered in the hundreds now, where it had once been in the teens. Apparently, there were also something like eight new evangelical start-ups every month, at a time when religion in general was in serious decline. People were not only free, but interested in alternatives – if presented in a reasonable light. The national Church, which had been hand in glove with Franco for so many years, was now paying the price for its deal with the devil, and Spaniards were abandoning their traditional religion in droves and looking for something new. For many, that only meant modern secularism, while for others there was still something in the human soul that yearned for the transcendent and eternal. Their continuing instinct was that there had to be something more to the universe than the atoms that made up their kitchen appliances.

From the moment David and Mariano arrived at the *palacio*, everything was sumptuous, luxurious and grand. First of all there was a very acceptable lunch staffed by lesser lights, then they were ushered into a lavish conference room.

At last the minister appeared, full of apologies that he hadn't made it to the lunch. He certainly looked distinguished, as a government minister should, though perhaps not in his full power-dressing regalia. A light suit, a pale-lemon tie, a full head of lightly greying hair, glasses and a totally in-control demeanour. The one thing that surprised David was his apparent age. For a retiring minister he actually seemed quite young – maybe not too far off David's own age, give or take a year or two. So maybe it was an early retirement to take up a lucrative post with a bank or corporation. There was also something familiar about his face or manner that David couldn't quite place. Maybe they had met before in the passing, or maybe he just recognised the minister from pictures in the papers.

A mixed bag of people was gathered around the table: major and minor faiths, from the ancient traditions of Judaism to the modern and slightly whacky. *Well*, David reflected, *better than an auto-da-fé and burning at the stake*. Coffee and exquisite little Viennese biscuits were served over small talk.

Finally, the minister coughed politely and shuffled his papers. "*Señores y Señoras*. It's my very great pleasure to welcome you to the ministry today," he oozed. "I'm sure you will be aware that as Shadow Minister for Justice I took a keen interest in matters of faith and observance. However, now that the election is over – and we've won – I've simply been holding the reins until a younger face can take over. Now we've got Señor Torres here lined up," he gestured to his left, "I've definitely decided to retire, so this will be our final get-together.

"I must confess to having very mixed feelings about this. On the one hand it will be a great relief to leave the constant squabbling and politics behind – particularly as the level of public trust we enjoy seems to be at a very low ebb these days."

Most of the gathering politely looked down, though David kept his eyes on the minister with interest.

"On the other hand, it has been my privilege to work with many diligent and visionary leaders – particularly in the spiritual field. By which I mean yourselves, among others. This I will miss. It is absolutely this government's intention that those of all faiths and none should feel equally at home in modern Spain – as the constitution guarantees, in fact. So, down to business, which mainly means me listening to you for a change. What are your interests and concerns? How can we help each other?"

The sly old fox, David thought. *When he says, "your interests and concerns", what he means is, "How we can serve the interests and concerns of the government and ruling party while thinking this is all for our benefit?" Well, he's a politician. What did we expect?*

The afternoon dragged on in a predictable manner. The chief rabbi spoke about anti-Semitism – both of the criminal and civil varieties – for which there should be no place in a multicultural state, and which should be very firmly dealt with.

"How right you are," the minister replied. "Alfonso, add a note to the cabinet agenda. Anti-Semitism: an integrated response."

The imam wanted to make clear that while irresponsible hotheads had succeeded in reversing 100 years of more positive attitudes to Islam in the West, the vast majority of Spanish Muslims did not want a new caliphate established in Cordoba or Syria, and simply wanted to get on with their neighbours, earn an honest living and pay their taxes. But that required anti-discriminatory measures from the government, too. It was a two-way street. While every effort was being made to fight extremism in the Muslim community, Muslims needed to feel they had an investment in a state that welcomed their presence.

"Without a doubt," the minister said in the warmest, most soothing tones. "Alfonso, change that agenda item to religious tolerance in general and the crime of hate speech. Now, the evangelicals. What can we do for you?"

The minister was looking closely at David. David, in turn, looked to Mariano, who looked back at him and nodded. David smiled across the table and took a sip of very good coffee to buy himself a few seconds. What he said in the next few minutes might have a significant impact on the progress of an evangelical point of view in Spain for years to come. It was a weighty responsibility.

"Nothing at all, Minister," he finally said. "We have a variety of representatives who meet with your officials on various committees. We think the work is progressing well. In general, we simply ask for the freedom to practise and share our faith – which we have. Beyond that, our main interest is to benefit Spain as a whole; not just our own interests. For example, the church I used to be part of – which my colleague here now leads – is very involved in assisting people who have problems with drugs and alcohol. We want to help them become healthy, productive, contributing members of society. Good husbands – they're mainly men – good fathers, good workers and good citizens. If we can achieve that, we'll be very contented."

The minister raised his eyebrows. This meeting was supposed to be a parting gift from a powerful man about to return to private life, with some largesse to distribute. *Surely they understand that,*" he mused. "*But the evangelicals don't seem to be asking for anything – they just want to play their part in building a tolerant, progressive society. How quaint. But interesting, too. Maybe they could prove to be useful as marginal allies for the Party.* He thought it through quickly. *Yes, that would do nicely.* He filed the idea away for later, while smiling blandly through all the successive flannel from the remaining guests.

"Now, Pastor David – if I might call you that," the minister said as papers were gathered up at the conclusion of business. "I hope you don't mind me prevailing on you a little longer. I'm about to head out to the airport to take care of some personal business in Zurich. I understand you're staying in Torrejón. If it would suit you, I'd like to take a little detour and drop you off on the way. How does that sound?"

Hmm, David thought. *Interesting.* David looked at Mariano, who again nodded. "Of course, Minister. Mariano and I came together, but that would be very convenient. So long as it doesn't take you out of your way."

"Not at all. Alfonso, could you arrange to have the car out front in ten minutes? Thank you."

Mariano shook the minister's hand.

"Dinner tonight – 8.15, isn't it?" David asked as Mariano made to leave.

Mariano grinned. "It is. Don't worry, I'll be on time!"

The intervening time was insufficient for another coffee; however, the minister did produce a very acceptable cream liqueur and even offered a nice cigar, which David turned down with thanks.

***

The conversation in the limousine was initially light and general. David wondered what was to come.

"Let me say, I was very impressed with your attitude in the

meeting, Pastor David," the minister eventually announced. "Very unusual and refreshing. These meetings can so often turn into shopping trips for those we're obliged to invite. It's their one, very infrequent chance to get their complaints on the table and try to bend the minister's arm. We come and go a bit, of course, but it's never going to go down in history. But your approach was entirely different. No demands and no complaints. Instead, you seemed to be saying, 'What can *we* do for *you*?' Did I read it right?"

David looked out of the window as Calle de Alcala slid smoothly by and took his time before answering. "I'm sure you're well aware, Minister, that Jesus said: 'My kingdom is not of this world', and we still believe our main calling is to try to offer a spiritual alternative that changes men and women from the inside out. However, that has implications for the outside as well. We think it perfectly in harmony with spiritual renovation that we begin to behave differently in society. In fact, you might sometimes hear the phrase 'Belong, Believe, Behave'. We want to create supportive communities that people want to be a part of; communities that can open their minds to see the world in a different way and come to believe some new things. That has to have an impact on how they behave in society. I think we've gone beyond dress codes and music styles, but we do care about keeping the law and paying taxes. Do you follow me?"

"I do indeed, Pastor David. Fascinating. And I couldn't agree more. The plain fact is that some of our traditional observances in Spain have become only that. Superficial observances, while corruption and self-serving go on under the surface, as they always have done. This is exactly what the next Minister f Justice will try to change during his or her residency. But I'm sure you'll appreciate that it's not just a question of changing and enforcing the law. What we're talking about is a change in culture. Encouraging people to invest in the nation and work for the common good, not simply doing the minimum required to stay on the right side of the law. But it's very unusual so hear another voice so much in harmony with our own. As you probably know, I shall be leaving office soon – in fact, this is my last official use of ministerial transport. However, with your permission, I'd very much like to maintain this link and encourage my successor to keep in touch with you and your people. If you don't mind, of course."

Well, well, David thought as they continued the run out to Torrejón, chatting informally about family and holiday destinations. *I didn't see that coming. Does he think I'm in a position to build closer ties between the evangelicals and the Party, and to bring in the Protestant vote next time around? He certainly doesn't miss a trick; I'll give him that.*

They arrived outside the apartment block just as Gillian was heading out to get some fresh air. The chauffeur jumped out and fetched David's case, then held the door open for him. Gillian had to pinch herself when she saw her husband climbing out of the limo. David took shameless advantage of the situation by introducing her to the minister.

"*Encantado*," the minister said in his most gracious tones, and vice versa.

Then the car purred off towards Barajas airport.

David and his slightly starstruck wife went inside and pressed the lift button.

"I wish I'd known. I could have changed."

"Don't worry. I'm sure he won't remember either of us in half an hour. Nothing is without a purpose for a man like that. He wants something from me… I'm just not sure what it is yet."

"I hope you at least managed to steal the coasters," she laughed as they went up in the lift.

David dumped his case in the corner and flopped into a chair while Gillian made coffee.

"OK, tell all," she commanded as she handed over a cup.

* * *

Mariano and Maria picked David and Gillian up at eight that night, and they all took the Renfe together to Puerta del Sol station. It had once been designated 'Sol Galaxy Note', but times had changed and it was now 'Sol iPhone'. They wandered around, taking in the lazy atmosphere.

"So, what did you make of the minister?" Mariano asked as they headed up towards the Plaza Mayor. "An honest broker or bent as a hook? Or something in between?"

"I think he's what we would call a smooth operator," David answered. "I imagine he probably has some skeletons in the cupboard, but he's keeping them well under lock and key. He's certainly charming and affable."

"And on the make?"

"Of course. He seemed to think we could secure the evangelical vote, but I guess you can't blame him for trying."

"And a nice lunch, too?" Maria put in. "So, not an entirely wasted day!"

"Without a doubt," David agreed. "That kind of thing is always interesting, even if there doesn't seem to be a particular benefit right away. You file it away and one day it takes on a new significance."

They wandered around the equestrian statue of Carlos V in the Plaza Mayor, enjoying the street performers and keeping an eye out for pickpockets. An elderly man with an enormous nose was playing "A Walk in the Black Forest" on crystal glasses, while further round a guy with a bucket of soapy water and a loop of chord on two sticks was entertaining children with the biggest soap bubbles they had ever seen. It struck David that maybe the economic crisis which began in 2008 might at last be almost over and people were beginning to feel more confident again, willing to spend money and wander around, relaxed and happy.

They got home late after a bit of a pub crawl, seemingly determined to outdo one another with tapas, and fell into bed. Their flight wasn't until mid-afternoon, so they could sleep late. Gillian had put the new term's prep to the back of her mind. David felt he had helped push the agenda on a bit, at no personal cost, since Mariano had insisted on paying everything from flights all the way down to filo pastry *empanadas*. With a fresh round of drinks in every bar, they had probably knocked off well over half a bottle each, and the world seemed a happy place. They fell into a deep, contented sleep that even the sound of passing police sirens couldn't disturb.

The next morning they woke slowly and languidly, had coffee in bed, followed by another cup, and only then got up and started pottering around. Mariano was due at eleven thirty to get them to the airport in time for what would just about pass for lunch at an airport restaurant, still in plenty of time to catch their flight. Then the tram in from Edinburgh airport, maybe some shopping, a walk around the Meadows, a simple supper at home, back to bed again after a tiring travel day, then back to normal the following morning.

About half an hour before Mariano was due to arrive, they started packing up the minimal stuff they'd brought for a short-notice weekend.

"Oh, by the way, David," Gillian said in the middle of trying to delicately fold a long dress, "do you still have the boarding passes?"

"Em, yes, I think so. They should be in the front of my notebook. It's in the case over there."

Gillian lifted the case onto the bed, clicked the locks open and lifted the lid.

The next ten seconds might have been the longest in her life.

"David," she said quietly. "I think you'd better come and have a look at this."

The case did not contain a notebook, boarding passes and a Bible, as it should have. Instead, it was full to the brim with €500 notes. Thousands of them.

Chapter 6

Torrejón

Mariano turned up on time, ignored the lift and bounded up the stairs. Gillian opened the door at the first ring.

"Well, here I am. Bang on time," he announced with a grin. "All ready to go."

She led him through to the living room.

"I don't think we're going to the airport," David said slowly.

"What, lost your boarding passes?" Mariano joked, still not noticing the sombre mood.

"Well, in a manner of speaking," Gillian said quietly. "Look what we found instead." She opened the case on the dining room table.

Mariano let out a long, low whistle. David explained that his and the minister's cases must have been very similar, and that the chauffeur had obviously picked up the first that came to hand from the boot of the limo and handed it over.

"So, this isn't my case or my money, and the minister has our boarding passes and my Bible!"

"And it wasn't even locked," Gillian put in. "That's how confident they are."

"Remember I told you about the minister saying he had some personal business in Zurich?" David added. "I bet this was it. A case full of money to lodge in a private Swiss bank account. Money that couldn't be paid into a regular Madrid bank and transferred in the normal way because it's not supposed to exist. We can't prove it yet, but this is dirty money, Mariano. I'm sure of it. The pay-off for years of faithful, crooked service. He's about to retire. Last use of the official car and all that. And his last duty – though whether you'd call it official, I'm not sure – is banking his retirement fund, thanks to the Party and probably a web of backhanders that would make the Mafia look like the choir."

Mariano sighed heavily. "I can see why we're not going to the airport," he said slowly. "Just as a matter of interest, what was in your case?"

"My Bible, a notebook, pens and pencils. A box of *turrón* I was taking back for our church secretary."

"And the boarding passes," Gillian added pointedly.

Mariano sat down, put his elbows on his knees, clasped his hands and looked at the floor.

"Have you counted it yet?" he eventually asked.

"I don't even want to touch it," Gillian replied.

The case was still open, dominating the room by its significance more than its size.

"So, what are our options?" Mariano asked after another long pause.

"Give it back and pretend nothing happened, I suppose," David began. "That would be my personal preference. This is nothing to do with me. I only came for the weekend!"

"I had to stop him from taking it to the nearest police station as soon as we found it," Gillian put in. "We've both had too many adventures in the past few years, and neither of us wants any more, but you can't simply pretend it hasn't happened. Another option might be to give it back, then tell the press what we've done so at least somebody else knows."

"Or," David went on, "keep it and say nothing…"

"We can't do that!" Mariano exclaimed.

"Of course not. I'm just going through the options. Keep it and say nothing or keep it and say something."

"Who to?"

"Well, that remains to be seen, but basically the first choice to make is whether to give it back or not."

"If we're going through all the options," Gillian remarked, "is there one that says, unlikely as it sounds, that the money is somehow legitimate and we're guilty of a crime by not giving it back?"

"Hmm, I suppose that is technically an option," David agreed. "And at least in Scotland there's a crime of theft by finding. So, if you're right, we might be guilty of something for keeping it. But assuming it's not legitimate money, we would certainly be morally implicated if we did give it back – much as I'd like to!"

"And the erm… the 'keeping it' options?" asked Mariano, who'd had less time to come to terms with the new situation than David and Gillian, and was still flummoxed.

"Well, obviously this is very much bigger than us." David at least seemed certain of that. "When I say 'we', I mean anyone other than *them*. So, we give it to the police or the press, or somehow put it into safekeeping while all hell breaks loose."

"You think it will?" Mariano asked.

David nodded his head wearily. "I can't imagine how it wouldn't."

"But if we're talking about political corruption here, you can't simply hand it over to the police, can you?" Gillian asked, aghast. "Would that not just be equivalent to handing it back to the minister? I mean, he is the Minister for Justice, isn't he? Doesn't that mean he has responsibility for the police? They'd just pass it back to him."

"Not quite," Mariano pointed out, now slightly more in control of himself. "In Spain the police actually come under the control of the Ministry of the Interior."

"But they're all going to be cronies, aren't they?"

"I imagine so."

"So, not handing it back has to mean giving it to someone who's going to properly investigate and has the resources to withstand the pressure till the matter's resolved," David concluded.

"Not Warehouse 66, then," Mariano said resolutely. "We simply don't have any of the resources to deal with something like this. We need to work out who does and hand it over. End of story."

"Hmm, you may be right," David conceded, "but I doubt it's going to be that simple. We're involved, and I'm not sure it's going to be easy to get uninvolved. But in the meantime, it's sitting on your table, Mariano. They're going to want this back very badly, and I'm sure they'll do whatever they need to do to get it. If it's illegal money, I think we have to assume that keeping the law isn't going to be very important in how they go about getting it back."

"So, where does that leave us now?" Gillian asked, bringing them back to reality.

"Where does that leave us?" Mariano repeated. "Up to our necks in serious trouble, I'd say."

Nobody disagreed.

Just then, David's mobile gave a noisy buzz against the glass coffee table and a few bars of "Take Five" sounded. Nobody moved. It buzzed and rang a second, then a third time. David gave Gillian a helpless glance and picked it up. He tapped to answer, then tapped again for speakerphone. Then he laid it down on the surface in front of them.

"*Hola*. David Hidalgo…"

"Pastor David," said a voice in honeyed tones. "You can probably guess who this is. I think there's been some mistake. I appear to have a briefcase that belongs to you. I imagine my driver gave you the wrong one yesterday, and you have mine. I'm sure you'll agree we need to restore these items to their proper owners, no?"

Again, nobody spoke.

"Pastor David?" the voice repeated. "Pastor David Hidalgo…"

"Speaking," David confirmed.

"So, if you don't mind, a car from the Guardia Civil should be outside your apartment about now. Your own case will come by courier to whatever address you want. I'm sure you can understand the importance of my ministerial papers. These are confidential matters of state. While the mistake may not have been yours, it would be very unfortunate if you were to become involved in matters of high-state policy. Do I make myself clear? The contents of the case are restricted and highly confidential. Failing to return government property immediately would be a very serious offence, with very serious penalties. I'm sure you understand."

Still nobody knew what to say.

"Pastor David, I hope you take my meaning," the minister repeated in a voice that was now less honeyed politician and more like a street fighter used to throwing his weight around.

Finally, David spoke. "Of course we'd be happy to return your case, Minister," he said.

Gillian gasped.

"It's a very nice case. Similar to my own, but probably a bit better quality. However, there is the small matter of the contents."

"You've opened it," the voice on the phone said in a flat tone that was more statement than question. "In that case, you will realise very well that the contents are government property. Don't even think about being foolish. Simply open the door, hand over the case – *and* its contents – and leave the country. Very simple, very easy and no consequences."

David paused again, then finally spoke. "Minister, as a pastor, I take very seriously the need to return lost or stolen property."

"Excellent." The minister's smile of relief could be heard over the phone.

David wasn't finished. "But just in case the contents happen to have been lost or stolen from somebody else, we'd be happy to return them once their status has been verified. You have my number and I think my email address. Once you can provide that information I'd be delighted to do as you ask. But until then, the contents will be in safekeeping."

"How dare you?" The last of the smooth operator had left the minister's tone. "How *dare* you? You have no idea what you're doing. This isn't a Sunday school game. Hand it over or suffer the consequences!" Rage had taken over from persuasion and subtle threat.

"When you provide the information I've asked for, I'll be happy to," David replied calmly. "You must know that questions are being asked nowadays about Party cash. You know how to contact me."

The minister was silent; no doubt furiously absorbing this unexpected complication.

David went on. "And one other thing, Minister."

"*What?*" The word was spat out like a blasphemy.

"If you wouldn't mind looking after my Bible. It was a gift from my wife." He hung up the call.

David and Mariano sat looking at each other.

"I guess we're not giving it back, then," Mariano said at length.

Meanwhile, Gillian, who had been fiddling with her own phone, showed more presence of mind and pulled back the curtains to look down to the street below. "Guardia Civil just parked," she said, as if she were referring to the milkman. "I think we'd better make a move."

Mariano roused himself. "So, what do we do now? If we stay put they come knocking at the door. If we try to leave the building, we get picked up even more quickly. I can't see another option."

"The devil and the deep blue sea," said Gillian sombrely. "Well, that was a short-lived blow in favour of standards in the Spanish state. I suppose we get deported now and that's that."

"If we're lucky," Mariano commented. "I think they'll actually throw the book at us now. Get ready to face the music."

The sound of doors being banged or demolished downstairs started to drift up and seemed to be getting closer. It sounded as if they had only a matter of minutes, at best.

"Hang on," David suddenly said. "Didn't you say that you had other church members in these blocks, Mariano? Isn't there another flat we could go to that might have a bit more cover than this one?"

"We do have an elderly member living upstairs – Margarita – but I don't see what difference that's going to make. All we do is involve somebody else with the police. She's not going to be able to stop them searching... and finding."

"Well, it's got to be better than here, anyway," Gillian said, picking up a bag. "Come on – grab that case!"

Thirty seconds later they had left the flat, locked the door and pounded up two flights.

Margarita Garcia was eighty-three but still alert and robust. "Pastor Mariano?" she said, opening the door. "What a surprise!"

"Not a pastoral call, "I'm afraid," Mariano said tersely. "Do you mind if we come in? I'll explain in a minute."

She stood well back, wiping flour from her hands onto a floral apron, as they tumbled inside. Mariano explained in hushed tones in the hall as David and Gillian went through to the tiny living room and tried to keep watch out of the window as unobtrusively as possible.

"On the run from the police? How exciting!" the old lady could be heard to say. "Reminds me of my father during the Civil War. He was a pastor too, you know. Coffee, anyone?"

The sound of a bell ringing two floors below was clearly audible, particularly as it was repeated half a dozen times. Then a pause, followed by an almighty crash and shouting. Another pause. Then the unmistakable sound of more doorbells. They had broken down the door, found nothing and were now going from door to door. Anyone not in or not quick enough was going to have a serious repair bill. Sirens could be heard in the distance, drawing closer. Tyres squealed as a second, larger vehicle drew to a halt on the street below.

Gillian peered over the edge of Señora Garcia's window ledge and kept up a running commentary. Eight armed officers had piled out. It looked like two had taken up station in front of the building as the rest poured inside. Downstairs, the sound of doorbells, doors being opened or broken down, shouted instructions, denials and more shouting were getting clearer and clearer.

"I think we'd better skip that coffee, *Señora*," David said, trying to keep his voice as normal as possible. "And we need to disappear for a few minutes till the Guardia are past. At least under a bed. Any ideas?"

"Why of course, *cariño*. Why didn't you say so to begin with? And we can do better than a bed. That's the first place they'll look. Oh, this is exciting!" The old lady whisked up the three extra coffee cups she had been laying out and popped them back in the dresser, leaving only her own on the coffee table, and led them through to a spare room done out as a study. One wall was lined from top to bottom with shelves of theological books, church histories, missionary biographies, dictionaries and devotional studies.

"This was my father's study," she explained in a totally unhurried way. "You know, he was a master carpenter as well as a pastor. Franco tried to round them all up or terrify them into crossing the border to France, but my father was made of sterner stuff. He made this. Hasn't been used for a long time, though. He'd be tickled to think of it being back in service! Would you mind just passing me that stool?"

David, who was by now only barely holding the panic down as the sound of the Guardia seemed to have moved up a floor, passed her a small perching stool and helped her up. The *Señora* steadied herself.

"Now, which one was it?" she muttered, as if trying to choose her favourite cheese at the supermarket. "*The IVP Dictionary to the Bible*? No, not that. *The Lion Handbook*? No. Nestle-Aland's *Greek New Testament*? Not that, either. *Young's Analytical Concordance*? Oh yes, that's it. Here we go." She reached up, grasped a tome the size of one of the larger volumes of the *OED* and swung it out, pivoting on the lower edge of its spine. There was an audible click and then the entire run of shelving it was sitting on popped out by about a centimetre.

"If you can just help me down, young man," she addressed herself to David as the doorbell gave a jarring series of rings. "Yes, there we are. Now, pull here."

The entire run swung out without a single squeak, as if the oil were as good as the day it had been finished.

"In here now. There we are."

Behind the shelving was a space no more than eighteen inches deep to the back wall but running the full width of the room. It was dark and dusty, but dry. The trio filed in with their bags, not quite believing what was happening. The light died as the shelf clicked back into place, just as the unmistakable sound of the front door giving way reached them.

"I hope she remembers which book opens it again," David whispered, laying down the briefcase and pulling out a handkerchief to stifle a sneeze.

Sounds from the hall, living room, kitchen, bedroom and the room where they were concealed were clear enough in their volume and intent. The officers concerned may not have known what was in the minister's case, but they knew there *was* a case, that it was important, and that they'd been tasked to find it and to detain the two or possibly three individuals who had it in their possession. They did their job as thoroughly as they could, unencumbered by respect or politeness even for an elderly woman.

Margarita Garcia did her best impression of a bumbling, forgetful, flustered old lady superbly well. She offered them coffee three times, thought she knew the captain's father, insisted on opening all the kitchen cupboards and the door of the washing machine, since they had said they were searching for something or other, and as a good citizen she wanted to help as much as she could. While not actually manhandled, she was pushed brusquely to one side while they carried out their own search. Underneath beds were indeed checked, along with the airing cupboard, wardrobes and the balcony.

Once satisfied, the captain gave a perfunctory, "*Gracias, Señora.*" Then they were off to the next front door.

The sound of doorbells and battering rams continued around the landing. Señora Garcia sensibly left a full twenty minutes, until the noise has subsided and she had seen the officers leave the building, before going back into the office. The sound of the little plastic stool scraping over the parquet flooring was followed by puffing and groaning, then suddenly there was a crack of light from floor to ceiling as the section of shelving popped open again.

"Señora Garcia, you are a veritable *caja de sorpresas*!" Mariano said with feeling as the trio sat down on office chairs and a tiny sofa. "I knew your father had been a pastor, but I didn't know he'd been on the run. It's incredible!"

"And did you ask?" Margarita said with a kindly smile but an undeniable hint of mild reproach.

"I did not," Mariano conceded. "I apologise."

Margarita snorted. "Ha! No need for that. You're a busy man and I'm just one elderly member. You have more fish to fry than that. And Pastor David," she continued. "I joined the queue to speak to you yesterday, but my legs aren't what they once were, and Pepe was waiting to give me my lift home, so I had to give up and take a seat. But I wasn't expecting a pastoral home visit, I must say. Señora Gillian, I don't think we've formally met, though of course everybody knows about the love of our founding pastor's life. *Encantada.*"

"*Igualmente*," Gillian replied, smiling. "Likewise. *Caja de sorpresas* is a box of surprises, isn't it, Mariano?" she asked.

"It is. And to say that you are simply a lone elderly member does not begin to do you justice," he added, turning again to Margarita.

"We owe you a debt of gratitude," David put in. "You weren't ever in the French Resistance, were you?"

Margarita laughed. "Never," she said, "but I was in the *Franco* Resistance. Maybe that was similar. Anyway, I think I was interrupted in the matter of coffee. My nephew bought me a beautiful Italian coffee maker last Christmas. It's too fancy just for one cup, but since I have company I'll open the good coffee and we'll see how it does. Come away through to the living room. We can put our cloaks and daggers away now!"

David, Gillian and Mariano seated themselves in the crowded living room, among heavy dark furniture in the old Spanish style that David guessed must also have come from her father. The events of the past half-hour still hadn't sunk in and nobody knew quite what to say, so they sat in silence.

In the kitchen, the coffee maker started fizzing, spluttering and wheezing. Margarita was back in no time with a tray of tiny cups, one jug of coffee and another of hot milk, alongside some brown sugar and a plate of almond biscuits.

"Now, how do we all like it?" she asked, as if the morning had been entirely taken up with nothing more than a spot of light dusting.

Gradually, her story came out in response to Mariano's thoroughly repentant questioning.

"My father came to faith as a teenager," she said. "He was in love with a girl in Cuenca, where he grew up, but the priest had also taken an interest in her. She became pregnant, and in those days if the priest was involved it was the girl's fault because nothing could be said against the Church. My father was furious but he still loved her, and they planned to run away together and pretend to be married. He would raise the child as his own and they would try to put the past behind them. But the Church was powerful and it put pressure on the girl to enter a convent to keep her quiet. It was all too much, and she jumped off the bridge over the gorge just outside the bishop's residence. My father was distraught. He thought, 'If that's the Catholic Church, then I want nothing to do with it.' Not saying there weren't many lovely, godly men in the priesthood, of course, but the tendency was simply to move the bad ones and hush it all up.

"Then a couple of Dutch missionary ladies came to the town when he was in his thirties. He was intrigued, because in those days the simple fact was that nobody knew there was any alternative way to be a Christian but in the traditional Spanish way. You know, we are the one country in Europe that was almost entirely untouched by the Reformation. My father decided that, since you have to believe something and he had absolutely no confidence in the usual faith, he'd throw in his lot with the new religion. Then he married one of the missionaries – my mother – which kind of made it a bit final. They moved to Madrid, I was born, he opened a carpentry shop and made doors, windows, shelving, that sort of thing. By the time he became a pastor, Franco was winning the Civil War. Once Franco was fully in power, he relentlessly persecuted anyone who was different. Communists, of course – or those that might be communist, which wasn't the same thing – artists, writers, community leaders who tried to resist in any way, and anyone who wasn't part of the new religion – National Catholicism. My father decided he had too much invested to run away, so he brought his tools home one day and built some shelves in the spare room."

"I'm glad he did," Gillian put in.

"Indeed. It was a godsend. So many times they came knocking on the door and my mother had to say she wasn't sure where he was. I think a lie in that situation is probably permitted."

David had to look down. Margarita seemed to have inherited all of her father's dogged determination and grit. She and the whole family had come through hard times, but like iron sharpens iron it had not broken her but left her all the stronger. The contrast with his own father, who ran away and threw bricks from a safe distance, didn't escape him. He had always thought moving to a safer location was totally logical and sensible; however, here was a simple man who hadn't had the international contacts and connections his father had built up, but had been determined to stay and fight it out. Even if it meant hiding behind the bookcase.

"So, I was raised in the faith, but I also chose it for myself," she concluded. "They say God has no grandchildren. You can't get it from your father or mother – you have to find it for yourself."

Gillian helped herself to another of the delicious crumbly almond biscuits, then took a sip of coffee. "So, what do we do now?" she asked simply. "However ingenious the bookcase is, we can't live here forever like Anne Frank."

"True," David agreed gloomily. "I'm afraid I haven't thought that far ahead."

"And there are a couple of things I don't understand before we even get to our options," she continued. "Like how they could direct the Guardia Civil to the flat. We could have been anywhere – on the way to the airport, for example, or even out of the country."

"Hmm, I hadn't thought about that," Mariano admitted. "He would have known the address from dropping you off here.

"But how did they know we were *in* the flat?" Gillian insisted.

"Mobile phone signals, I imagine," David replied. "I wondered why the minister was taking so long to get to the point. I'm guessing they needed some time to trace the signal. I think it's pretty common technology these days. Didn't they even use that to get Pablo Escobar, the drug baron, thirty years ago? I suppose it must be quicker and more accurate now."

"So, when he said the Guardia Civil were on their way to the flat, they knew you were there. If the signal had been from Barajas airport they would have gone there instead."

"Probably not," David countered. "They have Guardia Civil at the airport all the time. If I'd answered there, we'd probably all be in custody now, ready to be charged with something horrendous. It's a good job you arrived on time, Mariano, not too early."

"Well, I'm Spanish," Mariano smiled. "At a push I can be on time. Early? Never!"

"So, no using mobile phones, then," David cautioned.

"Anyway, we're here," Gillian again brought them back to reality, "and we've got the minister's dirty money. We might be safe for the time being, but not for long. They're certainly going to have the building watched, so we can't just walk out. We've no idea who to confide in or what to do with the money. And I've got lectures to prepare! Any ideas?"

"That's a lot of questions," David replied slowly. "I guess we just have to take them one at a time. What's first? Who do we give it to?"

"Oooh, let's count it first," Margarita put in, rubbing her hands like the crazy granny in a comedy film.

David shrugged. "Why not?" he said.

So they did.

It took a while, even though it was all in denominations of five hundreds. They laid it out on the coffee table in piles of fifty notes, each making up €25,000. One, two, three... the piles kept adding up. By the time they were finished they were looking at sixty neatly squared piles of cash: €1.5 million.

"Well, I think we can say that the minister must have been very diligent and the Party very grateful," Gillian concluded, looking at it all.

David picked up the apparently empty case and examined it, perchance another million or so might have been hiding there. The main compartment was clear except for a single, sealed envelope. Shrugging his shoulders, he picked it up and opened it. It had a complement slip inside.

He was about to lift it out when Gillian intervened. "No! There might be fingerprints. Don't touch it."

Margarita went to fetch some tweezers from her patchwork sewing kit.

Then they laid the letter out on the table next to the money. It bore a single message: "A long and happy retirement, *Señor*. From your friends, Marcos, Lucas and Juan."

Mariano shrugged. "Not much we can do with that, is there?" he said. "Three of the four gospel writers. Nicknames or code names."

"Hang on," said Gillian. "There's something else in here. Margarita, do you have a pair of gloves I could put on?" Gillian had picked up the case and was looking not at the main compartment but at the document wallet in the lid. "Look," she said, drawing out a thin, multi-page document with clear plastic covers and a black plastic spine.

Wearing the white linen gloves provided by Margarita, she opened it and began turning pages. Each had a single-word heading corresponding to the compliment slip, this time adding the missing writer – *Mateo* – alongside Marcos, Lucas and Juan. Below the title was a column of figures apparently showing inputs and withdrawals.

"I'm not an accountant," David said slowly, "but I think we've got more here than just the money belonging to one man. This looks like a record of the entire system. All the payments to all the recipients. For some reason they all have biblical code names. Why it's in the case I have no idea, but this feels like it must be important – maybe even the key to the entire operation. No wonder the minister wants it back."

Mariano said nothing. Gillian let out a groan and rested her forehead on the heel of one hand. David laid the folder down and rubbed his temples.

The only one who didn't seem appalled was Margarita. "Hurray!" she shouted, clapping her hands. "Wonderful! Now we can lock them up and throw away the key! My father would be dancing in the streets. This calls for a toast. Champagne, anyone?"

Chapter 7

Lozoya

The return flight from Zurich was met by airport security and the now former minister rushed through the VIP lane, even though he was technically no longer entitled to do so. The Party treasurer met him in a limo with a soundproofed rear compartment. He did not look happy.

"A million and a half!" he began. "How on earth—"

But the ex-minister cut him off. "Shut up!" he snapped. "You know perfectly well what happened. I hope the driver's been sacked or fined, or both."

"It's not just your money that's the problem," the treasurer persisted. "The records of the entire system were in there. What on earth possessed you to take them as well? I'm past caring about your pension fund. That document exposes all of us. And there was a little good luck slip in my handwriting with my prints all over it. Your carelessness could end up bringing us all down!"

The former minister ignored the accusation. "That's a detail," he said. "That document won't do anyone any good. The need of the moment is to get our hands on Hidalgo and his cronies. The Guardia couldn't find them at the block in Torrejón, but the building's under observation. Nothing goes in or out without our say so."

"Under what pretext?"

"Financial irregularities. Embezzlement. Tax evasion."

"That's ironic."

"Well, it doesn't really matter. The Ministry of the Interior is on the case. We pick up Hidalgo and his sidekicks. Get the money and the payment records back. And I go back to private life. No harm done."

The treasurer shifted his position uncomfortably and stared out of the window. "That is a best-case scenario," he suggested drily.

They drove into town in silence until they got to Party headquarters, coming in through the back entrance. The treasurer left the former minister in the porch for a minute while he disappeared into the main ground-floor office.

Two minutes later he returned. "I've sent the accountant home," he announced. "A couple of minutes and the coast'll be clear. Lucas is on his way and Juan'll be here as soon as he can. I can tell you now that they are not happy men!"

Half an hour, later four men were sitting around the table. 'Mateo' had, until recently, been known to the outside world as the Minister for Justice. 'Marcos' was well known in political circles as the Party treasurer and 'Lucas' was known to Oscarito as his boss, the office manager. The fourth, 'Juan', was a study in contrast to the other three. He was not well educated, well dressed, or well groomed. And instead of a bit of middle-aged spread, he looked about twenty years younger than the others but forty kilos heavier. He was silent during the ensuing discussion, simply cracking his knuckles.

"Well, gentlemen," Mateo began, "recriminations are pointless and a waste of time. What we need to do is set priorities. I can't imagine a higher priority than retrieving the case."

"And the accounts summary inside it," Marcos added.

"Quite."

"And perhaps an almost equal priority is to keep these events out of the public domain," Lucas commented, wiping the sweat from his brow.

"And what about the Prime Minister? Should he be informed?" Marcos asked. "I hardly think that counts as the public domain."

"It doesn't," Mateo agreed, "but I think we need to keep the doctrine of plausible deniability in mind. Should the worst come to the worst, the Prime Minister is the symbol of the Party in the public mind and in the minds of the voters. I submit that he should not be informed unless it becomes necessary to explain other information that may have come to light."

"Agreed," Lucas commented. "However, we also need contingency plans. The ideal is that the case is found and recovered, and Hidalgo and others expelled with dire warnings. But what if we find Hidalgo and not the case, for example, or – even worse – we find neither. Hidalgo must never be allowed to speak. I recommend giving authorisation to use maximum force. The matter can always be justified subsequently."

"Under no circumstances," Mateo was firm. "You are suggesting murder, which takes us into entirely new territory and simply leads to more difficult questions. No, we find him, we find the case, we deport them all, then we close the matter."

"All very well for you to say," Marcos retorted. "Not everyone has your international connections to find a safe haven somewhere else. When push comes to shove, all options have to be on the table. If it's us or them, I say we do what we have to do!"

Mateo inclined his head in acknowledgement but said nothing more. He had learned over the years when to speak and when to stay silent.

* * *

David, Gillian and Mariano spent much of the rest of that afternoon listening to Margarita's stories from the days of Franco, which, while horrific in themselves, served to raise their spirits. It felt like scenes from the life of *The Scarlet Pimpernel*, and made the forces now on their trail seem a little less frightening. If she could survive and live to tell the tale, maybe they could, too. After all, a man who could lose €1.5 million and a highly confidential document that might be key to the whole corrupt conspiracy might not be that ruthlessly efficient. Inevitably, the subject eventually turned to what to do next. They had come to the conclusion that use of mobile phones would be out of the question, and even Margarita's fixed line might be subject to surveillance.

"No problem," she said brightly. "I'm sure we can use Pepe's upstairs. He suffered under Franco as well and sees the present lot as fascists in disguise. He'll be pleased to help."

"You mentioned Pepe once before," Mariano commented. "Do I know him?"

"Not yet," Margarita replied. "He runs me to church, then goes off to a bar to have a coffee and read the paper before picking me up again. We have lunch together sometimes. He really wants to make it a bit more than that, but he knows I won't want to marry unless he's a fellow believer. I don't put any pressure on him, but I hope he'll come inside with me some day. Then we'll see."

"How long have you known each other?" Gillian asked.

"Oh, years and years," Margarita replied. "He used to have the hardware and *electrodomésticos* shop round the corner. His son runs it now. Everybody here buys their cookers and fridges from him. Come to think of it, I could do with a new fridge. One of those huge American ones. I'll tell him that as a sweetener if he shows any reluctance to lend a hand."

"Well, that would be a help, anyway," David remarked. "I'm sure Maria's wondering where you are, Mariano. And we'll need to get word back to the UK that we've been unfortunately delayed. Would it be possible to speak to Pepe sometime soon, Margarita?"

But Margarita was staring out of the window. "I wonder," she said, more to herself than anyone else. "I just wonder... Wait here. I'm just going to pop upstairs to see Pepe about that new fridge..."

David, Gillian and Mariano weren't going anywhere, but they hadn't expected Margarita's kitchen appliances to be the most important thing on the agenda right now.

Mariano thought he'd have a look at the old one, but it wasn't all that old and seemed to be functioning perfectly. He put more coffee on while they waited.

Margarita was back within ten minutes. "Pepe says it's no problem. You can use his phone as much as you want. He has a contract with 200 free minutes and he thinks his son might be able to bring me a new fridge this afternoon."

"Sorry, Margarita," Mariano began. "Thanks for checking out the phone, but you've lost me on the fridge."

Margarita smiled with an evident twinkle. "I'm sorry," she said, "I've been having so much fun. It's just like the old days. I have to remember you're new to this. I asked Pepe to get his son to bring me the biggest fridge he could possibly find. He told me they do this huge thing the size of a double wardrobe. One side is fridge, the other side is freezer. Very posh. It has an ice cube maker and a drinks chiller. Constant cold drinks in Madrid. What we would have done for that when I was a girl!"

"But where could you possibly put it?" Mariano asked, still completely confused and wondering if Margarita wasn't quite as sharp as they'd thought.

"Nowhere," she continued, undeterred. "Pepe's son will bring it here in his van with someone to help him. It'll come in a huge, reinforced cardboard container. The Guardia Civil will either sit and watch him deliver it or they might even make him open a corner to prove it really is a fridge. They get it into the lift somehow – or up the stairs – then they come to my door and ring the bell to deliver my wonderful new fridge. But I tell them I never ordered a new fridge. Somebody must be playing a trick, so they have to take it away again. This time the Guardia Civil already know what's in the box and, if necessary, Pepe's son can shout and swear a bit and say the customer has changed her mind."

By now, David was smiling. "You are an old fox, Margarita," he said. "Sorry it took me so long. Very clever. A fridge comes in and we go out."

Margarita clapped her hands again. "Wonderful!" she said.

"Though I have to tell you, Pepe got there a lot quicker than you. The only problem, of course, is whether it'll fit in the lift or not. If it does, you're exactly right. If it has to go down the stairs, then it's probably going to be more practical to get in once it's already down on the ground floor. But that's a minor detail."

Gillian was looking at Margarita with an expression comprising equal elements of admiration, amusement and horror. "Are you joking? We escape from a modern police force in a kitchen appliance box?"

Margarita nodded happily.

"Well, I only hope you're going to use sticky tape and not a staple gun!"

To get things rolling they filed up to Pepe's flat and were welcomed as if they were anti-fascist resistance fighters. Pepe insisted on opening a bottle of fine sherry he had been given by his own father, handing round tiny glasses and toasting "death and confusion to the enemy".

Then Mariano picked up the phone in the hallway and dialled. "Assuming we get out in one piece, we're going to need somewhere to lie low and think what we're going to do next," he called through to the living room as he waited for the other party to answer. "I've got some ideas about that."

By the sound of it, he called Maria first, then made three more calls. He looked happier by the time he came back in. "All sorted," he announced. "We're going for a short break in the mountains."

Gillian was next. She called a neighbour in Edinburgh who kept an eye on things when she was away, then her head of department. Something unexpected had come up. She'd be out of the country for a few days longer, but everything was under control and the lecture series would be ready on time, no problem. Finally, David let one or two key people at Southside Christian Fellowship know – and asked for prayer, saying that unfortunately he couldn't explain any further.

It was no more than half an hour before there was a knock at the door and an absolutely enormous box appeared – pushed, shunted, walked and wheeled by a younger, taller version of Pepe and a burly delivery guy. It just fitted in through the doorway, though getting it down the hall and into the living room was another matter. It had to slide horizontally along the parquet flooring before being heaved upright again and edged around like a foundation stone for the pyramids being inched into place. Once in the living room, all furniture was pushed to one side and the box was carefully pulled apart, taking care not to damage the edges. There were a couple of polystyrene protecting strips and plywood reinforcement. The fridge itself seemed even bigger once they got it out. It was a deep shade of burnished bronze and seemed to have more lights and baubles than a Christmas tree.

"Very fancy," Margarita murmured, standing back to admire it. "And what was my discount to be, Pepe?"

Pepe smiled and nodded. "The very latest,' he said. "Anti-frost, self-cleaning, energy-efficient, Wi-Fi connected. You can control the temperature from Hong Kong if you want. It even has a defrost compartment. You can put things in there that you might want to take out and turn it to defrost using your phone so it'll be ready when you come home. Though I think it costs more than my grandfather paid for his first farm. More of interest to us, it comes in a very sturdy box!"

All phone calls made and Pepe junior assuring them it fitted fine in the lift, they manhandled the box back out of the living room and along the outside corridor. With the lift doors wedged open, the box was edged in with one side still open, then lifted so they could fit a set of wheels underneath. Feeling like she had suddenly found herself stuck in an episode of *Dr Who*, Gillian stepped in first, followed by David, then Mariano, who apologised for the closer-than-comfort contact.

David leaned back out and gave Margarita *dos besos*. "You have been fantastic," he said. "If not for you, we'd all be in jail right now. Your papa would be proud of you."

She blushed slightly, tossed her hair in a distinctly girly manner and for the first time seemed lost for words.

After that, everything went dark. They crouched down to make everything more stable and felt the lift drop. Then they heard the door open and felt themselves being wheeled out. There was a nervous moment as the box seemed to catch on the lip of the doorway, then a bump as they dropped down onto the pavement. After that, the sound of the tail-lift of the van and a conversation with lots of swearing on the one side and understanding grunts in response. Apparently, working men, whether police or delivery drivers, were as one against the common enemy of fussy housewives who couldn't make up their minds what colour they wanted. The trio felt themselves being tipped precariously onto the lift, then more shuffling into the van. Finally, the doors slammed shut, the engine started and they were off.

Five minutes and couple of corners later, they felt the van pull up. The doors were opened and Pepe and his son helped them out.

"That was incredible, Pepe," David said with considerable relief. "I think that counts as my weirdest means of transport by quite some margin."

"Happy to help," Pepe senior beamed. "Margarita tells me you were the founding pastor of Warehouse 66."

"Something like that," David replied. "With many helpers."

"Well, glad to meet you. Margarita keeps trying to get me to come along and I tell her I'm not really a churchgoer, but I've got a surprise for her. I'm planning to come in three weeks' time."

"Why in three weeks?" Mariano asked.

"Because it's her birthday," Pepe replied, tapping his nose. "I'll come to church, which I know will please her, then we'll go out for a great lunch, then I'll ask her to marry me. So, if you wouldn't mind preaching a sermon – whichever of you it is – about the wonders of true love, I would be much obliged. Anyway, I think this is where you get out of the box, so to speak. Good luck."

"And good luck to you," Mariano said, shaking his hand.

When they finally climbed down, they were greeted by the smiling face of Jorge, one of Mariano's leadership team, leaning on the wing of his car.

"On the run, I believe," he commented, grinning. "We have your hideout all ready in the mountains. Did you know you've been on the news?"

* * *

They took the A2 back towards Madrid, then the M40 ring road and finally the A1 *autovia* north towards Burgos. Jorge drove his battered old Skoda with Mariano beside him and David and Gillian in the back. Like every other car in Madrid, old or new, it had bashes and scrapes on all four corners, owing to the *Madrileño* habit of what Gillian called 'contact parking', which made fairground dodgems seem tame.

Mariano filled Jorge in on events in rapid street Spanish Gillian found she could only vaguely follow. However, she knew the story, so it wasn't any loss. David added a few points for clarification. Jorge asked to see the object of all the hassle and David popped it open. Jorge craned around to look, let out a low whistle, then turned back at the shrill sound of a car horn blaring at him and pulled back into his lane without batting an eyelid.

"Wow! I've dreamed of seeing this much money all my life," he joked. "Now we've got it and we don't want it. Ha! You can never win!"

"By the way, I've probably missed it, but where are we going?" Gillian asked once the explanations had finished.

"I'm sorry," Mariano apologised. "Lozoya. It's a little village in the mountains. Some people from Madrid keep a place up here to get away from the heat. Maria's cousin Sebastian has a little house. He's a believer – totally reliable – and he's agreed to let us have it while the family's away on holiday."

"How long do they expect to be away?" Gillian asked, but nobody replied.

They continued north for about an hour before turning off to the left just after Kilometro 68. Thereafter, the country road wound higher and higher through scrubby brush and rocky outcrops on the route known as *La Garganta de los Montes* – "the Throat of the Mountains". Low down to the left were the deep blue waters of the Embalse de Perilla reservoir, part of the network of water supply put in place to serve Madrid during the Franco years. The only good thing he ever did, in Jorge's opinion.

By the time they arrived in the village of Lozoya it was dark and there was little to be seen. Jorge followed the GPS around twisty village streets, a very tight bend and further up another steep rise almost beyond the confines of the village, then slowed at the last house in the street and pulled over. The property was behind a high wall with locked metal gates. He got out, closing the car door quietly, then unlocked the gates and pulled in. The car was quietly emptied of occupants and luggage – including the all-important attaché case – then with brief embraces and *besos*, it backed out and Jorge's tail-lights disappeared back down the hill and around the bend.

Bags were dumped in the living room and Gillian carried out a quick survey. The house itself wasn't luxurious, but it fitted the bill of a second home for a middle-class family. The kitchen was well-enough equipped with all the necessary appliances, gadgets and a cupboard full of second-best plates. Another cupboard contained store ingredients such as olive oil, herbs, tins of sardines and some rice and pasta, but nothing fresh. There was one unopened litre of UHT milk. The fridge was empty but smelled OK.

David found cups and a kettle and started on some coffee. Gillian finally came across two packets of what claimed to be quick carbonara. She shrugged and proceeded to read the instructions, stealing some of David's boiled water.

Twenty minutes later they were sitting around a dining room table with a bottle of not-too-bad Ribera del Duero, plates of hot pasta, rice crackers and a dish of oily sardines.

"Cheers," David said, trying to make the best of it. "Here's to the Spanish Resistance."

The meal was largely eaten in silence, as nobody had any energy for small talk. Then Gillian managed to find sheets and light duvets and made up two beds: a single and a double. Mariano again phoned Maria to confirm their arrival in a ten-second call, without mentioning where they were, just in case.

Finally, in bed with the lights out, David and Gillian had their first quiet moment of the day.

"David," Gillian spoke softly into the darkness.

"Hmm?"

"What are we doing here?"

"I think it's called lying low till the heat dies down. Hiding from the forces of darkness, which these days means those in charge."

"Yes, I worked that out. I mean why us? You're an ex-pat and I'm a foreigner. Why are we charged with exposing Spanish corruption? Why not some brave investigative journalist or honest cop who knows what they're doing and is willing to take the risk? I can see the importance of it all, but why us? I just want to be home, getting on with the great vowel shift and open syllable lengthening. And if I have to know about what's going on, I want to read it in the news, not be living it." She let out a long sigh, then David heard her voice choke up. "I'm really fed up with this sort of thing, you know. I just want to be home, leading a normal life…"

David was still and silent in the darkness, except for reaching out for her hand. "I totally agree," he finally said. "That's what I want, too. But it doesn't seem to be what's coming our way. And to be honest, I think we're probably past just handing it back, anyway. We know something we're not supposed to know – and like you say, we didn't even want to know it. But I'm not sure what the alternatives are now."

They lay together in the silent darkness.

"So evil still triumphs when good men do nothing?" Gillian asked.

"I guess so. But if we believe in any higher power that has casting rights, maybe we have a part in the production, whether we want it or not."

"Huh," Gillian answered. "I wish I'd flunked the auditions."

Then a thought occurred to her. "Do you think marrying you was the audition?"

David managed something like a laugh. "Maybe. It was your big chance to say no, and you didn't."

"Remind me. What did I say?'

"I think it was for richer, for poorer, in sickness and in health, in a cosy flat in Marchmont or on the run in Spain. Something like that."

"Well, we are richer. That's certainly something."

"So maybe we missed one of the alternatives," David reflected. "Keep the money, go home to Edinburgh and live in luxury."

He could feel her smiling, even in the dark.

She rolled over and cuddled in. "Sounds perfect," she said. "A house in the Grange with a garden, a gigantic red setter and garden furniture from John Lewis."

Now David laughed. "That would be boring," he said. "You'd want to work."

"I could find enough to occupy myself."

"Doing what?"

"I don't know. Playing with the kids in the garden."

There was a second's silence that seemed to stretch on and on.

Then David spoke, barely audibly. "I don't want to get the wrong end of the stick," he said. "Are you saying what I think you're saying?"

"I think so. It's looking that way."

"I noticed you passed on the wine at supper. That's why."

He felt her nod. "Uh-huh."

"I don't know what to say. That's wonderful."

"Early days yet. We'll see. But if all goes well, can you promise me something?"

"Of course. If I can."

"Promise me we'll let somebody else be the good man who stops evil flourishing while we look on and watch it happen. Deal?"

"Deal. I love you, Dr Lockhart."

"You'd better. And any descendants you might have!"

Chapter 8

Town and Country

Oscarito saw it on the news and immediately felt something go hard and heavy in his chest, then drop into the pit of his stomach like a bag of cement. He was finishing a coffee and a piece of cake when his hand stopped halfway to his mouth. The report described how a foreign religious cult leader by the name of David Hidalgo had embezzled €1.5 million of government funds and was now wanted, along with other known co-conspirators. The report did not go into details of how the crime had been committed but did show an unflattering photo of the alleged criminal mastermind.

Oscarito immediately realised that he had been cheerfully chatting with said alleged criminal only a few days earlier and had found him relaxed, friendly, welcoming and thoroughly respectable. Chatting with Mariano later, he'd been given to understand that David Hidalgo now pastored a small church in Edinburgh, having founded Warehouse 66 many years before, and was back in Spain for an informal farewell meeting with the Minister for Justice.

Of course, the details about the money were fascinating, having many points of interest in relation to his own job and what had been going through his mind lately. After all, he was quite closely related to a large sum of money himself. In fact, Oscarito had helped Señor Ibañez remove exactly that sum from his office safe and stack it neatly into a brand-new black leather attaché case. The office manager had offered no explanation as to where or to whom this money was destined – and Oscarito had known better than to ask.

Then, the previous evening, he had basically been thrown out of the building – in the middle of his after-hours shift working on the gold star donors' accounts – for some top-level confab (for which, he had noticed, the car park at the rear of the building was full of dark limousines). Walking down towards the gate he had even caught sight of the Minister for Justice and Señor Ibañez drawing curtains in the back room. Perhaps there had been raised voices, but he couldn't be sure.

So the facts were these: there was an attaché case with €1.5 million in it; the Minister for Justice, who was a long-serving Party grandee, was retiring; David Hidalgo was to have had a meeting with the minister; €1.5 million had gone missing from somewhere and David Hidalgo was accused of purloining it, but he had only just come back to Spain for a flying visit and had appeared totally at ease in full public view. Finally, what looked to be a rush meeting with several big Party players had been convened the night before the news went public. *Coincidence?*

Oscarito thought back to his decision not to play the lottery because of the appalling odds against any given number coming up and decided that this looked remarkably similar. The chances of all these facts and events being entirely unconnected might even make the lottery look like a sure thing. Besides, he was already convinced that the Party was operating well on the wrong side of the law, both in its means of raising funds and the way the identity of these donors was disguised.

Going back to his father's round peg, round hole philosophy, Oscarito accepted that as far as his gifts and personality were concerned, events of high political machinations and skullduggery were definitely not his shape of slot; but even he was beginning to feel taken advantage of. Not only was he the last to know what was going on, but he was being treated as if the contents of a bottle labelled poison could be poured onto his paella right in front of his face and he would still be expected to smile and eat it up. That was, to say the least, beginning to irritate him. In general, he had tended to follow another long-time dictum of his father's: "Keep your head down, look after number one and don't draw attention to yourself." That might be a very apt and appropriate strategy in street sweeping, but here he was sweeping up another kind of dirt that had more of a tendency to stick.

Then an even more uncomfortable thought occurred. If the law was being routinely broken by his superiors and he was the accountant keeping track of it all, where did that leave him? Was the man who cleaned up the blood also guilty, along with the man who fired the gun? He continued his train of thought. Assuming that David Hidalgo was neither the leader of a dangerous religious cult – Warehouse 66 had seemed noisy but innocuous – nor a mastermind embezzler, and (this was an important *and*), somehow he was able to show that he had become involved for either innocent or accidental reasons with the same €1.5 million he – Oscarito – was acquainted with, and (yet another important *and*) the misbehaviour of his bosses and their colleagues was eventually brought to light, would *he* not be equally culpable for knowing and saying nothing?

His mind wandered while the TV news went on to the weather – more of the same. Without any effort, he found himself imagining the scene in court with a stony-faced judge up on his bench and a slick, smarty, hotshot lawyer in front of him saying, "Do you really expect the court to believe, Señor Fernandez de la Roda, that you regularly worked on accounts that even the sweepers of the street could guess were being raised illegally, and yet you, an educated, qualified, intelligent man thought you were just adding up blue beans?" He would stammer, stumble or mutter something while the court fell about laughing, just before the judge banged his gavel and sent him down for eternity plus twenty-five.

As these ominous thoughts bounced around in his brain, Oscarito realised he would be entirely unable to work this morning or even look his boss and colleagues in the eye. With all the evening work he had accumulated a mountain of overtime, so he concluded that before deciding anything else he would take the morning off. The rest of the accounts were well up to date and creditors could certainly wait another day.

After phoning in and leaving a message for Señor Ibañez, he made another coffee, had another piece of cake, turned on the air con as the Madrid morning heat began to build, and sat back to think. He did not want to go to prison and didn't think he deserved to. Since Oscarito had been on a higher salary he had finally got his own place, and he didn't want to swap it for a ten-metre-squared cell. Latina wasn't posh Salamanca, but it was OK and he didn't see why he should lose it. The only sense he could make of the €1.5 million was that it had somehow passed from the possession of the Party grandee into the possession of David Hidalgo. He couldn't begin to imagine how, but on present evidence Hidalgo seemed to be at least a more honourable man than those who had lost it. The loss would of course be a matter of substantial concern but also embarrassment to the Party, who would want it back as quickly and quietly as possible. So surely it had only hit the news because Hidalgo wasn't going to come quietly. The fact that he was a wanted man meant it could be a fair working assumption that he still had the money and that the powers that be did not know where he was. That was a good thing and a bad thing. A good thing in that there was still a chance the whole affair could be brought to light, and a bad thing in that David Hidalgo was now feeling like the only ally – besides Marta, of course – Oscarito had. But if the police couldn't find him, how could he?

Suddenly, Oscarito began to feel the fog clearing. The fact was crystallising in his mind that instead of being either the dupe and the dummy or the culpable accomplice, there was a third option. He could go on the offensive. After all, nobody knew the inside situation better than him – with the possible exception of the main perpetrators. He was the man who counted the beans, and that had to carry some weight. Going to the police was clearly going to be the equivalent to sticking his head in a gas oven, but maybe he could go to the press. There were campaigning investigative journalists who were building their careers by trying to root out government corruption. But what would he say? Would they believe him? What evidence did he have?

The thought of trying to smuggle the Gold Star book out of the office made his blood run cold. Who knew what the big boys would stop at when they were playing for such big stakes? No, it had to be David Hidalgo. No one else would do. If the money he was on the run for was nothing to do with the Party's slush funds, then ultimately he would look a fool, nothing more. But if the money David Hidalgo was being sought for was the same money, he – Oscarito – knew about, then Hidalgo might know what to do next or at least might know how to make use of this information. But where to start?

He finished his coffee and called Marta. That was his only link.

"Oscarito! This is a surprise. I've just dropped Marco at school. Are you at work?"

"No, I'm not. I'm taking the day off. Can we meet? There's something I'd like to discuss with you, but not on the phone."

Marta lived in Coslada – a low-rent, largely immigrant neighbourhood on the opposite side of Madrid from Latina – so they agreed to meet in the centre of town. Marta suggested La Mallorquina, a *pastelería* and coffee shop on the Puerta del Sol and a Madrid landmark for over 100 years. Oscarito never went out for coffee or cream cakes and needed to have its location explained in detail. The *pastelería* part was downstairs and there was always a queue for fantastic, thousand-calorie cakes and excellent takeaway coffee. The tables were upstairs, where waiters in spotless white jackets served a mixture of wealthy ladies of leisure and Erasmus students wanting to soak up the atmosphere.

The pair agreed that whoever got there first would bag a table and wait. To Oscarito's relief, Marta was already seated in a corner with a large frothy coffee and a sweet *hojaldre* puff pastry in front of her by the time Oscarito arrived. He had become rather anxious, wondering how he might go about bagging a table, but he needn't have worried. She beamed him a smile and a wave as soon as he emerged from the stairs and cast an eye around, looking for her.

"Over here!"

He walked past the other customers, keeping his eyes fixed firmly on the floor, then sat down and ordered only a *Poleo-Menta* peppermint tea. He wasn't in the mood for anything exotic.

Marta took his hand and smiled encouragingly. "What's the crisis?" she asked.

"Did you see the news this morning?" he replied.

"No, I was taking Marco to school. What is it?"

"They're saying that David Hidalgo has embezzled €1.5 million of government money, and that he's wanted by the police."

Marta gasped. "What? No!"

"Keep your voice down. It was on the news. I'm not saying it's true, just that they're looking for him."

Marta put her cup down and looked around, as if seeking out something normal that still made sense. Her lovely, sticky *hojaldre* had somehow lost its appeal.

"But how does that affect you, Oscarito?" she asked. "And why did you want to meet?"

He looked briefly exasperated then caught himself, realising that what was now so obvious to him might not be at all obvious to someone else.

"You haven't forgotten what I told you the other day, have you? You know, about the office?"

"No, of course not."

"Well, I think that somehow David Hidalgo has got himself caught up with the same thing. That money might be the very same money I was told to count out and put in a case last week. I think it's not government money; it's dirty Party money. And if that's the case, I have to do or say something about it. I don't want to go to jail if it all comes to light, when I've been right in the middle of it and never let on."

Marta let out a long, low breath. "I see," she murmured, unable to think of anything more to ask or say.

Oscarito sipped his tea and tried to practise the breathing exercises his doctor had prescribed for panic attacks.

Finally, Marta spoke again. "And have you thought of going to the police?" she asked. Judging by the look on his face, she realised that might not be the best move. "No, I suppose not," she conceded. "Then what about the papers?"

"I did think of that, but I've really got no evidence. I can hardly smuggle the accounts book out and leave it with them for a fortnight while they check things out. No, the only person I can speak to is David Hidalgo. Somehow or another we're both involved. If we could share what we know there might be a way forward. And I'm tired of being the meat in the sandwich, knowing it's wrong but not being able to do anything. I just want to tell someone else and get them to take over. Hand the whole thing over to someone else who'll know what to do. David Hidalgo seems like a guy who would know, but nobody knows where he is. You're connected with the church, but I've only been once. I thought you might know how to get in touch with him."

Marta put her coffee down. "Let me think," she said. "I have no idea where he might be – maybe back in Edinburgh – but Mariano would know. I've been to their house once. We can ask Maria…"

* * *

About seventy kilometres to the north, David, Gillian and Mariano were also sitting round a table having coffee. Sometimes a good sleep can clear the mind and make things look better in the morning. It hadn't had that effect for them this morning.

David had woken feeling a weight on his mind but also something happy, though he couldn't remember what it was. Then Gillian had made a sleepy noise next to him and he'd remembered. What had eluded him in his twenties and thirties might now be coming true in his fifties. He hoped it wasn't an illusion, and that he'd still have enough energy for fatherhood. Having a teenager around when he was in his seventies was far from ideal, but they could cross that bridge when they came to it.

David had got up, mastered a badly behaved shower and shaved, before putting the kettle on and taking Gillian a cup of tea.

Mariano had emerged as he went back down to the kitchen, and David had told him the news while rooting around for something that might serve as breakfast.

"Congratulations, *caballero*," Mariano had said. "I'm very glad. You'll be great parents, no question."

"Thanks," David had responded. "Maybe I'm being overcautious, but it strikes me that this is yet another reason we shouldn't be in this position. Whatever else applies, I doubt the stress of being on the run is good for expectant mothers."

"Indeed. We can talk about it later, though. In the meantime, congratulations again. A week or two and you'll be back home and this'll all be a minor detail. New life is more important."

Gillian had wandered through at the sound of voices, hair all over the place and a crumpled dressing gown on out of her weekend bag. "Morning everyone," she had whispered blearily.

There had been more congratulations and kisses all round while David gathered dry toast, biscuits and a jar of apricot jam, then made some fresh coffee.

About an hour later, Gillian and Mariano had got to the point of being able to face the day, and they all sat down together to see where they were.

"I was listening to the news while you were in the shower, Gillian," Mariano began. "Not good, I'm afraid. They're accusing David of embezzling €1.5 million and say the police are following a number of active leads as to his whereabouts."

David, whom Mariano had already told, was nonplussed. "It's the photo that upsets me most," he said, "and the bit about 'leader of a religious cult'. I'm not the leader – Mariano is!"

Gillian smiled, but she knew her husband and his sense of humour. She knew he was worried.

"I guess that means the gloves are off," she remarked. "So, what do we do now? It's traditional to make a run for South America with our stolen millions, isn't it?"

No one had an immediate answer. The events of the day before already felt like some sort of caper that had happened to someone else, like a scene from the Lavender Hill Mob. Hiding behind the secret panel in a trick bookcase. Escaping from the police in the packaging of a fridge. How ridiculous. But now they were in their temporary refuge, wondering when there would be a knock at the door, with neither a way out nor a plan. Any route through passport control was obviously out of the question. And at the very least, Gillian ought to be paying a visit to her GP for whatever important but routine tests went on these days.

"Would it be an idea to start with what we have going *for* us instead of just what's *against* us?" David began.

That seemed to go down OK, so they began.

"I suppose we're not stuck for cash," Gillian offered with half a smile.

"Maybe that's not as mad as it sounds," David followed up. "We've got what everyone's looking for, not the other way around. That's bound to give us some bargaining power."

"We've got breathing space," Mariano suggested, "for a couple of weeks, at least."

Gillian groaned. "I hope it's not going to take that long!"

"What else do we have?" David persisted.

"Friends," Mariano said. "Lots of friends and contacts, both personal and through Warehouse 66. People who don't believe the news and wish us well. The Party may have the power of the state at its disposal, but it also has lots of enemies who would like to see it brought down."

"Like whom?"

"Well, like some sides of the press, I suppose. Other parties.

There are bound to be some people in power who suspect what's been going on and don't approve. Maybe even some people at Party headquarters."

"You mean like a well-intentioned mole?" Gillian asked.

David looked thoughtful. "Bit of a coincidence, but I think I met someone on Sunday who has some sort of Party connection. Marta's boyfriend. Was it Orlando?"

"Oscar," Mariano corrected him. "No, *Oscarito*, I think. I've no idea what he does, though."

"I'm sure he said he was an accountant," David continued.

"Well, that may be interesting, but it doesn't really help in the meantime," Gillian said.

"OK – let's leave that sticking to the wall," David agreed. "Maybe the press is our best chance, then…"

"Whatever we do, though, we need to know what's going on," Gillian stressed. "Can we access the internet? That would be key to getting in touch, as well as to keeping tabs on things."

"I'll look," Mariano offered, and went off hunting down the back of the TV and on various shelves around the house. "Found it," he shouted after a few minutes. "Just wait. I'll plug it in."

"I'll get my laptop," Gillian said and disappeared.

"Is that going to be secure?" Mariano asked. "I'm not a technical genius, but if they can track a mobile phone could they not get the location of a laptop?"

Gillian shook her head. "Not this one," she said. "I think you can normally track down the owner of an IP address, but actually getting your hands on that person depends on the owner being at the same location the service provider bills them at. Obviously, a laptop moves around a lot. Anyway, we have a friend in Edinburgh who insisted we upgrade everything after a few adventures last year. He's put some software of his own on here that makes us more or less invisible online. We can receive and send emails and browse – all the normal stuff – but otherwise nobody knows we exist."

"I wish the police didn't know we existed," Mariano said.

Gillian turned on and typed in the passkey Mariano had found. "Bingo!" she said. "I'm online. Now, what do we want to look for?"

"Actually, I think we should hang on a bit," David interrupted. "We were talking about resources. So we have the internet, that's great. But just before we get caught up searching for stuff, I think it would be good to finish the inventory. So far we've got a case full of money that we can demonstrate came from the Minister for Justice, and there may be other fingerprints in there. There's also that document with the figures – you know, the Mateo, Marcos, Lucas and Juan one – whoever that might refer to. We've got some breathing space here. We've got friends and connections, and now we've got internet. Anything else?"

"The phone call from the minister asking for his money back?" Mariano offered. "I suppose that's evidence, even if it's just our recollection of it. Did anyone write it down while it was still fresh?"

"Oh! I am *so* stupid!" Gillian suddenly burst out. "I completely forgot." She took out her mobile and opened it up. "As soon as I heard the voice and realised what it was about, I thought it might be useful to have a record. I'm really lazy in lectures – I just record stuff all the time instead of writing it down."

She laid the mobile on the breakfast table and opened an app. The first ten seconds or so were missing, but the rest was pretty clear. It was chilling to listen to the whole thing all over again.

David sat back, visibly rocked at hearing the exchange replayed. "Did I really say that?" he asked. "That he should look after the Bible you gave me?"

Gillian smiled. "I was very proud of you."

David poured another cup of coffee. "So now we have a voice record, cash, possible fingerprints and maybe someone who works in Party headquarters – though whose side he might be on we don't know. What else?"

Mariano chipped in. "We've spoken about contacts. I know reporters who've been trying to nail the Party for years on rumours of slush funds, backhanders, bribes, sweeteners and even control of actual criminal rackets. They've been persistent, but firstly it's not been easy to get hard evidence, and secondly the justice system is so incredibly slow in Spain that it can take years to get to court, then years more for appeals to be heard. In some cases the whole thing takes so long that alleged crimes can no longer be pursued because they fall outside the statutes of limitations."

"You mean there are limits on the time between an alleged crime being committed and when it comes to court?" Gillian asked.

"That's right. More than the prescribed number of years and it has to be dropped. So it's in any criminal's interests to stretch things out for as long as possible, and the lawyers are experts at it. Anyway, I'm no lawyer or reporter, so one way forward might be to get in touch with someone who is, and is interested in investigation and possible prosecution, and then let them take things forward."

"To be honest, I like the sound of that," David admitted, putting down his cup and sagging in his chair. "I've had far too much of this sort of stuff lately. I went back to Scotland for a quiet life. That's the last thing I've had!"

Chapter 9

Babylon

"You really can't be serious," the ex-Minister for Justice was saying into his phone in Señor Ibañez's little office at the back of the general office within Party headquarters. "A *piso* block with one way in and one way out and you couldn't find them? Incredible. He's not the invisible man, you know... No, I'm not, but even a layman can see it was bungled. How is it possible?... No, I do understand, I'm just a bit worked up. This isn't *Monopoly* money. And getting out of jail costs more than €100... OK, OK. Calm down. I realise you're doing your best... How many?... I see. Well, that does seem a substantial response. So, how long do you think?... No, I know you're not. But do you have any... I see. Well, we'll just have to wait, then, I suppose. By the way, well done with the news piece. That should help... OK, I'm available on this number any time, day or night... OK, I'll wait to hear from you. Thanks."

He clicked his phone off, dropped it onto the desk and rubbed his hands through his hair. "I suppose you got the gist of that," he said to the office manager. "'No progress', 'every effort', 'lines of inquiry...'. All the rubbish they tell the public, but we all know what it means. Hidalgo and his friends got out of that building somehow and nobody knows where they are now. No mobiles, no reported sightings and nothing at ports of entry. The papers all have the picture but half of them are refusing to print it because they think the public interest is more to harass the government. By now I should be halfway to the Caribbean with the *Señora*, not baking in Madrid looking for my money."

Ibañez said nothing. There was nothing to say.

"Do you think the accountant's safe?" the ex-minister suddenly asked.

The office manager shrugged. "As safe as anyone can be. He's an idiot. He shows absolutely no interest in anything except numbers and seems oblivious to what they actually mean. I've put the frighteners on him a few times and I think he was shaking in his shoes. There's about as much chance of him taking an interest as… well… as him taking an interest in the new cleaning lady!"

* * *

"So, can we phone Maria right now?" Oscarito asked anxiously.

Marta shrugged and pulled out her phone. "I don't see why not," she said, trying to be cheerful. "I think I've got her number."

"OK, but not here. Too public. Let's go downstairs – at least out into Sol."

They paid and left. As usual, Sol was a human maelstrom, particularly at the corner of Calle Mayor, where *La Mallorquina* was located – all compounded by almost permanent scaffolding up around the facades. Oscarito shuddered and kept his eyes on the small patch of pavement in front of his feet to avoid the gaze of, or, worse still, physical contact with, the horde of humanity around them. They edged their way out, then took the next left down Calle Arenal, which was much less crowded, and found a rare vacant bench. If anyone was following or trying to overhear a conversation, this might be a bit safer – hiding in plain sight, as they say.

Marta called Maria.

After a couple of rings, Maria answered, her voice tense and strained. "Let me call you back," she said once Marta had introduced herself.

Seconds later, Marta's mobile rang.

"Sorry about that," Maria said. "I've had a mountain of calls from the papers, the police, people at church, even other teachers from my school, all wanting to know what's going on and where David and

Mariano are. I just needed to be sure it was really you. I suppose you want to know the same thing."

"I do, but there's something more. I'm with Oscarito. You know, I brought him to church on Sunday…"

"Yes, I think I remember. I'm sorry, there were so many people."

"Don't worry. Anyway, I don't know if you picked this up, but Oscarito works – well, he works somewhere important in relation to all of this. He wants to talk to David. He thinks he might know something that would help."

Maria was silent for a few seconds as she took this in. "That sounds interesting," she said cautiously, "but let's not talk on the phone. Where are you?"

"Arenal."

"OK. I was planning to come in anyway. Stay where you are. I'll be about forty minutes… if the metro isn't on strike again."

* * *

"So, in terms of contacts, then," David continued, "who do we have – discounting the accountant?"

"Do you know Filipe?" Mariano asked. "He's not what you'd call super committed, but he sometimes comes to church with the kids. He's on his own now and I think he sometimes feels the need for adult company at the weekend. He works for one of the big national dailies and they've been trying to nail the Party for years. I think he'd be trustworthy and would certainly want to know what we know. He could put out the other side of the story in the press and see what the reaction is. I don't think we should allow the government a free ride on this."

"Excellent," David said. "Do you have his contact details?"

"Only on my phone, and we don't want to be using phones here, I guess. I could find him easily enough online, though, and drop him an email."

"Anyone else? Anyone in the police, for example?"

"Yes, definitely. Alfredo is a captain in the Guardia Civil. He's actually part of our leadership team, as of the last elections. I'd trust him with my life. He may not have anything to do with the inquiry, though, which I suppose is going to be either a national or a city police matter."

"And can we contact him?"

"Certainly. I guess the same applies. I can email him."

Gillian finally launched the browser on her laptop and clicked open her own email account. Not much there. Routine departmental circulars; an end-of-summer barbecue at the luxury New Town residence of her colleagues, Stephen Baranski and Fran McGoldrick; various fashion offers; and the latest news about Alexa, the Amazon voice assistant David had given her for Christmas. Then she clicked open David's email. That was a bit more interesting. Among all the spam there were anxious inquiries from friends all over Spain – and even some in Scotland who had heard the news. Then at the bottom of the list the subject line read: "Are you OK? What can I do?". It was from Alfredo Sanchez de la Vega, Captain in the Guardia Civil.

"Ha! How about that?" David exclaimed when Gillian showed him the message. "The very man who might come in handy. I met him at church, didn't I?"

Mariano nodded. "You did indeed. Burly guy. I think you got the Alfredo bear hug. He asked me for your email, but I thought he was just wanting to keep in touch. Anyway, like I say, I trust him completely. If he wants to come and meet us to talk, I'd say we should go for it."

Gillian clicked to open it and they read together. It was as, Mariano had suggested, an offer to meet, talk and give any advice needed.

"OK. That might be the first establishment guy on our side. I'll take your word for his trustworthiness. Now, how about the press? Should we email Filipe?"

Gillian began to type the message in Spanish but Mariano took over when her use of the subjunctive turned out to be *un poco flojo*

– a bit weak. That suited Gillian fine, and Mariano rattled off a quick summary suggesting they'd be happy to meet if Filipe was interested.

"Can we trust these guys with our location?" Gillian asked a little nervously.

"Well, we could meet them in the park if you're not sure," Mariano replied, "but I think they're both really honest, reliable people."

"Look, here's another one popped up," Gillian remarked, still looking at David's email inbox. The name and email address were unfamiliar, but the subject line – "David Hidalgo: message from a friend" – attracted her attention. She opened it.

They read silently together: "Dear Señor Hidalgo. You may not have many friends right now. I am one. I am watching you. The Blackbird."

Mariano looked to David for some explanation, but there was none.

David scratched his head, drained the last of his coffee and looked out of the window. "No idea," he said at last. "None whatsoever. The email address looks Spanish, but I can't remember anyone it might connect to. Can't think of any nicknames or identities. Well, I suppose we need all the friends we can get, whoever it might be."

"And besides friends, there's something else we really need," Gillian commented.

"What's that?" Mariano asked.

"Lunch. I'm going shopping."

* * *

Maria arrived on time and found Oscarito and Marta exactly where they had said they would be. They decided to go for lunch while they thought about things. Everything around Puerta del Sol was hugely overpriced, so they took the metro back to La Latina, Oscarito's *barrio*, where he quickly found a quiet restaurant where nobody would bother them. It was one of those places where if you ordered

red wine and your companion ordered white, you got a giant carafe of each – as well as a two-course meal, *postre* and bread – all for €12.

Oscarito felt himself calming down in his own environment with a glass of red inside him. He told Maria what he knew. Then she told him and Marta what she knew. Jorge had come back after the 'special delivery' and told her everything, so she knew where they were and that they were well.

"I'm driving up there tonight," she said. "Maybe you should come with me, then you can explain."

Oscarito shook his head. "Can't tonight," he said. "My mother's birthday. I didn't go into work today but I'm trying to be absolutely normal, as much as I can. If I miss the birthday Mum will be upset and demand to know why, and Dad's bound to tell all his Party friends. I'll come tomorrow after work. Can I bring Marta?"

"Of course. I'll give you directions."

* * *

Gillian found the village shop and bought supplies. She explained that she was visiting a cousin who had a holiday house. The little shop was well stocked and had a good variety, so she bought bread, milk, fresh meat, eggs, yoghurts, vegetables, cereal and some drinks. Enough to dig in for a bit.

She cooked lunch while Mariano used the laptop to check his emails. He found a message from Maria explaining what Jorge had told her and that she would come out that night.

"Is that wise?" David asked. "She might be followed."

Mariano shrugged. "I don't know, but Maria and I have always gone through everything together. I think I'd like her advice and counsel before we do anything irrevocable."

David knew the feeling and didn't push it, but he privately hoped her email hadn't been hacked, that she wouldn't attract unwelcome attention and that she'd didn't try to call any of them on the way.

They ate lunch and, with nothing better to do, went and sat outside. The bungalow had a large *terraza* with bushes and flowers – both planted and in pots – and on the other side a swimming pool with a canopy over it, like a giant poly tunnel.

"Ah, what a pity," Gillian said. "I wish I'd brought my dippers."

Mariano thought they might dip into the bottle of white instead, which was by now well chilled, and no one objected. They raided the cupboards again for some savoury biscuits and sat around the pool as the afternoon wore on into evening.

"When's Maria coming?" David asked Mariano as the crickets got going once the heat had died down.

Mariano looked at his watch a little anxiously. "She said half past five, so she really should have been here by now," he said. "She's usually very punctual. Not like me."

"Maybe she's not familiar with the road and is taking it easy," Gillian suggested.

Mariano didn't argue.

However, half past five turned into half past six, then half past seven.

Finally, at half past eight, Mariano's mobile rang. "Yes, speaking," he confirmed, then his face went white. "Yes, of course. Of course I'll come. I'll be there in forty minutes." He turned the phone off and looked around helplessly. "Maria's been in a car crash," he said in a daze. "Multiple injuries. She's in *Ramón y Cajal* hospital. I have to go and see her."

The following discussion was one of the hardest David had ever had in his life, including those where he had comforted the dying, the bereaved, those who had lost a child or had a disabled baby, those with terminal diagnoses, and those who had lost businesses and livelihoods or been caught up in criminal activity.

Mariano sat with his head in his hands and just kept repeating, "No, I can't... I *have* to go."

Finally, Gillian suggested a compromise. "We could use the house's fixed line," she said. "David could call Jorge. He could go and then call you. If she's in surgery or sedated she probably won't even know who's there."

This finally, very reluctantly, prevailed and David called Jorge, who immediately agreed and set off. He said he'd phone from the hospital, and less than an hour later he did so. Meanwhile, Mariano just sat there, white, shocked and staring into space.

"Not very good," Jorge began. "Broken leg and pelvis, chest compression injuries from the belt. Lots of bruising. However, they thought it might have been worse, so I guess we should be grateful. She was run off the road, without a doubt. She's sedated but awake. She told me about it. She thinks it was a black 4x4, though she's not absolutely sure. Caught her on a bend and pushed her right over the verge. The car turned twice and rolled down. Thankfully, it didn't go on fire. She was found by a guy coming back from a fishing trip. He called *urgencies* and they got her here as soon as they could. She's not in any pain right now, but they're going to operate to set things. I'll stay the night and call you in the morning, and I'll keep my eyes open. This isn't a game any more."

Mariano sat with his head in his hands. Gillian had a few painkillers in her bag but nothing else, so they hunted around a bit more and managed to pour some brandy into him, not entirely sure whether that was what you were supposed to do. They ate silently – though Mariano hardy touched his food – then David prayed for Maria and they all went to bed.

"What do you reckon, then?" Gillian asked once the lights were out.

"It could be unrelated," David suggested.

"But you don't believe that."

"No, I don't. I suppose it was to tighten the screw. Come quietly or something worse might happen."

"If you're right, it was pretty ruthless. They must be desperate."

"Absolutely. Whoever gave the order and whoever was driving – they could have killed her. It could have been murder. I think that's where we've got to."

The next morning Mariano was still looking terrible. His

conversation was monosyllabic, and he showed no interest in food or drink. Still, Gillian got a strong coffee down him and he gradually rejoined the land of the living.

Jorge phoned, as good as his word, and gave an update. All the bones were set, the trauma surgeon was happy, and Maria had passed a peaceful night. She wasn't awake yet, but everyone seemed to think the prognosis was good. "No more ice hockey!" the doctor had said.

After that, the trio decided the only useful thing to do was keep in touch with their press and police contacts to see if there were any replies. Word had got out about Maria's accident – though it could hardly be called an accident – and both David and Mariano's inboxes were full of expressions of shock and sympathy. Once they had dealt with these and cleared away the garbage, three further messages remained. One from Filipe, one from Alfredo and another from the Blackbird.

Gillian clicked on Filipe's message. He had written at some length about hearing of the charge, and how he had immediately felt it must have something to do with his investigations into government corruption. He described the background as far as he knew it, and everything seemed to fit. He wanted to meet to go through things in more detail. After that, he would speak to his editor and see what line the paper would take. He thought this might be the breakthrough they had needed to finally nail it.

"Do we let him come here?" Gillian asked the room.

"I trust him, and he'll be careful," Mariano said, "but let's read the rest before we reply."

She clicked on Alfredo's message. He had been more guarded and cautious than Filipe in the tone of his writing, as might be appropriate for a serving police officer. Naturally, he couldn't give an opinion on a legal matter he had no knowledge of, and he didn't really see how he could help, but he did wonder whether what he called the "Esther Hypothesis" might apply.

Mariano laughed for the first time all morning.

"Explain!" Gillian demanded, looking mystified.

"I've been preaching on the Old Testament book of Esther," he said. "It's the only book in the Bible that doesn't mention God at all. It's basically political. You probably all know the story, but what I've been trying to bring out is that the Jewish people are in exile in Babylon, and a very powerful minister is jealous of their influence and wants them destroyed. Esther is a royal queen – basically winner of the king's beauty contest. Her uncle appeals to her to do something, but the law is such that it's very risky to speak to the king without being invited first. Despite that, her uncle pressurises her and says, 'Who knows but you are here for just such a time as this.' She speaks up and the king is sympathetic. Finally, the guy who started it all is hanged on the gibbet erected for the Jewish leaders. I think Alfredo is being subtle but supportive, and maybe making a joke. He's saying perhaps all this has happened just to blow the whole thing wide open once and for all. He's saying maybe it's not an accident you got the attaché case. Maybe it's meant to be. And what it's meant to do is expose the Party and the government in a way they can't wriggle out of or delay."

"Big responsibility," David said quietly. "Not sure I'm up for that."

"Well, I'm not sure we've any choice now," Mariano went on. Alfredo's message seemed to have galvanised him somehow. "Esther spoke to the king, though it might have meant her death – and she got away with it. Like I said, God is never mentioned in the entire book, but the clear implication is that God is with her; specifically putting her in that place at that time to do that thing."

"Wow," Gillian remarked. "That puts things in a different light. I must say I've been seeing it all so far as a really inconvenient mishap. But if we're meant to be here – meant to be doing this – I suppose it does give you a certain amount of confidence."

David went to make more coffee, feeling the need for a breather.

Gillian clicked on the Blackbird's email. "This is really weird," she called through to the kitchen. "Listen to this: 'Señor Hidalgo. I am sorry to hear about last night's event. Keep focused. Don't give in. You still have a friend. I am watching you. The Blackbird.'"

David came back through and read it over her shoulder. "The

Blackbird?" he said, shaking his head. "Still no idea. Is 'last night's event' what happened to Maria? He says he's a friend and he's watching. Any thoughts, Mariano?"

They reread the text and then looked back at the message received the previous day.

"What do you think?" David finally asked. "Significant? Somebody in a position to help us or just a random online weirdo?"

"If 'last night's event' does refer to Maria," Mariano commented, "then the people who know are going to be limited to friends and church folk. I don't think it'll be known any further afield, and not by people we don't know. I'm not sure I like the idea of someone else – even if they claim to be a friend – knowing as much as I do. Or maybe more."

"What do we think, then?" David continued. "Is it really a friend? Should we say something back?"

"I don't know why, but I'm thinking of the source they called 'Deep Throat' in the Watergate investigation," Gillian mused. "He was an inside source who got in touch with Bernstein and Woodward – you know, the two reporters who broke the story – and kept them on the right track. He would drop hints, then comment on the stories they filed."

"Wasn't he finally identified just a few years ago?" David asked.

"Yes. It was confirmed that it had been an assistant head at the FBI. Mark somebody, I think."

"So you think this could be an inside source who may be sympathetic to our cause?"

"Maybe. That's one possibility. Or it could just be mind games to confuse us or to trick us into giving away information. Or any other possibility."

"And you're sure that your laptop's secure?" Mariano asked.

"As much as is humanly possible," Gillian replied.

"Then why not just say something? So long as we don't let whoever it is influence our decisions, I don't think there's anything to lose."

"OK. What do we say?" Gillian asked.

David sat down beside her at the laptop and pulled it in front of him. "Since it's apparently addressed to me, maybe I should reply. How about this? Short and sweet: 'Who are you? What should we do? David Hidalgo.'"

"As good as any," Gillian agreed. "Let's see what we get back."

In the absence of any immediate reply, they turned to practical things to take their minds off the money in the case, Maria in the hospital, warrants for their arrest, TV news and photos in the paper. First they did dishes and then they explored the rest of the house, browsed through the bookshelves – a favourite hobby of Gillian's – and lounged about, trying to be normal.

David found a Bible and decided to reread the book of Esther, staring into space from time to time as he tried to recall anything that might be connected to blackbirds. He thought about the English nursery rhyme about 'four-and-twenty blackbirds' but couldn't get it to make sense. There was something about a sixpence – money. A pocket full of rye didn't seem relevant at all. Then the blackbirds in a pie, who started to sing when they came out. Was the Blackbird party to some information that he was going to 'sing'? Then the part about the king in his counting house counting out the money. Well, that certainly fitted. The queen was partial to bread and honey, but maybe that was just there for the rhyme. Finally, the maid was in the garden hanging out the clothes – dirty washing – money laundering? And it was the blackbird who pecked off her nose. But anyway, all that was English, not Spanish. He shook his head to clear the cobwebs. Something seemed to be tugging at the corner of his mind, but he couldn't flush it out. He went back to the adventures of Esther. Which subject made less sense in their situation was a moot point.

After lunch they went back to the question of Filipe. The consensus was that they should speak to him, since there was no one else to speak to. Alfredo seemed to have turned them down and the Blackbird might be singing somewhere, but not in a way they could understand. They had to take a risk; there didn't seem to be any other choice.

David drafted an email telling Filipe to contact Jorge and come out that evening. The rest of the day was spent restlessly waiting.

* * *

David was sitting outside with a glass of *tinto de verano*, a wine cocktail, he had managed to cobble together when he first noticed headlights coming up the hill. *Great, Filipe*, he thought. *Right on time*. He told the others, then went to unlock the double gates.

Mariano thought Filipe drove a VW Passat but wasn't entirely sure, so he wasn't too concerned when he made out what appeared to be a small Jeep. Maybe it was just passing traffic. Then the car slowed and made to pull in. David didn't recognise either of the faces inside and felt a panic rise inside him. It was a young man and woman. Mariano came out and stood beside him in some sort of defensive gesture, then relaxed.

"It's Marta," he said, "and her boyfriend. Oscarito, isn't it?"

The car parked in the drive and Marta and Oscarito got out. They had thought they were expected, but it soon became clear they were not.

David was unhappy that their location seemed to be so widely known. "They should put it on a bus route…" he muttered as they all went indoors.

Marta explained that she and Oscarito had met with Maria, who had promised to let everybody know they were coming. Maybe she'd forgotten.

"So you didn't hear?" Mariano asked.

"Hear what?"

"About Maria?"

"No. What?"

Mariano explained, then the implications sank in. Had Marta, Oscarito and Maria decided to travel together they would probably all be in hospital now – or worse – and anyone paying attention would have realised the Party accountant had started batting for the wrong team. Oscarito shivered. All he had ever wanted was a quiet corner where the numbers added up. Now they were adding up well enough but giving an answer he didn't like.

"OK," David began, not entirely with the patience of Job. "Now you're here, I guess you must have some information that might be relevant."

"I... I think so..." Oscarito stuttered.

"He definitely has," Marta added emphatically, gripping his hand.

They went inside, and once again Oscarito told the story he sincerely wished he knew nothing about.

When he got to the bit about helping Ibañez pack the attaché case, Mariano went into the other room and produced it.

"This one?" he asked.

Oscarito nodded. "If not that one, then one exactly identical."

Mariano clicked it open. Oscarito had seen the money before, but Marta hadn't and she visibly paled.

Over the next hour, Oscarito talked about the dead donors; other sums that seemed to come in less frequently but in much bigger lumps; and how large sums went in and out monthly but with no documentation of any kind by way of bills or receipts – very contrary to good accounting practices. Then he explained that the Gold Star Donors book was completely off the radar as far as any official audits were concerned. He described the late-night meeting, and how he had been kicked out to make way for a fleet of limos.

"I'm not supposed to put anything on the computer," he concluded, "but I hate adding up manually. I make mistakes, then it's impossible to find out what the mistake is, and you end up doing the addition twenty times. So I'm afraid I took a risk and set up a spreadsheet. Nobody knows about it except me – and you, now." He took a memory stick out of his pocket and laid it on top of the case full of money. "This is the Gold Star Donors book," he said.

Gillian looked at it. So small, but with so much significance.

"Wow, incredible! You've done really well, Oscarito. This could blow everything wide open. Congratulations."

Marta glowed and squeezed his hand, but Oscarito did not look any happier.

"After what you've told me about Maria, I guess they'd kill me if they knew I'd taken that," he said. "Can I stay here with you?"

Before they had time to react, another vehicle was heard outside. Mariano disappeared, then came back a few minutes later with a short, stocky man who looked like a Blues Brother, except for the absence of the pork-pie hat. His shirt collar was open, the gap filled with neck. A thin black tie was just about holding the two sides of the collar together. Further down, other buttons seemed less secure. The waistband of his trousers was buried beneath a belly of sumo proportions. The effort of getting out of the car and climbing three shallow steps into the house had already brought him out in a sweat.

"This is Filipe." Mariano introduced him without giving a surname.

"Sorry I'm late," Felipe puffed. "The editor caught me going out and wanted to know what was up. I had to give him some excuse, which took a while. So, what's going on?" His eye caught the open case on the table.

"*Madre mia!*" he said slowly. "I see *something's* going on."

Oscarito groaned at the thought of having to explain everything all over again, but David stepped in and recounted what they knew and what they suspected as succinctly as he could, all the way from the accidental swapping of cases to the attempt on Maria's life, the Gold Star Donors book full of the deceased and never existed, and Oscarito's memory stick of accounts.

Filipe sat there, shaking his head from time to time or asking simple, factual questions to clarify. His less-than-impressive appearance was soon forgotten due to the astute questions he asked and links he made that others hadn't noticed or didn't understand.

David finally finished and Filipe sat back, mopped his brow and let out a long breath.

"I don't think I've ever actually seen a smoking gun before," he commented, "but I think that's what we have here right now. I've spent half my career trying to nail the Party for backhanders, illegal fundraising and slush funds. I can't see any reasonable explanation other than illegal donations from donors who don't exist and a briefcase stuffed with money for an outgoing Party stalwart. To be honest, we're used to stories about envelopes stuffed with money, but an entire case breaks some new ground. I'll have to speak to the editor, but I'm positive he'll want to run this. I think we've got enough here to put them all away for a long time – if the courts can act quickly enough. The first thing of course is that we need to get this money into some sort of safekeeping, and we need to get them to call off the dogs on the phoney charges. We've got good relationships with some of the investigating magistrates and prosecutors, so I think we can make progress on both counts. By the way, I appreciate the substantial risk you guys have been taking. With a bit of luck, the worst may be over."

No sooner had Filipe finished than David tensed. *What was that?* He had wondered earlier if he'd heard the sound of a vehicle, but it had seemed to dwindle and he'd dismissed it. Now he couldn't be sure what he was hearing, but it was something metallic and it was close. A car or van door closing? The front gate quietly opening?

He held up a hand for silence, then both doors to the small sitting room burst open simultaneously. Mariano looked up with a sudden adrenalin surge, instantly recognising Alfredo, the Guardia Civil captain from their leadership team.

Mariano was just on the verge of saying, "Alfredo, it's you! You just about gave me heart failure!" when he saw David looking over his shoulder. He twisted around. Another officer he didn't recognise was standing at the kitchen door with a pistol drawn. Mariano looked back to Alfredo and saw that he had also pulled a gun out.

"Alfredo! What's going on?" he asked.

"*Señores y Señoras*," Alfredo replied quietly. "You are all under arrest."

Chapter 10

Ruta Nacional A1

David had been right about the sound of an engine. The Guardia Civil van had been parked about 100 metres down the hill.

Without a single unnecessary word, Alfredo ordered the fugitives to gather up their things. Mariano gave him a hard look, then did what he was told. There were five officers in total, all armed, and their every move was covered as their cases were packed yet again.

Gillian was in a daze as they were escorted out. *What on earth is going on?* According to Mariano, Alfredo wasn't just an occasional churchgoer, nor even just a committed member of the congregation. He was part of the leadership team. Yet here he was with his gun out, herding them down the hill into what would have been a Black Maria in Britain. All six, including Filipe, were handcuffed, so the officers had to carry their bags in one hand and drawn weapons in the other. Running was out of the question. Alfredo himself was carrying the attaché case with the money in.

So that's it, the game's up now, Gillian thought, trying not to fall in the dark with her wrists handcuffed. *And just when things seemed to be getting clearer!* Somebody with a significant public voice had been about to take up the case. Endemic corruption in the Party and the government would have been exposed. Charges would have been dropped and the truth would have come out. There would have been indictments and a date set for trials, but they still might have got home for the start of term. Now it was all over – it looked like they were heading to a police cell for the night. *Then what? A rigged trial on trumped-up charges? A verdict? A sentence? This is getting ridiculous.* She tried to stop her imagination. *Think straight, Gillian! This isn't Stalinist Russia. Surely the truth will come out somehow.*

David trudged towards the van with uniformed officers on either side. Mariano, Filipe, Oscarito and Marta came behind, with the other two officers behind them and Alfredo bringing up the rear. Nobody spoke. What was there to say?

The rear door of the van was unlocked and the prisoners were manhandled in, followed by three officers. The fourth got in the driver's door and Alfredo sat beside him.

The run back to Madrid was also silent. Oscarito sat slumped, with his head bowed. He had a good idea of what was about to fall on top of it. Marta tried to smile at him, but he ignored her. Mariano was looking half horrified and half confused. David was inscrutable. He was staring up at the roof of the van, his expression neither happy nor unhappy. If anything, he looked as if he were trying to tease out some tricky but intriguing problem and might be making progress. At one point Gillian thought she noticed the trace of a smile on his lips, then dismissed the idea. The only conversation occurred when one of the officers made some unintelligible remark to his colleague, who glanced at Gillian, guffawed and said something equally unintelligible back. She was glad she didn't understand.

They retraced their route to the A1, then south again, back to the city. After about forty minutes they felt the van turn off the motorway, pause at the lights, then start off again into a maze of stop-start city streets. What *barrio* they were in even Mariano couldn't follow.

Finally, they bounded over a speed bump, turned sharply right up a ramp and came to a stop. Gillian felt a shiver, and not just from the cool Madrid night.

One of the front doors opened and closed. Footsteps came around and the back door was yanked open. It was Alfredo.

He caught David's eye for the briefest of moments, then addressed himself to the guards in the back. Gillian found the Spanish too quick to follow, but there was something they didn't seem happy about. Then further exchanges. It was becoming an argument. Finally, Alfredo let rip with a stream of obscenities, some of which even Gillian recognised. Then the guards reluctantly got up and climbed out of the van. The back doors were closed again without explanation, the passenger side door opened and closed again, and they were on the move, down the ramp and back out into the Madrid night.

Gillian looked inquiringly at David. "What's going on?" she whispered frantically, simply to be met with a terse command to shut up from the front.

David shrugged.

This time the trip took less than twenty minutes and they continued in silence. When they finally came to a stop the horn fired off a couple of beeps, then it sounded as though a heavy iron gate was being opened. They pulled in and came to a stop.

"Well, whatever's going on, and wherever we are, I think it feels like a double-page story," Filipe remarked.

When the engine was turned off, both front doors opened and closed. Then Alfredo pulled the back door open and helped them out, one by one.

"What's going on, Alfredo?" Gillian demanded, but she only got a half smile and a raised eyebrow.

Without a word, he went round each of them and unlocked their handcuffs, which he passed to the driver. There was no evidence of firearms.

Gillian rubbed her wrists to get the circulation going and looked around. They were in a darkened courtyard surrounded by high walls. A series of arches softened by creepers defined a cloister along one side of a two-storey building.

"Is this your safe house in the city?" Filipe asked David, who merely stretched his arms and rubbed his wrists.

There were soft lights upstairs, but only gloom at ground level. The driver went back round to the front of the van to dump the six sets of handcuffs, then came back, hopped into the back of the van and passed down David and Gillian's bags. Only then did a crack of light show an opening door under the arches. A middle-aged woman with glasses, hair in a bun and a plain grey dress came over and gave Alfredo *dos besos*, then led them to the door.

Gillian again looked at David. "Where are we?" she hissed. "Will someone please tell me what's going on?"

"I think we're about to find out," David whispered. He picked up the bags and followed the woman.

Mariano shrugged and came with the others. Gillian heard the van starting up again and driving out, then the heavy iron gates being pulled shut behind it.

The hall inside was beautiful. It was spacious and oak-panelled with red cardinal tiling underfoot and a modest but perfect little chandelier. David put the bags down and took Gillian's hand. The woman who had led them in disappeared through a door at the end of the corridor. Alfredo closed the massive wooden outside doors.

They only had a few seconds to wait before a tall, slim figure emerged. He had a leonine head of pure white hair and was wearing smart cavalry twill trousers and a casual lichen green cardigan over a mauve polo neck. He immediately came up to David and gave him a warm *abrazo*, followed by the *dos besos* reserved for only the closest of male friends and family members.

"Pastor David," he said in a gentle, lilting accent. "*Mucho tiempo, amigo!*"

David took a step back, the better to look at the man opposite him. "How are you, Carl?" he asked. "Or should I say, 'Your Grace'?"

* * *

The sherry was dry as a bone – too much for Gillian, who had taken a taste before remembering she shouldn't be drinking – but everyone else seemed to think it was the very best. They were seated in a large, comfortably furnished living room, also with warm oak-panelling and soft lighting. She still felt as if she were in a fog.

"I wasn't sure if I had completely misjudged you, Alfredo," Mariano was saying. "Your email sounded positive, but I accepted you couldn't get involved professionally. Then the moment you came through that door with a gun in your hand, I was thinking, who on earth is this man I thought I knew?"

Alfredo smiled, and instead of a policeman doing his job without a trace of emotion he took on the appearance of a favourite uncle. He shook his head. "I know. I really apologise, but it had to be convincing."

Gillian stared at the ceiling and held up her hand. "Enough!" she said. "Does everyone know what's going on here but me? Will somebody please explain? I can see we're not in jail, but where on earth are we?"

"Somewhere safe," the white-haired man David had called Carl said. "This is my home. You are among friends. You'll be safe here for as long as it takes to deal with this unfortunate situation."

A thought occurred to Gillian and she voiced it. "Are you the Blackbird?" she asked.

Carl looked bemused and laughed. "I've been called many things, but never that. No. I don't know who the Blackbird is, but I'm certainly not him. My name is Carl McMaster. For many years I was a priest in the Catholic Church. First in Ireland, then I did some work at the Vatican, then I had a specific remit here in Spain and now I am retired. They must have thought I'd done OK because I got a retirement promotion."

"So, you're not Spanish, then?"

"Goodness, no. I'm as Irish as a pint of Guinness. Which makes me think. Maybe that sherry isn't to your taste. We have some cold Guinness in the fridge. Or Murphy's if you prefer…"

Gillian couldn't contain herself. The release of tension, the incongruity of a Catholic bishop in Madrid called Carl McMaster, whom David had greeted like an old friend, the fact she was being offered a pint of Guinness instead of whatever they give you in jail – it was too much. She suddenly felt herself crumpling. She leaned forward and put her head in her hands.

Carl was immediately on his feet. Then he crouched down beside her. "I'm so sorry," he said softly. "It's all been too much, hasn't it? It's unforgivable of me." He nodded to the plain woman with the bun. "Maybe just a cup of tea, Teresa? Thank you."

David pulled his chair closer to Gillian's and put his arm around her shoulder while she shook. Mariano and Marta looked on sympathetically, while Oscarito continued to stare around him. He looked as if he had just died and was in the holding space between heaven and hell, and hadn't yet been told his final destination.

Once the cup of tea arrived and Gillian had collected herself and fixed her mascara, David spoke up.

"I'm not sure I've got all the threads, but I'll have a go," he began. "Chip in if I miss something out."

"Explaining where we are might be the best place to start," Gillian said, trying for a smile.

"OK. Our host is His Grace, Carl McMaster, OSB, Bishop of the Church of Rome – or maybe it would be more accurate to say thorn in the side of the Church of Rome."

Carl waved his hand, pooh-poohing the suggestion.

"I don't know your recent history, Carl, but I'll see if I can summarise up to when we last saw each other."

"Summarise away," Carl replied. "Isn't it Burns who says 'to see ourselves as others see us'?"

"Well, if I remember correctly, you were born of Irish Protestant stock but to a family of staunch unbelievers. As I recall, your dad was a trade union leader in the Harland and Wolff shipyard in Belfast."

"That's right," Carl confirmed. "The yards were tough. My dad was a welder. He became a communist in the 30s and never looked back. Hence the name they lumbered me with!"

"Anyway, after growing up in a family of hard-line atheists, you studied philosophy at Trinity and began to doubt it all."

"Right again. I think it was CS Lewis who said that a young atheist really can't guard his faith too carefully. The feeling that there was something more than the materialists allowed for just kept growing on me. So I finally gave in and joined the Christian Union."

"But that wouldn't have been Catholic, would it?" Gillian interrupted.

"Indeed," Carl confirmed. "It was evangelical. We used to go to Grosvenor Road Baptist Church on Sunday mornings and have an open-air service on O'Connell Street at night. I think I've still got the bruises from the rotten cabbages people used to throw at us."

"But how could you possibly have ended up as a bishop?" Marta asked.

"Because I could see that the great majority of Ireland's Christians were Catholic and that the opposite sadly wasn't true. So, the only way to change things was from the inside. Protestants berating Catholics was old news and had no effect. But a priest might have more chance of tackling superstition and sometimes downright paganism, and could try to break through the nominalism to some sort of personal faith. So I converted. My father was horrified and so was the CU crowd. It was incredible. I was vilified from both sides."

"But you worked through it and worked your way up," David continued.

"I suppose I did," Carl conceded. "Did my apprenticeship in a West of Ireland parish and seemed to show enough promise to get a desk job in Rome, then a move here. People say the Catholic Church is monolithic and unchanging, but that's completely untrue. There are pressure groups and currents and lobbies, like in any organisation bigger than a rowing crew. I got involved with renewal movements, promoting personal Bible study, marriage courses, Alpha – things like that. I like to think I've gently pushed things in a positive direction."

"And that's how Carl and I met," David continued. "I was invited to speak at a renewal movement meeting Carl was chairing. In fact, I can still remember the topic. You asked me to speak on 'Can a Protestant be a Christian?' It was so funny because the boot is normally on the other foot from our side."

"I remember," Carl confirmed. "Then we went for a drink together and couldn't stop laughing. The whole bar must have thought we'd gone mad."

"And maybe we had. So you retired in Spain."

"I did. With Teresa, my lovely wife of twenty-seven years."

Now Gillian's mouth really did fall open. "Eh? I thought I was confused before, but I really am now," she said. "You're a Catholic bishop but you're married?"

"Yes," Carl said carefully. "Tricky, isn't it? I do my best to follow Catholic teaching, I really do. But sometimes your heart decides otherwise. Teresa and I met in Dublin but married in Edinburgh. She was my housekeeper. It's quite common, you know – priests and housekeepers. We fell in love. I tried keeping it a secret, but eventually word got out and I was given a stern talking to by the archbishop. I think the gist of it was, 'I'll turn a blind eye, just don't cause a scandal.' And I was whisked off out of the parish to somewhere I couldn't do so much damage and didn't have to fulfil the duties of a parish priest. Eventually I was posted to Rome. I already had an interest in renewal groups, and in due course they sent me to Spain to help the movement."

"And you and Teresa?" Gillian asked, determined to get it clear in her mind.

"Well," Carl replied, looking fondly at the quiet woman sitting next to him. "Once the authorities found out, I thought that would be the end of things. We both accepted we'd never be able to live as a couple. But then I came to Spain where I wasn't known. I needed a housekeeper and suggested the woman who'd been looking after me in Ireland. Nobody seemed too upset by that – and no one seemed to connect the dots. By that time, the archbishop in Ireland had died and my 'scandal' appeared to have been forgotten. So Teresa came, and she's been here ever since."

"And you and I got to know each other and worked together where we could," David concluded. "Which I suppose gave you the idea, Alfredo…"

Alfredo was in the act of pouring himself another glass of the bishop's fine sherry and nodded. "That's right," he said, having let the liquor slip smoothly down. "I saw the charges on the news like everyone else. Obviously, it was all just trumped up. They were looking for volunteers to join an ad hoc team to track down the illusive David Hidalgo and company. I thought I might be able to help – you, not them – so I signed up. I figured your whereabouts would come out sooner or later, so if I didn't come out and pick you up, somebody else a lot less friendly would. I asked Jorge, who told me you were in Lozoya. They gave me a team of five but one of them went off sick, so I pulled in Victor, our driver." Here, Alfredo raised his glass to his absent colleague. "Victor is a brother and agreed to sign on when I explained what was going on. My apologies for the rough handling. We had to make it look like the real deal."

"Was there a problem with the others at the police station?" Gillian asked. "The ones who weren't in on the ruse?"

"Yes, you noticed. They were at the point of smelling a rat. I had to say we'd received orders to use a different high-security station. They objected to being dropped off – it was touch and go for a bit – but I managed to persuade them, against their better judgement. I knew Carl from some of our joint meetings and I thought his residence would be the perfect hiding place. Luckily, he agreed. And here we are."

"So what now?" Filipe spoke up for the first time from another corner of the room. "Are we still part of a criminal conspiracy?"

"I think in the meantime you are... and me, too," Alfredo confirmed. "I'm probably in the biggest shit of anyone here – as soon as my police colleagues figure out what I've done. But sometimes it's just what you've got to do. I'm near enough retirement, anyway. Victor has a year or two to go, though, so we're really still hoping to be heroes, not villains."

"Sorry, but that doesn't actually answer the question," Gillian insisted. "What do we do next?"

David came back in again. "I think we were just about to get to that before the sudden change of premises. As I recall, Carl, you have some pretty generous accommodation here for a 'single' man."

Carl laughed. "I do. Why on earth the Church insists on places like this for men who, frankly, should be happy with a room and kitchen, I don't know. Something about 'princes of the Church', I suppose. Anyway, the fact is I have six bedrooms, which I think is enough for the party."

"You were asking about staying, Oscarito," David remarked. "I think this solves your problem."

The accountant nodded, and for the first time looked relieved.

"But it doesn't solve mine," Marta said anxiously. "My son Marco is with his father overnight, but I'll have to be back to pick him up from school tomorrow. What are we going to do if the police are looking for me, too?"

David looked at Alfredo.

"He can come here if you want," Alfredo said. "Is that OK, Carl?"

The bishop nodded.

"So the problem is just getting him here," Alfredo continued. "I think things are going to get a bit bouncy once the rest of my team report and it becomes clear that we've all gone to ground. It might be safer to pick him up tonight."

Marta nodded. "I can see that. His father might not be happy, but I can make something up. I'll call him and explain."

"And I can email Jorge," Mariano chipped in. "He'll tell Maria what she needs to know."

"Which just leaves you, Filipe," David said, "and I think you're the key to what happens next. What do you reckon?"

Filipe hadn't spoken much in the course of this long explanation, but his brain clearly hadn't been idle. "Yes, I can see that," he said. "In one way this is what we've been looking at for years, but we usually try to keep things so the journalist isn't actually part of the story! I really need to get back to the office to work on this, but maybe I'd be picked up as soon as I set foot out of here. Depends how good their intelligence is. But I can't do the work I need to do unless I'm on the outside."

"Could you do it with a secure internet connection?" David asked.

Filipe shrugged. "Yes, to some extent. I can write something and send it in, of course, but there are colleagues I need to talk to and records I need to check that I can't access online. To do a good job, I really need to get into the office. Then later on maybe I could use any video app that's secure enough."

"Are you sure you want to take the risk?" queried David. "Half of Spain may already be looking for you if it's got out that you were with the 'outlaw Hidalgo'."

Filipe shrugged again. "If it's got out. Alfredo?"

Alfredo shook his head. "It will do, but perhaps not yet. I was the one leading the raid, and if you recall, I made sure I was the one who took down everyone's names. It's not likely the other officers could identify who was who, other than David and possibly Gillian, whose photos have been all over the news. I think we've got a bit of time to play with here."

David pondered this for a while, then nodded. "All right," he said. "If Alfredo thinks it's safe."

"Safe enough... for now," said Alfredo. "But I don't know how long that'll last. So get in and out as quickly as you can. Don't make a splash."

Filipe grinned. "I'll do my best to stay incognito."

* * *

Marta had been to collect the sleepy Marco and had taken him into the double bed in the room Teresa had shown her to. Oscarito had already been asleep in his room for a while by the time she got back. David had sat up for another hour or so with Carl and Mariano while Gillian unpacked – again – and tried to settle herself. Filipe had asked if he could have a shower – to everyone's satisfaction – and had thereafter disappeared.

Gillian had finally settled under the covers and David had joined her shortly after. It was another night in another bed – one they certainly hadn't been expecting.

"Maybe we'd have been better finishing the week with your parents," Gillian said quietly in a tone of voice David knew very well.

He smiled in the dark. "I think you might be right," he conceded.

"I'm definitely right," she said.

"Accepted. You're definitely right."

"On the other hand, do you remember what Alfredo said in his email? He called it the 'Esther Hypothesis'."

"Hmm. Sounds like another of those Bible puzzles, like *The Da Vinci Code* or something."

"I know it sounds glib, but I wonder if it isn't actually quite profound. What if we *are* here for such a time as this? What if Mariano's invitation – or even the minister's invitation – were all part of the puzzle? All part of a plan to bring the whole thing crashing down and we're *meant* to be a part of it."

David was silent for a while in the dark.

"Hard to be sure till it's all done and dusted," he eventually said. "But if you believe in providence at all – and I do – then that makes perfect sense. It's just the outworking I'm not so keen on."

"Meaning?"

"Meaning that yet again you've been caught up in some muddle I've brought upon you. Now we're on the run and in plenty of trouble, if not in actual physical danger, when you should be sitting around with your feet up attended by sympathetic midwives."

Gillian laughed. "I don't think I'm quite at that stage yet," she said. "And I'm a big girl now, anyway."

"And getting bigger?"

"Maybe. Just be careful with that line of questioning, though!"

David leaned over and put his hand on her tummy. "Wonderful," he said. He kissed her hair, then fell asleep, his hand still resting on the new life within.

Chapter 11

Residencia Oficial

Hiding behind Margarita's bookshelves had felt like some kind of cloak-and-dagger escapade. Then Lozoya had been an eyrie in the mountains; pretending to be safe and high above the action. Alfredo's arrival with a squad of armed guards had given the lie to that. If Alfredo could find them, then no doubt others would have, too. Now, however, in Bishop Carl's official residence – behind the high walls and with Alfredo himself keeping them company – it felt like the cavalry had come in and taken over. In many ways, it was an oasis in the city. Rush-hour traffic was jostling for position around about them, drivers firing off strident beeps, sometimes accompanied by less-than-friendly hand signals. Shoppers, businesspeople, workers and loafers were going about their normal business. Police cars were cruising around, watching out for felons on the run.

But behind the ivy-covered walls, David the pastor, Gillian the academic, Alfredo the policeman, Filipe the journalist and Oscarito the accountant were having breakfast. Mariano hadn't appeared yet and Marta had breakfasted early and was now on the point of taking Marco to school, with very strict instructions not to talk about where they were living.

David just managed to stop her at the door. "I'm not sure this is a good idea," he advised gently. "I know you've given very clear instructions, but all the same – something might slip out. Best keep him here for a few days. Maybe a bad cough or a dose of the flu?"

Marta looked at Marco, then back at David and nodded. She

knelt down and explained to Marco in a whisper, then gently eased his school bag from his shoulders and led him back into the living room.

Carl held court in the most delicate and gracious manner, making sure everyone had what they needed while Teresa went back and forward with toast, freshly grated tomato, cheese, *jamón*, fruit, *bizcocho*, chorizo and a constantly renewed supply of fresh coffee and hot milk. Carl had explained to David and Gillian that she had a slight speech impediment, which was always worse when she was nervous. For that reason, she hated trying to speak in company she didn't know very well. She would prefer it if they could just ignore her and she'd join in when she felt ready.

"Everyone sleep OK?" Carl asked once the serious business of breakfast was well underway. There were nods, full-mouth grunts and one or two intelligible replies, all in the affirmative.

"How long have you actually been here, Carl?" David asked. "I thought you had a small flat in Aluche when we were last in touch."

"I did. I was working with the diocese of Madrid, trying to drag some of the parishes at least into the twentieth century. I didn't have any particular parish of my own, and I could live wherever I wanted, given the modest budget. So, I got a *piso*, dressed normally, went shopping, made friends with the neighbours and tried to be relatively normal. But then somebody saw me at a local parish event in what I call 'military fatigues', and the word was out. It's amazing how people's attitudes change. Some immediately became deeply respectful – almost reverential – while others treated me with something approaching disdain or ignored me entirely. Only a few managed to just treat me like a normal person. It was quite a revelation. Anyway, to answer the question, I got to retirement age, then I was given a token promotion and this house. My 'housekeeper' moved with me, and we are now as you see us. I try to keep a low profile nowadays, but when Alfredo called me I knew I had to act. So here we are. More coffee, anyone?"

"But you've obviously kept up with some of the evangelicals, even in retirement."

"Oh, yes. My main links are still with the Catholic renewal groups, but I do go to Warehouse 66 from time to time, so Alfredo and I have got to know each other. Hence his call, I suppose."

Alfredo lifted his cup in acknowledgement.

Gillian cleared her throat. "Forgive me for asking, Carl, but you said Teresa was your wife of twenty-five years or so. I still don't see how that's possible for a Catholic priest – especially a bishop."

Carl took another piece of toast, coated it in olive oil, then spooned some tomato on before sprinkling it with salt.

"Yes. Curious, isn't it?" he remarked, as if talking about something as trivial as snowfall in June. "Do you mind if I tell the story, my dear?" he said to his wife.

Teresa smiled and shook her head on the way back to the kitchen.

"We met in Clontarf, a district on the north side of Dublin. Quite posh, really. I was a newly installed parish priest and Teresa was a young, single, trainee nurse. She taught Sunday school and also kept the manse in good order. I'd said I didn't want a housekeeper, as I found the simple manual tasks of cooking and cleaning a welcome diversion from the emotional weight of pastoral work. However, Teresa was very kind and used to bring fresh bread and treats from time to time. One thing led to another, as they say, and that caused a bit of a crisis. As you know, the Catholic Church gives value to traditional teachings as well as to the scriptures. The traditional teaching was very clear, but it made me go back to the scripture itself and start asking myself some fundamental questions. I came to the conclusion that celibacy may be helpful in some cases but certainly isn't required. It's an invention of the later Church, not of the apostles. So I invented something, too. A retreat in Edinburgh. Teresa took a city break and we arranged the formalities. When we got back it turned out that I did need a housekeeper after all. And by the way, that's not for publication," Carl said with a grin in Filipe's direction.

The journalist held his hands up in surrender.

Gillian shook her head in amazement. "That's incredible. It's really none of my business, but it must be a huge strain to maintain what is essentially a pretence. Do you both feel OK about that?"

Carl paused and took a deep breath. "It can be a strain sometimes," he admitted. "Obviously, we chose not to have children, which we both would have liked."

David seized Gillian's hand under the table.

"But given the choice of not spending my life with the one I love or doing it under some strain – well, I prefer this. To be honest, I think it's almost an open secret now, and the Church has a long-established practice of turning a blind eye. Steady as she goes, don't rock the boat, firm hand on the tiller, if I can use a few English expressions. That can be a very bad thing, but in this case it worked in our favour."

"So, you think the hierarchy probably knows?" Gillian pressed him.

Carl shrugged. "I can't be sure. It's not something we really talk about. But the housekeeper–priest relationship is more often some sort of closet love affair than you'd imagine. I think we call it 'don't ask, don't tell' nowadays, don't we? And I think the Church has been rocked by so many scandals there simply isn't any appetite for more. Which sadly works in our favour, I suppose. Even in the most rigid of organisations there can come a point where sleeping dogs are preferable to what happens if you wake them up."

Teresa came back through with more toast and coffee, and laid a hand on her husband's shoulder. "There are… mmmany… people in mmmore… difficult ssssituations," she said slowly and deliberately.

Gillian smiled and nodded. "I'm sure," she said.

Gradually, the munching and sipping slowed down. Mariano finally appeared, looking as if he hadn't slept a wink.

"Morning," David said. "How did you sleep?"

He shrugged, pulled out a chair and looked around for coffee. "I've had better nights," he admitted. "I'm not coping very well with this. I think I'm going to have to see Maria soon, whether it's a risk or not." He took a sip of lukewarm *café con leche* and made a face.

Teresa immediately went to make more.

"Yes, I think we have a number of important decisions to make, *hermanos*," Carl said, summing up what everybody knew but didn't really want to acknowledge when it could be put off by another slice of cake or a piece of chorizo. "Let's let Mariano finish his breakfast, then maybe we need a counsel of war. The parish give me a lovely conservatory extension last year – I think it should still be cool enough. How about we reconvene in fifteen minutes or so?"

During the break while the table was being cleared, David pulled Mariano to one side. "I can't believe how insensitive we're all being," he said. "Your wife was in a serious accident and you can't go and see her, yet we're all talking about trivialities in comparison."

Mariano shook his head. "No, they're not trivialities," he said, "just not my highest priority. I couldn't get to sleep last night. I kept thinking, 'What if she'd died?' Then I asked myself why they didn't just follow her to Lozoya instead of attacking. They could have got us all easily without actually harming anyone. Why?"

David shook his head. "I've no idea," he admitted. "Maybe it was a mistake. We already know that although they may be powerful, they're not actually that bright. I think it fits into a pattern for people who think they're invincible. They can do what they please and there are no consequences. I think they wanted us to throw our hands up and give in. You know, turn up at a police station somewhere and accept that the game was up. Admit everything and hope for leniency. Maybe the attack was a warning. They could have followed her and it might have been effective, but it wasn't sufficiently stylish. Or maybe she guessed someone was on her tail and was slowing up to turn and come back, so they thought, 'Let's have a go, anyway.' I don't suppose we'll know until you can speak to Maria. Or maybe she doesn't know, either."

Mariano drained his coffee cup and put it down. Then he cupped his hands around his mouth and let out a long slow breath, staring straight ahead. "I don't know," he said quietly. "I just don't know. In many ways, Maria is a much stronger person than I am. She always copes and keeps cheerful. I get down and can't think of the way ahead."

"Well, I think you have a perfect right to be feeling pretty low right now," David countered. "Don't beat yourself up."

"The only thing I do know," Mariano continued, "is that exposing government or party corruption might be important, but it's not worth the life of my wife. Maybe that's a selfish attitude, but I can't help it. It's not worth it." He took out a handkerchief and loudly blew his nose.

David looked away. "I know," he replied. "Remember I've been there myself. Anyway, it's not going to come to that. We won't let it. Come through to the conservatory and let's see where we're going. Maybe having a plan – *any* plan – might help you feel better."

Carl and Teresa's conservatory took the idea of a city oasis to another level. There were plants and flowers everywhere. David recognised African violets, orchids, vines and creepers, Japanese bonsai, flowering cacti and delicate alpines, as well as a dozen varieties he had no name for. They jostled for space on the window ledges, stood in cane pots on legs and hung from the roof. He thought he might not have been surprised by a 'tyger, tyger burning bright' peering through the undergrowth.

Teresa brought yet more coffee and a plate of tasty ginger biscuits. David remembered Gillian telling him that ginger was good for choppy waters. He hoped it might help.

"You want to do the honours, David? Bring us up to speed?" Carl suggested.

David shrugged and sat a bit more upright. Gillian was alert and focused. Mariano looked awful. Oscarito was studying his footwear. Filipe was already perspiring freely but sitting with a pad and pencil on his lap, looking like he was in an editorial meeting. Alfredo looked the most relaxed of them all – the most used to crime briefings. Carl was the genial host; not personally involved but providing facilities.

"Everybody happy with that?" David asked. "OK. Well, where do we start? How about if Filipe gives us a rundown of the context? I think you've been following this saga for a while."

The reporter nodded. "Sure. Well, it is a saga. There have been rumours and allegations for at least ten years. You have to remember that people in Spain divide very strongly on party lines. The civil war still feels like yesterday to some, and it still defines a lot of loyalties. Socialists are socialists forever and can't imagine being anything else. Nationalists likewise. Right and left wing are like the football team you support – in fact, that actually governs whether it's Athletico or Real for a lot of people. It's impossible for some people to imagine changing, and the political parties have grown cosy with this.

"There's a small number of floating voters who essentially decide each election, and since Franco died it's basically been a game of ping-pong. One, then the other, without any other parties making much of an impression. I think that's engendered a spirit of entitlement. The parties are entitled to be in power alternately. The rule of law and the actual statutes governing fundraising, for example, or what is or isn't corruption, feel like a bit of a detail to the senior people. It's always been this way and it always will be. There are jobs for the boys – handsome retirement packages, as I think we've seen – and life goes on. Journalists like me tend to just nibble around the edges, making accusations that are hard to really prove and trying to whip up some sense of public indignation.

"The public, on the other hand, is typically involved in its own lower level of backhanders and sweeteners, so people have mixed feelings. If you get a plumber to sort your shower out it'll cost you twenty per cent more if you insist on a receipt. Spanish society runs on *enchufe* – connections and favours; the black economy. So, on the one hand people claim to be disgusted by political corruption, but on the other they shrug their shoulders because everyone has their nose in the trough to some extent. Nobody who really knows what's going on is willing to talk on the record because they're benefiting too, and the merry-go-round keeps on turning. However, with the right scale of scandal I think attitudes might change, and this case full of money might be our biggest breakthrough yet.

"We've got the *result* of the sum, you might say – now we need the *working*. We need to know where this money came from, who gave it, why, for what services rendered and with what expectation of a return. Then we can start to push for well-grounded charges against the guilty parties. Those who gave the money and those who received it. To be honest, we need both sides of the equation to really nail it. I'll be going back to the office if I'm allowed. Sadly, even in a Western democracy there are times journalists have been made to feel like public enemy number one. So, we've had to build up ways and means to keep out of sight. We've got some safe locations and ways to move about the city incognito. I promise I'll keep a low profile. Then we'll start trying to join the dots. It'll be up to the editor how we play it, though. I'll keep you posted."

"Oscarito?" David turned to the accountant. "If anyone, you're the man who could help us most with the details."

Oscarito had been keeping his eyes fixed firmly on the floor. Now he spoke, still without making any eye contact. "I'm not going back, if that's what you want," he said in a flat monotone. "No way, José."

"What do you think would happen?" David asked as tactfully as he could.

"They'd kill me, for sure. They tried to kill Maria. I haven't been to work for days, without a good excuse. They've probably guessed already. I set foot in that door and I'm a dead man. I'm a hopeless liar. If they ask me where I've been I can tell them in hospital, but they'd guess. You don't know what they're like. I'm staying here or I'll go abroad. There's no way I'm doing anything more. I can tell you what I know, but you've already got the figures."

"Right," David said cautiously. "OK. Well, let's leave that on the back-burner. As far as I know, you're free to come or go whenever you want." He looked to Carl, who nodded, so he moved on. "Alfredo, what's your take?"

The captain of Guardia Civil cleared his throat. "Just here to keep the peace," he joked. "No, they were looking for volunteers to join the *policía judicial* team to apprehend the notorious David Hidalgo, so I pricked up my ears. Then as soon as I heard about the accident with Maria I decided you needed a hand. Jorge told me where you were, so I got a good mate who hates the constant background static of corruption as much as I do, then we booked out a van and the rest is history. Sorry again about the pickup. I had to make it look good for the other guys."

"And sorry to sound paranoid, but what of the other guys?" asked David. "You said yourself that it's just a matter of time. That they'll eventually start asking questions and raising the alarm when the fugitives they went to arrest never made it to a police station. They might not have questioned it overnight, but what about today? Or tomorrow? When will they start looking for us again?"

"To be honest, I'm sure that's already underway. It was all I could do to get them out of the van in the first place. I'm sure they would have been complaining to the first senior officer they came across. However, the aim was not to call off the hunt indefinitely – just to make sure the quarry was somewhere the hunters couldn't make a kill – and I think we've done that. Frankly, I don't give a shit what the rest of my colleagues think about it. It's done. That's what matters."

"What about Victor, then?" Gillian asked. "I mean, he helped you, so he's bound to be in serious trouble now."

"Well, Victor's an old campaigner," Alfredo said with a wry smile. "But unlike me he has a wife and family, and can't just disappear. He'll think of something. Maybe I held him at gunpoint till he drove here, and then he was forced to stay the night. Whatever. Anyway, he was up for it, too, so I guess he'll have to think of his own excuse. And he needed to take the van back. However, as far as my contribution is concerned, I guess I can keep you straight on police procedure and what they might be doing, but not much more. Like Oscarito. I'm probably a bit stuck here till the dust settles. Unlike

Filipe, I don't have a safe house to go to and I'm well known to the cops who are looking for us all. No wife and kids, though, so it's not the worst assignment I've been on. Probably have to start thinking about another career, though."

David broke a ginger snap in two. "Let's hope it doesn't come to that," he said. "Maybe you'll be a national hero. So, next round the table. Gillian – do you want to add something?"

"Oh, I'm just here for the ride," she answered quickly. "I haven't any inside knowledge or information. I should be preparing my next year's lectures. This man here," she addressed herself to the group but nodded in David's direction, "promised me a quick weekend in Madrid, then home in time for tea. It's not quite working out that way. But if I can get an internet connection I'll just sit in the corner and get on with my lectures till you brainboxes arrive at a solution."

David raised his eyebrows. Right now he couldn't have felt less like a brainbox, but he took the point. He was well aware that the deal hadn't worked out as he'd assured her. Getting away from his dad had seemed such a welcome prospect, he had to admit that he hadn't thought about anything else. On the other hand, this hadn't been entirely predictable. "So that leaves you, Mariano," he continued. "Any thoughts?"

Mariano shook his head. "Nothing,' he said. "I can entirely see that this is a good thing to be doing, but – for me at least – it's at a very high price. I've already said to you, David, that I'm not sure how long I can hide here. I need to see my wife. She needs me, and to be honest I need her. Sorry if that sounds a bit pathetic."

"OK. Entirely understandable." David nodded sympathetically.. "Anyway, that's where we're up to. Now, where do we go next?"

"Not quite." It was Carl, who had been quietly listening but now seemed to be rousing himself. "David mentioned to me what you put in your email, Alfredo. The 'Esther Hypothesis', I think you called it. Nice thought. I was very impressed by that. I'm familiar with the story, of course, but I've never heard it put quite that way. Can you tell us what you said and what you meant?"

Alfredo shrugged. "No grand idea," he said. "Mariano's been preaching through Esther at church. It just seemed appropriate to the situation. I didn't want to say too much in case it came back to bite me, but I wanted to give some sort of encouragement. I think we all agree – or most of us, anyway – that life has a meaning and each of us has a purpose. The Esther story just makes that a little more specific. The Jewish people are going to be massacred. Esther is Jewish, but also part of the royal household. Her uncle is trying to put a bit or pressure on her to act, so he says, 'Maybe that's your life's purpose at this moment – to save the people. You're in a position where you can make a difference. Not everyone can. And maybe all the others are depending on you, so get on with it.' I didn't think about it a whole lot; it just seemed to fit.

"Maybe I'm going to disagree with Filipe here, but not everyone is on the make. Many, I suppose, but not everyone. There are people who care about honesty, fairness and a level playing field. And if we can do something to make things better, we should – although there may be a personal cost. I'm saying all this without having dependants like you, Mariano. But each of us might have to pay a different cost. For me it might be my job. It might even be time in jail – though I hope not. But I just think there are times when you feel like, 'This is my moment. If I don't do something I'll regret it, and nothing will ever change.' So I've got to take a risk and act. Of course, that's all based on an assumption – what I'm calling the Esther Hypothesis – that there is this moment you have to act or the bad guys get away with it forever. As a police officer, I can't accept that, so I'm here to do what I can."

"If I might be permitted, David..." Carl interrupted.

David nodded.

"Some of us around this table are men and women of faith," Carl continued. "That usually means certain beliefs, but I always think it's much more about trust than doctrines and dogmas. Alfredo's phrase struck a chord with me right away, and I'm not sure that's just down to my way of thinking or state of mind at the time. The

Esther story is essentially about secular palace intrigue, but I take it it's also about being in the right place at the right time and doing the right thing.

"Not everyone has that chance – the chance to make a significant difference just by virtue of being in the right place at the right time and doing the right thing. That's both an awesome responsibility and a tremendous opportunity. In my experience, far too many people, both religious and not, naturally tend to look after number one as a default position. Not many find themselves with a suitcase full of money dropped into their laps – now safely under lock and key upstairs – but it doesn't really matter if it's that amount of money or just a trivial opportunity to right a wrong or give some help. I'm in my seventies now, and I observe a world becoming more and more individualistic. Even in Spain families aren't as close as they once were. Couples are less committed – there's that horrible phrase 'serial monogamy'. An entire generation of children brought up between separated parents. We still have no real idea what that's going to look like when they try to make relationships themselves as adults. Anyway, that's another problem. If you can forgive the preaching, all I'm saying is that the right thing at the right time is something that only comes along once in a while. You have to decide if this is one such occasion. What you do is up to you, but if you feel this is indeed something given to you, then you should act with courage and confidence. That's it – sermon over."

There didn't seem to be much more to say. Mariano went to phone Jorge to find out the latest. Oscarito found a newspaper and took it off to a corner to do some number puzzles to keep his mind off other matters.

Alfredo looked for a TV to see if there was any footage from the previous night's Champion's League. There was no rerun of the football, but there was a newsflash about a group of fraudsters on the run – apparently having embezzled over €1 million. He called the others over and they watched, mesmerised, as the details unfolded. The reporter was clearly enjoying the unlikeliness of it all.

An evangelical pastor, a former pastor and his wife and a serving police officer – probably aided and abetted by others. The money they had stolen had actually been intended for social programmes for the poorest in the community, which made it even worse. They were now believed to be holed up somewhere in the Madrid area, and might be armed and dangerous. Members of the public with the nearest knowledge or suspicions should contact the hotline number or any police station. Photos then flashed up. Mariano at church. David opening a drug rehab centre. Gillian from her departmental web page. And Alfredo in uniform, displaying the result of a drug bust.

If any sobering effect was needed, this provided it. Gillian sat with her head in her hands. David got up and turned the TV off, then sat beside her. Carl simply shook his head and stared into space while it all sank in. Alfredo seemed the least bothered, perhaps used to warrants and wanted lists.

"That's all just propaganda," he said dismissively. "Relax. It's one thing to go fishing, quite another to catch a fish." And with that he pulled an old history of Real Madrid from Carl's bookshelf and settled down to read. Carl went off to wash dishes with Teresa, leaving David and Gillian alone in the conservatory.

"I'm sorry," Gillian explained. "That's just rocked me. Do you think the Hidalgos might stay together and free long enough to raise junior?"

"You won't get rid of me that easily. We're like Rodgers and Hammerstein, Bing and Bob, Morecambe and Wise – together for ever."

"Or maybe more like Bonny and Clyde!" She took a deep breath and straightened up. "Anyway, I guess the show has to go on. Now, what do you fancy, boy or girl?"

"Actually, I was hoping for a puppy," David replied dryly.

She made a face.

"Well, since I have a brother – whom I'm actually supposed to be looking for in the midst of all of this – a girl would be lovely," he said.

"And I had a sister, so I want a little boy."

"OK. Let's just be conventional and say that so long as mum and baby are well, we'll be ecstatic."

"Deal."

"How do you feel about it?"

Gillian looked around for inspiration. "I've really got no idea how to feel. A bit clever, I suppose. We were saying if it happens it happens, but if not that's fine, too. But now it's happened I'll be really disappointed if I don't make it the whole way. I'll certainly be what they call a 'mature' new mum, though."

"Well, I'll aim to be as immature a dad as possible and make jokes all through the labour."

"I bet you will, too. And your sermons will be full of birth and baby allusions now, I suppose. That's if you're not too sleep-deprived to stand up."

"Hmm, that'll be a new sensation. Along with everything else. I hope I'm not such an old dog that I won't be able to learn new tricks."

"As far as I can see, the last three years have been nothing but new tricks."

"How am I doing?"

"OK so far But if we could restrict the new tricks to changing nappies that would be appreciated.

"Deal."

* * *

The ex-Minister for Justice got up, leaned across the desk towards the Party treasurer, and pointed a finger in his face. "Do. Not. Lose. Your. Nerve!" he said with an intensity that brooked no debate. "This is a setback, nothing more." He was a veteran of a thousand political battles, run-ins with the quality press, flashy exposés from the rags, mistresses who had threatened exposure and uppity juniors who wanted to dethrone the old campaigner. He had learned the art of not being phased by the unexpected. "Lose your nerve now and we can throw in the towel. Do what you please with your own future, but you're not pulling me down with you. Smile and keep positive and it'll all slide by. Trust me, I've seen it all a hundred times before."

"And if they go to the press before we can get to them?" the treasurer asked.

"So what? It's an allegation. It's proof of nothing. To prove wrongdoing you need a dodgy donor and a wrongful recipient. You might choose to handle Party funds in cash in an orange box. So what? Until somebody speaks up to say they gave money wrongfully or we received it wrongfully, there's no proof of anything. Read my lips. There is *no proof*. And the donors will be the last to complain because they've got even more to lose."

"And the accountant? He hasn't been in for two days now. What if he's jumped ship as well?"

"If he has, we'll find him. He's signed a contract that gives us carte blanche to hang him by his balls if he so much as talks in his sleep to his girlfriend – though I don't suppose he has one. Don't worry, and don't lose your nerve. It might take some time, but there's nothing serious that can go wrong."

The treasurer tried to smile and to look as if he believed this. The way he saw it, there certainly were a few things that could go wrong. His shirt collar seemed to have grown uncomfortably tight all of a sudden. He loosened a button and wondered how long it would be before he was sweating it out in court.

Chapter 12
Battle Bunker

Filipe left before lunch and came back late that night. He was looking gloomy. They all gathered in the conservatory again, which seemed to have become the battle bunker. For the others, the time since the morning meeting had been spent in relative quietness. Marta had kept Marco busy with drawing and games, then, to give Marta a break, Teresa had taken him into the kitchen to help her bake a cake. Carl had taken his turn to entertain the child, too, allowing him to 'help' in the garden. Oscarito had sat in the corner most of the day, doing his number puzzles. Alfredo had found a history of Athletico in Carl's library to balance his affiliations and had been a happy man sitting in a quiet nook. Mariano had been like a caged animal, spending most of the day either locked in his room or walking the floor.

"Progress?" David asked once everyone was assembled.

Filipe shook his head.

"Blood out of a stone," he grumbled. "We've followed up on every name we've got. We've told them we know the Party is floating in dirty money and that we're going to pass evidence to a prosecutor. The sensible thing to do is come clean early on – turn state's evidence while that's still on the table and get immunity – but nobody's buying. In terms of specifics, we're pretty sure there were building contracts agreed on kickbacks. There are some close personal links between senior figures in the Party and some of the big construction companies. Motorways, apartment blocks, hotels all going back to the last time the Party was in power. Contracts were awarded above the lowest tender, but it was always claimed it was the issue of quality that pushed up the price. The suspicion, of course, was that the quality wasn't any better than any other, but the contractor got a more lucrative deal if there was a plain brown envelope stuffed with money in the treasurer's pocket while the documents were being signed."

"Is there nothing we can do until somebody decides to volunteer information?" Gillian asked.

Filipe shrugged. "It's a bit of a bluff, to be honest. If everybody stays clammed up, the prosecutor would have to tackle the Party directly and demand to see a paper trail for the cash. They could no doubt invent something plausible.

Oscarito shook his head. "No, they couldn't," he said. "Not if they look at the Gold Star Donors book. That's the paper trail. It's an original document with made-up names."

"But you have all that on your memory stick, don't you?" Mariano asked.

"Well, I do," Oscarito conceded, "but it's only a spreadsheet. I could have created it from my imagination. If they had the handwritten book it would be a lot harder to deny."

"Where is the book?" Alfredo asked.

"In a safe in the office manager's office. Someone would basically need to break in to get it."

"Unless it was someone who was authorised to look at it…" David suggested.

"Oh, no!" Oscarito saw the trap he'd laid for himself and was emphatic. "No way. There's no way I'm going back inside that building!"

"Well, look at it this way," David suggested. "You've got as much to lose as any of us and more to gain. You're the only one so far who's actually committed a crime by breaching your confidentiality clause."

David felt guilty turning the screw, but in this case thought it was worth it. Oscarito immediately looked miserable and made David feel almost as bad for having been the cause.

"What we need," Filipe continued, "is someone who's been paying the Party but didn't actually want to be. I mean money changing hands for no appreciable services rendered, which they'd be happy to blow the whistle on."

"Why would you pay and not get anything?" Gillian asked.

"Lots of reasons," Alfredo countered, laying down his football history. "That's what protection rackets are all about. Pay up or else something bad *will* happen. I'm not saying the Party has been involved in something as openly criminal as that, but that would be one example of someone who'd be delighted to tell all if they could safely do so. Another would be any sort of activity that needed government or Party permission to keep going, so you pay up simply to be allowed to do whatever your business is."

"How would that work?" Gillian asked. "I mean, why would anyone pay a bribe simply to be allowed to conduct their legitimate business?"

"I didn't say *legitimate business*," Alfredo came back with a smile. "I just said *business*. It should be the role of law enforcement – which is a branch of government – to shut down any illegal activity. However, there's always money to be made by a rake-off from turning a blind eye."

"What sort of thing?" Gillian asked, intrigued.

"Oh, there are lots of possibilities," Alfredo was happy to elaborate. "Illegal gambling; anything to do with drugs; prostitution, of course; selling fake goods; counterfeiting; smuggling; people-trafficking; false passports and other sorts of papers; online scams; loan sharks; tax evasion – you name it. All highly lucrative and all illegal. But they go on. So you have to ask yourself whether it's always just down to police incompetence that no one is ever caught or are they getting help from a higher power?"

"Is there any evidence of actual collusion?" Gillian asked again.

"Well." Alfredo sat back and ruminated. "Depends what you mean by evidence. I would say there is *evidence*, but not what you'd call *proof*. Cops on the street hear things and see things that don't add up. We're sometimes told to back off – that there's another operation underway they don't want interrupted, or they want to get to the mastermind behind it all, not just the bit players. What can you do? The word comes from on high, so you have to back off or get another job. But if I were a betting man – legally, of course – I'd be prepared to bet there's some money changing hands to keep the routine cops off their backs."

"And if you were to place all your money on a single number on the roulette wheel?" David inquired.

Alfredo thought for a minute. "Hard to say. If I were pushed, I'd say prostitution and the people-trafficking associated with it. The law's so lax in Spain, and prostitution is so widely accepted that nobody gets upset about it, so there's no public demand for tighter controls. However, there are some things that aren't allowed, and that is without a doubt an inconvenience for those involved. If the law enforcers were to make their lives a bit easier in these areas, I think the criminals would certainly be willing to pay."

Gillian sat forward in her chair. This was getting interesting. "Sorry, but I'm not familiar with the situation. I thought prostitution was illegal everywhere."

"Not at all," David came in. "Different countries can have totally different approaches. I don't suppose anyone thinks it's actually a good thing, but some societies criminalise everything, and some just the prostitutes, some just the punters, and some only the pimps and madams. Some think that criminalising everything doesn't make it go away but just pushes it underground, which makes it more dangerous for the girls – and sometimes the boys. They're less likely to work in public and more likely to be where they can find themselves in greater danger."

"What about Spain, then?" Gillian asked.

"I think the situation here is that it's just the pimps who control the girls. Is that right, Alfredo?"

Alfredo nodded. "Prostitution has been part of the culture in Spain basically forever," he said, "and it's now very widely accepted.

You can tell that easily enough from the number of places that call themselves 'clubs' that sit on the outskirts of every reasonable-sized town. They're basically brothels and everyone knows that; the police, the town councillors, the neighbours. And it's entirely permitted. The girls are supposedly self-employed and just pay rent for use of the premises. What the law says you can't do is 'employ violence, intimidation, trickery or abuse, exploiting an abuse of power or based on the needs or vulnerabilities of the victim to force them to engage in prostitution or maintain such a practice'. I had to crib it up for a course last month. So, the girls are essentially free to work but shouldn't be forced into it. Which of course is what pimps do, and is the heart of people-trafficking."

"Very impressive, Alfredo," David said, "but I think we're getting a bit off track here. How could that help us nail the Party for kickbacks?"

"No, this is good," Filipe came back in. "If the Party has in any way been taking cash to go easy on people-trafficking – which is clearly against the penal code – then we'd have them. It might even show up in Oscarito's Gold Star Donors book. And there must be somebody who knows what's been going on and would be willing to talk."

Gillian tucked a stray lock behind her ear and leaned forward again, concentrating. "Sorry," she said. "I'm still not getting this. Why would someone involved in people-trafficking and paying bribes want to expose it all? They might want to get away with not paying, but they'd be more at risk of simply being arrested and charged. Wouldn't they be fairly happy with the situation, so long as they could go on exploiting the girls?"

"Yes, they would," Alfredo agreed, "but not all prostitution means people-trafficking. There are legal – not sure you could actually call them legitimate – but at least legal operations that might be unhappy with the way other groups are working illegally and being protected."

"And if some of those might be willing to talk," Filipe added, also gaining momentum, "then they're likely to know more than anyone else what's really going on. After all, it is their industry, I suppose you could say. If they were willing to talk and link us to gangs that seemed to be getting some protection, that might link back."

"And how would we connect to anyone like that?" Gillian asked.

Nobody answered, so she looked to David, whose eyes were half closed as he sat staring up at the ceiling.

"I think I may have mentioned the Blackbird," David remarked slowly. "I've been getting emails from someone calling himself that. He – I'm assuming it's a 'he' – says he's a friend and that he's watching us – or watching *me*, to be more specific. Ring any bells for anyone? No? Well, anyway, we took a risk yesterday and replied."

"What did you say?" Alfredo asked.

"I just asked who he was and what we should do. And today I got a reply. It said two things that I think might connect with this conversation. I'm not saying we should do anything an anonymous emailer we know nothing about suggests – it's just that what he said does fit in with what we've been saying."

"So, what was his advice?" Alfredo continued.

"He said two things: follow the money and talk to those who want to talk to you. Ignore the rest. Now, it seems to me that following the money is pretty standard advice – maybe even a cliché. So, anyone could have said that. But only talk to those who want to talk to you sounds more like the result of some experience. I've no idea if this is an insider in the Party who doesn't like how things are going, someone in the police who knows more than they should or someone else in Spain who's somehow got hold of my email address and wants to join the drama. But what they're saying right now seems to make sense. So far, Filipe, you've been talking to people who really have no good reason to want to talk to you. They would be implicated just as much as the Party – whether they get off with a plea deal or not. I just wonder if we should shift the focus and find the sort of person Alfredo's been talking about. Someone who's been forced to pay up, but not willingly. Maybe that would be more productive."

"That sounds like it might make sense," Filipe put in. "However, could I just make a plea that whatever we decide, we leave it till the morning? I've been hard at it all day and I'm completely wiped out. Would that be OK? Just to sleep on it?"

"Of course," Carl chipped in. "I think a good rest might do us all good. In light of that news report this morning, we seem to be pretty high on the wanted list, but I'm not sure there's anything we can do to make things safer. I can get groceries delivered, and none of us has a job we need to go to... so all we can really do is sit tight."

"I'm sure that's right," Gillian agreed, "though I have to say it doesn't feel the least bit safe, all the same. I have no idea how the police go about that sort of thing, but I can't help imagining posters up everywhere with our smiling faces on them. Officers checking out anybody who knows us, anywhere we might go for help, trying to pinpoint mobile phone signals... Sorry to sound so gloomy. It's just my imagination running riot. I'd love to be here in happier times, but right now I'm just finding it impossible to relax."

"I believe the word is 'catastrophising'," David commented. "I only know that because I do it myself. It means that anything you can imagine always leads to imagining something worse, then something even worse after that, and so on. We can't fool ourselves that we're safe here, but in the absence of anything we can do about it, we should try to focus on the present and not imagine the myriad ways things could go wrong. You know, try to live in the moment and all that."

"And on that subject, do we have plenty of milk, Teresa?" Carl asked. "Excellent. So, how about hot chocolate all round?"

Carl and Teresa went to fix the nightcap and left the group in silence, pondering it all. David was still staring at the ceiling, a thoughtful look on his face.

"Oh no," Gillian thought. "I've seen that look before..."

David wouldn't admit to anything that night as they got ready to sleep, but Gillian was sure there was something on his mind. At any rate, leaving that on the back-burner, the earlier part of the day had been reasonably relaxing. She felt as safe as was possible at Carl's official residence and had got to know Teresa a little. Teresa had seemed much more willing to speak one-to-one than in a group, and once she began to relax her speech problem was hardly noticeable at all.

"I love your house," Gillian had begun once they were alone earlier in the evening. "It feels a bit grand, but really comfortable as well. Were you able to sort it the way you wanted?"

"To some extent," Teresa had explained. "We brought some of our own furniture – a few things we've had s-s-ince Dublin, in fact. They gave us a budget for redecoration. It was only once we'd moved in that we found out that the previous occupant had left under a very big black cloud, so the neighbours were suspicious at first. But we feel very much at home now."

"Please forgive me for asking," Gillian continued, "but isn't it an incredible strain not being able to behave like a normal married couple? If I understand what Carl was saying, you've had to live all your married life pretending to be something you're not. Not holding hands in public, for example, and not showing any outward affection. That kind of thing. Of course, it's nothing to do with me, so just tell me to mind my own business if you like."

Teresa was thoughtful for a few moments. "To be honest," she began, "it's not something I get the chance to talk about much, so I tend not to think about it. It's our life and we're together. There are many priests who would give their eye teeth for what we have. Nobody has publicly accused us as yet, so, as Carl said, a blind eye is turned and we get on with things. We're both officially retired, anyway, so we can choose what we do and who we interact with. We have to be discreet outside, but we're like any married couple behind closed doors. We manage."

"You seem to manage very well." Gillian smiled. "I don't know if you're aware, but David and I have only been married a fairly short time. Even with the best will in the world and the greatest advantages, it still takes some adjusting. I think you've done incredibly well."

"Thanks, that's nice to hear. As I said, I don't have this kind of conversation very often. The only regret is that of course we could never have considered children – not without leaving the Church. That's a regret." After a pause, she continued tentatively. "Now it's my turn to ask something that's none of my business. Do I hear correctly that you may be expecting?"

Gillian couldn't help but smile. "I think so," she said. "I haven't been to the doctor yet, but the test turned blue, so I think that confirms it. But it's very early days. I'm definitely going to be an older mum, so I'm not expecting a completely free ride. I just hope I can get to the end OK."

"Well, modern prenatal care is much better than it used to be. I'm a nurse midwife by training and I try to keep in touch with things. Older mums have very much better outcomes than in my day. I'm sure you'll be fine. And how's David with the news?"

This time Gillian laughed out loud. "Well, he's not the sort of man who does cartwheels in the street. I think he's delighted, though. He and his first wife were never able to have kids, and that was very difficult for them both. We're both delighted. But it'll mean another upheaval, of course. And David is a bit older than me, so maybe he won't have the energy he once had!"

"Well, if you can't do the time, don't do the crime."

That made them both laugh.

* * *

The next morning, David ate his breakfast with the same thoughtful look on his face and Gillian sat watching him like a hawk. Alfredo and Filipe joined them and, as if by unspoken mutual agreement, they all kept off the subject of bribery, corruption and crime in high places. Carl and Teresa were busy filling their online shopping trolley with essentials and one or two treats for delivery later that day. Mariano hadn't appeared yet, and Marco was still in bed, playing on his tablet, when Marta brought Oscarito to the table, as if leading a condemned man to his doom.

"Oscarito and I have been talking," she began. "We think it's time he went back to work."

Oscarito said nothing. He studied his croissant as if trying to work out what surface area it might have if it were carefully unrolled.

David raised an eyebrow. "Really?" he said. "Well, I think that's good news for the investigation – if I understand it correctly. Am I right, Oscarito? Does that mean you might be willing to help?"

Oscarito nodded gloomily. "I should go back," he said.

"But surely you'll be arrested as soon as you set foot in the office," Gillian exclaimed.

Oscarito glanced at Marta. "Maybe, but not necessarily," he said.

"How come?" Gillian persisted.

Marta took up the story. "Remember when we were arrested in Lozoya and they didn't even take names and addresses? I suppose we all thought that would happen when we got to a police station, but then we never did."

"Exactly." Alfredo put in, "and very deliberately."

"So, you are known, David – and Gillian, I imagine. But as far as Oscarito and I are concerned, the other officers had no idea who we were, and I would think that they still don't."

"That's right," Alfredo confirmed. "In a situation like that formal ID is normally done at the station, along with fingerprints and mugshots. And the formal charging. Until that point, people are merely suspects. So, I'd go with Marta and Oscarito's idea. Unless some information has come in from another source, there's no reason to suppose anyone would have any idea that they're involved."

"I hadn't thought of it like that," Gillian admitted. "Sign of a guilty conscience, I suppose!"

"But how am I supposed to get the book out?" Oscarito continued. "That's what I can't work out. Ibañez is always last out on the nights I'm dealing with the Gold Star accounts, and he sees that it goes back inside the safe. How on earth am I supposed to get it past him?"

"What about a dummy book?" Gillian asked. "Could you buy another book exactly the same and put the wrong one back?"

Oscarito shook his head. "He always has a look to see what the latest figures are. He treats it as if it were his own personal bank account."

"Maybe not too far from the truth," Filipe put in.

"So, I can't photocopy it, I can't put a dummy book back... and once it's in the safe I can't get at it. Unless we break in at night and blow the safe up."

"I don't think we're at that stage yet." David commented. "I totally accept what you're saying, and you're showing a lot of courage just to be willing to consider it. I think we need some way of getting the book out after it's been locked up. Then you could put a substitute back in its place, which might hold them for a few days and give us more time to get it to someone who'd be willing to investigate officially. Anyone got any ideas how we could reopen the safe?"

There was a pause, then Alfredo spoke. "Maybe," he said. "We've been having a weird kind of crime wave recently involving men taking covert videos of women in situations where they shouldn't. Changing rooms in shops, gyms, swimming pools, toilets in bars and even domestic showers. I suppose they get a kick out of it, but they can also sell the results to adult websites."

Gillian shuddered. "That's horrible," she said. "How do they get away with it?"

"Well, the ones we catch don't get away with it. Somehow the victim gets suspicious and has a closer look at whatever the camera is disguised as. Clocks are popular. Or it could be the spine of a book, a children's toy or a wall ornament. We're getting to the point now where it might be nothing but a button or a coat hook, though these are more limited in their facilities. Anyway, the point is that technology has made it easy to film almost anything, almost anywhere."

"So?" Oscarito asked, unimpressed.

"Well, the office safe – does it work with a key or a combination?"

"Combination.

"Good. There might be a way, then."

"Can I guess where you're going?" David interrupted, intrigued.

"Guess away."

"We equip Oscarito with something very unobtrusive – maybe a book or something – with a camera inside. He works on the Gold Star accounts, and at the end of the evening takes them into Ibañez's office, along with whatever item we give him. He gives the book to Ibañez and lays the item down. Ibañez puts the book back in the safe and closes it. Everything is filmed. Oscarito goes back into the office, saying he's left something behind, and collects the camera object. Then back here we look at the video and see what the combination is, then the accounts can be removed some other time. How's that?"

"Hmm, pretty close. But there's a problem with what you've described," replied Alfredo.

"I know," Gillian spoke up. "Closing a safe doesn't need the combination. You only need the combination to open it. Oscarito has to have forgotten something that forces Ibañez to reopen the safe and put the missing item in. Then we have a film of the process."

"That's it," Alfredo confirmed. "Of course, there are lots of points where it might go wrong, but it's the only thing I can think of, short of brute force, and that would immediately alert the Party to the fact that they're being investigated."

"Think you could do that, Oscarito?" David asked.

Oscarito was looking more and more like a man on the way to a firing squad. Marta watched him closely and gripped his hand. He nodded almost imperceptibly. She squeezed his hand again.

"And I would be willing to get the book later on while I'm cleaning," she said. "There's never anyone around then."

"How do we get a camera like that?" Gillian asked.

"Oh, that's easy," Alfredo replied. "We've got fifty of them down at the *comisería*. I can easily get Victor to go in and let us have one for a night."

"Is that not going to be tampering with criminal evidence?" Gillian asked. "Sorry if I'm nitpicking."

"Not really," Alfredo countered. "The real evidence is the USB stick they put in the back. The unit itself may have fingerprints, but that's usually less important if we can show that the item belonged to the suspect anyway. The evidence is the memory stick and the data on it. Let's aim for a book – that's something Oscarito could be carrying. Now, what could you have forgotten that would mean Ibañez would have to open the safe again?"

"Now *that* I can do," Oscarito said. "The book's been in use so long it's half falling apart. A page or two could easily fall out. I could notice as I was going back to my desk, then return and get Ibañez to open the safe to put the pages back in. I'd have to leave the office while he was doing that, of course, then go back in. The hard part will be leaving the book in the right place to film it. It's going to look suspicious."

"Put it on top of his filing cabinet," Marta suggested immediately. "I have to dust that every night. I probably know the layout of his office better than he does. The safe is directly opposite it. He's right-handed, so he'll turn the combination with his right hand, which means the view from the left should be clear. If you were to lay the book on the cabinet aimed at the safe, I don't see why it wouldn't work. I'll take the dummy book in with me. You phone me as soon as you've seen the video and have the numbers. Then I do the swap and bring the real book back here."

"Fantastic," David said. "Were you ever in the Romanian secret service, Marta?"

"Well," she said with an entirely straight face. "I could tell you, but then I'd have to kill you."

David wasn't entirely sure she was joking.

They finished the last of the coffee and Gillian started carrying things through to the kitchen while David went looking for Mariano. He came back a few seconds later with a note in his hand. He found Gillian halfway to the kitchen carrying a pile of plates.

"Look," he said. "I was worried this might happen."

Gillian put the dishes down and read aloud:

David.

Sorry to do this to you and sorry not to be able to tell you in person. I have to be with Maria and see how she is. If I can get in and out I'll be back by lunchtime. If I don't make it, something may have gone wrong. Hope you can find a way forward with things.

Sorry.

Mariano

She pursed her lips and shook her head. "I was worried, too," she said. "They'll pick him up straightaway, won't they?"

"I imagine so. If he'd asked me, maybe we could have worked something out. Just walking into the hospital is going to be equivalent to walking directly into a police station, I'm afraid. I hope I'm wrong, but that's my guess."

It didn't take until lunchtime. Jorge phoned and broke the news. Mariano had barely made it into the room where Jorge had been keeping Maria company and kissed her on the cheek before two armed officers arrived and cuffed him. Then Maria had got herself into a state and ended up worse than if he'd never appeared. They'd had to manhandle him out of the room. Maria had tried to get out of bed to intervene and had fallen, pulling a drip stand down on top of herself and dislodging stitches. Jorge hadn't elaborated on how bad it was.

Shortly after Jorge's call, Victor arrived with an early edition of *Don Quixote: Volume One*. Or at least, it was meant to look like it. The camera lens was embedded into an elaborate tooled design on the spine, which took even those who knew what they were looking for some time to spot.

Alfredo gave Oscarito the tour. "Obviously, it doesn't record all the time. To start it there's a tiny button at the top of the spine and to stop it another likewise at the bottom. You'll have to make sure you put it near enough the edge of the cabinet to give a wide angle, otherwise we'll mainly just get the flat surface it's laid on. I think we'll only get one shot at this, so you'll have to get it right."

Oscarito had been looking like a dog expecting nothing but kicks up to this point. Now he looked like another kick had landed. Marta squeezed his arm, but to no avail.

"Oscarito, you're looking terrible," Filipe put in.

"Thanks!"

"No, I meant it positively. You've been off sick for a few days. Now you're going back, but you're not completely over it. You really do look sick. You'd fool a doctor."

"Fantastic," Oscarito said without enthusiasm.

* * *

"Excellent," the former Minister for Justice said. He put down the phone and took a sip of his morning coffee. The office hadn't opened yet and they were alone.

"What?" Ibañez asked.

"They've got the pastor. Picked him up at the hospital."

"Hidalgo?"

"No, I'm afraid not. The other one. Mariano something or other. Anyway, we're doing well. The plan is working. One down, two to go."

"Don't you mean three?"

"How three?"

"The accountant hasn't been in for three days now. I'm beginning to smell a rat. I don't think it's a coincidence."

"Well, supposing he does jump ship, all he knows is a column of numbers. The Gold Star book is still in your safe and there's nothing on the computer. No prosecutor on earth would be interested."

"I hope you're right," Ibañez replied, sighing heavily. "I'm beginning to feel nervous about this."

"Well, don't. Dodgy deals and funny money are ubiquitous in

Spain. And it all takes years to come to court, anyway. There are a lot of hurdles to cross before you need to feel anything other than optimism."

Just then, the outside door could be heard opening and closing.

"Keep your voice down. That's the secretaries arriving. Eavesdropping and gossip are the two things they're good at."

But a few seconds later, as the two men sat in silence finishing their coffee, there was a knock at Ibañez's office door, and it swung tentatively open.

"Oscarito," Ibañez said. "You look terrible!"

"I know, Señor Ibañez. I've had a bad few days of flu. I'm not really over it yet, but I was worried about the accounts getting out of date. I'll do as much as I can today, then I hope I can get back up to speed tomorrow."

"Well, don't overdo it, man," Ibañez said. "Don't want you dropping dead on the job."

"No, sir. But actually, I'll feel a lot better when everything's up to date. If you don't mind, I'd also like to get the Gold Star Donors book up to date after hours tonight. I'd feel better if it was right."

Ibañez shrugged. "On your own head be it. I can only stay till eight this evening, so do as much as you can before then. The rest can wait."

"OK, sir. I'll do my best." Oscarito half closed the door.

The sound of his chair being pulled out, his computer being switched on and his lunch being taken out of his case could be heard through the gap.

"There you are. What did I tell you?" the former minister whispered, a look of glee on his face. "Not as bad as you thought. *Si o sí?* We'll get through this *and* we'll get the money back. I guarantee it. I've got a very good feeling this morning. You'll see."

"Yes. No doubt I will."

Chapter 13
Calle Montera

David Hidalgo emerged blinking from Sol metro station and looked about him. He half expected to see 'wanted' posters on the walls and police officers looking in his direction, speaking seriously into handheld mics. Neither were to be seen. It was in fact, as far as he could tell, a perfectly normal, busy, sunny, Madrid town centre day. Tourists and those who fed off them were going about their business. Spider-Man, Bart Simpson and an Indian fakir were fighting for attention and cash from wandering passers-by. Erasmus exchange students and au pairs were giggling and showing off their extremely limited Spanish, as if they had just decoded the Enigma machine. The morning sun was warm but not yet oppressive. Tourists were taking selfies, as if the price of data storage had plummeted but was about to rocket again – so better use it while they've got it. A girl was standing on a red box playing the guitar and singing about Jesus. So, a normal day in Sol.

David headed for Calle Montera – one of the rays of the sun radiating out from the semicircle that is Puerto del Sol – meditating on the concept of reluctant agreement. Clearly, agreement can be wholehearted, enthusiastic and non-existent. But if it's reluctant, is it fair to call it 'agreement' at all? Well, perhaps it depends on how reluctant. Gillian had been very reluctant. Thankfully, it hadn't degenerated into a full-out row, but he had known when he left Carl's comfortable refuge that he wasn't really going with her blessing.

Filipe was an enthusiastic agree-er. "What a brilliant idea," he'd said. "We need something to break the log jam. This could be it. If you have the connections you say you have, these might be exactly the sort of people who'd want to talk."

Alfredo had been less enthusiastic. He'd had what he called 'business dealings' with the sort of clientele David was proposing to engage with. He knew that trust was a commodity in very short supply, and that when it ran out there was a very short trajectory between being under suspicion and being under a bus. Carl didn't give an opinion but told him to be careful, and Oscarito was already gone by the time they'd had the discussion.

All of this had left Gillian feeling very uncomfortable. She had been uncomfortable about being in a minority of one, about being the only negative voice, but she had been even more uncomfortable about the plan itself, and particularly about the word 'dead'. She had apologised around the room but made it clear that she and David needed to talk about this in private.

"This is not your job," she had begun as they went into the conservatory together, leaving the others feeling subdued and uncomfortable around the breakfast table. "I know you're going to talk about Esther and being here for a moment like this, but that was then and this is now. Solving the problems of corruption in the Spanish state is not your single-handed responsibility. We are not guilty of any crime, and that'll come out if we're arrested. And there are those whose job it is to solve real crimes, like political corruption. Alfredo, for example. Even Filipe. Oscarito has uncovered wrongdoing, so maybe even he has a responsibility. Why does it always have to be you? You were given the wrong case. So give it back! I'm fed up with running and hiding. And you don't only have a wife to consider now. Think about that!" She turned and stared out of the window.

David said nothing for some minutes. "What can I say?" he eventually began. "This situation is not of my choosing, but if we all just sit here it's not going to get any better. We'll be picked up sooner or later. Filipe said nobody's willing to put their head above the parapet, but Oscarito has put himself in some personal danger, Mariano is already in custody and Maria almost died. I'm not suggesting this recklessly, but I just don't think doing nothing is an option any more. What I'm suggesting is not meant to be heroic and it's not meant to be reckless. I have some contacts from my Madrid days. I'm planning to have a couple of conversations and see if there's any interest. If not, I'll come right back here and we'll try to think of something better."

"If *you* don't get picked up on the way as well."

David shrugged. "It's a risk, but sitting here waiting is only a slightly lesser risk. We didn't want this, but this is what we've got. The Esther connection could just be somebody's imagination, but you know I'm not a big fan of meaningless coincidence."

They sat in silence for a bit.

Finally, Gillian took David's hand. "I'm feeling pretty vulnerable right now," she said. "It's probably something very primitive, but having a new life to think about changes your outlook slightly. Do what you think is right. I know you'll be careful."

"I will," he said. "It's not my idea of fun, either, you know."

* * *

The lottery stands were as busy as ever. Kids on skateboards whizzed past. A bunch of teenagers walked in the opposite direction, tossing a nice leather wallet between them. It didn't take much imagination to guess where that had come from. A huge advert for the Apple Watch hung over three storeys of the frontage of one of the buildings that made up the arc of the setting sun.

David allowed himself to be distracted as he wandered up the street. Madrid had been the setting for some of the best and worst days of his life. He wasn't sure into which category the following few hours might fall. He walked past Diago's fan shop with more designs than even the Madrid heat seemed to merit. Further up, it was souvenir tat. Then a KFC already doing business. Then a shoe shop, a chemist, the latest fashions in an international dress shop chain and a couple of street cafés. Then the street opened into a wider avenue occupied by delivery lorries and the first outposts of what he was looking for. He kept turning over in his mind the Blackbird's advice: follow the money and talk to those who have a reason to talk to you – not those whose best interest it is to keep their mouths shut. That seemed like good advice, whoever it came from. That was what he was going to try to do this morning.

A chunky dark girl with a short black dress and bare legs was leaning against a parched tree, a cheap fake leather handbag over her shoulder. A few yards further on, a pale stick figure with bleached blonde hair, lipstick the colour of blood and a tight red leather skirt stood in a doorway. A fat man in a dirty T-shirt that had once been sky-blue and jeans that had never fitted stopped to talk to her. He looked nervous; she was trying to smile.

David passed them both and kept on up the hill, not exactly sure what he was looking for, but trusting that he'd know it when he found it. He wandered past a few more girls, not really noticing. Then a girl with skin the colour of milk chocolate and hair tightly bound into bleached golden-blonde cornrows. Not this one, either. He pressed on but also noticed a thick-set, Cuban-looking man with a white T-shirt, black jacket and trilby hat leaning casually against the lamppost on the opposite side of the street, picking his teeth but watching everything like a snake outside a nest of mice.

David ignored him and walked on, scanning from side to side. Then he saw her. Tanned but light-skinned. Tastefully highlighted hair, the colour of the different shades in a framed sand picture, hung halfway down her back. She wore a skin-tight, shoulderless snakeskin dress, just extending to the top of the thigh and no more. She had bare legs and strappy, high-heeled sandals. Somehow, she reminded him of a young Barbra Streisand. The uniform might have been exchanged with any of the girls, but her expression was different. Unlike the others, she wasn't already looking bored and resentful, shifting from one foot to the other, exhausted from standing for hours. Instead, she was doing her best not to look terrified, as if only the greatest possible powers of self-restraint were keeping her from abandoning her spot and running as fast at those heels would allow for the metro, a cafe, a taxi, a hole in the ground... anything that would get her off the street.

"Hi," he said.

She almost jumped. The look in her eyes was like that of a frightened rabbit. "Hi."

"Are you busy?"

"N... no."

"Are you working?"

"I guess."

"What's your name?"

"You can call me Barbara."

He took that as a good sign. "How much for an hour?"

"Depends what you want."

"I want to do anything I want."

"Two hundred, then."

"That seems like quite a lot."

"For anything you want, that's the price."

"And that does mean *anything*?"

"Within reason. No children or animals. Nothing that leaves a mark."

"Otherwise, anything I want?"

"Within reason."

"And I don't need to tell you now? I can decide as we go?"

She nodded dumbly, as if she were giving permission to be tied to the railway tracks in exchange for money to feed her family for a week. Horrifying, but necessary.

"OK, sounds cool," he said. "Where do we go?"

"I have a *piso* near Callao."

"Do we have to go there?"

She shrugged. "Depends. I'm not going to Barcelona."

He smiled at her attempt at humour. "It won't be as far as that, I promise. And it'll be safe. Honestly."

"Anyone else there?"

"Nobody who'll trouble us."

"OK."

He retrieved his wallet and pulled out four €50 notes.

She straightened up and pushed the money down her bra. "You don't need to pay till we're done, you know."

"I know, but I want to pay you now. In return for anything I want to do."

She looked around without a smile, made eye contact with the Cuban man across the street and picked up her bag. "So where do we go?"

"Here." He took her elbow and steered her across the street and into a café.

She looked confused as he pulled out a chair for her and saw her seated before going round to the other side of the table and pulling one out for himself. She looked at him blankly. Was he mad or just bad like the rest? Was it something even worse than she had expected in a particularly cruel way? Was he going to ask her to do something perverted in public? She'd only heard about that happening once before and the police had been called. It hadn't ended well.

The waiter came over and nodded at them.

David raised his eyebrows towards the girl. "What would you like?"

"What do you mean?"

"To drink. Coffee? Glass of wine? *Tinto de verano?* A vermouth?"

She shook her head slightly, as if recovering from a blow. "Erm...Vermouth, I suppose."

"Red or white?" the waiter asked with a smirk.

"I don't know," she muttered, still confused. "Red?"

"And the *Señor*?"

"*Café con leche. Grande.*"

The waiter headed back towards the bar. David noticed him

talking to a colleague and nodding in their direction. They laughed as if they had just seen a dressed-up monkey pretending to be human.

Once the initial shock had passed, Barbara looked properly at David for the first time. "What's this all about?" she demanded.

"You said we could do anything."

She didn't reply.

"Didn't you?"

"I guess."

"Well, this is what I want to do."

"What? Just have coffee?"

"Yes. And talk."

"That's it? You don't want to…?"

He laughed. "Certainly not. I'm married and I love my wife very much. I don't need any more. I just want to talk."

She was still looking uncertain, as if she couldn't believe her luck. Two hundred for just talking. This guy was obviously an idiot. She would have done just talking for fifty. However, you shouldn't complain about good luck. At least she could sit down. Then a thought occurred. "Are you police?" she asked abruptly.

He shook his head. "No."

"An investigator, then?"

"Nope."

"Social services?"

"Nope."

"So, what are you?"

"Actually, I'm nothing in Spain. I live in Scotland right now, and there I'm a pastor."

The light seemed to dawn. "Ahh," she said. "I understand. You had me a bit confused there for a bit. You're a *pastor*. That's an *evangelista*, isn't it? You want to convert me. To save me. You have a mission to rescue the world."

David's coffee and Barbara's vermouth arrived. David pulled open the tiny packet that came with it, which had an even tinier biscuit inside, and took a nibble.

"Well," he began. "It is sort of my job to be of help to people, but that's not why I'm here today."

"You just want to talk? That's crazy. Well…" she seemed to think again. "I suppose that's better than… the other thing. So, what do you want to talk about?"

"You. And me. And the world. Whatever. But there is one qualification."

She put her head back and shook her hair over her shoulders. "Ah, I thought so," she said. "Here it comes."

"No, nothing bad. At least, I don't think it's bad," he said.

"What, then?"

"I'd like you to tell the truth."

She laughed for the first time in a way that sounded natural. "That's funny," she said. "The truth? I can't remember the last time I told anyone the truth."

"Well, that's what I'd like," he said. "You can ask me anything and I promise to tell you the truth."

"Really?"

"Really. Or I won't tell you anything at all. What I'm saying is, I won't lie to you."

"That'll make a change. OK, then," she began. "How about this one? What's your wife like in bed?"

David had to laugh. "Touché," he said. "She's very good, but I'm not saying any more than that. Is that fair?"

She laughed, too.

"My turn now," he said. "What's your name?"

"I told you. Barbara."

"Lose a life," he said. "What's your real name?"

She smiled again, beginning to enjoy the game despite herself. "Sandra. I haven't told anyone that for a long time."

"Good," he said. "Now we're getting somewhere. Now, where are you from?"

"Budapest. Really! I've been in Spain two years. I tried working as a waitress but kept losing my job because I didn't have good enough Spanish. Then I found a job where I didn't need to speak. I mean, you have to make kind of moaning noises, as if you're enjoying it, but you don't exactly have a stimulating conversation. In the meantime, I learned Spanish anyway."

"Would you like to go back to being a waitress now?"

She put her head to one side and shook her hair again. "Don't know. I haven't really thought about it for ages. I'd have to kick the drugs before I could afford it. Now I'm telling you too much. See, you fooled me into telling too much truth."

"Gets addictive, doesn't it? The truth, I mean. Not the drugs."

She smiled again. "Maybe. Now my turn."

David noticed the Cuban-looking guy watching them closely, but he was out of Sandra's line of vision. David smiled at him in a friendly way until the man dropped his gaze. Then he ignored him. "Ask away."

"OK. Erm... what's Scotland like?"

"Nice. I live in Edinburgh. It's a great city. Really international. Historical. Can get a bit touristy in the summertime. You don't go there for the weather, though."

She took a sip of her vermouth and for the first time leaned back and relaxed into the chair. "Sounds like Budapest," she said.

"Did you grow up there?"

"Yes. I don't remember the communist time, though, if that's what you're going to ask. You know, they have a theme park in the city full of all the old statues. In most of the former communist countries they just blew them up, but in Budapest they gathered them together and put them in a theme park. You can wander round and take photos. There's Lenin looking invincible..." She struck a pose. "And a Soviet warrior clasping a Hungarian soldier in an embrace of everlasting friendship. They're behind the times. They don't know we hate each other now. You can buy tins of fresh democratic air in the gift shop. It's hilarious."

"Would you like something to eat?" David asked suddenly.

She thought for a second. "Yeah, OK. Croissant *a la plancha* with apricot jam. And a coffee."

"Are you sure they do that here?"

She nodded. "Yeah, sure. Lots of the girls come here when they've finished a shift."

"You work shifts?"

"Of course. You can't be expected to spend half the day on your feet and the other half on your back. I'm on early this week, then late next week. I prefer early. For some reason the real brutes come out later. In the morning you get an old guy whose wife has just died or a college student whose friends are teasing him because he's still a virgin. That's not so awful. The guys who want to tie you up and hit you only seem to come out at night. I don't know why."

"Does that happen a lot?"

"I wouldn't say a lot, but some of them want to act out stuff they've seen on the internet. That can be risky. Once you're tied up there's no way of stopping them. Even if you haven't agreed to something and you're shouting the safe word, they just ignore you. And it can be painful for days after, so you have to take some time off. Then you're not making money and they're not pleased."

David gestured the same waiter over and ordered two coffees, along with one sugary doughnut for himself and a croissant *a la plancha* with apricot jam for the *Señorita*.

The waiter smirked again at the mention of 'the *Señorita*'.

"Something funny?" David asked.

The waiter straightened his face and went for the order.

"Who's *they*?" he asked once the waiter was out of earshot. "You said, 'They're not pleased'."

"Well, you don't really think I'm self-employed, do you?"

"But as I understand it, you can sell sex in Spain but pimping is illegal."

She laughed again, this time bitterly. "You wish," she said. "And I wish, too. See that guy over there? He's on the early shift, too. Carlos. A colder-hearted creep you couldn't hope to meet. If the Buddhists are right, it would be great if he came back as a slug –

that's all he deserves – and I came back as an elephant. You can guess the outcome of that. And he'd deserve it, too. I hate him."

David took another sip of his coffee and sat silently.

"So, everyone's controlled," she went on. "He controls me. Agustin controls him. The Spider controls Agustin and I think the Gorilla controls her. That's what they say, anyway."

"Who's the Spider?" David asked.

"Ha! You really want to know?"

David paused and looked around again. Life was continuing as normal. It felt like they were in a bubble. Him and her, a table, drinks, sunshine. The rest of the world was a watery illusion that didn't make a sound. He guessed that not one in a hundred of those going up and down Calle Montera, smack bang in the middle of Madrid, really knew what was going on under their noses. They might notice the girls on the way past – well-dressed women looking down their noses and middle-aged men leering – but it merited as much attention as a sewer they had to step over. Nobody took any notice of the human flotsam floating along, then going down the drain.

"Do you trust me?" David asked abruptly.

"I'm not entirely sure I know what that means," she replied cautiously. "Trust you to do what? I don't think you're going to rape me on the street, if that's what you mean."

"I was thinking of something a little beyond that." He smiled. "Do you trust that I don't want to harm you?"

She looked into his eyes for ten or fifteen seconds without speaking. "I think I do," she said quietly.

"OK, then," he said. "I needed to ask that. Can I ask you a couple of other questions, and you promise you won't run away or throw your coffee?"

She smiled and nodded. "I won't do that. If I don't like it, I'll just finish the coffee and walk away. What do you want to know?"

"Who is the Spider?"

She was silent for a moment. "You didn't pay me €200 to ask me about spiders. What's going on? What do you really want?"

"I want to help you and to change some things. I said I'm a pastor and that's true. But right now, I'm something else as well. I've found myself in a situation I didn't expect and didn't want, but it's a position that carries a lot of power and a lot of responsibility. I have information that could bring down the government and that could put lots of people who pretend to be serving the nation – but are really only serving themselves and using lots of other people to do it – in jail. That would mean that the people they control could have another chance. Another chance to make better decisions in their lives.

"But I don't have all the information I need. For that I need to know some things that you know. You could decide not to help me, and I promise you'll never see me again. You can keep the two hundred and I'll even pay the bill. If you tell me what I need to know, there's a chance someone might find out you told me and that might be difficult. That's the risk you have to take. The risk I'm taking is that you'll not tell me the truth and send me on a journey that won't have a good destination."

"What can I tell you?" she asked again, staring rigidly at him, as if unsure whether he might disappear at any moment and unsure whether that wasn't what she wanted, anyway.

"Where can I find Marie Vey?"

The colour drained from her face. "How do you know?" she asked, aghast. "How do you know who she is?"

He smiled, despite the tension. "I guessed," he said. "Maria Victoria and I go back a long time – maybe twenty years. I didn't know she was your Spider, but I guessed. I need to find Marie Vey. Not to do her any harm. Ironically, I want to help her, too, in a sort of a way."

"You and the Spider are buddies, then? Is that it?" she asked, a cold wind in her voice.

"No, we're not. I promise you we're not. I'm a pastor in Edinburgh right now, but I spent more than twenty years as a pastor in Torrejón. My church was basically made up of junkies, alcoholics and ex-sex workers. Some not so ex. Marie Vey had employed a lot of them. When they decided they'd prefer a job that involves standing up – or at least sitting down instead of lying down – Marie was not at all happy with me. She tried to have me killed twice, then promised me half a million euros if I'd just leave her operations alone."

"Did you take it?" Sandra asked, intrigued in spite of herself.

David laughed again and shook his head. "I didn't. And ironically, that was the best decision I could have made. Marie seemed to come to respect someone who couldn't be frightened and wouldn't be bought. I guess I'm just a bit stupid that way. We came to an arrangement. I wouldn't go fishing in her business if, when she knew someone who was really ready to leave, she'd send them to me. Many of them came to church and really got sorted out. Not all, but lots. And I didn't try to make her life more difficult with the police.

"Anyway, you mentioned the Gorilla as well. I think we've established that Marie Vey is the Spider. I'm betting that the Gorilla is a police officer who's not satisfied with his monthly salary. He could make life very difficult for Marie but prefers just to make it slightly difficult by creaming off some of the cash for himself and turning a blind eye. What you maybe don't know is that I think the cash keeps on moving up the line. Eventually, a proportion of it reaches the government and the ruling party."

She shook her head in amazement and pushed her long hair back over her shoulders again. David noticed she had begun to look very attractive now that the hard, frightened look had gone.

"Really? How do you know this?"

"Before I tell you that, am I right?"

She nodded. "I was once in the office getting a total dressing-down after a customer had complained. Marie got a phone call. She looked at the name and decided to take it. She listened for a few seconds, then started shouting at him. She called him 'Gorilla' and a lot worse. I remember I was seriously impressed. I wished

I could insult someone and swear like that when I needed to! I've never seen her so mad.

"Once a month everybody had to get out, then a car would arrive and leave ten minutes later. Some of the girls would hide just to watch. The guy who got out was enormous. I guess that's why they call him the Gorilla. He would go upstairs, I suppose to meet with the Spider. Then he would leave with a bag. I think we can both guess what was in it.

"After a while, instead of just taking the money and leaving, he started hanging around, thinking he was entitled to spend time with one of the girls. That was even worse. He started asking for me. He's horrible. And the things he makes you do are horrible, too.

"The girls who work at the other clubs meet and sometimes we talk. The Gorilla – or somebody exactly like him – seems to have a similar arrangement with the others as well. Which means he's not just someone from another gang. He has his own protection. In my book, that makes him police. So, I think you're right. What are you going to do?"

David, who had forgotten his coffee in the conversation, took a sip and another bite of his biscuit. "Well, if you tell me where I can find her, I'd like to have a conversation with Marie. Maybe talk over some old times. Then I'd like her to help me nail the Gorilla and the other links in the chain. Right to the top. We have lots of pieces of the puzzle, but there's one missing. Marie could help me fit it in. Then I'd like to suggest we reconnect in the way we used to. Except with my successor at the church I used to be part of. Anybody that wants to leave, she passes to us. And we don't harass those who are happy with what they do."

Sandra laughed bitterly. "You think anyone's happy with what they do in this business?"

"No, I don't," he replied, "but I know that not everyone is ready to move on yet. When they are we can help, but I've found there's really no point in trying to offer help when someone isn't ready. I mean, until at least they think there's a problem they need to solve."

Sandra nibbled the last of her biscuit. "You know," she said, "when I was young I wanted to be a rock climber. No – really. I read books about it, I watched films. My favourite was *The Climb Up to Hell* about all the people who died on the Eiger. Where I'm at now, it's like being stuck on an ice field under an overhang and over a precipice with no anchor points and no climbing partner. You can't go on and you can't go back. I know I can't go back to when I was seventeen, looking for work in Budapest and thinking the West was like one huge Disneyland. I don't expect that. But I'd like to go on to something else. To get off this stinking, rotten ice field."

Her voice took on a hard, bitter edge again. "I'd like to get somewhere firm and level. Somewhere you could put down roots. Where nobody knows your past or thinks they can buy and sell you. I'd even like a friend. Some guy who'd be nice to me. And one night, if I didn't feel like sex, he'd say, 'That's OK, honey. Never mind. Have a bath. Let's go and see a movie, then get something to eat.' I don't see why that's too much to ask. I think there are some people who have it. Not all the guys out there are greedy perverts. I still believe there are good people. After everything I've been through, I still believe it. Crazy, I know." She paused and looked at David, full in the face. "I think you might be good people," she said quietly. "So, what do you want? The address or the GPS coordinates?"

Chapter 14

Headquarters

Oscarito passed the day in a bad dream. Numbers, which were normally his closest, most reliable friends, danced in front of his eyes and wouldn't keep still to be counted. They kept swapping identities with each other, so that every time he counted, the total came out differently. When he tried to read the name on a bill it became illegible. The amount seemed to magically transform between reading it and typing it in. When he looked back to check, nine times out of ten it had changed into something different again and he had to retype it. He had never had to do this before. In the middle of working through a pile of backlogged vouchers, he even tipped a cup of cold coffee over the whole lot – and his trousers – and had to jump up to get a cloth, knocking his desktop calculator onto the floor and spilling out the batteries.

"*Pobrecillo*," Rosa whispered to Alicia. "He looks awful. He should be home in bed."

"I know," Alicia agreed. "Even a robot needs repairs."

They had a quiet giggle, then went back to looking at Zara's autumn coats online.

Oscarito didn't even notice. He mopped up the mess, tried to separate out the sodden pages to dry, dabbed his trousers and went to the toilet for a moment of respite. He thought of texting Marta but decided not to. He'd probably only end up asking for her permission to give up and run away. When he looked in the mirror he realised that as well as being white as a sheet he was also sweating. And he had a headache. It was such a perfect set of flu symptoms he wondered if he really did have the flu. That would be a genuine excuse. *Sorry, Señor Ibañez, I think my flu is getting much worse. I'm going to have to go home. Just in case I give it to anyone else, you understand. I'll get back as soon as I can and catch up. Sorry I won't be able to do the Gold Star book tonight after all.*

In the middle of that movie playing in his mind, the toilet door opened and Señor Ibañez came in, already unzipping his fly.

"Ah, Oscarito. Didn't know you were in here. How are you feeling? I must say, you look terrible. Why don't you go home and rest? There's nothing so out of date that it won't wait. The Gold Star Donors book can wait, too. In any case, I can't stay as late as normal tonight, so you won't have much time to get a good run at it. Go home and come back when you're ready. We don't want this job to kill you, you know!"

Oscarito stopped and stared. What he wanted most in the world at that moment had just materialised in front of his eyes without any effort from him. He had been willing, he really had. It wasn't his fault that he was coming down with a summer flu – or maybe malaria – and couldn't possibly do what he'd agreed to do. Anyone would understand that. It was impossible. Even soldiers in the line of fire got sent back behind the trenches when they were sick. And he was quite obviously very sick. The secretaries had noticed and now even his boss had noticed. He could quite truthfully tell everyone he'd done his best but the office manager had sent him home. He'd had no choice.

However, at that precise moment, Oscarito surprised himself and did what might have been the bravest thing in his humdrum life up to that point. He thanked Señor Ibañez and declined. He told the office manager he probably looked a lot worse than he felt (the opposite was, in fact, the case) and that he'd rather deal with things properly before he took some time off. That part was at least true. If he could just get the outstanding bills paid, send out a couple of invoices, balance the ledgers and get the Gold Star book up to date he'd really be able to rest and recover.

Ibañez raised an eyebrow. "Oh well, on your own head be it. But like I said, we prefer to keep our employees alive. Don't die on the job, will you?"

Oscarito assured his boss that he would try not to – in this he was entirely honest. He dabbed a paper towel around his forehead and collar, then headed back into the office to the sound of a loud waterfall in the bathroom behind him.

Why on earth did I do that? he thought. *What am I, crazy?* He swivelled slightly in the chair and looked down at his case, parked exactly where it was always parked, on the right side of his chair between his desk and the Swiss cheese plant. He was sorely tempted to click it open and glance at the fake early edition of Cervantes, but he knew that no help would come from that source. He wiped his brow again and got on with trying to pull apart the sodden pages in front of him.

* * *

Gillian spent a miserable morning trying to concentrate on vowel sound differences between the west and east of Scotland. It was another feature of the great Glasgow–Edinburgh divide. Like London and Birmingham, Washington and New York, Madrid and Barcelona, they were traditional rivals; opposite in everything. The west had been poorer and more industrial, and had attracted immigrant labour from Ireland – which was poorer still and had no industry to speak of – and the influx of a different culture and different accents had affected the speech patterns of those to whom they came. Non-native speakers from other countries who came to visit the capital of Scotland and generally got on OK would go to Glasgow for a day visit and, as far as the language was concerned, feel like they'd landed on another planet.

Hence Gillian's research interest and lecture series. It was an interesting topic and well worth a place in Scots language studies. The only problem was that trying to put the series together was proving almost as impossible as non-native speakers asking for directions in Govan. She couldn't concentrate and was struggling to make it sound interesting – even to herself. She worked for three hours and completed two slides of a PowerPoint and one page of accompanying lecture notes. Her mind kept returning to David. If she didn't love that man so much, she would definitely kill him!

Alfredo was sitting like the Buddha, reading football books as ever. Either he had nerves of steel and iced water for blood or he was a very good actor. Filipe had once again left early to continue the search for someone willing to accuse the sitting government and its political party of criminal behaviour. Actually, there was a queue of people keen to do this, but generally without sufficient evidence. What was needed was someone who knew enough to make the charges stick. And people in that position would almost inevitably be implicated themselves. So why would they shop themselves just to bring down the business partner they were working so lucratively with? It was hardly surprising there had been no takers. Most people Filipe tried to speak to put the phone down without further comment. A few got shirty, and one or two abusive, but working in newspapers at least gives you a thick skin, so that didn't trouble him.

Teresa was at the hairdresser's, trying to act normal, and Marta had taken the risk of going home. She had sworn she would be in and out before anyone noticed. She needed to put out the rubbish or it would be at the point of crawling out itself.

That left only Gillian and Carl, who up to now had been reading quietly so as not to disturb her. Finally, Gillian closed the lid of her laptop and looked around. She caught his eye.

"Trouble concentrating?" he asked.

"It's not just hard – it's impossible," she groaned. "Despite trying to set the world to rights, I still have a job to do and the deadline's getting closer. I know what I have to do, but I just can't seem to beat the brain cells into submission."

He laughed. "Yes, they do seem to have a life of their own, don't they? When I was in Rome I had to work in either Italian or Latin.

Some days I think I produced two lines of sensible text and a ton of paper for recycling. If you want to talk, I'm here. *Crazy Horse and Custer: the parallel lives of two American warriors* is very interesting, but it'll be here when we finish."

She smiled at him. "You must have been a good parish priest," she said. "You have a very calming manner."

He gave a snort of disgust. "No, terrible," he said. "A very calming manner is the last thing more parishes need. They need a bomb put under them or a giant kick up the backside. When people are in trouble, yes, I suppose so. Maybe I was good at funerals. But I mainly wanted to have an impact on the living."

Gillian got up from the desk she had been working at and put her laptop back into its case. "Do you mind if I make some coffee?" she asked.

"No, of course not. I'll come and help. You need a degree in engineering to work our new coffee machine, but I think I've got it bullied into submission."

Five minutes later they came back through into Carl's living room.

"This really is a lovely, peaceful house," Gillian remarked. "You must be bored with us saying so. It's like a haven in the middle of the city. I feel like we're a bunch of hobbits in Rivendell hiding and recovering before the next step of our quest."

Carl laughed. "And the case of money is the Ring. Powerful but destructive. You have a way with words," he said, "as a linguist should. So, what can we talk about?"

Gillian took a sip of her coffee, then laid the cup on the coffee table. "Take your pick," she said. "Life, death, danger, risk, caution, recklessness, hope, despair, crime and punishment. I think we've got plenty to be going on with."

"Indeed. But those are universals. Anything specific on your mind?"

"Well, of course," she said quietly. "I guess I'm worried, but I'm also angry, if I'm honest."

"At David?"

"Partly. But at God, too. Mainly at God, in fact."

"How so?"

She pursed her lips and thought. "David has a bit of a disability," she began slowly. "I mean, everything is there and functioning reasonably well, but he has what I call a moral disability. He's completely unable to see something that is wrong or unjust and leave it well alone. Of course, I partly love him for that, but I'm also pretty fed up with it. Time and time again he seems to get pulled into things that aren't really any of his business, but he seems to think he can make a difference and should get involved. The way he sees it, it's his duty. The way I see it, let it be someone else's duty for once."

"Hmm, I see," Carl replied. "But that's David. That's how he is and always has been, as far as I remember. And I think you're suggesting that it's part of what attracted you to him. I guess it wasn't his looks – forgive me!"

Gillian laughed with a release of tension. "You could be right. Though I've seen worse."

"Anyway, if we're agreed that it's who he is, then I can understand you being in two minds about it. But you said you're mainly mad at God, not just at David. Is that right?"

Gillian nodded. "I think so. I'm mad that God – who's supposed to be in charge of things – seems to keep setting up these situations that David gets dragged into. I know it's life, and that life is full of imperfections and injustices if you pay attention – and most people don't – but all this business about 'you might be here for just such a time like this' really makes me mad. Why doesn't somebody else get the big pointy hand sometimes? We've had missing teenagers, fake churches, jihadi warriors, kidnappings and I don't know what else. It reads like Sherlock Holmes's casebook, and I'm really tired of it. We just about had a real row this morning before he left. The next time – if there is a next time – I might find myself going home and locking the door and letting him get on with it. I've really had just about enough!"

The Root of all Evil

As Gillian spoke, the words grew harder and harder. Finally, it was more sobbing than speaking.

Carl came over and sat beside her. "Ssshhh," he said quietly. "Ssshhh."

He let the storm blow itself out, then got up and gave her a box of tissues.

She blew, dabbed, wiped and did her best to fix her eyeliner. "Thanks," she said. "Sorry to blub."

"No need to be sorry; it's natural. I'm not sure I can say anything that'll help – despite my very calming manner! Maybe it's a bit like the mum's dilemma when her child gets bullied at school. What should she do? Ignore it or confront the bully? It's a dilemma. Ignore it and the bully gets away with it and goes on to bully someone else, or take a risk and confront it and you could go down fighting."

Gillian nodded. "I think that's a fair comparison. But my problem is, where's the teacher? If this is like kids in the playground or the classroom, and bad behaviour needs to be confronted – I agree with all of that – but then where is the teacher who has the ultimate responsibility? You hear people in church saying, 'Remember God is in control.' Well, my question is – so where is he? Is evil only confronted if one of the other kids takes the bully on – David, in this case? Doesn't the teacher have a role to play? After all, it's the teacher who sets the rules and has the power to enforce them. Why do we have to wait till the bell rings before everybody gets what's coming to them? Shouldn't it be happening during class time as well? I think it's a fair question."

Carl smiled at her. "A very fair question. You know, David and I have been friends and colleagues for more than twenty years. I know how much he suffered when Rocío died. I don't say this to embarrass you. I'm just so glad for him that he found you. I love the way you're willing to ask the hard questions but not with any sense of bitterness, if I read it right. You're just so open and honest with yourself – and in this case me – that no one could be offended. And I'm sure that includes God. Do you know the passage in the book of Proverbs about the righteous wife? She is more precious than rubies, the heart of her husband is glad in her, and she does him good and not evil all the days of her life. I know I'm not answering your question, but I just wanted to say that before I forget. I'm so glad he got you. You are perfect for him, and I hope he's perfect for you."

"Well, I doubt either of us is perfect," Gillian replied, finishing off dabbing her eyes. "But so far, so good."

"OK, so, to your problem. Of course, I'm as much in the light and in the dark as you on this. I don't really believe in proof texts and magic formulae that make all problems disappear. Some of our supposed theology and solutions to difficult problems I call 'fancy footwork'. It kind of deals with the problem in a superficial way but it's not satisfying, and it doesn't really feel conclusive. It sometimes feels like it's more just to get God off the hook than resolve the real human difficulty. That's pointless and it makes me angry.

"So, I'm afraid we have to start from the position that there are hundreds of extremely important issues that we don't have complete answers for and maybe never will. I've been as frustrated as you many times. Or at least as frustrated as I think you are. I never quite got to the point where Job's comforters recommended that he should just curse God and die, but I came quite close a few times. And remember at the end of the book of Job, when God showed up to respond to Job, God simply told him he didn't understand the issues enough to form a sensible question. That's always felt a bit dispiriting to me. So, even if I don't seem to be suffering exactly from your problem right now, I have been there. I, too, was rescued by the love of a good woman – maybe that's why I appreciate it when I see it. Anyway, rather than trying to say anything trite and unhelpful, do you mind if I tell you a story of something that happened once which really helped me?"

She nodded.

"When I was working as a parish priest in Dublin – before I met Teresa – I was actually just an assistant to a more senior colleague, and I was young and idealistic and enthusiastic, and I'm sure absolutely insufferable. Well, there was a homeless drunk who used to ask for money outside the church on Sundays. I decided that this guy would be my project. I was going to get him cleaned up, dried out, smartened up and back into a house and a job. I didn't expect he'd become prime minister, but anything short of that was fair game."

Gillian put down her coffee and sat forward attentively.

"I tried to pull in all the resources I could. I got social services involved, various charities, second-hand stores. The guy seemed genuinely grateful, and sat still while he had a haircut and shave, and while they weighed and measured him, fed him up, gave him new shoes, gave him the keys to his own flat etc., etc. Then, just when I was feeling pretty good about myself, do you know what happened?"

"Tell me."

"Social services called me one day. They'd gone round to check on him and do some cleaning, and found him gone. And not just him, but the cooker, the electric fire, the kitchen units, the worktops, the carpets, the doors and even some of the wiring. I went round immediately, of course. It was quite an impressive achievement. Every single thing that was moveable or could be made moveable had been moved. Some of it later turned up in second-hand shops on the other side of town, but lots was never seen again. Beds, blankets, every single stick of furniture I had got for him. It was amazing. I was kind of heartbroken but also kind of impressed. And I was very angry."

"At the man?"

"Yes... partly. But more at God, as you've said yourself."

"Why?"

"Because he hadn't backed my act. I thought the deal was that I did something and then God did something. I did the best I could, but of course we can't guarantee the final outcomes – we leave that to him. You know where Paul says, 'I have planted, Apollos watered; but God gave the increase'? Well, I thought I'd played my part and

God had singularly failed to play his. Does that have any resonance with what you're feeling?"

Gillian nodded again. "Yes, I think so. I come from a totally secular background, Carl. A lot of this God stuff has been pretty hard for me, to be honest. Some of the churchy culture drives me up the wall. But the heart of it I've come to accept. I mean, I've come to accept it as true and to accept it as my own. Not just David's religion, but my personal faith, too. I suppose if I'm to be brutally honest – and we are being honest this morning – I think I've done enough to deserve a bit of a break, you know? If I really call a spade a spade, then, underneath it all, I think God owes me one. I've done what I needed to do and more, and I've been with David through lots of these crazy things. Now I want a break. I was looking forward to a nice weekend in Madrid and getting my work done in good time, then back into another term. I enjoy my work; I think I'm quite good at it. I support David at church – and I think he's good at what he does as well. I think we both deserve a break. And to be honest, we're not getting it. Does that make sense? Are you allowed to say that kind of thing?'

"Yes, it certainly makes sense. As to whether you're allowed to say it, we haven't had a thunderbolt yet, so I guess we can press on. Anyway, to finish the story, I went to my boss, the local bishop and had a conversation a bit like this one. I moaned and complained – actually, I think I whined – much more than you've done. Why did God not help? Why did he do nothing in the situation? I had done everything this guy needed, but God had utterly failed to provide the necessary change of heart, which was beyond me and was what was ultimately needed. I was a saint and a martyr, and God was sleeping on the job. I think that was the overall effect."

"What happened?"

"The bishop disagreed with me."

"In what way?"

"He said that God had, in fact, done everything."

"What did he mean by that?"

"He said that everything I had done had actually been done by God. That made me even more mad, of course, but while I was shouting – you're not supposed to shout at a bishop – he calmly insisted that God had done everything. I demanded to know how he made that out, and he said that God in me had done everything for the homeless guy. Organised social services, bought the furniture, got the health check-up, made the meals. Everything. Well, I was so angry it took a while before I even understood what he was saying; far less came to the point of agreeing with him. But I think I'm far enough away from it now to see what he meant. The values I had and even the desire to help had come from a higher source. Does that make sense?"

"I see what you're getting at. I think I'll need to let that settle a bit before I can work it all out."

"I'm not looking for you to agree or disagree with me, and maybe I'm fooling myself in the search for a positive outcome, but it's another way of looking at things. You're a very intelligent woman. I'm sure you can do the rest and see if it applies. Just a thought. Ah, I think that's Teresa coming in. Any preference for lunch?"

* * *

Oscarito worked through the rest of the afternoon with the feeling that the case at the side of his desk was holding a ticking time bomb. If all went well, he would complete his normal day's work, take a coffee break, maybe stretch his legs in the little garden round Party headquarters, then go back in and ask Señor Ibañez for the Gold Star book. Then he would spend some time working on it until near to the time when the office manager had to leave. He imagined himself leaving a few loose pages carelessly on his desk and taking the remains of the book through to go back inside the safe. But in his other hand would be the time bomb. The facsimile early edition of Cervantes. Somehow, he needed to give Señor Ibañez the Gold

Star Donors book back with one hand while placing the camera – for such it was – on the filing cabinet facing the safe exactly as Marta had explained – having earlier pressed the on button.

After that he would go back into his own office and allow time for the safe to be locked. Then he would notice the missing pages and take them back through. Señor Ibañez would huff and puff and send him out of the room again while he reopened the safe and put the missing pages in. Then Oscarito would have to remember the missing camera book and go back in for it, apologise, take the book down and then go back to his desk, gather up his things and leave. Once back at the bishop's house they would take the memory stick out and insert it into a computer. Assuming there was anything on it at all, he was convinced that the video would only be of Señor Ibañez's ample backside right in front of the safe as he bent over it to spin the dial.

It didn't happen like that. When the time came, Oscarito did indeed ask for the Gold Star book and Señor Ibañez did indeed send him out of the office while he opened the safe and took the book out – after commenting once again that the accountant looked more dead than alive and should really go home immediately and leave the book for another day. Oscarito repeated his rehearsed speech about being sure he would sleep better knowing all his work was up to date. In fact, he was already contemplating the possibility – nay, likelihood – that if there was nothing useful on the video, he might have to come back the following day and try to do it all again. That being the case, he couldn't even agree to take the next day off to recover. This was so much above and beyond the call of duty that he would even have been suspicious of himself had he said it to himself. However, just as Oscarito was opening the book and preparing to loosen a couple of pages, Señor Ibañez emerged out of his office like a bear out of his cave, stretched and wandered idly over to his desk. By this time Oscarito had already taken the Cervantes camera out and laid it on the corner of his desk.

"Just to let you know before I forget, Oscarito," Ibañez began. "I do appreciate your loyalty and hard work. I want you to know that. It won't go unrewarded. Trust me." He gave Oscarito a wink.

As if that wasn't bad enough, the office manager noticed the hefty volume, leaned forward to see what it was and picked it up for a closer look. Oscarito almost had a heart attack on the spot.

"Hmm, this looks impressive," he muttered. "What is it? Ah, very impressive. *El Quixote; Volume One*. I didn't know you were a classical scholar, Oscarito. You are indeed a box of surprises. I wrote my thesis on Volume One. It was entitled: 'Quixote's Delusions and the Roots of Medieval Humanism: Cervantes and Erasmus – Parallel Medieval Minds'. Got a B-plus, too." He opened the tome and began to leaf through it.

This is it! Oscarito's mind screamed. *How can you actually handle it without noticing the wires down the spine?* He tried to keep his face straight but could feel the cold sweat trickling down the small of his back. "My, erm... my sister gave me it for Christmas," he stammered. "I'm trying to... to finish it before next Christmas."

"Very admirable," Ibañez said approvingly. "I know it's only a facsimile, but I must say it's a very good one. The type, the chapter headings, the plates, the binding. Very good. Spine seems a bit thick, but maybe that's the style. Actually, I wouldn't mind a glance through it if you don't mind, Oscarito. Compare it with some others I have at home. Just for a couple of days, you understand. If you don't mind."

Oscarito was never able to understand thereafter how he managed it. Neither could he remember the exact form of words. Something about having dinner with his sister that night. She would be bound to ask how he was getting on. He particularly wanted to have the volume with him that evening to show her. Any time after that would be fine. No problem at all, sir. As far as he could recall afterwards, Ibañez had merely shrugged and complimented him on doing his duty, once again asked him if he was all right, since he looked like he'd seen a ghost, then pottered back to his room.

Oscarito took out his handkerchief and mopped his brow, his

cheeks, his neck and under his arms, which really needed to be connected to the wastewater system, not dabbed with a handkerchief. He put in a few numbers in a blur, then took the book back through with *Don Quixote* under one arm, leaving a few pages on his desk.

"All done, sir," he said.

"Well, that didn't take long," Ibañez said, apparently wondering what all the fuss had been about for a job that had taken less than five minutes and could easily have been left for another day. "OK, then. Go and gather up your things, then straight home and into bed. Oh no, you can't. Your sister. I forgot. Well, if you can't cancel, I'd chuck her out immediately after *postre*, then a hot whisky and honey, and take the day off tomorrow!"

Oscarito looked around, glancing at the spot on the filing cabinet where he would have to place the camera in a matter of minutes. *Blast!* It has been clear half an hour ago and now it held a pile of lever-arch files and a cash box. It would be utterly impossible to put anything there beside it. Oscarito looked around helplessly. There was nowhere else. In the meantime, however, Ibañez was ignoring him entirely and had already turned towards the safe. He got down on his haunches and started turning the dial.

Oscarito couldn't believe his eyes. Eighty-three. Twenty-seven. Nineteen. Then the other way. Forty-five. Eighteen. Ten. A turn of the handle and the safe popped open. Ibañez casually laid the Gold Star Donors book on top of what looked like piles of €50 notes.

Oscarito slid out of the door before Ibañez had closed the safe. A flawless memory for numbers was a wonderful thing. On the other hand, as he put the camera back in his case, he remembered something else. Something Ibañez could easily discover.

He didn't have a sister.

Chapter 15

Kiss Club

David had to take a taxi, since the Kiss Club was off the Madrid public transport network and he didn't have access to a car. The taxi driver knew the location well, however, and gave David a sly wink as he got in.

"I'd come with you if I was at the end of my shift," he said. "Bar prices are high, but then you get what you pay for."

David smiled weakly and said nothing.

The building itself was in the form of a substantial two-storey country house painted black and red. All the windows had shutters, and all were shut. It had the normal "CLUB" sign on top of a pole, ten metres high in bright neon, but also the name of the club across the largest blank wall on the side of the building. "Kiss Club" was written in an art nouveau font with a graphic of two identical female heads and shoulders in the familiar American jazz-age style. They were exactly the same. Both looked like Maureen O'Hara. Hair and facial features were in black with curvaceous red lips, further emphasised by bright red neon. Two cocktail glasses with paper parasols and straws completed the design, except that everything was chipped and worn. One of the heads was missing an eye and one of the cocktails had a gaping hole in the bottom of the glass. Only one 's' of "Kiss" was illuminated, and the 'C' of "Club" was also missing. This made it spell "Kis lub", which didn't sound very appealing. Nevertheless, the car park was half full and it was not yet two in the afternoon. Maybe this was the pre-lunch trade; something to give the punters an appetite.

The driver gave David another wink as he paid. David decided not to leave a tip. The feeling he had as he headed towards the double doors reminded him of the first time he'd crossed the threshold of an evangelical church so many years before – "Abandon all hope, ye who enter here" – but there the comparison stopped. Salsa rhythms could be heard coming from inside, which became considerably louder when he pushed through the double doors.

There was a foyer with what looked like a ticket booth. A huge Latino-looking guy in a plain white shirt with no tie, a Maori tattoo over one eyebrow and a single gold earring sat behind the glass. He had a badge on that said "Juan". David reckoned the chances of that being his real name were less than the Spanish king really being called Gonzo.

Juan nodded with an upward jerk of the head. "*Buenos dias*. First time, *Señor*?"

David nodded back.

"Well, we have a special offer this week," Juan continued. "A book of drinks vouchers. Only €25 gets you ten drinks half price. It's a good deal."

"No membership, then?" David asked.

Juan shook his head with a clucking sound. "No membership. Though you can be barred for bad behaviour."

"And how do I pay for... other services?"

"Between you and the hostess. She'll tell you depending on what you're looking for. We've got some lovely girls in right now. First-timers. Real kissing and a choice of costumes. You'll love it."

"No doubt," David replied dryly. "I'll pass on the vouchers, thanks."

"OK, whatever. Just go right on in. The girls all have numbers on. Tell the barman who you'd like to join you."

David pushed through the second double doors and the salsa beat doubled in volume. At first he could hardly make anything out, the lights were so low. He stood for a few seconds to let his eyes and ears adjust. Compared with the sunshine and normal people going about their business outside, it felt like another planet. A hot, fiery planet inhabited by strange creatures of the night.

The room was maybe thirty metres long and twenty wide. A long bar lined one wall and the other was taken up with high-sided booths. A few individual tables dotted the remaining open space. There were staircases at both far corners leading to a balcony, in the middle of which was a closed door.

The girls did indeed have numbers on. Each had a circular card on their left wrist – like an enlarged wristwatch – with a clearly printed number in black on top of a pair of bright red lips and a circular border, also of black. The first David noticed was "29". So, there were at least twenty-nine 'hostesses' here at one time – maybe more. A couple of girls were sitting at the bar, the rest were in booths with their customers. Before any of them could slide off a chair and take David's arm, he went up to the bar.

The barman came along with a plastic smile. "What can I get you, *Señor*?" He had to more or less shout to be heard.

"Cuba libre and no company," David shouted back.

The barman raised his eyebrows, but he pulled a glass out from under the bar anyway. He poured in a measure of Bacardi and topped it up with coke, ice and a slice of lime.

"That's €12, *Señor*."

Now David raised his eyebrows but pulled out his wallet anyway. Three times the price on the street. Well, as the driver said, you get what you pay for. Mostly.

He took the tall glass, ignored the plate of crisps the barman had put out and went over to a vacant table. He pulled out a chair and sat. The salsa changed to *son cubano* but the beat went on. David took a sip of his drink – that at least was OK. He took his time to look around more closely. All the girls had matching outfits that fitted the red-and-black, art nouveau theme. They were dressed like 1920s cocktail waitresses with black, plunging necklines, short puffed-out skirts, patterned stockings with seams and high heels. The dresses were black and all the details red.

Those with customers were giggling coquettishly while sipping the €25 cocktails their companions had bought them, while the men seemed to be sitting with plain beers, which were slightly less extortionate at only €7, according to the list behind the bar. The walls bore copies of the faces from outside on top of a 1920s New York skyline with the Empire State Building, the Rockefeller Center and the Chrysler Building all recognisable. Little lights in the windows were actually tiny electric bulbs. David had expected pure porn and was a bit surprised. In another setting it might have been quite tasteful. Looking behind him, there was a TV high up in a corner near the door showing football. Incredible, but also in another way perfectly in place. The three Spanish obsessions brought together: wine, women and football. Real were one nil down to Raya Vallacano, which had been his local team in Santa Eugenia. *Go Las Rayas*, David automatically found himself thinking. He could perfectly well imagine a customer telling his date to shut up until they took the penalty.

He sat, slowly sipping, and watched customers come in, go to the bar, greet the barman like a brother, buy a drink and immediately be joined by a girl who looked as if she might have been waiting for them.

He imagined the conversation as the barman listened to the drinks order, then replied, *'Certainly, sir. Do you have a reservation?'*

'Oh, yes. Number 7.'

'Very good, sir. The perfect number, isn't it?'

'I think so. Well, it certainly was last time!'

Then they'd share a laugh while the barman called Samantha or Raquel or Veronica over.

From time to time, girls would also head towards the stairs, leading a guy behind them. Some of the men gave a quick, nervous glance over their shoulders, as if anybody cared. The business David wanted to do was up that staircase and through that door, but he wasn't entirely sure how to get there. He could chat to a girl, suggest they go upstairs, then abandon her and head to the office Sandra had told him about at the far end, but the club would certainly have security. If he was lucky, he'd simply be caught and thrown out, and the Spider in the office would probably never hear about the incident at all. If he was unlucky, he'd be frisked for a wire or a camera, ID and any spare change, and finally be dumped on the highway in a rather poorer state of health than when he'd arrived. He was well aware that most people would consider him a fool for coming this far, but then he thought maybe he should just trust to a fool's luck and ask.

He finished his drink and went back to the bar. The barman came over to him with an inquiring expression. Nobody comes to a club for cheap drinks, so what did this guy want?

"Another drink, *Señor*?"

David shook his head. "No. I'd like to speak to Marie Vey."

Now the barman really looked surprised.

"I'm sorry, *Señor*. We don't have anyone here by that name. The girls all have numbers. If you just tell me which number you'd like to speak to, I'll arrange it."

David smiled. "I'm not here to speak to a girl," he said. "I want to speak to Maria Victoria. I believe she may be upstairs in her office. We know each other. I know she's there, you know she's there and I know that you know. So I'd be grateful if you could go and tell her, please."

The barman wasn't looking surprised any more. Hostile and threatening would have been more accurate. "How do you know Marie Vey?"

"We used to work together – in a sort of a way. Tell her Pastor David wants to catch up on old times."

The barman didn't move or speak, but just kept looking. Then he seemed to make a decision. "Wait here," he said.

He caught the eye of a girl at the far end of the bar, who slipped off her stool and came round to replace him. Then he went up the stairs at the end of the bar and opened the door, casting a glance back at David, who hadn't moved.

One minute became two, became three, became five. *This isn't going to work*, David was beginning to think. A number of the unoccupied girls were looking quizzically in his direction, and he wasn't sure whether to smile back, ignore them or watch the football.

Instead, he kept his eyes on the door until finally it opened and the barman re-emerged, his expression unreadable. He came down the stairs in no hurry and went back to his place, eyes on David with the sort of expression that reminded him of a traffic cop who has just pulled you over. It was part swagger, part contempt, part frustration, as if left to his own devices he'd haul you out of the car and give you a good working over, then fine you to boot – but rules being rules he was required to restrain himself and merely serve you with a ticket for €200. The barman kept his eyes fixed on David as he slowly poured himself a *caña*, took a long, slow sip, hunted around under the bar for a cardboard coaster, laid it on the bar and stood his drink on it.

Without averting his gaze, he spoke to the girl who was still behind the bar. "Anastasia, take this *tonto* upstairs." He gave a nod towards the stairs and fired a parting shot as David slid off his stool. "You'd better have a good story, *tonto* – trust me!"

David wasn't sure whether to think of climbing the stairs as a "stairway to heaven" or like steps to the scaffold. Well, too late to turn back now, even if he'd wanted to.

Anastasia was a light-skinned girl with jet-black hair, vivid lipstick, and dark eyes, rimmed in black. She held the door open for him to pass, then shut it behind them. The corridor was as dimly lit as the salon below. It was about two metres wide and another thirty along. There were five doors on either side, each with a red light above. About half of them were lit.

At the far end, the twin of Juan the ticket man was standing, legs apart in a ready stance, hands clasped in front of him like bouncers the world over. He had an earpiece with a spiral cord leading to a pocket. He didn't look any friendlier than anyone else David had dealt with in the "Kis lub" so far. David certainly wouldn't be recommending this establishment to any lonely hearts he knew.

As he approached, the bouncer stepped forward and frisked him more than thoroughly. If there had been a spare Polo mint in his pocket it would have been found and accounted for. The bouncer nodded at Anastasia, who turned and headed back towards the stairs.

"*Gracias*," David said over his shoulder as she retreated, believing as he did in politeness – even to pretend cocktail waitresses.

Surprisingly she turned, smiled and gave a "*De nada*" – don't mention it.

The bouncer turned the handle behind him without letting David out of his sight and pushed it open. He nodded into the room.

David went in. "*Gracias*," he said.

The bouncer did not return the courtesy.

Inside, David had to quickly adjust his vision again. Instead of dim red lights, the office was bright, with large windows that weren't covered by shutters or blinds. The walls were a plain, slightly creamy shade, featuring some nice artwork. The floor was parquet with a few Mexican-style rugs. A couple of filing cabinets stood around and towards the far wall was a single dark-wood desk.

Behind the desk sat an enormous black woman wearing an African-style dress in a startling shade of emerald green with a matching headdress. She wore several strings of pearls, enormous gold hoop earrings and huge rings on almost every finger.

"Pastor David," she said warmly. "This is a surprise!" She got up from behind the desk, smiling, and gracefully shifted her considerable weight around towards him, arms held out.

David approached and took her hands, then returned the proffered *dos besos*.

She took a step back, holding his hands at arm's length, then, before he could react, she dropped his hands and landed an open-handed blow to the side of his head that knocked him more than two metres sideways. He banged his head against the sharp corner of a filing cabinet.

"I don't like surprises," she said quietly and walked back round to the other side of the desk as David felt a stream of blood from his forehead trickle down his cheek.

"Don't get blood on the carpets," she said, throwing him a box of tissues. "That's for all the good girls you robbed me of when we were last in touch. Don't do it again. Now, what can I do for you?"

David slowly picked himself up, pressing a tissue to his forehead and rubbing it down his cheek.

"Well," he began. "It's a pleasure to see you again, too, Marie."

* * *

Marta was surprised Oscarito wasn't there when she arrived to clean. His desk was clear but he was nowhere to be seen. She went through to the office manager's room and looked. The safe was firmly locked and there was no camera book. She shrugged. The plan had been for him to remain so they could go back to Carl's house together when she'd finished her work. Then they'd look at the video to see if they could make out the combination. The following day he'd stay off work and she'd take a duplicate book in her bag with her, then open the safe and swap the books once the office was empty. Oscarito would then phone in the following morning and tell his boss that he'd been told to take the rest of the week off. During that time, they'd just have to hope there wouldn't be any need to look at the fake book while the real one was being presented to a prosecutor and his team. Once it had been verified as the real thing – and copied – Marta would swap it back for the false one and hope no one was any the wiser.

She was going through this in her mind while emptying wastepaper bins and washing out dirty coffee cups. She almost dropped the aspidistra she had been carefully watering when Oscarito burst into the room.

"I've got it!" he shouted.

"What?"

"The combination, I've got it! He just opened the safe before I could leave the office. I've got the combination!" Oscarito was so excited he almost touched the dial.

"Stop!" Marta shouted. "Fingerprints! Don't touch it!"

She took a wiping cloth and insisted on noting the number the dial had been left at before turning it while Oscarito happily recited the numbers. It opened first time. There was the Gold Star book, exactly where Oscarito had seen Ibañez deposit it.

Again, Marta insisted on taking it out with the cloth over her hands, as you would take a hot dish out of the oven. She put it into her bag and lifted out the other book, which she'd put into the bag on a whim, just in case.

Oscarito was all for placing it in, shutting the door and getting out of the office as soon as possible, but now that the safe door was open, Marta insisted on having a closer look. The pile of notes underneath the book were indeed fifties. Oscarito refused point blank to let her take them out and count them, but it looked like tens of thousands of euros. Underneath them was a bunch of other documents. Likewise, she was all for having a look, but Oscarito declared that if she touched a single one she could say goodbye to any further involvement from him. Reluctantly, she agreed.

They left the office hand in hand, not noticing the black 4x4 across the road and the enormous dark-haired man behind the wheel watching them closely.

* * *

David recovered quickly, tucking the bloodstained tissue into his pocket.

Marie Vey had pulled out a chair on her way back to her side of the desk and gestured towards it. "No hard feelings?" she said in a totally friendly tone.

"If you say so," David replied and took a seat.

"So, how have you been?"

"Well, it may be hard to cover eight years in a few sentences, but really very well. You know I went back to Edinburgh after Rocío died?"

"Yes, I know. My condolences."

"Thanks. It was hard for a while, then I met someone. We married two years ago. We've just found out she's expecting as well. So, all systems go, I suppose."

"I'm glad. And what do you do when you're not making babies?"

David had to smile. Marie Vey had never had any difficulty in coming straight to the point, as he'd just experienced. "I'm still a pastor. Small church – nothing like Warehouse 66. It has its moments, though."

"None of the type of congregants you used to pick up from me, then?"

"As a matter of fact, there sometimes are. We got involved in trying to sort out a people-trafficking gang working from Belarus some time ago. We saw a good few of the gang locked up and a lot of girls either going back home or getting proper jobs in the city. A few come to us from time to time. It was very satisfying."

"I can imagine. As you know, I detest all of that stuff. We run a clean business here. Only willing workers. Free health care, regular testing and two weeks' paid holiday. We prosecute violent customers. We don't steal the punters' wallets when they're asleep, and people are free to leave whenever they decide they've had enough."

As she was speaking, Marie pulled open a drawer and took out a lighter and the longest cigar David had ever seen. She proceeded to light it and blow smoke over her shoulder.

"So, how's business?" he asked.

Marie shrugged and blew out another cloud. "I shouldn't complain, but it's frankly terrible. The punters are terrified of infection. With the internet, the girls can work self-employed and don't need the entrepreneur. And there are unscrupulous bosses bringing girls in from South America with the promise of easy money. You see their ads in the papers every day: 'New in town. Your dream come true. Seductive and compliant. Real kisses. Let our passion bind us together.' You know the routine. It basically means a forty-two-year-old housewife from Bogatá who'll do anything and provides her own ropes and handcuffs. It's horrible. It gives the genuine trade a bad name. Then there's the fact that everybody wants to charge top rates knowing we're on the verge of illegality. Those who are entitled to it – the hairdressers, the retailers, the decorators – and those who aren't. I'll leave that to your imagination. Oh, I should have offered you a drink. What would you like?"

"At the downstairs prices, a glass of tap water would be fine. Thanks."

Marie laughed. "You're killing me. How much did you pay?"

He told her.

She pressed a buzzer on the desk and ordered another Cuba libre and a refund, plus a whisky and soda for herself. "No ice and a clean glass this time." Then she turned back to David. "So, you didn't come here for a bang on the ear and expensive drinks, did you? What's it all about? Why are you even in Spain if you're happy in Edinburgh now and the little lady does the business?"

David winced but let it pass. "Well, we came over just for the weekend – my wife's here, too – but something a bit unexpected happened." He told her all about it.

"*Madre mia!*" she said, deeply impressed. "And you want me to help you launder the money?"

It had taken a little while to get used to Marie's direct style, David mused, but it certainly saved time. "No. We're hoping the money will be confiscated eventually – with fines and jail time for those involved – but right now we're trying to join up the dots. Where does it come from, exactly? How, how often, who are the middlemen and how does the Party keep it all hidden?"

The drinks arrived. The barman avoided David's gaze but at least wasn't insolent this time.

Marie sounded more cautious when she spoke again. "I'm just a simple country girl," she said. "Spell it out for me."

He did. "I accept that you run a clean business. It's not a business

I approve of, but nobody's succeeded in putting a stop to it in 5,000 years, so I'm not going to now. To be honest, I'd rather you were running it than some of the characters I've bumped into over the past few years. I tolerate it, Spanish society tolerates it and the government tolerates it. Of course, they tolerate sex work legally – and officially – but we know that they also tolerate sex work that's not entirely legal. Pimping and trafficking." David held up his hands before Marie had the chance to clatter him across the room again. "I'm not saying that's what you do, but some do. And they tolerate it – for a price. And I think they also keep off your back, even though you're not illegal – also for a price."

Marie sucked on her cigar and didn't bother to blow the smoke in another direction this time. "Who have you been talking to?" she asked quietly.

David sipped his drink and took his time. "It's the word on the street," he said in as neutral a way as he could.

"Dolores!" She spat out. "I guarantee it's Dolores. They know the rules. Half pay for a month!"

"It wasn't Dolores," David said wearily, "but it really doesn't matter who it was. I picked up some information, and I think what I know from all sources could be useful to both of us."

"Go on. I'm listening."

"Right. So can we agree that someone connected to the powers that be takes a rake-off? They come here once a week or once a month or however frequently. If you don't pay up, you get harassed and inspected every week – even though what you're doing is legal. And the price for being left alone is a percentage. Five per cent or ten per cent, or whatever it is."

"Fifteen," Marie said with disgust.

"OK, now we're getting somewhere," David followed up. "You put up fifteen per cent and the authorities leave you alone. I'm guessing it's a policeman of some sort. At least a captain – maybe higher. Probably needs to lose a few pounds. I'm told they call him 'the Gorilla'."

Marie looked up and blew her smoke towards the roof this time. "You *are* well informed," she said. "Go on."

"Well, I think it's pretty simple after that. My thesis is that the Gorilla isn't funding a country house and a motorboat in the Rias, though that may be part of it. He does the pickup here and gives it to someone else, minus his whack. That someone gives it to someone who gives it to someone – I don't know how many links – but eventually it ends up in a safe at the headquarters of the ruling party. A gentleman by the name of Gonzaléz is party treasurer. A Señor Ibañez is in charge of the actual cash, and at least one beneficiary is the man who, until recently, was Minister for Justice – ironically enough."

"All very interesting, *amigo mio*, but you haven't quite joined up all the dots yet. What specifically does this have to do with me? Corruption in high places is just about as old as our business. You won't change me and I can't change it. So, what are you proposing?"

David leaned forward and put his clasped hands and elbows on the desk. "You're right. We can't stop them all, but we might be able to stop this lot of hooligans and crooks. It kind of goes against the grain just to give the money back and act as if nothing has happened. In my opinion they do real damage, far and beyond just taking money that doesn't belong to them.

"Ordinary Spaniards can't see why they should be honest and pay their taxes when those who run the country are crooks. That filters down to every level. And because people work in the black economy – no offence intended – taxes aren't paid, health services suffer, people don't get the treatment or medicines they need, kids have to pay for their own schoolbooks or get none at all, university places are cut, roads go unrepaired and lack of investment in the economy means that businesses fail, so people are made unemployed. Then they can't even pay minimal taxes and the circle goes round and round. If we could nail just one high-profile figure and send him to jail – in a very public way – it might just make a little change that would encourage people to do the right thing and make their contributions. It might be a tiny drip, but on the other hand it might be joined by others, and that really could change things. For the better. And incidentally, you would save some money. You might even decide to use it to pay the girls' taxes. Stranger things have happened."

"Maybe – but not much." Marie said, smiling in spite of herself. "You really are an idealist, aren't you, Pastor David? You really believe in changing things for the better. I admire you, you know? Such a pointless, fruitless, unachievable task, but you keep on plugging away at it. Even losing your wife hasn't really changed you – not fundamentally. You're still the same guy who used to have whores high on junk sleeping in the back bedroom of your *piso* till they could find a place, so they had an address and didn't get sent to prison to go cold turkey. I don't know. What are we going to do with you?"

David didn't quite know whether this was a compliment or an insult, but he decided to take it positively and press on. "So, with your help, we'd like to send the Gorilla back to the jungle, if I can put it that way, along with his chain of command. It makes your life safer, easier and more profitable, and I get what I want – even if you think that's a waste of time. Win–win. What do you think?"

Marie took a final puff of her cigar and stubbed it out. She sipped her drink. She stared out of the window. She doodled on her notepad. She tapped a pen on the desk. She did a quick sum on a Post-it note.

Then she looked up. "What do I think?" she asked herself as much as him. "I think you're a fool who believes that people can stop being who and what they are and start being nice to each other instead. You think good intentions can change everything. *Your* good intentions. You want El Dorado or Shangri-la or whatever we should call it. Heaven on earth, the Garden of Eden, thy kingdom come. Well, 'thy kingdom' is not coming any day soon. History is littered with failed idealists. I'm a realist. I accept the world the way it really is and try to bend it to my benefit.

"The girls working in the bedrooms down this corridor accept that, too. They don't have to like the punters; they just have to accept that they'll never win a beauty contest or a talent show, but they do hold body and soul together – just about – and that's enough. That's their reality. Your reality is a pipe dream. A fantasy. Never-never land. However, like I said, I'm a realist. The Gorilla thinks he's invincible. He's a filthy, disgusting animal who makes the girls do filthy, disgusting things. So, for that reason, if for no other, I'll do what's required. Now, what do you propose? How can we nail his filthy, disgusting hide?"

Chapter 16
Battle Stations

It was late by the time David got back to what he and Gillian had taken to calling 'the Bishop's Palace'. He hadn't eaten since breakfast and was famished. The others had held off cooking until he came back – hoping he *would* be back – so there was nothing either ready or on the way to being ready.

Teresa was embarrassed, but then Gillian said what David, at least, considered the magic word: "Chinese?"

Carl knew an excellent local establishment – for once *not* called The Empire, Jade Garden or Great Wall – and phoned them. Teresa found an old menu in a drawer, and they ordered.

In the typical late Spanish style, Marco wasn't in bed yet, so he was surprised and delighted to be told he could have prawn crackers for supper.

Twenty minutes later, they were unpacking pork ribs in a sticky sauce, lemon chicken, king prawns, duck with cashew nuts and ginger, and fried rice '*tres delicias*'. Carl produced a beautiful Bierzo red wine from his cellar, far and above what the food merited, and they ate and drank like kings and queens.

Oscarito was cock-a-hoop and seemed to have shrugged off his flu symptoms in one fell swoop. He now considered his work over and was looking forward to at least three days off. Marta was more quietly satisfied, but was already thinking of the next step. Marco just sat at her side, stuffing his face and enjoying being around the grown-ups.

Carl was patient, wading his way through another refill of both plate and glass, waiting to hear David's account of his day without pushing him. Teresa was quiet at his side. Marta and Oscarito sat like teenagers, playing at feeding each other with chopsticks, with predictable and sticky results. Filipe had already told everyone that he had drawn a blank again that day, so, like Alfredo, he kept his peace, remaining professionally interested.

Eventually, the last crumbs of rice that had tried their best to avoid the chopsticks slid off their plates into much less hungry mouths and the table was cleared.

"So, what's been going on today? Oscarito?" Carl began, recognising that the accountant was so excited and pleased with himself he had barely been able to contain it until the end of the meal.

Oscarito produced the Gold Star Donors book with a flourish and was congratulated around the table. Marta held on to his arm and planted a kiss on his cheek at the conclusion.

"Well done, *Señor*," Carl congratulated him. "I think we could say that your number came up, no? Now, Pastor David. What have you got for us?"

David told the story of his day. Gillian listened closely, but only showed overt emotion when he described how he'd come to have a bloody wound on his right temple.

"But why?" she asked. "Marie Vey didn't have anything to be angry about. What was the point of that?"

"I think she just likes to establish the pecking order," David replied perfectly calmly. "In her world that matters. Once I'd mopped it up I wasn't that offended."

"So, she's on board to move to stage two?" Alfredo asked, just for confirmation. "I have a few guesses as to who the Gorilla might be, but I'd like to see if I'm right. I have some colleagues who are sick of it all who'd love to be involved in the sting. I can't wait to see the look on his face."

"And we have a prosecutor lined up," Filipe put in. "I haven't entirely wasted the day. Name of Daniel de la Morena Byass. He's worked on a couple of corruption scandals, and I think he's even more frustrated than the rest of us."

"Are you sure he's sound?" Alfredo asked cautiously. "He's not going to blow the gaff?"

"Not unless he's on the make as well. But from his previous efforts, I don't think that's likely."

"So, help me with the procedure," David said. "The investigating magistrate is independent of government and the police, but calls on the police for resources to conduct an investigation. Is that it?"

"Roughly, yes," Alfredo replied. "However, there are a couple of complications. First, however much the magistrate wants to see them all locked up, he has to maintain a semblance of independence. His commitment is supposed to be to 'impartial justice'. So, the magistrate instructs a prosecutor, who actually conducts the investigation. It's the prosecutor who deploys police resources to investigate potential crimes. And he can switch resources at any time if there's any doubt about the integrity of the officers he's using. There was a case in Lugo a few years ago where some police names came up in the course of an investigation. The prosecutor immediately switched to another force so there was no question of the investigation being hampered by bent coppers."

"But who can you switch to if the police are corrupt?" Gillian asked. "Do you get someone from another region?"

"Can do," Alfredo replied. "In this case I think they brought in officers from Customs. They have their own investigators who are just as professional and able as the police. Anyway, that's one complication. The other might be even more significant. In Spain it was decided decades ago that senior government and parliamentary figures needed to be protected from politically motivated false accusations, so a higher court was established that only deals with political matters. Now, the lower courts are going to be fine for the likes of Ibañez and Gonzaléz, but the ex-minister may be another kettle of fish. Normally, high-ranking officials and ministers cannot be tried by lower courts. Whether he would still qualify for the higher court, I don't know. The main problem is that it doesn't conduct its business very quickly, and I suppose it confers a sense of privilege – even in matters of justice."

"That's horrible!" Gillian declared, shocked. "Surely everyone should have equality before the law. And if they break the law, they should face exactly the same penalties and be processed in the same way. Sounds awfully like elitism."

Alfredo inclined his head in part agreement. "Ultimately, you may be right," he said. "The idea wasn't to preserve elitism, though. The original idea was to prevent frivolous suits against public figures and to ensure that they didn't waste time defending themselves against things that should never have been brought. So, before a case comes to the highest courts, it's already been tested to some degree – at least with regards to seriousness. Whether it's a good system or not, or whether we'd bring it in again, is open to question. However, it's what we have nowadays. I'm only flagging it up because I'm not sure if it applies to ex-ministers or only to serving ministers. It may or may not be an issue. I just don't think that as a Guardia Civil captain I'd be able to turn up with a few buddies and lift the ex-minister. That's all I'm saying."

"OK, so where does that leave us?" David asked. "I suppose the first priority is to get the Gold Star book to Señor Byass, then get it back in the safe. Can we do that tomorrow?" He paused for a response. "Yes? OK, great. Then we have to work out some way of apprehending Señor Gorilla. Marie told me his regular run wouldn't be for another three weeks. Clearly, we can't wait that long. I'm guessing that's going to be your job, Alfredo – maybe with a team supplied by the prosecutor. What do you think, Filipe?"

Filipe nodded. "I think so," he said. "Alfredo and I can visit the gentleman tomorrow. I think you and Gillian ought to come, too. And bring the money. The phone call you recorded would also be relevant, Gillian. Hopefully we'll get the go-ahead, then ideally

Alfredo can pick his team in a way that doesn't expose the operation. Then, finally, we entice the Gorilla to come and get some bananas and see what happens!"

"No team," Alfredo said flatly. "Let's keep it in-house. Just those of us here and a trip to a DIY store."

* * *

After hours, Ibañez, Gonzaléz, the ex-minister and a huge bear of a man in jogging sweats and trainers met in the party treasurer's office.

"So, what are we planning for?" Ibañez asked. "Aggressive attack, strategic withdrawal, retrenchment or something else?"

"Oh, none of the above," the ex-minister said in almost an offhand way. "I view this as a progress and stock-taking meeting, nothing more. I'm not aware of any significant progress made by the other side, and we even have some positives on our own balance sheet. You mentioned the accountant last time, Lucas." He addressed his remark to the office manager. "It seems your anxieties were a bit premature there, weren't they?"

Ibañez grunted non-committally. "Perhaps. He showed up back at work, despite a horrible dose of flu, and even insisted on staying late to do the Gold Star book. The only fault I could find was that he left a couple of loose pages out on his desk that I had to put back in the safe the next morning. I didn't bother to find the right place – just left them on top of the book. He can do that when he comes back. He's taking a few days off to recover. So, yes, it looks like things are OK on that front. *Gracias a Dios.*"

"Excellent. Now, Juan – how are things with you? Oh, by the way, I heard on the grapevine they've given you a nickname. They call you 'the Gorilla'. I wonder why."

The fat man made a bit of a grunt but didn't respond. It seemed he was used to being the butt of people's jokes and knew his place. "Everything's OK," he said with a heavy Puerto Rican accent.

"Marie Vey called me yesterday. She said fortnightly would be better for cash flow, so I'm going round again the day after tomorrow. She always pays good. And the others. All OK. Lucas has the cash."

"Exactly. Safely stowed away," Ibañez confirmed, nodding towards his office through the wall. "But what about Hidalgo? That's what's troubling me. Any news of his whereabouts?"

The ex-minister sighed heavily. "No progress on that front, I'm sorry to report. We've got the current Warehouse 66 pastor, but that hasn't done us much good. If certain parties had just followed the wife, we'd have had them all by now, singing like birds." He looked pointedly in the fat man's direction. "But instead, a moment of panic and the first thing that comes into his mind and we almost have a murder as well as everything else – which would undoubtedly have been messy. Well done, *amigo*!"

The fat man shifted in his chair. "She was pulling up. A Guardia Civil van had just passed us going the other way. I was sure she was gonna turn round and try to catch it and report me. I had to stop that. She'd have my number, then I'd have to explain why I was following her. I had to make a decision in an instant. We know the direction she was heading in. It must have been somewhere in the mountains near Lozoya. It didn't do no harm."

"Not so far," the Party treasurer said dryly. "I believe she'll live. But her husband has a good lawyer, and he's made absolutely no comment on the whereabouts of Hidalgo or the money. And as far as Lozoya is concerned, we had a Guardia Civil captain who claimed some inside knowledge and went up with a van-full to investigate. According to the team, they picked up Hidalgo, his wife and three other unidentified individuals and brought them down to Madrid, but the captain made everyone except his driver and the prisoners get out, then took off somewhere else. So, they were certainly in Lozoya, but now they aren't *and* we've got a rogue police captain to content with. The driver's been threatened with everything from dismissal and loss of pension to high treason but hasn't let anything slip yet. So, the best thing we can say is that it was a waste of time. So near, yet so far. They might still be somewhere in Madrid or maybe Timbuktu. Who knows? We've got the pastor, but he's not speaking either – in fact, he's kicking up a fuss about the accident."

Ibañez looked frustrated and worried, and wasn't in the mood to let it pass. "That's too easy," he said. "So near, yet so far! This isn't a game. We're talking about a lot of money and life and liberty here. This was complete incompetence. We cannot afford spur-of-the-moment mistakes. If you'd just held back a bit, Juan – and she hadn't guessed you were following her – we'd all be in a much better situation and—"

"Come now, gentlemen. Let's all calm down," the former minister interrupted. "This sort of bickering won't do us any good and doesn't take us any further forward. As far as we know, there's no paper trail that connects the money to the Party. I could easily have been choosing to take personal assets in liquid form overseas. That's not against the law. I have a very good accountant who will vouch for the entire process and could even concoct a series of withdrawals from those nice banks in Panama. I think the possibility of any successful operation against us is vanishingly small. But we need to get the cash and stuff the mouths of those who might cause trouble. I'm not averse to spending some of the money to that effect – even if it means scaling down some of my retirement plans. The *Señora* won't be happy, but I can deal with that. Anyway, while we're here it might not be a bad idea to see just where the balance stands. Marcos, do you have a running total?"

The Party treasurer looked to the office manager.

"Not in my head," said the treasurer. "Lucas – where do we stand?"

"Well, Oscarito was working on it last night. It should be more or less up-to-date. Let me have a look."

He got up and left the room. The sound of his office door opening was clearly audible. Then the faint sounds of the combination dial spinning and clicking. Then a grunt as he bent down to pull something out. Then silence.

He came back into the room and dumped a large folio accounts book with a gold star on the table.

"We may have spoken too soon," he said in little more than a whisper. "The Gold Star Donors book isn't here – this is a dummy. By now they'll know everything!"

* * *

At that very moment, Oscarito had another large, foolscap ledger open in front of him on Carl McMaster's table. David Hidalgo, Gillian Lockhart, Filipe, Alfredo and Marta gathered around him as he explained the detail.

"Every name has a set of pages. On a computer you wouldn't need this, of course, but in a book that isn't loose leaf you have to guess how many pages you're going to need for each account. If you run out, you have to allocate more pages further on, then the account gets split, which looks untidy – and mistakes can creep in. So, every name has some pages, and we can roughly relate the number of pages Señor Gonzaléz has allocated to the importance of the account."

"Are you sure?" Gillian asked, poring over the pages he had open. "You've shown us several accounts with just a single page but hundreds of thousands in only one or two transactions. Then there are multipage accounts with lots of little transactions. I would have thought it was the total that defined the importance of the account, not just the number of transactions."

Oscarito nodded. "You're right," he said. "When I say the importance of the account, I suppose I mean the amount of work involved in keeping it up to date and correct. I guess total contributions would be more important in the long run. There are a load of accounts in here that I haven't even touched. Look at this," he said, flicking a few pages back. "This is a single transaction for €198,243.17, dated two years ago. Nothing before and nothing since."

"Look at the name," Alfredo said, pointing it out. "Raven – in English."

"A code name?" Filipe asked.

"Yes, but not a very good one. I bet that's Hermanos Cuervo. It's a construction firm. Is 'raven' not the translation of *cuervo*, David?"

"I think *cuervo* is normally a crow, but it's near enough. Why do you think it would be them?"

Filipe answered before Alfredo could get in. "There have long been rumours about some sort of crooked deal between the Party and various construction firms when it was last in government. Cuervo was the most obvious suspect. It was responsible for the new hospital in Torrejón. The government paid way over the odds for it and Cuervo wasn't nearly the lowest bidder, but the government claimed it was the only bid that met all the tender document criteria. So they got it. And it looks like the Party got €198,243.17. I suppose that must have been a percentage of the job – unless they did something extra for seventeen cents!"

"I can see the Gold Star Donors book is going to be a gold mine," David commented. "So, we're taking it to the prosecutor tomorrow?"

"That's right," Filipe agreed. "Then we have to figure out what to do with the Gorilla."

"I've got some ideas on that score," Alfredo commented ominously.

* * *

"What on earth do you mean," Gonzaléz demanded, staring at the volume on the table in front of them. "What do you mean the Gold Star book isn't here? I can see it with my own eyes, right in front of me!"

"Open it up," Ibañez said.

Gonzaléz grabbed the book and opened it in the middle. Then he started leafing through the pages, going back and forwards, unable to believe his eyes. Every page was just as blank as the one before and the one after. The only mark in the entire book was the sticker on the front, which declared 'Gold Star Donors' in exactly the same font, size, colour and design as the original, right down to the gold star next to the title.

Gonzaléz closed the book and sat back, speechless and shaking his head. His mouth was open but seemed unable to form a word. The Gorilla looked blank, not understanding the significance of what was unfolding. Ibañez had turned a whiter shade of pale and Gonzaléz was shaking. Only the former minister seemed to maintain his composure.

"Well, this changes things a bit," he said heavily, as if he had just popped his head outside and felt the first spits of rain when they had been planning a nice walk in the country. "So, now it looks like Hidalgo might have two things that belong to me. We may have to step up our efforts, gentlemen. Juan, you visit Marie Vey and the others, just as you'd planned. Everything goes on as normal. Lucas, call my former assistant, Alfonso. He has access to some additional resources we might call 'extra-judicial' that can be deployed. They'll check for prints, etc., although I imagine our wonderful, loyal accountant has to be at the top of the suspect list. You'll need to check with his father, of course, and all known associates. I'm putting you in charge of finding him. Personally. He was *your* choice, so he's *your* responsibility."

From white, Ibañez had now turned a sickly grey.

"Marcos," the former minister continued, "you co-ordinate with the Interior Ministry to find Hidalgo. Tell them to throw everything they have at it. Mobile tracking, computer IP addresses, feet on the street, everything. And don't restrict yourself to Hidalgo. His wife came with him, and she's probably still with him now. If she's using a mobile, if she's using a computer, I want to know which one, whom it's registered to and where. Check the banks for deposits of that amount. Check international transfers. Check social media, postal deliveries, automatic cash machines. Anything that ties any of them to a location, address or person."

"And what about Mateo, may I ask?" Gonzaléz came back at

him, clearly not used to being given his marching orders. "What's he going to be doing?"

"I," the former minister announced perfectly calmly, "am going to be following some new avenues of investigation. "I hear that some of our former and indeed current donors have been getting more attention than they're used to or like from a particularly vociferous gentleman of the press. I intend to find out why. However, there's nothing more we can do tonight. I suggest we meet here again in twenty-four hours. And I think we should expect to be able to share significant progress by then or hard questions might need to be asked. Do I make myself clear, gentlemen?"

* * *

Gillian was exhausted from all the stress of the day and went to bed as soon as the discussion about the Gold Star Book had come to an end. Oscarito and Marta sat in a corner, held hands and giggled, which was something no one had thought they'd ever see. Filipe watched a bit of late-night CNN, then also retired. Carl and Teresa pottered around for a few minutes, tidying, then likewise disappeared, leaving only David and Alfredo.

"So, what does the future hold for the bold captain of the Guardia Civil?" David asked, not unkindly. "If it hadn't been for you, we'd probably all be trying to raise bail right now. It may have cost you your job, though. That's a big price to pay."

Alfredo finally managed to overcome the sticky catch on the drinks' cabinet and pulled it open, glancing over its contents approvingly. He selected an aged Ron Barceló and a nice crystal whisky glass, carried both back to the sofa where David was sitting and eased himself down. He poured a generous measure and savoured it. Only then did he sit back and strike a thinking pose.

"Probably store detective in El Corte Inglés," he said. "Ten euros an hour and a discount card. Will suit me fine. No stress. Make the Latino kids put back the nice leather wallets that stick to their hands, not to mention the respectable society ladies with a touch of kleptomania. Then I can wind down towards retirement.

"On the other hand, this might be the biggest bust in Spanish political history – of which I will no doubt be one hero among a select few. In that case, I'll milk it for all it's worth and become a hugely overpaid security consultant and find a slightly younger, gorgeous lady who's dying to consult someone on her future matrimonial security. Equally no stress and a happy retirement. Just more money, that's all."

David had to laugh. "I see you've got it all planned out," he said. "Good luck with all of that – if you believe in luck. Personally, I take a more optimistic view. Don't forget the 'Esther Hypothesis' – your idea, if I remember rightly. Carl's been going on about it, and it's kind of been circling around in my mind, too. If we take that line, you could say you were meant to be a part of Warehouse 66, meant to be acquainted with me and Mariano, meant to hear about the search for the elusive David Hidalgo and meant to borrow a van with a bunch of unwitting colleagues and come looking for us. No doubt just in time."

"Maybe," Alfredo rejoined. "I think these things always seem clearer looking back. When you're in the middle of it, nobody knows how it's going to play out. Once it's done you can claim there was only one likely outcome. I think I'll wait and see, and not spend my lottery winnings before the numbers come up."

"OK – agreed. So, on to the subject of the Gorilla. I guess you have some ideas there."

"I do. And I have an idea who it might be. Pretty disgusting creature, I have to say. I worked with him on a drugs bust a few years ago. The whole team came under suspicion when the total quantity of goods bagged and logged was different from the amount eventually handed over to forensics. Everybody was clean, but I had my suspicions. He was a greasy customer from the start. If the Party was looking for a bent cop to start some sort of protection from prosecution racket, I certainly think his name would be in the frame. Naturally, being a big guy helps with the intimidation. However, between you and me, I think he's a snowflake. A little bit of pressure in the right place and he'll melt in front of our eyes."

David grabbed a handful of the cashew nuts Teresa had left out. "And how do you propose to apply that sort of pressure?"

"You told me Marie Vey was willing to play ball, didn't you?"

"Yes, she is. And she has even more reason to be fed up with him than we do."

"Well then, I think after our visit to our legal friend tomorrow, you and I should pay another visit to the wonderful Kiss Club. Some preparations might be in order."

"What sort of preparations?"

"For what I have in mind, let me just say that a drill, a dozen or so nice, hefty screws, some steel angle brackets and plenty of that thick silver cloth tape might come in handy. I'll have a look in Carl's shed in the morning, but otherwise we can pop into a *ferretería* on the way."

"I'm intrigued," David admitted.

"You should be. Oh, and we'll need a knife or scissors, and some candles, matches, handcuffs and rope. Though to be honest, a sex club's probably OK for that kind thing."

Chapter 17

La Sala del Siglo de Oro

Early the following morning, David, Gillian, Filipe and Alfredo went to the prosecutor's office. Filipe had made the appointment; however, his editor had insisted on adding his weight and had shown up, too. They went in with the Gold Star book, Gillian's audio recording and a briefcase full of money while the others waited nervously outside.

They didn't have to wait long.

"I think that's what we call a result," Filipe announced, coming out less than half an hour later and giving David a high five. "The longest part of the process was copying the book. Now Oscarito can pop it back tomorrow and nobody will be any the wiser until the sky starts falling on their heads later on. The prosecutor says he's going to take steps right away to get the warrants rescinded so you don't need to be outlaws any more."

David nodded thoughtfully and Gillian smiled.

"So," Filipe continued, "maybe a drink is called for."

Since the warrants were still operative and Alfredo had gone AWOL from his job, they decided to keep things a bit low-key and found a tiny bar on Calle de la Cruz, just up from Plaza de Canalejas near Sol.

"Feels nice to be legal again," Gillian commented over a *café cortado*. "Almost, at any rate. Should we stay on at Carl and Teresa's? I feel they've been more than hospitable. I don't want to impose on them any longer than we should."

"I suppose that depends on how long we need to stay in Spain,"

David responded. "If the prosecutor's taking things seriously and sees that this is all a put-up Party job we may need to come back to testify, but I guess we'll only be a few witnesses among many once the dam bursts. Maybe Carl won't mind if we stay a few days more."

Alfredo tapped a *chorro* on the side of his coffee cup to knock off some of the sugar in a meaningless gesture towards weight loss, then dipped it into his coffee, took a bite and sat back comfortably. "I hope you're right, David," he remarked casually. "Remember, though, that the book identifies sums received from supposed donors – but it's all coded. As far as I can see, the names are all taken from bird species. So, we have Raven, Eagle, Finch, Buzzard and so on – no Blackbird, though," he added wryly.

"So, that means we – or someone else – will have to find out who these names refer to before a serious investigation can make much more progress. I still want to have an appointment with a certain hairy primate to find out about his little racket and ask him about the book, but to be honest he may not know much and it's not a foregone conclusion that he'll tell us what he does know... though I have some persuasion techniques that might encourage him. I wouldn't pack your bags just yet."

Despite Alfredo's words of caution, Gillian felt a weight rising from her shoulders. She was looking forward to going back to Carl's more or less a free woman, maybe doing some fun things around Madrid to justify the trip, then getting solidly down to the new term's prep, which was becoming more and more urgent. Once she'd got her head around it, she'd found herself relating more and more to Esther and her dilemma. The question Esther had faced was whether to do the right thing and maybe put herself in significant danger, or take the easy way out and survive but see horrible consequences for others. Gillian had reread the story several times over the past few days and couldn't help but admire Esther's courage. Granted, she had done what she did under pretty heavy moral blackmail from her uncle, Mordecai, but given the stakes, he had probably also been left with very little choice.

Then there was the key phrase, which she had read and reread, looked up in other translations, read the commentaries on and pondered. From memory, her favourite translation put it something like this: "If you don't speak up now, help will come from somewhere else, but you and your family will die. And maybe you're here for just such a time as this."

The passage seemed to suggest that Mordecai was confident that injustice would not be permitted to triumph, but that Esther had a historic opportunity to make her mark. To play a part in history. To make something of her life instead of just being a royal ornament and a sexual plaything.

As a twenty-first-century woman, Gillian could entirely see the point. For Esther, it hadn't just been about saving her people – as if that weren't enough – it had also been the chance to become something more herself. To rise above the limitations of her role. To 'make a difference', as the popular phrase went. Ninety-nine per cent of the time, Gillian was entirely content and satisfied doing what she did. With a love for words and language, she saw her job as passing on that love and fascination, as well as helping students understand more about the origins of the language and learn a bit about study, research techniques, using evidence and constructing a solid argument. But sometimes, just sometimes, she found herself wondering what else she might have been. A campaigning lawyer, maybe. An activist for women's rights in some exploitative society. A financial regulator stopping unscrupulous rip-off companies fleecing the naive of their life savings.

Somehow, she had found herself in Spain doing almost all of these things. And now that the heat was easing off, it did feel satisfying to be playing a part. Maybe the Party would come tumbling down. Maybe senior officials who thought they were impregnable would end up on enforced vacation. Maybe public confidence in honesty and paying your taxes would be somewhat restored. And maybe some part of that might be traced back to her involvement and choices. But the process was changing her as well. The idea occurred that maybe doing her job, playing in a flute group, going to an aikido class and supporting her husband in his work might not be enough.

Then she remembered... they were about to become a family. For a moment she felt a slight feeling of disappointment, then recovered. Maybe this was the nudge she needed. A change of role and responsibility could lead to other changes, too. Who knew whether she hadn't come to this point in her life – through all the discomfort of what they had recently been through – not just to have an impact on the Spanish state, but also to have an impact on Dr Gillian Lockhart? And who knew what that might be?

She drained her coffee. "Come on then, folks," she announced. "Still lots to do today. Drinking coffee isn't going to get it done. What's next, everybody?"

"Back to the office for me," Filipe replied. "I've got to start drafting the sort of report we might put together if the prosecutor decides to take action. Lots of background to research. That's the downside. It's going to be a busy few days!"

"Back to Carl's for me," Alfredo put in. "I've got most of what I need, but there are a few things he might have in his shed that could be useful. The sort of things that make gorillas talkative. Then Marie Vey's, I guess."

Since Calle de la Cruz was midway between a number of metro stops, they ended up taking advantage of a slightly cooler day and walking up Calle de Alcalá to the famous Cibeles fountain, then up Recoletos to Metro Colón. That put them on the brown line directly to Metro Esperanza near Carl's residence. Gillian took it as a good sign that the name of his nearest metro station meant 'hope'. She hoped things were drawing to a conclusion and that there would be minimal drama before things could got back to normal – if she could remember what normal was.

It didn't work out that way.

Turning the corner into Carl's street, the road was blocked by a Guardia Civil van about fifty metres down. Right outside the Bishop's Palace. Beyond that were several other vehicles. Armed officers were standing in the street. Gillian just caught sight of her silver carry-on bag as it disappeared into the back of a van.

"Uh oh," Alfredo muttered. "About turn, everyone."

At that precise point the officer with the silver case looked straight up at Gillian. There was a moment, frozen in time, as they observed each other.

Then he shouted, "It's them!"

Alfredo grabbed Gillian's arm and took off.

David stood rooted to the spot, looking blankly at the officer, and Alfredo had to go back for him.

Gillian's aikido training finally proved its worth, and Alfredo had been forced to maintain a certain level of fitness for his work. The most exercise David ever got was lifting down a heavy commentary. Luckily, Alfredo had spent time in the Esperanza *barrio* and knew his way about. By the time the Guardia had reached the corner the trio had already disappeared into an alleyway. Alfredo led them through the back entrance to a fruit shop, past the bemused customers, out the front door and into a *centro commercial*.

Gillian and Alfredo ran, while David panted along behind like a boxer coming out for the fifteenth round. They cut left at the fish counter, then through a flower shop, out the in door and upstairs to hardware and a huge Chinese bazaar. Once again, in one door and out another. Finally, they came out on the upper level and dived into a bar where Alfredo knew the owner.

"Pepe! A private room, please," he puffed.

"Sure, Alfredo. You need to go easy on the ciggies and *cervesa*, you know!"

As they huddled together in the back of the bar, the sound of police sirens going up and down the street could be clearly heard. Any time they grew nearer, Gillian felt her pulse and breathing quicken. Then they heard a couple of officers interrogating the owner. Her gaze was riveted on the door, as if it might swing open at any moment. It almost felt as if she should walk out and give herself up, just to break the tension.

Then the moment passed. Voices receded. After ten minutes, with the sound of sirens growing fainter in the distance, they began to relax. David had his elbows on the table, his forearms flat and his head in his hands. He slowly raised his head. What hair he had left was plastered to his forehead. Beads of sweat were running down his cheeks and he looked the colour of a robust rosé wine.

"What I do for the good of Spain," he wheezed.

Gillian was the freshest of the three but didn't look happy. "I'm fed up of moving house," she moaned, "and I'm so sorry for Teresa and Carl. I wonder how they found us."

"We may discover that in due course," Alfredo puffed. "The main thing now is damage limitation. What have we lost that's important?"

"Clean underwear," Gillian said gloomily.

"A laptop," David added. "Clothing can be replaced. Not having internet could be a problem."

"And I had to leave my phone with the prosecutor as evidence," Gillian added, turning to her husband. "But you still have yours, don't you?"

"Yes, but remember it only gets calls and messages – nothing more. And I really don't think it's safe to use it. So we're a bit incommunicado."

"I tried to get him a new one, I really did," Gillian explained. "'Why do I need internet on my phone?' he wanted to know. OK, this might be one such occasion. But at least we've still got the Gold Star book. If we'd left that at Carl's the whole thing might be over by now. And the money's in the prosecutor's safe."

"So, things aren't as bad as they might have been," Alfredo summed up. "Maybe internet access would be useful, but I think the more pressing point is where we're going to sleep tonight.

"I have an idea," David managed to say, recovering his breath. "Just don't invite your relatives for a visit…"

* * *

Marie Vey raised her eyebrows. "Are you serious?" she asked.

David said nothing.

She shrugged. "Well, I suppose we do have plenty of bedrooms. I just hope you're not too sensitive to noises through the wall."

The trio had gone shopping for essentials once it seemed they were in the clear, and had then taken a taxi to the Kiss Club. Next David had texted Marta and Filipe, using Marie Vey's phone, to let them know what had happened. He also tried calling Carl, but to no avail. Finally, Alfredo had insisted on stopping off at a branch of the Leroy Merlin hardware chain, and had come out about twenty minutes later with a big brown bag, offering no information about what it contained.

Marie Vey showed them into the bedroom nearest her office. "I can only let you have one," she said. "We have a business to run here. There's a double bed and I can get you a spare mattress. There should be enough space if you push the bed over."

The room was decorated in black and red to match the house style. The sheets were black satin and the pillows a deep ruby red. The floor was tiled, and the only other furniture was a simple armless chair and bedside tables. A box of tissues lay on one table and a tube of lubricant on the other. Gillian decided she didn't want to investigate what was in the drawers. There was no proper chest of drawers or wardrobe, but that was fine since they didn't have anything to store or hang. The only other features of the room were an enormous mirror on the wall at the foot of the bed and a variety of spotlights on the ceiling. An en suite toilet and shower room were through the one other door.

"Simple and functional," Gillian commented to no one in particular.

"We don't do meals but there's a restaurant across the street and down a bit, and you can get drinks at the bar downstairs. I've told them to charge in-house prices. I'm afraid I'm busy just now, so I can only give you about ten minutes, but if you want to talk about Mr Gorilla I could meet you again in around two hours. David tells me we could help each other on this, and I'm willing to hear what you have in mind. So, that's it, I guess. As we say to all our guests, 'Welcome to the Kiss Club. Enjoy your stay and may all your dreams come true!'"

***

Marie Vey listened carefully as David quickly explained what they had in mind.

"We know numbers, but we only have code names for the contributors," he said. "The Gorilla collects money from you and we think it goes through what they call the Gold Star Donors book. There are accounts for all the illegal payments the Party gets, but it's coded. We don't know what the names mean or who they relate to, so it's going to be hard to question separate companies and individuals."

"Let me see."

Gillian took the book out of her bag and put it on the desk. Marie opened it and began looking through. It didn't take long.

"Here," she said. "This is us. Regular payments on the fifteenth of the month. I used to have a club called The Flamingo. That's the code name they've used. Except we pay €10,000 a month. Only €9,000 shows here. I bet that swine creams off €1,000 for himself. If you hope to persuade him to talk, I'd like to be in the room. And by the way, how do you hope to persuade him?"

At this point, Alfredo picked up his Leroy Merlin bag. "I'll need another room," he said. "Probably without a bed – or at least with plenty of space. And I'll need a couple of hours to set things up."

"That's no problem," Marie said. "We have a couple of storerooms you could use or there's another bedroom that's being renovated. Do you want to see it?" She led him out of the room.

"Perfect," Alfredo announced when he saw the room on offer. "This fits what we're going to be telling him perfectly. Now, I'll need a very strong wooden chair. And an extension cord."

"I think I can manage that," Marie confirmed. "We have one bedroom done out in what we call *Siglo de Oro* – Golden Age-style

– that might suit you even better. The punters get to pretend they're medieval knights and the girls are damsels in distress. There's a huge wooden chair in there that I got at a junk shop. I think it's actually authentic. Would that do?'

"Great, I'll take a look. Now, you said the Gorilla had agreed to come early this month. When do you expect him?"

"Tomorrow at twelve."

"Perfect. I'll get to work this evening, if you don't mind. I'll let you know when I'm done. The chair might not be good for anything else afterwards, though."

"OK. Just keep the noise to a minimum, would you? Customers don't come here to listen to DIY in the room next door."

Alfredo was shown into the *Siglo de Oro* room and pronounced himself happy. Marie went back to work in her office, and David and Gillian went downstairs. As usual, the main hall was in low light, suitable for a limbo twilight world, regardless of what time of day it was outside, and it took a few seconds for their eyes to adjust. A few girls were in the booths talking to their clients. The same guy was behind the bar and one girl sat on a barstool waiting for custom.

"Sandra," David said. "Hi. Nice to see you. Can I introduce my wife, Gillian?"

"Old friends or recent acquaintances?" Gillian commented dryly, giving the girl *dos besos*.

"David bought me a drink and we had a chat. Nothing more, I promise you," the girl said, smiling. "He was a gentleman – something I'm not able to say very often about the men I meet in this job. And by the way, David, I want to apologise about the question I asked about your wife. I suppose I just wanted to shock you, but it was rude and uncalled for."

David nodded. "Forget it," he said.

"What question?" Gillian asked.

"Tell you later," David said. "Not in Calle Montera today, Sandra?"

"We work week about," the girl explained without batting an

eyelid. "It's supposed to keep things fresh in case the punters want to come back for more, though to be honest they sometimes prefer someone familiar." She spoke in a totally matter-of-fact way, as if she were explaining checkout shifts at the Co-op.

"I can understand that," Gillian remarked. "Not that I'm speaking from experience."

Sandra laughed. "Don't worry," she said, "this isn't everybody's preferred career choice. It wasn't what I told my mum I wanted to be. And it's something I hope I won't be doing for very much longer. Though, to be honest, we all say that. You couldn't keep doing this if you weren't fooling yourself it was only temporary; just till something better comes up. Actually, David, I've been thinking a lot about some of the things you said. You know, about the girls who wanted to get out and that your church had a programme. A halfway house and stuff. Maybe that's what I need."

"Maybe," David agreed, "but it has to be what you want. It's not my job to show you the error of your ways or anything, but we can work together. Sometimes we just need the right thing at the right time. I've experienced that a few times. Then you can find you're pushing at an open door, and it's a good feeling. Anyway, I think we're going to head out for something to eat. It's been a busy day. I hope you have a quiet night. Stay safe."

Sandra smiled. "I will. The *Jardín de Baco* – Garden of Bacchus – down the street is quite good. Ask for the *arroz caldoso con bogavante*. It's their specialty."

* * *

"Well, well. You do have a wide social circle, my dear," Gillian remarked, taking David's arm as they walked through the car park. "I suppose you didn't meet in the metro."

"No. It was that day I went fishing in Calle Montera. We had a very interesting conversation."

"And how did you decide which girl to take for coffee?"

David thought for a second. "I partly left it to providence, I suppose. I had an idea of the sort of person I was looking for, though I couldn't really tell you why. Anyway, it worked out OK. For us and I hope for her, too."

"Sounds like you made her think."

"Maybe. At the very least, we've got to try to treat people as human beings, not operatives – whether it's a waiter or a sex worker. I believe they're all made in the image of God, however far they might have wandered. There have been times when I've wandered a bit myself. And I believe there's always a way back, *gracias a Dios*.

The *arroz caldoso* was superb. It was new to Gillian and looked a bit like a paella crossed with lobster bisque. David explained that it literally meant 'soupy rice' and that it was very popular in Galicia – where his grandparents had lived – and was a celebration dish.

"Well, let's hope that's not a premature thought," Gillian remarked, trying to winkle a bit more meat out of a delicately pink lobster claw.

The rest of the meal was taken largely in silence, each occupied with their own thoughts and trying to process all that had gone on that day. David was still feeling the effects of the unexpected exercise and Gillian was busy pondering what life must be like for a sex worker called Sandra.

* * *

When they got back, Alfredo was just standing up and wiping his hands. He seemed satisfied. The aim of the *Siglo de Oro* room was to recreate the world of Don Quixote or Lope de Vega – or perhaps to be more accurate, a *bordello* from their era. The wooden floor was dark wood, as were the doors, skirtings and all the furniture. The walls were an attempt at sixteenth-century rough, plain-white plaster. A massive display unit for plates and glasses, with drawers for cutlery and linen, stood against one wall. Dark portraits in heavy gilt frames decorated the others. The bed was a huge four-poster with heavy damask drapes. A small, rustic, dark-wood occasional table was under the one well-shaded window, with rickety chairs on either side. A metal flagon stood on it, next to a couple of bronze goblets on a pewter tray. Two heavy iron chains hung around the walls, like strings for some sort of diabolical Christmas card. The only concession to modernity was an en suite shower room, which was more or less in a modern style.

In the middle of the floor, at the foot of the bed, stood the upright wooden chair Marie Vey had provided. Alfredo had made some modifications over the past few hours.

"That looks like an instrument of torture," Gillian commented, looking at the result.

"Exactly, and in keeping with the era. I call it the hot seat. I think our furry friend might find it strangely appropriate. Would you like the tour? These 5mm angle brackets are bolted to the legs and screwed to the floor. Anyone sitting here isn't going to take up their chair and walk. Then there are handcuffs attached to the arms. Pretty obvious what they're for, I suppose. And something similar for the ankles. Finally, a leather band that goes around the chest to keep the subject firmly against the back of the chair."

"OK," remarked David. "So, the Gorilla isn't going anywhere. I still don't see how that translates into getting him to tell us what he knows."

"Ah, well, that's because I haven't described the main feature yet," Alfredo went on, with obvious pride in his craftsmanship. At this point he lifted the cushion resting on the seat of the chair. "Under here is the major modification. The wooden base has been replaced by a steel plate. And underneath the plate, on the underside of the chair, is a tray a few inches lower down."

Gillian crouched down to have a look, then glanced up in shock. "I'm not sure I really want to have anything to do with this," she said. "Is that where the candles go?"

Chapter 18

The Seat of Learning

By dint of some clever negotiation, Gillian persuaded Marie Vey to let them use two rooms overnight, which suited everyone much better. Alfredo confessed to being a notorious snorer and Gillian thought the idea of sleeping in the *Siglo de Oro* room was quite cool. On the other hand, she wasn't comfortable with the thought of what might take place there in a few hours.

"How do you feel about all of this?" she asked David, sitting up in bed.

"About what?"

"The hot seat. I presume what's going to happen is that the steel plate gets hotter and hotter with the Gorilla sitting on it, till he has to tell what he knows or gets third-degree burns. Are you OK with that?"

David shook his head. "No, I'm not," he said, "but I'm also not OK with the cash he comes here to collect once a month, or with what Marie Vey tells me he makes the girls do as part of his personal pay-off, or with the blatant lying and distortion of the rule of law that underlies the whole thing."

"So, it's OK to break the law – I suppose we're talking about common assault here – it's OK to do that to prevent more serious law-breaking in future?"

David shifted around and pulled his pillows up a bit further. "This is all getting a bit philosophical, but I get your point. How far can we take the law into our own hands to stop something worse happening? I've debated that with students, but I must admit it's never been at such close proximity. The question is: is it OK to roast a corrupt policeman's backside in the interests of democracy?"

Gillian couldn't stifle a laugh. "Now you put it that way, it doesn't seem quite so serious. I suppose if I saw this in a movie I would be cheering."

"And you've got to remember that standards of what is acceptable punishment have varied hugely over the centuries. When I was at school, we still had the belt. I remember getting three for being repeatedly late for music and not singing songs from *The Gondoliers* with sufficient gusto. It was a leather belt, but when they hit you it felt like a plank of wood had come down on your palm and the mark would last for days. But that was thought to be entirely OK at the time. I can even remember when it was banned and everybody – kids and teachers, alike – thought that would usher in an era of chaos in schools, with kids doing whatever they pleased and teachers completely unable to maintain order. But somehow we survived. So, I understand the ethical problem entirely. But actually, I'm not that inclined to step in and insist we give him a cup of cocoa and ask nicely if he'd like to tell us anything. On the other hand, I also don't want to be there while it's happening. You can call me a hypocrite if you like."

"There are lots of things I could call you," Gillian said, snuggling down, "but that's not the first that comes to mind. Only one more question, then, and I promise to shut up."

"Fire away."

"Have you ever had sex in a brothel?"

David had been sipping the small nightcap whisky kindly provided by the bar downstairs. He spat a mouthful all over the richly embroidered – maybe even antique – quilt. "*Whaaaatttt?!*"

"No, sorry. Follow-up question. Would you like to?'

David looked at her in astonishment. "Butter wouldn't melt" was the expression that came to mind. "You are incorrigible!" he said in despair.

* * *

The man they called the Gorilla rolled up in a black 4x4 at eleven o'clock the following morning. No imagination was needed to see where the nickname came from. He struggled out of the driver's seat, already puffing, and waddled across the car park, belly out ahead like a billowing sail. He didn't obsess about his weight, reasoning there were always others much worse off. There certainly were others worse off, but whether they were *much* worse off was questionable. Still, there were some women who liked a big man, he had found. And he certainly liked big women. Though as far as that was concerned, he also liked middle-sized women and even skinny girls. With a bit of luck, there might be a skinny girl on the menu today, and he was looking forward to it. But fair's fair. He always knocked a bit off the bill if there were any payments in kind. The fact that the bill was considerably higher than the one he'd been delegated to collect, and that the extra went straight into his pocket, was beside the point. He was giving up some of his cash for the pleasure of some company. And that was what the Kiss Club was in business for, anyway, so what was the problem?

He started softly whistling the tune to "Guantanamera" – the classic hymn in praise of the Cuban girls of Guantánamo. What a pity the town had become famous for something other than lovely, sexy girls with skin the colour of coffee and flowers in their hair. They sometimes had Cuban girls in the Kiss Club, and he always made a point of asking for them as his first choice. What would he get today? He could hardly wait.

He waddled in the front door, nodding in a friendly way at the guy behind the glass, then went straight on through to the bar. There wasn't much going on pre-lunch, but that was fine. The fewer punters hanging about the better. There was always a chance someone might recognise him from police business, even though he wasn't in uniform, and that might lead to unnecessary explanations.

He greeted the barman happily and ordered a double whisky. "Is Marie Vey in?

"Yes, just go right up."

He downed the whisky in a oner, shook his head – making his cheeks flap like the jowls of an overweight pug – recovered his composure and headed for the stairs.

"Well, Marie. Good morning," he said, breezing straight into her office. "What a beautiful day. Do you think the worst of the heat is over? What have you got for me today?"

Marie Vey eyed him cautiously, said nothing and pulled open a desk drawer. She took out a large, sealed envelope and laid it on the desk. "Half the normal," she said, "since we're going to be seeing you twice a month."

"Lovely," he said, still beaming. "I hope you appreciate my flexibility and the fact that I'm not charging you double for travelling expenses." He laughed at his own joke. "You can leave it in the desk for now if you want. I've got a few hours free and I wouldn't want the cash to go missing in the company of a young lady. So, what can you do for me today? Any of the lovely *cubanas* free?"

Marie Vey shook her head. "I'm sorry, we're all out of Cubans. Sandra's free, though, if that would be acceptable."

The Gorilla grinned. Sandra was quite a special girl, and hers was often the face that came to mind when he was thinking about his next visit to the club. In fact, visiting twice a month suited him down to the ground. Double the action, double the fun.

"Sandra would be very acceptable," he smiled. "An hour?"

"OK, an hour," Marie confirmed. "We've been putting some special new facilities together. Maybe you and Sandra can try them out."

The Gorilla licked his lips. "Wonderful," he enthused. "Sounds intriguing. Show me the business."

Marie got up, forcing herself to keep perfectly calm and casual, and led the Gorilla along the corridor. They stopped at a door with an antique finish, featuring a fake gold handle and lettering.

"*La Sala del Siglo de Oro*," the Gorilla read slowly. "Sounds exciting. So I can be Don Quixote and Sandra can be Dulcinea? I hope you have the costumes. And make sure Sancho Panza doesn't

The Root of all Evil

stick his nose in where it's not wanted!" The Gorilla clearly thought himself very witty, chortling to himself as Marie Vey pushed open the door. He stepped through into the relative gloom of the *sala* and looked around. "Wow. You've really gone to town here, haven't you?" he enthused, taking it all in.

"We certainly hope so," Marie Vey replied, entirely truthfully. "Go on in while I get Sandra."

By the time the two women returned, the Gorilla was already sitting in the chair.

"This is great," he beamed. "It feels really authentic. I mean, the whole room. So, how does it work?"

Sandra stepped forward, smiling, and explained, "It's really quite easy. We've been thinking of adding some additional options to what we can offer at Kiss Club for a while, but we thought it would be kinda cool to do it with a Spanish flavour."

"Fantastic! Like the Spanish Inquisition comes to town. What fun!"

"Exactly. So, if I can just show you…"

"Sure, go ahead." The Gorilla was already rolling up his sleeves and holding out his arms.

"The handcuffs on the arms snap on just like this," Sandra said. "Then there are others for the ankles down here. I don't know if you noticed, but the chair itself is fixed to the floor, so no amount of struggling is going to move it."

"Cool!" the Gorilla enthused, already beginning to imagine a helpless body struggling and getting nowhere.

"And the final bit is this leather strap." Sandra held her breath and reached under two sweaty armpits to pull a thick, dark strap across the Gorilla's chest and click it into the hook on the opposite side. "So, there you are. Think you can get out of that?"

The Gorilla laughed with anticipation. "No way!" he said. "This is fantastic. I love it. Whoever's in the chair is completely at the mercy of whoever put them there."

"Exactly," said a new voice as the shower room opened and a

figure emerged. "You've got it in one, Rodrigo. How are you, by the way? Sitting comfortably, I presume?"

The Gorilla opened his mouth, which was about the only part of his body he still had complete control over, but no sound came out. "Alfredo?" he finally managed weakly.

"Ah, so you do remember me. How gratifying. It's been quite a while, and I wasn't sure if we'd reconnect. We worked nights together in San Blas, as far as I remember it. Didn't I have to turn you in for taking a cut in exchange for leaving the dealers alone? Yes, I'm sure that was how it went. And you got busted back to basics and had to work your way up again. But it seems you must have got a taste for it then, because you kept coming back for more. Though as far as I understand it, you're not only working for yourself this time."

Alfredo kept talking as he walked round in front of the chair to face the Gorilla. "Creaming protection money from a club would be something you'd need a bit of help with, wouldn't it? I mean, they could just complain and you'd be back on nights in San Blas. So you'd have to have someone higher up who'd set the whole thing up and was protecting you, and taking the majority of risk and the majority of income. So you're really more like an errand boy, aren't you? Not actually an entrepreneur of crime; just sort of a middleman. Or maybe more of a bottom feeder. Yes. I think that would be a better description, wouldn't it?"

As he spoke, Alfredo had been moving closer to the Gorilla's chair. The Gorilla had been turning his head to follow the speaker and was trying his hardest to get to grips with what he was hearing. What on earth was Alfredo doing here? Was he not supposed to have been on the run, having spirited off the very suspects Mateo, Marcos and Lucas were looking for? What was he doing here and what on earth was he talking about? This was hard work for a brain not used to deductive thinking.

When Alfredo got to calling him a bottom feeder, he knew that wasn't a compliment. He let out a roar and tried to lunge forward. His head and shoulders obeyed, but his chest and enormous belly were stuck. He tried to throw a punch but found his arms were immobile. He tried a kick but only succeeded in scraping the skin off his ankle. He let out another yell and started shaking his enormous frame from side to side, then back and forth. The wood of the chair groaned, and the joints flexed but held. The legs of the chair didn't even lift. It was an impressive performance but totally futile, and the Gorilla soon realised it.

He put his head back, panting. "Let me go," he gasped. "Let me go. You've no right. They'll come after you. I can help you... they'll listen to me. I can make it easier. I won't mention anything about this, I promise. Let me go. I've got a phone in my pocket. Just let me have it and I'll make a few calls."

"Let you have it?" Sandra repeated thoughtfully. "Let you have it? Sure, I'll let you have it. Like you've been letting me have it." She smacked him across the side of the face with every atom of energy she could muster.

His head snapped round. His expression wasn't so much one of pain as of total surprise. It was so long since someone had dared to raise a hand in their own defence that he couldn't quite believe it. He looked at her uncomprehendingly, then let out another roar and began to struggle and thrash about again, to the extent that Alfredo started looking a little nervously at the brackets holding the chair to the floor, and Marie Vey began to wonder if she needed a bit of additional muscle on hand.

But this second storm blew itself out like the one before. A few minutes later the Gorilla was puffing harder than ever and sweating from every pore. His shirt, which had once been light blue, was now almost entirely dark. His face was streaming and his hair was plastered to his forehead. Alfredo tried not to think about what might be happening elsewhere about his person.

"So," Alfredo said, "are we ready to play? That's what you were expecting, wasn't it? A bit of fun with Sandra, maybe, except I think the idea was that she was going to be in the hot seat, and you'd be having all the fun. Sorry it hasn't worked out like that. However, fun *is* still the name of the game."

The Gorilla's head had slumped onto his chest. "Water," he said. "Can I have a drink of water?"

"And the magic word?" Marie Vey asked.

"Please. Please can I have some water?"

Marie nodded to Sandra, who went into the shower room and came back with a plastic tumbler. She raised it to his lips, only to have him lunge forward again and try to bite her hand.

She jumped back, then dashed the water over his face. "Drink that!" she shouted. "You filthy swine!"

"Tut tut," Alfredo remonstrated. "That is not gentlemanly conduct, Rodrigo. Primitive, we might say. Though maybe that's all we should expect from you, being a primate and all. Remember, you're supposed to be a gentleman from the Golden Age. If you can behave as a gentleman should, we can be nice. Or not. It depends on you."

"What do you want?" the Gorilla finally asked, desperately trying to wipe the sweat off his face onto his shoulder.

"Answers," Alfredo replied. "Details. Names and numbers. Causes and effects. You are certainly not the sharpest knife in the box, but I want to know everything you know. I want to know anything I happen to be curious about. Is that clear enough?"

The Gorilla raised his head and looked at Alfredo with the first sign of understanding slowly dawning. "Go to hell!"

"Ah, well – which of us is going to hell isn't actually on the agenda this morning. While the *Sala del Siglo de Oro* may not be hell, it's not going to be the earthly paradise, either. And it might get quite warm. So, let's get down to brass tacks."

Alfredo further confused the prisoner by reaching in between his legs, grabbing something and yanking. Thankfully, it wasn't what the Gorilla initially feared it might be. Alfredo pulled out the cushion and threw it across the room. What was the point of that? the Gorilla wondered. The surface he was now sitting on was hard and cold. What was it? Marble? Metal?

"So, as I was saying," Alfredo continued, "brass tacks. This is a game called 'Who Wants to be a Real Man?' Real men take responsibility, you know. They take responsibility and they keep their dignity intact. And everything else."

Alfredo went over to the huge dark-wood unit and pulled open a drawer. He lifted out something about the size of a shoebox, along with a small lighter. He laid the box on the bed and opened the lid. He took out a small tea light candle and placed it on his open palm.

"My mission today, Rodrigo – or Mr Gorilla, whichever you prefer – is to bring light to dark places. Illumination, if you will, in place of ignorance. And I do confess to a degree of ignorance. For example, I'd like to know the identity of all the code names in the Gold Star Donors book."

This immediately got the Gorilla's attention. "What do you know about that?" he barked.

Alfredo turned back to the unit and lifted a book out of the still open drawer. He held it in front of the Gorillas's face. "Lots," he said. "Lots and lots. But not everything. So, you can help me by filling in the blanks. Then I want to know where the money went after it came in from those we call the Gold Star Donors. Who got what? When and how? And who authorised the payments? Was the Prime Minister included or just deputies? Was the Party chair aware of what was going on or just the Minister for Justice and the Party treasurer? You get the idea, Rodrigo. I'm a curious man and I know you can help me."

The Gorilla shook his head. "I don't know anything," he muttered. "I went to meetings, but I didn't really follow what they were saying. I just did what I was told. That's all I know."

Alfredo sucked his teeth. "I'd love to believe you," he said, "I really would. But I don't."

"Why not? It's the truth."

"Because you're a lying skunk," Sandra put in with feeling. "As well as being a filthy animal."

"And a greedy pig," Maria Vey added.

"So, here's how the game works," Alfredo went on in the most matter-of-fact of tones. "Every time you tell me you don't know something and I remain unconvinced, we light a candle in the name of truth and justice to roll back the darkness of ignorance. Like I didn't believe you at all just now." He took the candle he still had in his hand, sparked the lighter and lit it. "And we send the candle to where it can do the greatest good. That's to say, to the place of greatest darkness. Where the sun doesn't shine. Namely, under your enormous backside."

He leaned forward and slipped the candle onto the tray beneath the metal plate that formed the seat of the chair, while the Gorilla twisted round, craning his neck to see what was going on.

"So, every time you tell me something I don't believe, we add a candle. I suppose we could get twenty or thirty in there, no problem. And every time you tell me something I do believe, we remove a candle – in honour of pushing back the boundaries of darkness and ignorance, and to show our appreciation for your openness and honesty. Of course, once the hot seat is good and warm, taking one candle out isn't going to make much difference very quickly. So, it's a good idea to think not only about the flame of truth at that moment, but how it might be shining in a few minutes' time or longer. Get the idea?"

"And what if I don't know?" the Gorilla said with a new note of pleading in his voice.

"Like I said, you have to convince me. It's that simple. Since we haven't been communicating very well up to now, I think we need to make a good start. I don't want to be here all day. Do you think six would be enough?"

"They'll kill me if I talk," the Gorilla moaned, tears suddenly forming.

"Ah, yes. The perennial witness dilemma," Alfredo replied without a trace of sympathy. "They might kill you if you do and I might kill you if you don't. Or, at the very least, you're going to be lightly toasted and probably not a real man any more. Though I doubt any of the girls here will shed a tear over that."

Chapter 19

Home Fires Burning

By mutual agreement, David and Gillian stayed out of the *Sala del Siglo de Oro*. They didn't want to be present, and Alfredo didn't want them there either. Instead, they sat downstairs among the few comings and goings around the booths and the bar. The punters mainly treated them as if they were invisible.

David thought he might have recognised one or two, but on reflection hoped he hadn't and tried not to give anyone too close an inspection. Gillian, on the other hand, was fascinated – horrified, but also fascinated – trying to tell from their appearances what sort of men would pay for sex in the middle of a weekday afternoon. Most were in jeans and T-shirts, but there were others who looked more like bank managers or lawyers: well dressed and moneyed. These were the most clearly embarrassed of all. They came in, glancing nervously around, and tried to pick a booth as far from anyone else as possible. They usually settled for the first girl who approached them and didn't bother troubling the bar with numbers. The girl would get the drinks so the guy didn't have to budge until it was time to move on to other things.

Alfredo spent so long 'interviewing' the Gorilla that some of the guys they had seen come in also went out, not looking appreciably happier or more relaxed. The cash transactions having already taken place, they made a beeline for the door without making eye contact with anyone.

This was in marked contrast to the working-guy types, who generally greeted the barman, chatted with a few of the girls, selected the one of their choice, had a few drinks and a laugh, then headed upstairs, hand in hand. When they re-emerged, they were likewise full of fun, joking with the girls and the barman. One guy actually winked at Gillian, which made her blush to the roots of her hair.

From time to time, Sandra would trip lightly down the stairs to give them an update. It wasn't long before they had their first name. Then ten names. Then fifteen. Eventually, the Gorilla was desperate to tell them everything they wanted to know and even some they didn't.

The picture emerging was of a vessel rotten from top to bottom. The rot had set in during the previous term of office and solidified while money was tight during the opposition phase. Now they were back in power, the idea was simply to start up again where they had left off. It looked like most of the bigger construction firms, about half of the city's prostitution and illegal gambling circles, and a few of the drugs rings were in on it. That didn't count wealthy individuals paying for access to departments and ministers, or lobbying firms willing to pay for information and influence. Finally, at three o'clock, the club doors closed so that the girls and other staff could nip out for a bite. Neither David nor Gillian felt very hungry.

"Do you think a career in the police makes people indifferent to violence?' Gillian asked as they sipped their coffee and nibbled some crisps.

"I don't see how it couldn't," David replied. "You're certainly a witness to violence, and I suppose the subject of it sometimes. And using a legitimate degree of force to get someone to 'accompany you to the station' must be par for the course."

"And violence to get suspects to tell you what they know?"

"I know. I'm not comfortable with it, either, but to be honest I can't think of any other way forward. Can you?"

Gillian shook her head. "I've thought this through a hundred times – whether there might have been another way. Some other sort of softer threat. But everything I've heard about these guys tells me that what 'normal' people might respond to just doesn't apply. I guess I'm guilty of thinking that other people – even the bad guys –

think and feel more or less the way I do, but I suppose that simply isn't true. I guess there are times when you have to hold your nose and do what needs to be done. I just hope we find out what we need to know before we have to call an ambulance. I imagine by now they're having to literally hold their noses upstairs. And what about us? We were quite a merry band for a while and now we're down to three. Who's going to be next to drop off the radar?"

David shook his head. "I've no idea."

"First it was Mariano, then we lost Carl and Teresa, and maybe Marta and Oscarito if they were there at the time, and Filipe's off doing what he does. So now we don't dare to risk using mobiles to call anyone or find out where they are. It does make you feel a bit isolated. And now our best friends are a madam, a prostitute and a policeman with an inventive imagination for torture. This isn't going to look good in your annual report, you know."

This made David smile and relax very slightly.

At that moment, the door to the upstairs balcony opened and Alfredo appeared, looking weary. He joined them and sat down, wiping his brow.

"Can we ask how things are going?" Gillian asked tentatively.

Alfredo scratched his head and groaned. "That man might just be the biggest scumbag I've ever come across," he said. "I know it's maybe unrealistic, but I still try to expect better from serving police officers. We sometimes say, 'If walls could speak.' Well, I've been listening to a lump of lard speak for the last three hours and it does wear you down. It comes out drip by drip, and you have to try to separate out the truth from what he thinks might be enough to satisfy the interrogator and take the heat off. Literally, in his case. I've probably been party to a thousand interrogations. This one will go down in the annals as the slipperiest and most unpleasant."

"You mean because of the methods you had to use?" David asked.

"No, that was nothing. More bluff than anything else. If he'd steadfastly refused to say a word, we could hardly have left his backside like well-done crackling. We merely warmed up the seat a bit when he showed any reluctance. I mostly just lit a few more candles then laid them on the floor. He'll have a suntan where the sun doesn't normally shine for a few days – nothing more. But it was enough that he was worried about a burned bum and toasted testi—"

"I think we can fill in all the alliterations!" Gillian interrupted him.

"Yes, well. Anyway, it was ninety per cent threat and only ten per cent discomfort, I can assure you. And to be honest, that's the case with almost all good interrogations. Violence takes us down to the same level as them. That's something you always have to watch out for."

"So, what's the situation now?" David asked. "What's happening?"

"Well, if you can believe it, we're applying a bit of first aid. I'm pretty sure we've exhausted all he knows, and we were in danger of slipping over into him inventing stuff simply to give an answer to protect his nether regions. That doesn't help anyone. So, we got him out of the chair and handcuffed him the other way about; kneeling, facing the seat. I left Sandra spraying aftersun onto his ample backside. If she decides to follow that up with the odd kick to a delicate part, I wouldn't blame her. But to be honest, I think she just feels sorry for him now. He's a pathetic creature."

"And the next steps?" David continued.

"We tell it to the judge, along with documentary evidence that matches what we've found out here. I think we've actually got that with the donors' book and the file that was in the case. Anyway, I don't think we need to let fears about the use of mobiles stop us dead. We can use the fixed line here reasonably safely, I think. I was too busy frightening the living daylights out of the Gorilla to be able to write everything down, but Marie Vey produced a recorder, so it's all on tape. I think we should go out for a late lunch, then try to gather the team together this evening and get ready to move in the for the kill."

"And the Gorilla?" Gillian asked. "What happens to him?"

"Oh, he stays here, for two reasons," Alfredo replied. "First, we don't want him running back to Mummy and telling them all to leave town. But second, I think he knows he's probably safer here after all the beans he's spilled. Besides, walking, driving and even standing up might be a bit delicate for some time to come!"

* * *

Ibañez looked at his watch, making no attempt to hide his impatience. "Everyone was supposed to be here by nine," he grumbled. "Where on earth is he?"

Gonzaléz lifted his phone, tapped and swiped. "According to this, he hasn't looked at his phone since eleven thirty this morning," he said. "That's not a good sign."

"Where was he supposed to be at eleven thirty?" the ex-minister asked.

"I don't know exactly, but he was supposed to be doing the rounds of the clubs this week," Ibañez explained. "He could have been visiting any of a dozen, or maybe he just lost his phone. He's such an idiot, anything's possible."

"OK, gentlemen," the ex-minister advised, clearing his throat, "let's press on, anyway. There's lots to talk about and, frankly, I think we can live without Juan's contributions. So, how would we describe the present situation? I think we've seen a number of encouraging developments."

"Well, yes and no," Gonzaléz reluctantly agreed. "Yes, in that we've hounded them out of another bolt hole. The former bishop and his 'housekeeper' are, I believe, helping the police with their inquiries. He won't be getting his church pension much longer, at the very least, since it turns out he's actually been married for over thirty years. There might even be an argument for clawing back everything he's been paid during that time – as well as benefits in kind, like accommodation and transport costs. He hasn't been fulfilling the most basic obligations of celibacy, so he hasn't been a legitimately qualified priest. Which means he should not have been receiving the salary of a priest. I think he comes from an evangelical background, doesn't he? Well, he can go right back there as far as

I'm concerned. I've had some discussions about that already. So that's a positive.

"On the other hand, we didn't manage to pick up the main quarry in the raid. That means Hidalgo and company are still at large. However, there are fewer and fewer places for them to run to. It's surely only a matter of time now.

"As far as the Gold Star book is concerned, I have no idea what must have been going through Oscarito's mind when he decided to make off with something as important as that. We know he's little better than an adding machine, so I suppose he thought that taking the book might add up to blackmail, or perhaps he intended to sell it to someone with more brains than he has. It's inexplicable. Anyway, there's a warrant out for him as well. That shouldn't take long. Then we can throw the book at him!"

"The Gold Star book, I suppose," Ibañez added dryly.

González ignored the comment. "The only danger I can realistically foresee is if Oscarito were to be in touch with Hidalgo. Thankfully, there isn't any chance with that. They don't know each other and they have no connections. And don't forget, there are loyal Party members all over the city and in every part of the legal system. I've got my sources. If it genuinely looks like things are getting serious, I'll know it before the shit hits the fan. Then steps can be taken."

"And what about the press?' Ibañez asked. "Was there not something about that last time?"

"Nothing to worry about there, as far as I know," the ex-minister put in. "There was some reporter snooping around a while ago, but that seems to have died down. I think we can be pretty confident that none of our wonderful donors are going to be declaring their Party contributions any time soon. And the names in the Gold Star book are all encoded, so neither Oscarito nor anyone else will have any idea who the names connect to in the real world."

"So, summing up, then," Gonzales said, "the bishop and his wife have been thrown into outer darkness, it's only a matter of time before we get Hidalgo and his futile little band of fugitives, the current pastor of his church is already under lock and key for conspiracy to defraud the government, the press are toothless, Oscarito is hawking a document that'll be meaningless to anyone outside this room, and a policeman who decided to take pity on some criminals in his custody has just said goodbye to his career and his pension. That all being the case, I don't think there's too much to worry about. It's surely just a matter of time. In fact, the main thing that's bothering me right now is why my bin hasn't been emptied and my desk given a good clean!"

"That's remarkably sanguine of you," Ibañez commented dryly.

"Well, whatever he's done, I'm still sure Oscarito doesn't have the imagination to do what we're all worried about. Relax! Remember – he's a robot."

"Hmm." Ibañez was unconvinced. "Well, it turns out he had the imagination to invent a sister I've discovered he doesn't have. I'm hoping that's as far as his gift for creativity goes!"

* * *

"Are you saying it's just a matter of time, then?" David Hidalgo asked.

"Well," came the answer. "Like in the UK and the US, we maintain a presumption of innocence until proven guilty, but the wheels of justice probably turn even more slowly here than in your country. However, I wouldn't disagree with your assessment. The amount of evidence you've managed to accumulate is really impressive, and when we put it together with what we already know – or have suspected for a long time – it gives us a very strong case."

The company around the table was probably the oddest combination ever to have got together at one time in the Kiss Club – bearing in mind that people from all strata of society paid occasional visits there. Since it was Maria Victoria's establishment, she seated herself at the head of the table. David Hidalgo and Gillian Lockhart sat opposite her at the far end. Using Marie Vey's fixed-line telephone, they had managed to contact Oscarito, Marta and Filipe, who were all sitting on one side. Oscarito and Marta had been out shopping when the raid took place, and Felipe had been in communication with the prosecutor all along. Alfredo and Sandra had places on the other side, along with a youngish man in an impeccable suit and tie, an impeccable haircut, impeccable fingernails and impeccable €1,500 designer glasses. Finally, a dishevelled, hugely obese figure in handcuffs sat on a bench against the wall looking miserable – and very uncomfortable.

"Understood," Gillian put in. "I think it's the same all over the world. But would you mind just explaining the process, Señor Byass? If you don't mind."

"Of course, no problem," the impeccable Byass replied. "In Spain we have what is called an 'inquisitorial system' rather than the adversarial system you have in the UK. That means the examining or investigating prosecutor has the role of investigating any crime that might have been carried out in their jurisdiction – unless the matter has to go to a higher court. The investigating magistrate appoints a prosecutor, of which I am one. So, I carry out an investigation – aided by resources from the various branches of the police service – and then present the evidence, in written form, to a court. That's fine, as far as officials of a political party or indeed ex-ministers are concerned. The problem might be if this reaches right up to serving ministers – even perhaps including the Prime Minister. In that case I can go no further, and the matter has to be decided by a court specially convened for the purpose.

"As Filipe has maybe told you, we've had an interest in investigating political corruption for years, but this is undoubtedly the biggest breakthrough we've ever seen. The cash, the voice recordings, the trumped-up charges, the misuse of police resources, the general harassment you've been suffering, the evident racketeering" – here he looked very briefly in the Gorilla's direction – "and the bribes and pay-offs connected with government contracts, as well as identity fraud concerning many of the smaller donors. All of that clearly amounts to the most egregious public misbehaviour you can imagine. It's exactly what everyone is Spain thinks goes on, but it's been very difficult until now to actually prove anything against the big players. I have to say that if we're able to pull this off, the whole nation of Spain will owe you all a very significant debt of gratitude."

"What happens now?" Gillian asked. "Are we still going to be picked up by the nearest overenthusiastic cop we lay eyes on?"

The prosecutor shook his head. "No, I don't think so. All warrants were cancelled this afternoon, as soon as Filipe let me know about the... erm... 'confession' obtained from your 'suspect'. The bishop and his, erm... 'housekeeper' have been released, as has your colleague, the pastor. The first charges being prepared are in connection with the attempted murder of the pastor's wife. Then the heavier work will begin. We'll have to pull in all the names mentioned in the Gold Star Donors book and look at paper trails for the cash they gifted to the Party. Besides that, we'll be checking out the names obtained via identity theft and other means. To be honest, the Gold Star book will go down in the history of Spanish investigation."

"And then there are the Mateo, Marcos, Lucas and Juan records we found in the case," Gillian added. "Any thoughts on that?"

"Well," Byass paused, choosing his words carefully, "I believe we have a confession – or maybe it's an allegation – from one of the gang. Our friend 'Juan' has already agreed to turn state's evidence in exchange for some leniency. That'll make it very difficult for the remaining three, whom we believe to be the Party's office manager, the Party treasurer and the ex-Minister for Justice."

"I hope they're not going to be allowed to make a run for it," Gillian commented.

"I certainly hope not," Byass reassured her. "Warrants are being prepared right now. I don't see any reason why they wouldn't be picked up as a matter of course."

***

González and Ibañez had just stood up to go when the ex-minister's mobile went off. He pulled it out, looked quizzically at the screen, then tapped to take the call.

"Yes?" he said, listening without giving anything away. "OK," he said finally. "Thanks for letting me know. That's very helpful."

"Anything?" Ibañez asked.

"No, nothing of any significance," the ex-minister replied nonchalantly. "My car needs to go in for some work. They think it's going to cost more than was expected."

"I hope it doesn't break down on the way home," González joked. "Or are you off on other business?"

"No," the ex-minister said with a smile. "That's it for tonight. Back home to the *Señora* and a cup of hot chocolate, I suppose. However, I may need to go over some papers tomorrow. Do you mind if I just gather up a few things? I'll lock up when I'm done."

Ibañez and González would have been surprised by the ex-minister's behaviour over the next hour had they stayed behind a little longer. As soon as everyone else had left, he went into the little storeroom where the cleaning materials were kept, quickly found a roll of heavy-duty refuse sacks and peeled off two. Then he went back into Ibañez's office, pulled open the filing cabinet and started pulling out folder after folder and dumping them into the bags. Once they were full, he dragged them into the general office and emptied them out in the middle of the floor.

Next, he went back into the storeroom and hunted right at the back. He knew exactly what he was looking for and soon found it. Next to a rusty old barbecue unit stood two full sacks of charcoal, a large plastic bottle of lighter fluid and an unopened packet of firelighters. These he carried back into the general office. With a sharp knife, he sliced open the bags of charcoal and dumped them next to the pile of papers. Then the firelighters went on top and the whole pile was soaked with lighter fluid. Finally, he took a lighter out of his pocket and was just about to spark it when he suddenly thought better of it and paused, setting the lighter down on Oscarito's desk.

Instead, he went back into Ibañez's office and opened the safe. He placed his attaché case on the desk, took everything out and started calmly and systematically filling it with cash from the safe. When no more would go in, he shoved the remainder into his jacket pockets. All other documents from the safe he carried through to the main office and dumped them onto the pile.

Then he picked up a desk phone, pressed for an outside line and dialled a number. "Hello? Emergency services? Yes, fire brigade please. Hello? Yes, I'm a resident in Vicálvaro. I've just noticed smoke coming from a factory at the end of our street. Calle Las Santeras, 47 2/A. Yes, I think it's actually a paper factory, but it's right next to a residence for older people. And there's a lot of public housing round about. Lots of kids, you know. Of course, it may be nothing, but it looks quite serious. In fact... in fact... yes... I can definitely see flames now. Wow! There was just a huge explosion. I think this is going to be a big one. Definitely. Everything you've got, I suppose. I'll start going round the neighbours and evacuating. Absolutely! Police, too. And some ambulances as well. Of course, no problem at all. Glad to help. It's what any public-minded citizen would do. I hope you can get there in time. My name? Ibañez. Victor Ibañez. Have you got that? Excellent. And thank you for all your wonderful work."

The ex-minister put the phone down with a smile of satisfaction and turned to the pile of papers on the floor. "Goodbye, cruel world," he muttered and sparked his lighter, starting a tiny flame at the corner of a single sheet.

Then he turned his back and walked calmly out of the office, making sure to lock the door securely behind him.

A warm, rosy glow was already reflecting in the rear window of his black Mercedes as he pulled out of the drive and headed in the opposite direction from his normal route home.

Chapter 20

Garden Party

"More sherry, anyone?" Carl McMaster was circulating with a bottle of very nice, very expensive and very exclusive Jerez. "Anyone? And remember, there's plenty more where this came from!"

Everyone at the gathering was in a relaxed and happy mood, and his guests were very willing to relieve him of the very nice, very expensive, very exclusive contents of his bottle. Oscarito and Marta sat like lovebirds on a tiny two-person sofa, with Marco perched on one end feeling very grown up. Filipe and his wife Sonia were chatting in the corner with Alfredo and Sandra, who had put on her best formal dress and reduced her normal make-up by half. She had her arm through Alfredo's and was looking radiant.

Filipe's editor had stopped by for a few minutes on his way to another event. While he had said how glad he was to finally 'meet the team', it was David Hidalgo he followed around the room with an expression of considerable interest and curiosity.

Marie Vey was chatting with Teresa over a low coffee table, nibbling tiny squares of *membrillo* on equally tiny *tostadas*. Both held their glasses out for more as Carl walked past. Mariano and Maria were on the other, bigger sofa. Maria still had a leg in plaster and elbow crutches beside her, but she seemed to be coping well with Mariano hopping up and down to get her a drink or something to nibble. Next to them sat Margarita Garcia – owner of the bookcase hidey hole. Gillian and David were sitting near her, heads together, talking quietly amid the buzz of party conversation.

"So, everybody got a drink?" Carl asked the company. "Good. Now, I'd like to propose a toast to absent friends. Thinking particularly of the honourable Señor Byass, who made all of this possible. Unfortunately, he didn't feel it appropriate to attend our little celebration; however, he is assuredly here in spirit. To absent friends!"

They all drank, then went back to whatever point in the conversation they'd paused at. Marco took a massive slug of his coke and fresh orange, which his mum had told him was a cocktail called a Muddy Puddle.

Gillian glanced around the gathering and smiled. "He who fights and runs away…" she began.

"Lives to fight another day," David completed her thought.

"Were we right to run and hide?" she asked, squeezing David's arm.

"Of course. What else could we have done? All's well that ends well, I suppose. Or whatever other happy refrain you can think of."

"It's a bit of a pity so much of the evidence went up in smoke along with Party headquarters. Now Oscarito and Marta will have to look for new jobs."

"I'm not certain, but from what I hear that may not be necessary," said David mysteriously.

"No? Why not? Are they running away to Budapest together?"

"No. Staying in Madrid as far as I know, but Oscarito was saying that he's going to have a crack at his own accountancy firm, with Marta as financial co-wizard."

"Wow, that's fantastic! She'll provide the human touch and he'll be happy crunching numbers all day long. Perfect."

"I think so. Well, I hope so, anyway."

"So, maybe something good will come out of all of this."

At that point, Carl came over to top them up again.

"Carl, sit down," Gillian said. "We don't want more drink; we want your company."

He smiled and did. "That's very kind. I'm going to miss having a houseful of such interesting guests."

"I'm sure Teresa won't. It must have been like catering for a summer camp."

Carl smiled and looked over to where Teresa and Marie Vey were deep in conversation, though what they were talking about he couldn't imagine. "Actually, no. She enjoyed it, too. When you don't have kids it's not just the kids you miss but their girlfriends or boyfriends, too. And their other friends. And *their* kids, in due course. A big house can be kind of a lonely place. Having it full of fascinating people was good for us."

"Even considering that we were all on the run and you were harbouring fugitives?" she asked.

"Even in that event." Carl laughed. "I knew you were all dangerous desperados, but we were willing to take the risk. And as it turned out, we were on the side of the good guys after all."

"What happens to you two now?" David asked. "I heard there might be awkward questions asked."

Carl shrugged. "Maybe," he said, "but I have no regrets. Teresa and I were in love and still are. And in terms of my behaviour, my allegiance is to scripture first and the institution of the Church second. And I simply don't see the need for singleness in scripture. We did what God intended, even though the Church doesn't approve. But I also think I was right to continue in the Catholic Church. That was where God called me to make the biggest impact. I'd like to think I've been a moderate influence for good."

"More than moderate, I'm sure," Gillian insisted. "But is it true that you might lose your income? Somebody said that might be on the cards."

Carl shrugged again. "Who knows? It's in the hands of God. As I've already mentioned, the Catholic Church has a supreme talent for turning a blind eye. In some cases that turns out to be disastrous, but maybe in our case it would be a modest recompense for helping unmask a load of corruption and abuse that for once doesn't involve the Church. We'll see. And what about you two. Or is it three?"

Gillian smiled. "It's been a very stressful couple of weeks, but

I think we've made it through intact. We'll go home as soon as we can get booked, and then we'll try to get back to normal – though I keep saying I've forgotten what normal feels like. I'll get a GP appointment, and if all goes well everything will change again in six months or so, and there'll be a new kind of normal. I hope I've still got the energy at my age."

"And what about you, *amigo*? Still got enough energy to be a dad?"

David grimaced. "Right now, I doubt it. But what can you do? I believe Teresa told Gillian, 'If you can't do the time, don't do the crime.' I hold my hands up as a guilty man!"

"Well, please keep me in the loop. I'd love to come over and add my blessing. If I'm still in holy orders…"

"Even if you're not, you'd be completely welcome," Gillian put in. "The idea of standing up in church and having you bless the baby would be just wonderful. Please come."

"OK, I will. That's a promise."

They sat back and viewed the rest of the guests in quietness and satisfaction. Then Sandra looked over and winked at David.

"Just a minute," he said. "I think I have some mingling to do." Holding a plate of Teresa's tiny crispy sardines, he crossed the floor in her direction. "Excuse me, *Señorita*. Can I tempt you with a little something?"

"OK. But only one – then I'm finished with temptation forever."

Alfredo seemed to be deep in discussion with Filipe, so David felt justified in taking Sandra's arm and leading her away, guiding her through the room, along the hall and out into the balmy night. They found a comfy bench outside and sat down.

"Forgive me for leading you astray," he said, "but we haven't had a proper chance to sit down and talk. I wanted to thank you for taking a risk on one more guy off the street and trusting me. Without that I wouldn't have stood much chance of finding Marie Vey and, through her, finding out what the Gorilla was up to. Then we couldn't have got all that information out of him and – well, you know what all of that led to."

She smiled a bit smugly. "I know. To be honest, I was in two minds for a bit. It was a bit disorientating. People like me are so unused to being treated like real human beings rather than just a means to an end. I wasn't sure what it was all about, and I've been told so many lies through the years. People tell you to trust them, then you do and they treat you abominably. Someone who does what they say and doesn't take advantage is rare. I'm glad I did, though. Very glad." She twisted round and kissed him on the cheek.

The moonlight was shining on her face and David thought it was almost as if she were glowing with an inner light. He told her this.

She looked down and smiled.

"It's none of my business to pry," he went on, "but I'm wondering if something else went on in that room while you were trying to get information out of the Gorilla?"

"You guessed," she said. "Another strange experience. To be honest, all I wanted was to hurt that man. Badly. For all the hurt he'd caused me and others. But Alfredo wouldn't let me, eEven when we had him in a place where he couldn't defend himself. Where I could give him some kind of payback for what he'd done. Alfredo stopped me. That was surprising. For people like me, cops are the enemy. Brutal, conniving, always taking advantage and demanding instead of protecting. And if the bad guys fall down the stairs on the way to the station – that's too bad. Police can be even more brutal than the punters. At least you know what the punters are about, but the police are supposed to help you.

"So, first of all I met you, and you paid your money but didn't want anything other than to try to make a bad situation better. Then I met Alfredo and he was the same. We had the chance to talk a bit while we were letting the Gorilla think over his options. Alfredo was nothing but gentle and respectful. He treated me like a human being as well. Can I say he treated me like a lady? That's how it made me feel, at least."

"So, what happens next?"

Sandra looked pensive. "I'm not entirely sure. It's a long time since

I've had what you might call a 'normal' relationship. Our first date could be going to church. I haven't done that for a long time, either."

"How did that come about, if you don't mind me asking?"

"I don't mind at all. I seem to remember you paid for true answers! You're maybe still a few euros in credit. Alfredo wanted someone else in the room with him to witness what went on – not you or Gillian – and I volunteered. Once we'd got all the information we could, we were both exhausted. Marie Vey has a time-out room, so we got a couple of cold beers and went for a sit down. I told him I admired the way he'd gone about things – like when he stopped me from attacking the Gorilla. Then he said he hadn't always been like that and told me a bit about himself and about church and how he'd changed so much since getting involved with Warehouse 66. He called it a 'faith journey'. Then he asked if I'd like to see what it was like, and I said yes. Simple as that. There's a lot of stuff I need to get rid of. *I* need to change as well. There are memories I want to leave behind, and I need to quit the drugs. I thought I'd give it a go. And we've been texting and phoning ever since. I've told Marie Vey I want to quit, and I think she's OK with that."

"Well, well. Fascinating. Can we meet back here in a year's time and see how it's going?"

Sandra laughed and it sounded happy, open and relaxed – almost carefree. "You bet."

"Come on, then. Let's go back in or Alfredo will be getting jealous."

Inside, the party seemed to be showing no sign of slowing down. Sandra went and took up her station next to Alfredo, who looked round and nodded at David, as if to say: 'I know, and you know, and I know that you know, and that's cool.'

Given what Sandra seemed to be saying about a new start, David decided he'd better touch base with Marie Vey as well and sat down at the table with her and Teresa.

"You two look like you're deep in conversation," he began.

"Plotting and planning," Marie Vey said archly.

"Can I get in on the secret?"

"It's still just an idea," Teresa said, with only the mildest trace of her speech problem. "I've just been making a few suggestions that might help the girls at the club."

David raised an eyebrow.

Marie laughed. "Don't worry, we're not talking about sexual technique here. Teresa's done a lot of classes with young women who've never really had a chance to learn some of the basic things about looking after themselves and having their own place. I run a business, but I accept that the girls I employ won't be doing what they do forever. So realistically they need to train for another – maybe younger – profession and it would help their confidence a lot if they had some other skills."

"What sort of things do you do, then?" David asked Teresa.

"Things I learned from my mum, but I guess many of these girls never had a stable upbringing. Cooking, baking, some craft things, filling out forms, budgeting, basic healthcare... that sort of thing. What any independent person needs nowadays – male or female."

"All the girls get time off every week," Marie continued, "so we're going to start on our slowest day and see who wants to learn. It'll all be free, and we'll do it in the meeting room. Maybe nobody'll show up, but we'll see how it goes. Just so long as they don't all leave to become cooks and accountants. I run a legitimate business. Not everyone approves, but it brings together supply and demand. I'm not going to change that, but I've always tried to run things in a humane way. Now that we're not paying off the government I can afford to invest in the lives these girls may lead when they move on – as all of them eventually will. In fact, Sandra's already said she wants to go."

"I know. She just told me."

"You see! You are a malign influence in my life. I should never have agreed to see you!"

"But think of all the money we've saved you!"

"Well, there is that. Just don't expect me to show up at church any time soon."

"Stranger things have happened."

At that point, Carl appeared on another round, this time with red in one hand and white in the other, and the conversation drifted on to other things. It wasn't long before Gillian caught David's eye and nodded towards the door. They wandered out into the night, hand in hand, and sat on the same bench under the vines, which were creeping around the elegant facade of Carl's residence.

"Satisfied?" Gillian asked.

"I suppose it's in my nature never to be entirely satisfied, but this comes pretty close."

"You did a good job."

"We all did."

"So, do you think you were here in Spain for just such a time as this?"

"I don't feel like an anointed deliverer, if that's what you mean. But maybe the little part we played was planned for us. Who knows?"

She took his arm and pulled herself a bit closer. "I'm still fed up with drama," she said, "but I have to say that this last ten days seems to have been worth the stress in terms of the final result. Do you know, they're saying it might bring the government down and lead to new elections?"

David groaned. "I only came for a meeting with the minister. That was all. Honest!"

A solitary cloud drifted over the moon, softening the light.

"I wonder where he is now," Gillian mused.

"Who?"

"The ex-minister. Apparently, they've picked up Ibañez and Gonzaléz, and the Gorilla was already in custody. But your friend got clean away."

David held up his hands in horror. "Not my *friend*. Anything but."

"From the pictures on TV, I think he looks a bit like you, actually."

"I don't see it. Anyway, he has the benefit of a much more expensive coiffeur, I suppose. Apparently, he's really ugly when he takes his wig off. "

She laughed. "So, back to work on Monday."

"I hope so. And you'll have to break the news that the Scots Language Department will be losing its most talented, most popular and best-looking lecturer."

"Oh, is someone else leaving?"

He gave her a dig in the ribs. "That's what I get for being nice!"

"Well, I'm sure it'll be a happy announcement. Anyway, it'll only be temporary – I'll be back as soon as I can. Luckily, I have a husband who works a one-day week, so he can do all the baby care and still fulfil his other obligations."

"You know, you really don't deserve me!"

She leaned back and sighed happily. "That's actually true. And you don't deserve me. But somehow we make it work, however difficult it can be. Anyway, I think I've had enough for today. Ready for bed?"

"I think so. Maybe I'll just have a quick walk around the block first, though. Unwind a bit and try to process it all. So much has happened and keeps on happening. Sandra and Alfredo seem to be an item now. Oscarito and Marta have plans. And apparently Teresa's going to start giving life-skills classes at a sex club. Can you imagine it?"

"I can. It's all totally lovely. I love it. OK, see you in ten."

David went back in for a jacket, then slipped out without anyone noticing. He opened the latch on the gate and passed into the shadows of the street. He didn't notice a shadow on the other side of the road as it turned to follow him.

Carl's residence was one of the few small detached houses in the area. The rest of the street was normal Spanish inner-city tower blocks of six or eight storeys. Walking along the avenue, David passed a fruit shop, a lottery ticket seller, a little corner shop, an *electrodomésticos* showroom and a dress shop.

Across the street, two figures were rummaging through a huge roadside rubbish container. They looked like they might be father and son. The younger, slighter figure had climbed inside and was passing stuff out for the older man to sort and to decide what was worth keeping or might be sellable. Sewer rats of the city. All so, so normal for Spain.

It was as if the past week or so, which had lifted the lid on hidden horrors, had settled back down again. Maybe nothing was really different. There might be some political and criminal repercussions, but once it was no longer a headline, people would go back to the normal Spanish preoccupations of football, drinking and chatting with friends. In the minds of most Spaniards, politics and corruption went together like ham and cheese, and that would never change. Still, it seemed likely that a least a few flies would be temporarily brushed off the *bocadillo*, and that had to be positive.

Privately, however, what pleased David most was what seemed to be going on between Sandra and Alfredo, and what Teresa was cooking up with Marie Vey. *Clever, clever women*, he thought. *All quite, quite different, but each determined to take advantage of the situation and bring about positive changes; in one case in her own life, in the other maybe in the lives of many.*

Teresa seemed to be such a simple, modest woman that you couldn't imagine there was much below the surface, but David had seen the twinkle in her eye during her conversation with Marie Vey. She was setting it out in such a simple, non-threatening way, who could object? It was just a couple of hours to teach the girls how to make a good Spanish omelette and sew on buttons or fill in a form, but of such things life changes could be made. So innocent and innocuous. David could tell Teresa was starting with a teaspoon, but her goal was to undermine the walls that kept these girls in a place of horror and exploitation. Despite all that Marie Vey had said, she was fundamentally trying to legitimise the sale of human flesh. He hoped Teresa's initiative would go well and start a chain reaction.

The night was still and more bearable now the sun was down. David decided, on a whim, to go a bit further and headed for the park. Half a dozen teenagers were enjoying the *botellón* outdoor drinking ritual of Spanish youth. He skirted the group and made for another bench about 100 yards further on, near some bushes. The shadow followed.

Just as he was about to have a seat, enjoy the balmy evening and reflect again on the last few weeks, a figure emerged quietly behind him. He heard the footsteps and turned. His first thought was to head for the light, as muggings in the park were not unknown. But the figure approached and held up his hands.

"No gun, Pastor David. No knife. No police bodyguard. Nothing. Just little old me."

"What do you want?"

"Just to talk. We've a bit of catching up to do, don't you agree?"

The ex-minister sat on the opposite side of the picnic table and very deliberately brought his arms up and placed them in front of him, hands clasped. "Since we're both going to be leaving the country soon, I thought it might be appropriate to see each other one last time. It will surely be the last."

"I suppose so. Unless I see you in court on TV."

"Aw. No need to bring unpleasantness into the conversation; we're both civilised human beings. In any case, I think that's pretty unlikely. An old campaigner always has a means of retreat planned, however well the battle may be going."

"Where will you go?"

"Far enough. And nowhere near Scotland, you can rest assured. Which is a pity, in some ways. I spent many good years in Scotland."

"Really?"

"Yes, really. Just on the outskirts of Edinburgh, in fact."

"You're joking?"

"Not at all. I even went to school there. My father was Spanish and my mother Scottish, you see. I was brought up there but found the atmosphere too cold and restrictive, so l left for Spain as soon as I could. Quite a close parallel with your own story in many ways, no?"

David remained silent, looking closely at the ex-minister. "You're lying," he said at length.

"No, not at all. I'll admit that I'm a politician, so I don't always feel bound by the strictest bounds of truth, but on this occasion that's what it is. The truth."

"So it's you, then?"

"Yes, after all these years. Surprised?"

David was lost for words. "I didn't recognise you," he finally managed.

"You weren't meant to," Roberto replied perfectly calmly. "Plastic surgery is marvellous these days. And surprisingly affordable, too. Cheekbones. Nose. Lips. Hairline. And *voila*! Your little brother becomes another human being entirely. Then a new passport and some modification of official records and we're good to go."

"But politics? I thought you were only ever interested in making money."

"What's the difference?" Roberto shrugged. "Businessmen go into politics and politicians join the board when they lose their seat. I chose to combine the two. A bit of private enterprise in public life. And it was going really quite well until that ill-fated ride to the airport. But I did enjoy our chat – that wasn't a lie. I know you're a biblical scholar. I thought of it like Joseph meeting his brothers in Egypt, when he recognised them but they didn't recognise him. It must have been fun. That meeting we had – I could hardly contain myself. You were so earnest and serious. So anxious to do good for all those drug addicts and other dregs of society. If only you'd known who was sitting at the head of the table. That would have taken the wind out of your sails, I'll bet."

"Is that why you were always so focused on money? Because it made you different and gave you status? You weren't among the dregs of society – you were calling the shots. From that standpoint, politics would be a natural progression, I suppose."

Roberto amused himself by knocking some crumbs from a previous picnic off the table. "You understand the psychology very well. But without experiencing it, it's impossible to really feel the power of the drug. Lackeys jumping to do your bidding. 'Yes, Minister. No, Minister. If you wouldn't mind, Minister.' And everyone looking for a favour. Women find it irresistible, of course. It really is quite addictive, believe me. However..." here Roberto sighed heavily "... I suppose I'll have to adjust to private life before deciding on a future direction. We are young men, David. We still have a world of possibilities in front of us."

"Where will you go?" David asked again.

Roberto laughed lightly. "I think you're an honourable man, brother, but I don't trust you that much. Somewhere far away."

"South America, then?"

"Maybe. Or maybe Lapland. I could reorganise Santa Claus's routine. I really think Christmas is underdeveloped. Or Kazakhstan. Or Timbuktu. You'll never know because we'll never meet again. This is it. Hail and farewell!"

David glanced round at the teenagers, still giggling and shouting – roaring drunk by now but still pouring it down their throats. "Do you not have any inclination to see the old man just one last time? You must feel something or you wouldn't keep sending the Christmas cards."

"Those are for our mother. The old man can go to hell and roast, for all I care. You were always his favourite. Nothing I did was ever enough. I went back after making my first million and he poured scorn on the whole thing. Called me a lackey of the ruling class. So I decided then and there, screw you! I'll make myself part of the ruling class that can buy and sell the likes of you."

David shook his head. "You are so mistaken," he said. "He was never done beefing you up. You were the miracle money-maker. I was a travelling salesman hawking cheese and wine. Maybe the truth is that neither of us measured up. I think it's a Scottish affliction. Maybe he caught it, having lived there so long. You can praise a child to another child, to your friends, to the blokes at the pub, but never to the child in question."

Roberto was pensive. "Maybe you're right. We're both victims. The fear of children that were 'too big for their boots' was so pervasive that it seemed better to raise a child who had absolutely no self-respect than one who might think too much of themselves. They call it the 'tall poppy syndrome', don't they? Everyone who grows too tall has to be cut down to size. Or do you think he just didn't have the necessary gene to show love and generosity?"

"Maybe. Though Mum still seems to love him."

Roberto looked scornful. "She tolerates him. I defy you to say that anyone would live with him – with what he's become now, anyway – by choice."

"And how do you know what he's become now? You haven't seen him for forty years."

Roberto paused, smiling slightly. "Not actually true," he said softly.

"What?"

"I've been back. Every few years, when I felt the itch. A waiter at a hotel. Serving in a shop. A few hundred euros and most people are willing to let you play out your fantasy."

"Did you ever see me?"

"A few times. I wanted to speak to you, I really did. But there was something stopping me. I found I couldn't give up my disguise."

"Giving up control is the essence of faith, actually."

"So I've heard."

"Anyway, off to pastures new for you. And the *Señora*?"

"Oh, she'll find someone younger. In fact, I understand she already has."

"Another politician?"

"A ballet dancer, I believe. He's on the make and so is she, in a different way. I think they'll both be disappointed."

The kids across the park were getting louder and louder. There was the sound of a bottle smashing, followed by raucous laughter and shouting. Then a fight seemed to be breaking out. David felt the evening would be no more surreal if he were to go over and join them for a friendly drink.

"So, brother," Roberto concluded. "The ball's in your court now. You might choose to shop me, and I wouldn't blame you. I don't know why, but despite the risk I just felt I wanted to speak to you face to face. We've been batting away in our different courts and it looks like you've won. Still, isn't it the custom to shake hands at the net?"

David smiled. He was finding it difficult to associate this intelligent, affable gentleman with the money-laundering embezzler who took a weekly rake-off from prostitution rackets. He was beginning to feel like the victim of a charm offensive; something else the ex-minister was very good at. "I believe so. You know, when I last spoke to Dad, he was going on about you yet again. He wanted me to try to find you. I told him that was a ridiculous idea when the police and private investigators had failed."

Roberto raised an eyebrow. "But here we both are. Lo and behold, you've succeeded in your mission. Yet again. You do have a habit of that, you know. I've been following things in the Scottish press, and I just wanted to meet the guy behind it all. To see if you were the same brother I left behind so long ago."

"Well, clearly not. Neither of us is the same. How could we be? And personally, I'm glad about that. But what about you? Are you happy with what you've become?"

"I was pretty happy until you came along," Roberto said with a brisk laugh. "But that's a very profound question. I think we need to let the dust settle a bit, then I might think about it again. Anyway, as I said, the ball's in your court. Are you going to get your friend Alfredo to treat me to the hot seat as well?"

David grunted. "I should, but I doubt I will."

"You're not going to phone the police?"

"I don't think I am. But not for your sake. And not for Dad's either, actually. For our mother. It would be a very bitter blow for her, which she doesn't deserve. As far as they're concerned, my quest will have been a failure. The Christmas cards might still keep coming, but I'll have no insight as to where they're coming from. Will you keep in touch?"

"Based on what you've just said, I might. You're easy to contact. and I can disguise where the emails come from. I won't exactly be showing up in church, but you might hear something from time to time. Anyway, speaking of time, I have a plane to catch. And the lovely Señora Gillian is waiting for you. This last week has cost me a lot, you know, but in some ways I'm not unhappy. Believe it or not, I'd rather have lost to you than some faceless bunch of judicial accountants and bean counters. *Mucha suerte, hermano.*"

And with that, Roberto stood, turned and disappeared into the shadows without looking back.

Well, well, David Hidalgo thought, walking back towards the bishop's residence.

Then it stuck him that Roberto was too clever a foe just to stop him for ten minutes of idle conversation, and he hurried his pace. What had he engineered while keeping his long-lost brother occupied somewhere else? But the building was still there, the last guests were leaving and Gillian was waiting for him, sitting up in bed, deep in a history of the Celtic nations. Maybe he was becoming too cynical and always suspecting the worse. Maybe a man with no roots, no history and no family could be forgiven for simply wanting to make contact and to talk without any nefarious purpose.

"All calmed down now?" she asked.

He paused before answering, then said, "I guess so. The night air is good for clearing the head."

"Meet anyone?"

"Bunch of kids getting stoned in the park. And a homeless guy who thought he'd like to reconnect with civilisation again. Claimed I was his long-lost brother."

Chapter 21

Edinburgh

It was only on the flight back to Edinburgh that it sunk in how short a time they had actually been away. Less than a summer holiday, yet it seemed like months or years. They got in late, took the tram into town, then walked up Lothian Road and over the Meadows to Marchmont.

Gillian fumbled for her keys. "Don't say I've lost my keys now," she muttered, before finding them and opening the door.

She went to run a bath while David gathered up the post. Nothing of interest. He had been hoping there might at least be a mysterious postcard from Caracas or Buenos Aires, but there was nothing. There hadn't even been time. He undressed, slipped a dressing gown on, went into the darkened living room and stood at the window.

The noise of kids drinking in the park floated up, but this wasn't Madrid. Maybe kids were just kids in any country. There was no Roberto. Nor was there Oscarito, Marta, Marco, Carl, Teresa, Marie Vey, Sandra, Mariano, Maria, Alfredo, Filipe or Margarita. He sighed. The adrenalin levels were dropping to healthy levels again now that life had a chance to return to normal. Then he remembered that everything was going to change again in a few short months in ways he couldn't even imagine. *There's probably a good reason why nature gives babies to younger men*, he thought with a twinge of apprehension. *That'll be another challenge to rise to.*

He stood and took in the Edinburgh night. Taxis. Partygoers. Late-night shoppers in this new 24-hour city. Cyclists coming back from the university library with panniers loaded with notes for their theses. Young couples, hand-in-hand, striding up the hill. Behind them, much slower in pace, was an elderly couple – also hand-in-hand. *Nice*, he thought. *I hope we're given the grace to grow to that age, still loving and helping each other.* He did a quick sum in his head. *When I'm eighty, my child will still be at university. Wow. I'll need a Zimmer to get to the graduation.* David grimaced.

Where will Roberto be then? he suddenly wondered. *Still on the run under an assumed identity – another one – instead of going about his happy, contented business, with a lifetime of achievement and friends around him.* He realised it might have been very different had the ex-minister's driver not got the wrong case out the back of the car. *Well, we all make our bed and lie on it. Speaking of which...*

He went through to the bedroom and turned on the bedside lights, then into the kitchen and made two hot chocolates. He took them through to the bathroom, where Gillian was stretched full out in hot water, eyes closed.

"Chocolate?" he said.

"Hmmm, the magic word," she murmured, slowly rousing herself. "What do you think about a water birth? We could have low lighting and James Taylor."

"Not in person, I hope."

"No. The only one I want is you."

"I'd recommend someone with better qualifications for the task. A new spiritual birth is one thing – babies on the way is entirely another."

"Hmmm, I feel so content. Dreamy. I'm almost falling asleep here. But I'd better get out before the water gets cold. Hand me that towel, will you?"

He did, then wandered back into the bedroom and was just preparing to take off his dressing gown when he heard a cry.

"David! I'm bleeding!"

Physicists tell us that time is relative. They proved it that night in the run to the hospital when time stood so still that it felt like an eternity.

Normal service clicked back in again as they got to the A&E desk. A team was waiting and Gillian was whisked off. Juan, a restauranteur and David's closest friend in Edinburgh, arrived shortly after and prayed with him. It took about forty minutes to get the news.

A doctor appeared in scrubs. "Mr Hidalgo?"

"Yes."

"I'm so sorry."

David felt it like a physical blow and almost staggered. "What do you mean? What's happened?" he managed to say.

"Oh, nothing serious. It's just taken a bit longer than expected to get things sorted. We're a bit short-staffed right now."

David took a deep breath and tried to straighten up, the adrenalin rush still washing around. "What are you saying? How is she?"

"Fine. And the baby's fine, too. Nothing to worry about. These things sometimes happen in the early stages of a first pregnancy for an older mum. It's entirely routine, but we'll keep her in overnight till we get things back into balance."

"Thank God."

"Do you want to see her?"

"Of course."

Gillian was sitting up, looking pale with a drip in and various monitors clicking and beeping. "Well, no end to the drama," she smiled. "You OK?"

"I am now. Five minutes ago I wasn't so good. Juan came."

"I'm glad. That's what friends are for. Apparently, this is not uncommon, but nothing too much to worry about, they say. There's a drug I'll have to take from now on, but other than that it's just regular checks and back here if anything untoward happens."

"Like if the pound rises above €1.40?'

"Don't joke. You might set it off again!"

"Sorry."

"Anyway, I think I'm fine. Go home and get some sleep. See you in the morning."

* * *

The next morning, David phoned his mum and dad, who were still in the holiday house, and gave them some edited highlights. He also took the chance to ask his mum how things were health-wise.

"Amazing, really," she replied. "Your dad finally confessed that he'd been to see a doctor. They told him he didn't have long. He showed me the letter. But he seems to be defying predictions. He's physically weaker, but in a much better mood. I'm sorry he wasn't in great form when you came down."

"Not your fault. To be honest, you seem to cope with it incredibly well. We don't know how you manage it. He gave me advance warning of the diagnosis."

David could hear her putting on her brave face.

"Did he? Well, we're coping. And he actually seems brighter overall."

"So, what made the change?"

"Not entirely sure, but I think it might have something to do with you. He was trying to follow things in Spain through some contact or other. I've no idea how he knew what was happening. I didn't inquire too much, but he was on and off the computer all day. He knew something of what had happened even before you phoned. And now you're the blue-eyed boy."

David wasn't sure what to say. "Well, that'll be a first," he eventually managed.

* * *

David's parents had insisted on coming up to Edinburgh to see Gillian, so he took them along when he went to see her. The doctors had decided to have her stay another night, so she had called ahead for him to bring some stuff.

After meeting and greeting and congratulations, David and his dad went out to the cafeteria for something that claimed to be coffee and some genuinely quite nice sticky buns. When they got to the till, Ricardo added a couple of flapjack slices, complimented the girl on her hair, insisted on paying as if it were a privilege and left a tip.

His son raised an eyebrow but said nothing.

As they looked for a place to sit, David politely inquired about matters of health.

"Oh, I think 'riddled like a Swiss cheese' is the best way to describe it," Ricardo replied nonchalantly as they found a corner table. "But the painkillers pack a punch, so I'm bearing up. Anyway, enough about me. I gather you've been a busy boy."

"Baby or Spain?" David asked, not quite sure what he meant.

"Oh, both. I mean, congratulations again. It's what you've wanted for so long. Gillian will be a great mum, without a doubt. And we'll try to be at least acceptable grandparents – if I'm around that long. But I'm afraid I was thinking more about your adventures in Spain."

"Mum said you'd been following events. How did you know?"

Ricardo took a sip of the poisonous coffee. He didn't smile with satisfaction, but at least he didn't spit it out. "I keep my eye on the Spanish news websites. It seems you've achieved what I never could and brought the whole rotten edifice tumbling down."

"Kind of you to say so, but I didn't know there had been much in the press yet. I think the result still very much remains to be seen."

"But it's going that way…"

"Yeah, maybe. The prosecutor we were in touch with seems to think he's got the smoking gun they've needed for years but never found. So it could be significant."

Ricardo eventually managed to break through the cellophane wrapper of his flapjack slice, but instead of going into a tirade about the many lies told about easy-peel packaging, he simply took a bite, gave a little 'mmm' sound and took another sip of coffee. Through the slurping and munching, he kept to his theme. "I actually still have some contacts in the press world. People are saying you're a hero."

"Hardly."

"Well, modesty becomes you, but really. What I heard was that you'd found a stash of money, traced its origins, tied it back to a protection racket, got a confession out of a key player and handed a folder of secret accounts to the authorities. That doesn't sound like 'hardly' to me!"

A little warning bell was beginning to ring at the back of David's mind, but he wasn't quite sure why. "You seem to be remarkably well informed," he said.

"Well, ear to the ground, nose to the grindstone. Like I say, I still have some contacts."

David shifted in his seat and thought he'd push the boat out a bit more. "What sort of strategy would you have followed if you'd been in our position?"

Ricardo took another bite of his treat. "This really is good, you know," he said. "I'll have to get your mum to lay in some supplies."

"And what would you have done in my place?" David pressed him.

"More or less what you did, I suppose. I would have avoided getting picked up, cultivated some talkative friends, joined the dots and followed the money. That sort of thing. And I would have prayed for a bit of luck – which you also seem to have had."

This is getting surreal, David thought. *He rarely pays and never happily; never tips; never compliments anyone; never likes what they give him; certainly never compliments me; and never mentions 'prayer' except as an insult. What's going on?*

"So, follow the money, talk to those who want to talk to you, get some documentary evidence, cultivate the press and – if possible – a prosecutor, bring in the expertise you think you lack and keep one step ahead. Would that be about it?" David pressed him.

Ricardo saw the trap, but too late. He shrugged. "I suppose that sums it up. Anyway, that's not important now. What's important is that you did it. Do you know, I've spent most of my life hoping for someone to do what you've just done? And the fact that it's my own son who seems to have made the breakthrough... Well, that's the icing on the cake." He took another bite and smiled. "Delicious."

David had heard enough and wasn't about to be diverted by flattery. "Does the nickname 'the Blackbird' mean anything to you, Dad?"

Ricardo stopped, mid-munch, but quickly recovered. "Blackbird?" he mused. "Blackbird? Isn't that what they used to call the SR-71 – that US spy plane? Yes, I'm sure it was."

"Is that all? That's the only thing? Nothing connected with Spain? Nothing about journalism?"

Ricardo avoided his gaze. "I think I'll get another of these," he said and headed for the till.

David let out a long sigh. What to do now? He was ninety-nine per cent sure. He could confront him and complain about interference in his affairs. He could do a big 'how dare you?' – which was definitely tempting – or he could simply let it go. What was to be gained? Here he was, having horrible coffee with his dad, who for once in his life was not complaining about anything, and strangest of all was actually being complimentary. Unconditional love and acceptance had never been stock-in-trade in the Hidalgo household, but for the first time he could honestly remember, this was looking a bit like it.

Ricardo came back, sat down, and handed David a coffee refill and a flapjack slice of his own. "So, what happens now?" he asked. "I suppose you'll have to go back and give evidence."

David paused to consider, then decided just to play dumb and let it go. "I suppose so," he said, smiling. "I asked if I could maybe do it by video link and they thought that might be a possibility."

"Once the dust settles, I think you should write it up. It would make quite a story. You know, like *All the President's Men* or something. You could call it *All the Minister's Men*."

Throughout David's childhood, youth, student days, early career, journey to faith, pastorate in Spain and work in Edinburgh, he had always known something was missing. He had tried to ignore it, deny it, compensate for it and look elsewhere for it. Now, in a moment of revelation, he realised what it was – and that for the first time ever he had found it in an overpriced hospital cafeteria over horrible coffee and flapjack slices, which pretended to be healthy but were actually dripping with sugar and fat.

"Dad," he said. "What do you really think about what's happened?"

Ricardo stopped smiling and munching and put his coffee down. "This is really vile stuff," he said ruefully. "How they get away with calling it coffee I'll never know."

David relaxed. This was more like the father he knew. "I mean about what's happened in the past few weeks."

Ricardo paused, glanced around the room at the weary and worried relatives, cleaners on their break, and equipment and drug reps trying to summon the energy for another onslaught on the NHS budget. He put his coffee down and studied the surface of the table in front of him.

"You know, I'm not really used to this kind of thing," he began. "My father never believed in praise. He used to bang us round the ear and say, 'That's what you get for nothing, so think what you'll get for something.' He thought that was funny. So, I'm sorry to say that I probably did the same with you boys. Maybe life's a bit like writing a novel. It's only when you get to the end that you finally understand the beginning. But at least with a novel you have the chance to go back and correct your mistakes. Not so in life. I know I haven't said the things I should have said. Now the time I have left to do so appears to be very limited. So, however uncomfortable it is, I'm going to say it. And don't interrupt.

"I'm proud. Of you, of Gillian, of what you've achieved. This is what I used to live for, and I lost it. I didn't have the impact I wanted to have. How could you in Franco's day? I tried, but I failed. I don't suppose you really understand it, but I came to Scotland from Spain a bitter man. He had won and I had lost. He held all the cards and I was a nobody, but I had hoped the truth would somehow come out and win the day. It was a total fantasy; I can see that now.

"Once I got here, I tried to snipe from the sidelines and maybe I managed to wing a few of the hangers-on… but the old man himself? Not a scratch. It's not easy when the one thing you've directed your life towards turns out to be completely beyond your reach. Like the guys who climbed Everest. If they'd got to the top, utterly at the end of their resources, and discovered another peak behind it that nobody had noticed, another 5,000 feet up – what's that supposed to feel like? Well, I didn't have sufficient oxygen to climb any more, so I wrote about flamenco for *National Geographic* and links between the Spanish Armada and the Northern Isles for *The Scots Magazine*. Not exactly trash, but it was as far as I was concerned. It wasn't what I was born for.

"Somebody mentioned a little quotation from the Bible to me recently – you know it's not my favourite book. It was something about someone being born 'for such a time as this'. Well, I thought I might have been born for such a time as Franco's, and that I could single-handedly bring the roof down – like Samson in the temple, if I'm permitted another biblical allusion to a real Bible scholar. Anyway, it didn't happen, and that wasn't easy. And now, well, the dominoes are beginning to fall at last, and it's satisfying to watch. I know the Party isn't part of the Falange – the *fascistas* – it's supposed to be a democratically elected government and a legally regulated political body, but at the end of the day that doesn't make much difference. They are corrupt bloodsuckers on the body politic of Spain, and it looks as if they're going to be plucked off and dropped into the bucket of salt, where they belong. And if I couldn't do it, then who better than you?"

David was silent for a moment. As a believer and a pastor he certainly should have believed in miracles, but this was one he thought he'd never see. "I appreciate that, Dad," he said quietly. "Very much. You're right that I didn't understand how all of that must have felt for you."

Ricardo nodded. "How could you?" he said quietly. "Anyway, it's over now. I feel like something got finished somehow. Different actors in a different play, but at last somebody was left standing in the final act."

They sat and ignored their coffee in silence for a few minutes.

"And the Blackbird?" David finally asked, unsure if he should push it.

Ricardo gave a wry smile. "I think they retired that plane, didn't they?" he said with an entirely straight face. "I heard it flew one too many missions."

David nodded and studied his father's face. He thought he just about detected the remains of a frustrated past in his expression, but it was faint and fading. The man in front of him seemed strangely at peace – even despite the plastic cup of washing-up water in front of him.

"Oh, one final question," Ricardo suddenly said. "I don't suppose you came across anyone who had heard anything about Roberto? Any last known address, last sighting, associates, that kind of thing?"

"Hmm, 'fraid not," David replied. "There was nobody who answered to that description."

"Ah." Ricardo sighed regretfully. "I suppose that would have been too much to hope for. I was always worried that an excessive love of legal tender might be his downfall. Oh well, at least we can hope that he wasn't mixed up in any of this nonsense. Anyway, I think we've given the ladies long enough to bad-mouth their men. Let's try to limit the damage."

They walked back to the ward. Gillian was sitting up, and both women were laughing until the tears rolled, though neither shared the joke. Once she'd recovered, Helen gave her son a long, hard look and raised her eyebrows, but he just smiled and gave her a kiss.

"All OK, Davie?"

"Perfect, Mum, thanks. And thanks for coming up. Remind me how long you're staying in Scotland."

"We fly home on Friday, but we'll probably be back before long. We have some plans."

"Oh, intriguing."

"Yes. Your dad has finally got fed up with sun, sand and golf. We're thinking of downsizing to a small apartment in Spain and buying again in Edinburgh."

"Wonderful, Mum. That's great."

"Your mother thinks she'll be nearer John Lewis and Jenners," Ricardo said, tongue firmly in cheek.

"Nearer the grandchildren is what he means."

"Grandchildren?" Gillian said, aghast. "Let me get the first one out first!"

* * *

David came back the following day and took Gillian home. She was still walking a bit gingerly but seemed content.

"You and your dad had a good chat the other day, I gather," she said.

"Yes, you gather right. It was very surreal, but I learned a lot."

"Like what?"

"Like who the Blackbird is, for example."

"Someone he knew?"

"Closer to home than that."

"Your father? *Ricardo?* You're kidding!"

"Well, he didn't come right out and admit it, but it was as good as. I looked the name up when I went home and it turns out there was a young reporter in the 1960s they used to call the Blackbird."

"Why that?"

"Because they said he used to wait till the rain, then swoop down, get a hold of a worm and hang on to it until he'd pulled it out of the ground. And he was associated with the man who is now Filipe's editor. I'd bet a double fish supper that when his old colleague found out I was involved in something he got on the blower and alerted Dad, then they kept in touch. So everything Filipe knew, his editor knew, and everything his editor knew, my dad found out quite quickly afterwards. I guess he couldn't resist trying to help things along, but I don't mind. Initially, I thought: 'Can't you keep from sticking your big oar into my life, even after all these years?' But then I realised he was trying to be helpful in his own way. And I suppose maybe it did help to galvanise me into action before I went to speak to Sandra. That conversation made all the difference, and maybe Dad should take some of the credit."

"Did you tell him that?"

"Not yet, but I will."

"You'd better be quick. He's not a well man."

David nodded grimly. It took a few seconds to recover himself. "Anyway, I think it's pretty well established that Ricardo Hidalgo was – and is – the Blackbird. This was his last swoop!"

"Well, well. Hard to imagine now."

"True, but I can imagine it a lot more easily after our half-hour in the cafeteria."

"You must tell me the full story."

"I don't know if I can even remember it all in order. It just seemed like one of those magical moments where time stands still and everything unfolds as it should. In a way, I don't even want to examine it too closely. It was what it was, and I think it helped us both a lot."

"Well, I'm glad. Now, Mr Gallant, you need to help me out of the car, up the stairs and into an easy chair. I've been told to take it *very* easy. Think you can manage that?"

David groaned. "Oh, I don't know," he said wearily. "Crime-busting is more my line."

"Yes, so I hear. Well, I'm hoping an old dog can still learn new tricks. There are going to be lots of new tricks for both of us."

"I'll take it in my stride," he said slowly, climbing out of the MX5, gradually straightening up, stretching a bit to get the muscles moving, then helping Gillian out. "I bet we were born for such a time as this!"

Postscript

"OK, one last big push now, Gillian. You're doing fantastically well. Final push! That's it – wonderful!"

Dr Gillian Lockhart collapsed back onto the pillow, her face running with sweat, her hair plastered around her forehead and a look of utter exhaustion on her face. But there was also a hint of a contented smile on her lips. "Is it over?" she asked.

"That's it. Well done! And relax. You are now a mum!"

Señor David Hidalgo pulled out another moist wipe from the packet and mopped her brow, then leaned over and kissed her on the forehead. "Well done, Mum," he whispered. "And here's something else for you."

He pulled something out of his pocket and revealed an eternity ring. "Like it?"

Gillian smiled through her exhaustion and slipped it as far as it would go onto her swollen finger. "It's beautiful. Thank you."

"Least I could do. You've done all the hard work."

A few more moments of suspense were needed for weighing, tagging, checking and cleaning, then the midwife came back in and handed Gillian a tiny dark-haired bundle.

"Congratulations," she said. "A beautiful, healthy, perfect baby boy. Well done."

Gillian took the bundle and laid it on her breast. She gazed down, pulled the blanket back a bit and looked down at a pair of dark eyes, which were not yet focusing but seemed to be looking up at her.

She glanced round at her husband behind her shoulder. "Did I do well?" she asked.

"Completely and utterly. I couldn't have done better myself."

"Thanks for helping," she whispered. "Love you."

"And I love you, too."

"And we both love you," she added, looking down. "Welcome to the world, little David. Now, between us, let's see if we can keep your daddy out of trouble."

* * *

Ricardo Hidalgo died three weeks later, before he and Helen had had the chance to further their plans for a place in Edinburgh. They said it was heart failure in a cancer-weakened system, brought on by prolonged use of strong painkillers. The body was brought back to Edinburgh and a strictly humanist service was held, followed by cremation. David was allowed to say something – nothing religious according to Ricardo's strict instructions – just the affectionate comments of a family member. As he sat waiting for his moment with a piece of paper in one hand and holding his mum's hand with the other, David realised his comments would be so different from what they would have been had he not gone to Spain and had the Blackbird not started singing again after so many years of silence.

When his moment came, he walked down the aisle, stepped onto the platform, put his paper on the lectern, then ignored it. "I'd like to tell you about a man I really only got to know a few weeks ago," he began. "A man I am now very proud to tell you was my father."

He looked up. Dr Helen Hidalgo was looking at him, eyes shining. She smiled and he could very easily imagine what a young, dashing, determined young Spanish journalist had seen in those eyes to fall in love with. He looked at Gillian sitting next to her and remembered what had made him fall in love with her. And now she had a baby in her arms. Full circle. Life goes on. One life ended, another begun. Of course, his father wasn't a believer in any sort of afterlife, David was well aware of that, but still he hoped the Blackbird might still be singing somewhere. Just so long as he didn't start sending parenting advice!

When everything was over, they walked out into the car park. There weren't many mourners – just Helen, Gillian, David, Juan and Alicia from La Hacienda restaurant, Marjory MacInnes from Southside Christian Fellowship, and a friend of Gillian and David's, DI Stuart MacIntosh. Three cars were enough.

But there were four cars in the car park. The final one was a big black Mercedes. A tall, darkly dressed figure stood beside it. This time David recognised him. He was surprised but not as stunned as he would have been a year earlier. He made eye contact and gave a quick upward questioning jerk of the head. The figure replied with an almost imperceptible nod.

"Mum," David said softly. "I think there's somebody else here you ought to speak to."

Helen gave a heavy sigh. "Do I have to?" she asked. "It's been a tiring day. I just want to go home and rest."

"This way," David said, leading her gently by the arm.

They approached the stranger, then, about three metres away, David released her arm and let her walk the final few paces herself. He could see the figure take her hand and whisper something in her ear. She staggered slightly, but he easily caught and held her. David could see her shoulders start to shake. *It's appropriate*, he thought. *Something lost and something found.*

Maybe he should have been phoning the police. Maybe he should have been whispering in Angus MacIntosh's ear. He should certainly tell Gillian all about it, and surely he would. But not today. Today was personal. It was for something else – something maybe even more important. After all, you only get one good try at a second chance.